AN ETHNIC
AT LARGE

*A Memoir of America
in the Thirties and Forties*

by Jerre Mangione

G.P. Putnam's Sons, New York

Copyright © 1978 by Jerre Mangione

SBN: 399-11774-1

Library of Congress Cataloging in Publication Data
Mangione, Jerre Gerlando, 1909-
  An ethnic at large.

  Includes index.
  1. Mangione, Jerre Gerlando, 1909-   —Biography.
2. Authors, American—20th century—Biography.
I. Title.
PS3563.A47A47   813'.5'2   [B]   77-27447
ISBN 0-399-11774-1

PRINTED IN THE UNITED STATES OF AMERICA

FOR PATRICIA, in the 22nd year of our marriage.

And in memory of these unforgettable friends who became part of this memoir:

Leonard Brown,   Elizabeth Batterham Burke, Coburn Gilman, Earl G. Harrison, Helene Hartley, Edward Havill, Josephine Herbst, Evelyn Hersey, Burges Johnson, Kenneth Langford, Corrado di Niscemi, Mitchell Rappaport, William Rollins, Jr., Charles Edward Smith, Carlo Tresca.

A Note, and Some Acknowledgments

Chapter Thirteen of this memoir, "Concentration Camps—American Style," describes a virtually unknown segment of World War II history: the internment program conducted by the Department of Justice for some ten thousand individually apprehended aliens of German, Italian and Japanese nationality. For reasons explained in the text, this program (unlike the mass internment program of the West Coast Japanese and Japanese Americans, which was simultaneously operated by the War Relocation Authority) was not made known to the general public, even though the media were aware of its existence.

Throughout the war years, I directed the public relations program of the Immigration and Naturalization Service, the custodian agency for the internment camps. In the course of my duties, I visited all of the major camps, and spent considerable time talking with members of their supervisory staffs as well as with some of the German, Italian and Japanese prisoners.

A grant from the Earhart Foundation enabled me to supplement and substantiate my memory of that experience with specific data obtained from Department of Justice records. The same research effort yielded various forgotten facts regarding the department's nationwide registration and fingerprinting of all aliens in 1940, an event which forms part of Chapter Eleven, "Washington at War."

I also acquired valuable information about the operations of the alien enemy internment program from some of the persons who were involved with it, namely Edward. J. Ennis, Esq., who headed the Department of Justice's Alien Enemy Control Unit; the late L.M.C. Smith, a special assistant to Attorney General Francis Biddle; Dr. Amy N. Stannard, who administered the Seagoville Internment facility at Dallas, Texas, and Sarah G. Lewis, a member of her staff; Abner Schreiber, Esq., who was on the supervisory staff of the camp at Santa Fe, New Mexico; and Ivan Williams, who was in charge of several of the camps in Texas and New Mexico. My thanks to all of them, especially to Mr. Williams, who was unusually helpful. I am also grateful to Charles Gordon, former General Counsel of the Immigration and Naturalization Service, who helped me track down the archives of the alien enemy internment program to the Federal Records Center in Suitland, Maryland; and to Livingston Biddle, Jr., who helped me get permission to examine them.

For some of the historical data in Chapter Six, "The Left-Winged Whirl," I am indebted to Daniel Aaron's excellent study, *Writers on the Left.*

As for the book in general, I am beholden to Thomas C. Cochran, the late Loren Eiseley, Vartan Gregorian, and Edward P. Hutchinson, friends and colleagues at the University of Pennsylvania, who by their deeds and attitudes encouraged me to undertake this project. To Yaddo and to the MacDowell Colony I owe much gratitude for providing the solitude and hospitality I needed for writing large portions of the manuscript. I am grateful, too, to Bernice Ferst and Louise Lux for their copyreading expertise, to Rebecca McCombs for her proofreading, and to Linda Kosmin for her bibliographical assists.

Finally, I want to thank my wife, whose wholehearted support made this head-on confrontation with the past possible.

J.M.

Contents

AN ETHNIC AT LARGE

ONE

Growing Up Sicilian

Before my parents considered me old enough to go beyond the picket fence that separated me from the children on the street, I would peer through it for hours, longing to play with them and wondering what they could be saying to one another. Although I had been born in the same city as they, I spoke not their language. English was forbidden in our home—for reasons of love. Afraid of losing communication with their own flesh and blood, my parents, who spoke only Sicilian, insisted we speak their tongue, not the one foreign to them.

The feeling of being an outsider may have begun with that edict. Or it may have started when, finally allowed to go beyond the picket fence, I found myself among jeering strangers—the sons of Polish, German, and Russian Jewish immigrants who lived on the same block. Their loudest taunts were directed against my baptismal name of Gerlando, which they reduced to Jerry as soon as they had accepted me. From this action came the awareness of being doomed to lead a double life: the one I led among my drove of Sicilian relatives, the other in the street and at school.

There was also a third life, the one I lived with myself, which gradually was to dictate the secret resolve to break away from my relatives. It was largely based on para-Mitty feats of the imagination that could easily transport me into agreeable realms far removed from the harsh realities of my everyday existence. (One winter I galloped over the snow-packed side-walks of our neighborhood in the moonlight, believing I was a god disguised as a horse; in another season I kept rescuing my beautiful third-grade teacher from the flames about to consume her while she slept.) My fantasy life was well nourished by the piles of books I brought home from the public library, most of which I read clandestinely in the bathroom or under the bed since my mother believed that too much reading could drive a person insane.

As I tried to bridge the wide gap between my Sicilian and American lives, I became increasingly resentful of my relatives for being more foreign than anyone else. It irked me that I had not been born of English-speaking parents, and I cringed with embarrassment whenever my mother would scream at me in Sicilian from an upstairs window, threatening to kill me if I didn't come home that minute. If I rushed to obey her, it was not because I was frightened by her threat (there was nothing violent about her except the sound of her anger), but because I did not want my playmates to hear her Sicilian scream a second time.

My fondness for privacy, which my relatives considered a symptom of illness, added to my feelings of incompatibility. I was offended by their incessant need to be with one another. If they could have managed it, they would probably have all lived under the same roof. Only the families of my Jewish playmates approached their gregariousness, but they were recluses by comparison. My relatives were never at a loss for finding reasons for being together. In addition to parties for birthdays, weddings, anniversaries, and saint days, there were also parties when a child was baptized, when he was confirmed, and when he got a diploma. The arrival of another relative from Sicily or the opening of a new barrel of wine was still another pretext for another gathering of the clan.

Pretext or not, on any Sunday or holiday a score of relatives would crowd into our tiny house at the invitation of my father, whose capacity for hospitality far exceeded his income, to partake of a Lucullan banquet consisting of at least three meat courses and, at Christmas and Easter, *connoli*, the masterpiece of his art as a pastrymaker, his original trade in Sicily. As long as the celebrations were held indoors away from public scrutiny, I could enjoy them, especially when my relatives were swapping stories about Sicily. But in the summer months, when they took to serenading one another in the dead of the night, waking up their non-Sicilian neighbors with their songs and mandolins, or when they invaded the public parks with their exuberant festivals, I would be tormented with the worry that they were making a bad impression on the Americans around us. The most excruciating moments came when the Sicilian mothers in our party, not caring how many Americans might be watching, bared their breasts to feed their infants.

A mindless conformist like most children, I was incapable of appreciating my relatives' insistence on being themselves, or realizing that this was their way of coping with an alien world that was generally hostile. Nor was I aware of how much antagonism they had endured and how much they had been slandered. I learned long afterward (not from them) that at one point the public's image of Sicilians in Rochester was so sinister that the immigrants had felt compelled to prove they were a civilized and moral people, not criminals involved with the Mafia or the Black Hand, as the press would have the community believe. As evidence of their good character, the Sicilian community decided to enact the Passion Play. Included in the large cast were milkmen, masons, ditchdiggers, shoemakers, bakers, tailors, and factory hands, among them some of my relatives. The date set for the elaborate production was Columbus Day, 1908. Although invitations were mailed to hundreds of

American community leaders and their spouses, only a few showed up. Fortunately, their enthusiasm for the quality of the production generated such excitement that the Sicilians were encouraged to stage a second performance. This time the auditorium was packed with both Americans and Italians, among them my father and my mother and to some degree, myself, for I would be born in a month's time. The lines in the drama were spoken in Italian but the Americans were as deeply moved by the performance as the rest of the audience and joined in the prolonged applause. The next day came the big payoff: the same newspapers that had been headlining Sicilian crime on their front pages devoted the same kind of space to praising the Sicilian community for making such an impressive contribution to the city's cultural life.

But it takes more than a play to change public opinion. Within a year the press was back to its old routine of unduly emphasizing crimes that involved Sicilians.

Of all our relatives my father was the most sensitive about the honor of Sicilians. So much so that on learning that Boy Scouts carry knives, the weapon that was commonly associated with Sicilian homicide, he forbade his sons to become Scouts. Not understanding his concern, the image of Sicilians as knife-wielding criminals rather appealed to our Hollywood-nurtured love of melodrama, but we saw no evidence of it among our relatives. Although there were about a hundred of them, only two ever came to the attention of the police, and in both instances they were victims rather than culprits. The most tragic was my mother's favorite brother Calogero, a gentle, dreamy-eyed father of two young children, who was killed at a wedding party when he tried to stop a fight between two guests, one of whom had a revolver. The killer was sent to the electric chair but this did not diminish the grief of my relatives, especially of my mother, who all of her life spoke of the murder as though it had just happened.

The second victim was my Uncle Stefano who, abhorring manual labor, had been operating a small jewelry business from

his living room which catered to a clientele of Sicilian immigrants about to be married or engaged. The business was
beginning to prosper when two of his *paesani* invaded his
apartment one morning and, after tying him to a chair and
threatening to blow off his head if he did not reveal the
combination of his safe, took all of his jewelry including the
wedding ring he wore. He was untied by a Jewish neighbor
who heard his cries. The neighbor, without consulting him,
then telephoned for the police.

The arrival of the police officers horrified Uncle Stefano as
much as the robbery itself. Eventually he and the rest of my
relatives were to make a distinction between the American
police and the blatantly corrupt police system they had known
in Sicily. But at the time all policemen were regarded as
obstacles to justice. When questioned, Uncle Stefano gave the
police a vague account of the robbery and refused to guess at
the identity of the thieves. As a result, the newspaper accounts
broadly hinted that he himself may have plotted the robbery in
order to collect the insurance. No one had bothered to check
out the fact that there was no insurance. My uncle was
completely wiped out.

In an attempt to recover the stolen jewelry, Uncle Stefano
visited a *paesano* who was reputed to be a power in the
Rochester underworld, and gave him all the information he had
withheld from the police. The *paesano* expressed horror that "a
gentleman as honest and as respected" as my uncle would be
robbed by two of his compatriots and promised on his honor to
do everything possible to restore the jewelry. A few days later,
with much apologizing, he reported that the thieves, on seeing
the newspaper accounts of the robbery, had taken fright and
left for Sicily. Unless they returned, which was unlikely, there
was nothing he could do.

None of my relatives considered it strange that Uncle Stefano
should have gone to a *mafioso* for help; nor did they doubt that
if the police and the press had not interfered, he would have
recovered the jewelry. While they did not condone *mafiosi*,

they held that when you could not trust the police to deal with you with enough respect, you placed your trust in those who could enforce your rights as a respected person. In the vocabulary of my relatives the words "respect" and "honor" were interchangeable and sacred.

Convinced that our teachers made no effort to teach us the meaning of respect, my father distrusted American schools even more than the police. He held them responsible for promoting such shocking customs as that of boys and girls dating without a chaperone or young people marrying without their parents' consent. The American school system, for him, symbolized everything that outraged him about his adopted country. His diatribes on the subject were of such eloquence as to make us feel guilty for daring to like any of our teachers. Beneath his fury was the conviction that they were encouraging immorality, disrupting family life, and undermining his position as the head of his family.

Like other Sicilian fathers, he never permitted his children to forget that they were living under a dictatorship, albeit, in his case, a loving one. In the eyes of his Sicilian peers, he was regarded as a maverick. He allowed his children to address their parents with the familiar *tu*, a concession rarely granted to children of Sicilians. And instead of spending his leisure time with his cronies drinking and playing cards, as was the habit of most Sicilian fathers, he preferred the company of his immediate family and would seldom go anywhere without them. He differed from the others in still another significant respect: despite his easily triggered hot temper, he never lifted a hand against his wife or his children.

Although he was of small stature, he conveyed the authority of a giant as he exhorted us to disregard the "nonsense" that the teachers stuffed into our skulls. Repeatedly we were reminded never to succumb to teachings that would cause us to disobey our parents. One evening, in a voice pregnant with moral significance, he read aloud to us the newspaper account of a Sicilian neighbor who had caught his daughter secretly dating an American; the neighbor had trailed the couple and, while they were kissing each other good night, pounced on the young man and bitten off part of his ear. "The teachers of that girl are to blame," my father told us, "for not teaching her to respect the wishes of a father."

Later, when my father discovered that his own daughter was seeing an American medical student on the sly, I expected a burst of temper that would badly scald my sister. But nothing of the kind happened. He simply asked her to invite the young man to the house. Then almost as soon as they were introduced, my father asked him point-blank whether he intended to marry his daughter. The bewildered young man paled and stuttered, trying to explain he was too young to think of marriage. In that case, my father told him, he was also too young to court his daughter. And that was the end of the romance.

As much as my father ranted against American schools, he and my mother yearned to send one of their sons to college, something which, they reminded each other, only the rich could afford to do in Sicily. Here it was not such an impossible dream. They chose me since I was the eldest and also because of my passion for reading, which they mistook for scholarly aptitude. I disappointed them at once by refusing to become either a doctor or a lawyer which, like most immigrants, they considered the only truly prestigious professions. Uncle Stefano urged that I become a pharmacist and presented me, on my next birthday, with an elaborate chemistry set. Because I was fond of him, I managed to show some interest in the possibility, but it literally went up in smoke when I almost set the house on fire while tinkering with hot test tubes.

My true ambition, which I tried to keep secret from my parents as long as possible, was to be a writer. It seemed to me that I had no talent for anything else; that, moreover, it offered the fastest avenue of escape to the world outside that of my relatives. The hope of becoming a writer was easily nurtured by my addiction to reading, but it may have first taken root at the age of ten when Uncle Peppino, who had a penchant for non-

Italian widows, wealthy ones especially, began commissioning me to ghostwrite his love letters. The first of the letters, for which I received a dime, must have been a disaster. In my vast ignorance of women, I had stressed my uncle's passion for the widow's properties rather than his passion for her. When there was no reply to the letter, my uncle attributed the woman's silence to her cold Anglo-Saxon nature and addressed himself to other widows. There were some responses, enough to encourage both of us, but nothing much came of them. However, another correspondence I undertook for an immigrant cousin who had fallen in love with a Polish-American girl proved quite effective. After the third letter, they eloped, and my dreams for a writing career went soaring.

Apart from the dimes he paid me, I felt a special affinity for Uncle Peppino, mainly because he was an iconoclast by nature constantly at odds with his relatives for his un-Sicilian behavior. It delighted me to learn that shortly after his arrival in the United States he declared the Catholic Church a force for evil and joined the Baptist Church, which he found far more cheerful and where, as he put it, he could concentrate on his worship of God without having to ration it among a large roster of saints, whom he dismissed as superfluous intermediaries. He remained in the Baptist Church only long enough to make certain that all of his children became Baptists. After that he explored various religious sects, finally settling for the Holy Rollers, whom he came to regard as God's solace for widowers.

His relatives could not take his church life seriously; sooner or later, they predicted, he would return to the arms of the Mother Church. They attributed his flirtations with religious sects to an American "madness" which they were confident would pass as soon as he found a good Sicilian wife to care for him and his six children. What they failed to understand was his craving for venturing beyond his Sicilian world and exposing himself to new ideas and customs. Since I shared the same craving I could understand it. Yet I perceived that, except to take on a new religion or a new American mistress, he would not venture far. Although he had the brains and brawn to surmount the barriers of his environment, even to become a Moses of his people, his lack of English, together with his lack of interest in improving his status, would prevent him from developing into anything more than a gadfly philosopher content with being a bricklayer, playing a noisy game of poker and *briscola*, and taunting his relatives with the unorthodoxies of his not-so-private life.

Unlike Uncle Peppino who relished publicizing his experiences with "Americans" (that is, non-Italians), I instinctively became closemouthed on the subject, fearing perhaps that my mother or my father might detect my scheme to put my Sicilian life behind me as soon as it became feasible. Except for whatever Italian girls came my way who would let me kiss and pet them, I usually gravitated to contemporaries who were not Italian. Throughout most of my teens my closest friend was Mitch Rappaport. He was nearby, minutes away from our home and seconds away from St. Bridget's, the church my mother ordered her children to attend every Sunday. Mitch, a burgeoning skeptic like myself, was my savior. When I began secretly boycotting St. Bridget's because the priest who listened to my confessions had taken to castigating me for reading the novels of Anatole France, I would take refuge at Mitch's house and stay there until mass was over. On such occasions Mitch, the brightest of my contemporaries and the valedictorian of the two schools we attended, would regale me with outrageous parodies of biblical stories which he invented on the spot. A few minutes before mass was finished, I would dash from his house to the church, just in time to intermingle with the congregation as it poured out of its doors, making certain I was seen by relatives who would be likely to tell my mother what a fine, churchgoing son she had.

Mitch and I were kindred spirits yet quite different. While I churned with anxieties that kept me lacking in confidence, he was consistently calm and self-assured. Yet his parents were immigrants with as little education as mine. They spoke Yiddish to each other and broken English to their five children. I marveled that Mitch, unlike myself, accepted their foreign mannerisms with no embarrassment; he was obviously content with his lot. But what I most envied about him was his easy way with girls. Although he was far from handsome—he had the wide mouth and thick lips of a clown—he could always engage the attention of any girl and keep her amused. So superb was his poise that he could pretend he knew how to dance and hold a girl in his arms without moving anything more than his lips. His partners, engrossed in what he was saying, never seemed to mind. He called it the "Why Dance?"

It was Mitch who, on learning that I had become enamored of a girl called Claudia Westfall in my Latin class but lacked the courage to speak to her, prodded me into inviting her to a school dance. Claudia had violet eyes and long blond tresses. She also had acne, but I placed her on so high a pedestal that it was seldom visible. To my astonishment she accepted. As the date of the affair approached I became so excited that I could barely think of my studies. But from the moment I called for Claudia, the evening was a flop. Her parents squelched me with their coolness as soon as they realized I was Italian, not Irish, as they had been surmising from the sound of my first name. Their feelings must have been transmitted to Claudia. During the long trolley ride to the dance, she sat silently and rigidly, indifferent to my desperate attempts at conversation, apparently mesmerized by a soap advertisement.

The situation did not improve at the dance. Although we danced extremely well together (my mother had taught all her children almost as soon as we learned to walk), hardly a word passed between us. Yet I noticed that when she was dancing with some of the other boys, Claudia, the sphinx, became Claudia, the laughing, flirtatious chatterbox. When I delivered her to her door after another long and silent trolley ride, she smiled at me for the first time that evening and called me "a wonderful dancer." Before I could reply in kind, she had pecked me on the cheek and disappeared inside. The compliment and the peck were not enough to assuage my tattered pride. Certain that, like her parents, she considered Italians beneath her, I never dated her again.

The fear of being discriminated against was prevalent among the children of Italians I knew. Some pretended their parents were French or anglicized their names when they applied for jobs at factories like Eastman Kodak and Bausch and Lomb, which then favored anyone else but Italians, Jews and blacks. Others followed the example of their parents and rarely made friends outside their own ethnic group. My own inclination was to associate mainly with Jews who stimulated my intellect more than the Italians I knew. Mitch was not my first Jewish friend. Before him came a freckled redhead named Morrie Levenberg who tutored me in math and Latin (my weakest subjects) and got me a part-time job hawking newspapers at a Main Street newsstand which he and his brother operated.

At Morrie's suggestion I joined a boys' club called the "Aurorans," which consisted of fourteen Jews and me, in a neighborhood settlement house. Financed by funds contributed to the city for charitable causes, the club was my first inkling that our neighborhood was officially regarded as a slum inhabited by disadvantaged families. The extent to which we were disadvantaged did not occur to any of us until our director, a volunteer social worker who was an affluent WASP, took us to his exclusive country club one evening and treated us to a sampling of how the rich spend some of their leisure: a tobogganing party in the moonlight followed by the most luxurious repast we had ever seen. It was enough to make us feel disadvantaged the rest of our lives, especially after we learned that no Jew or Italian was ever permitted to join the club.

Not until I moved from junior high to high school did I become aware that it was possible to have friends who were not ethnics. The first of them were my Anglo-Saxon English teachers who, realizing with what intensity I concentrated on trying to master the language I was forbidden to speak at home, did whatever they could to encourage me. The chairman of the English department awarded me my first literary prize, a Baldwin apple from his own orchard which he presented with all the pomp befitting a Pulitzer. Accepting it in the same spirit, I could not persuade myself to eat the apple but kept it until it was fit for the garbage can.

Another of my English teachers, the faculty adviser of the high school weekly publication, made certain I joined its staff, with the result that I immediately fell into the company of a band of iconoclasts who called themselves the "Conceit Club." They reveled in their cynicism, bragged of their agnosticism, and shamelessly used the pages of the *Clarion* to flaunt their opinions. Twice the publication had been suspended by the high school principal, the first time for publishing a vitriolic editorial attacking the local Hearst newspaper, which was demanding the expulsion of some University of Rochester students who had formed an atheist club known as "The Damned Souls"; the second time for printing a review of a violin concert which likened the violinist's performance to "the squeaks of a dissipated rat."

At first I was wary of becoming closely associated with such reckless characters, afraid they might commit some indiscretion that would get all of us expelled. Yet once I discovered that the bond which held them together was the determination of each person in the group to become a published writer by the time he reached the age of twenty-one, nothing could keep me away from them. There were five of them: three Anglo-Saxons and two Jews, my old friend Mitch Rappaport and Jerry Joroslow, the editor in chief of the *Clarion*, who had come to the defense of "The Damned Souls."

Joroslow, the wittiest and most handsome member of the staff, had himself become an atheist. On one occasion he tried to prove to us, by means of differential calculus, that God could not possibly exist. When his explication went unchallenged, he dared each of us to rise and declare that if God existed, he strike him dead on the spot. His dare was laughed away when someone observed that if God existed, he would have had more sense than to permit the invention of anything as stupidly complicated as calculus. I was often out of my depth, but the excitement of their company prodded me into trying to win their favor. I launched a weekly column of literary and philosophic observations named "Fumes," and I found time to squeeze out pieces of fiction which I could present as evidence that I was worthy of their company. Nothing I did ever overcame the disdain of one of the Anglo-Saxons, but I became friends with the other two, especially Ed Havill, the most talented writer of the group.

Our guru was Arthur Haney, a tall and sallow blond with green eyes and elastic eyebrows, which habitually signaled skepticism whenever he was listening. Haney, who had read far more than the rest of us, exerted a more powerful influence on our impressionable minds than our adult teachers. So extensive was his reading that English teachers were reluctant to tangle with him, aware of the malicious pleasure he took in class letting the other students know that his knowledge of literature surpassed that of the teacher.

His classroom chutzpah was matched by the titillating auto-biographical tidbits he fed us from time to time, such as the information that he was born a bastard and had never known either of his parents, or the revelation that the middle-aged woman with whom he lived, who claimed to be his aunt, forced him to share her bed every night by the simple expedient of refusing to provide any other. His objection to sleeping with her was not a moral one (he would have us understand he was contemptuous of all morals), but that she was too skinny and too old. He was quite certain she was not his aunt but a former servant in the family of his unknown father who was being paid to look after him; every month she received a check for his upkeep from a New York law firm.

As if this were not enough to impress us, one summer night

he announced that on the previous evening he had succeeded in deflowering a virgin whom we all knew as a secretary in the English department. No one else in the group had gone as far with any girl. Elaborating on the story of the seduction, Haney told how he had lured the girl to the top of an abandoned astronomical laboratory on the pretext of pointing out the major constellations, then plied her with Madeira (stolen from his aunt's supply) while he caressed her. Halfway through the wine bottle, she was "begging to be relieved of her cherry." When Havill, who knew the girl to be a stubborn puritan, voiced his skepticism, he led us to the top of the observatory tower, promising to show us "proof positive." There, in the light of the moon, he displayed the empty bottle of Madeira and, most telling of all, pieces of a bloodstained petticoat. These he slowly dropped, one piece at a time, over the parapet of the observatory, all the while leering at us.

Being too young to be certain of anything, we were easily influenced by Haney who seemed sure of everything. In all of us, with the exception of Mitch, he instilled a disdain for convention which clung to us long after he had married the virgin he had seduced and fathered three children. There was a spellbinding sophistication about him which made us believe that to be in his presence, absorbing his erudition and irony, was to learn the secret of how we might triumph over the banalities of our everyday life.

Influenced by Haney, our outward stance was to take no one seriously. The high school yearbook, edited by Mitch, devoted a full page to such Conceit Club pronouncements as "Modesty is the worst policy" and "Our purpose is spreading the gospel of perfectibility of man by offering ourselves as examples of that perfectibility," and was followed by a list of teachers and celebrities who met with the club's approval and a list of those for whom it had no use. Yet behind such juvenile joshing was the intense earnestness of six teen-agers determined to make their mark in the world of arts, one so contagious as to transform my somewhat ambiguous notion of becoming a writer into a specific goal.

It was not an ambition I could discuss with my parents, for since they equated a college education with a standard profession (they did not consider writing a true profession), they might summarily veto it. It was difficult enough for a poor Sicilian family to make the "sacrifices" necessary to send a son through college, they would argue, without having him squander his education on anything as ephemeral as a writing career.

I must have complained of them to my friends. "Why don't you run away with us?" Ed Havill suggested one hot July afternoon. He and a friend had been talking of their plans for escaping the "claustrophobic atmosphere" of their homes by living as hoboes. "It's the best kind of experience a writer can get," Ed added. "How about it?"

The idea of abandoning my parents shocked me. Although escape was in my mind, I could not imagine being indifferent to their feelings. Since, by Conceit Club standards, such an admission would smack of sentimentality, I found another reason for turning down the invitation: I could not afford to quit my summer job.

That was no lie. From the time I was thirteen I had been supplementing my father's meager wage with earnings from part-time jobs. I did not mind; the jobs were another means of exploring the American world. My first was ushering in a burlesque theater called The Family, for which I received five dollars a week and two free tickets. The money I gave to my mother, who was under the impression I was employed as a cashier in a cigar store; the tickets went to my friends. I was too inexperienced to appreciate the off-color humor of the comedians who performed at The Family, but the chorus girls and their gyrations excited me and occupied a prominent place in my fantasy repertoire long after I quit the job.

The next summer, at the age of fourteen, I worked as a busboy in an elegant hotel restaurant. Its polyglot staff included a French widow (my boss) who was having an affair with the German headwaiter; a black dishwasher who talked like Huck Finn's Jim; and a Canadian cashier named Mr. Verity who showed me photographs of bare-assed boys, then made passes at me. There was also a big-breasted young Polish cook who would caress me while I deciphered for her the pornographic love letters she received from an Irish lover living in Buffalo. Because of some romantic notion that I should not come between them, I did not press my advantage with her, nor could I respond to her. When, at the end of the summer I left the job to return to school, the cook bade me good-bye by pulling me into a dark mop closet and kissing me with her tongue in my mouth. When she was finished, I stuck out my hand for a farewell handshake.

The only job I came to hate was digging ditches in the Eastman Kodak plant under the sadistic supervision of a foreman named Leary. I wanted to quit after the first excruciating day, but since it paid more than I had ever earned (thirty dollars a week), at a time when my parents were badly in debt, I felt compelled to stick it out. By some act of Providence, a few weeks later I contracted a severe case of poison ivy while clearing some land of its weeds. It laid me up for almost a month, but enabled me to leave the job with a clear conscience.

As soon as I recovered, I answered a classified advertisement for "young men with dancing ability" to perform in the musical Sally, which was being produced by the Lyceum Players, a local repertory company that starred professionals. Apparently my lack of self-assurance did not extend to my feet for I was promptly hired for the chorus line, and placed under the tutelage of George Cukor, then a fledgling director. For the next two weeks Cukor, an impatient and demanding taskmaster, scolded and drilled his charges several times a day until he had whipped us into a synchronized team that could perform with enough precision to escape the brickbats of the local critics.

The role of Sally was played by a brunette named Dorothy

Burgess, who seemed genuinely relieved on opening night that we could hoist her in the air with apparent ease. The featured male star was Louis Calhern, who drank incessantly but who, onstage, was the essence of controlled insouciance.

My sudden immersion in the theater generated such a state of euphoria in me as to arouse the fears of my mother, whose leaps of intuition never failed to astonish me. From the outset she disapproved of the job, claiming that theater people were a disreputable lot, not fit company for a seventeen-year-old. Why couldn't I find myself another busboy job instead where I would associate with "nice" people? But I sensed that her genuine fear, one which she was too prudent to voice, was that I might decide to become an actor or a dancer. To register her disapproval of any such notion, she refused to watch me perform, nor would she permit any other member of the family to do so.

There was, of course, some justification for her fear. A stage career struck me as an ideal means of escaping Rochester, and at the same time myself. Without considering whether or not I had acting talent, I was fascinated by the prospect of spending my life assuming a variety of roles that were antithetical to my private self, which I considered dangerously overburdened with Sicilian melancholy. I had no doubt that I was among the most melancholy of creatures, especially after the discovery that my paternal grandfather Gerlando, whose portrait my schoolmates often mistook for that of Edgar Allen Poe, had drowned himself in the Mediterranean one Christmas Eve when my father was still a child. I suspected that my grandfather's fate, which my father had twice tried to attain, could well become my own.

Acting, I reasoned, was a far less lonely activity than writing and could dispel my melancholy and possibly save me from myself. The idea gained momentum when the manager of the Lyceum Players hinted that he might be able to place me with a Broadway musical which was going into rehearsal in the fall. But after performing in three productions, once as an extra in a comedy starring Miriam Hopkins (*The Poor Nut*), I concluded that the stage was not for me. The prospect of enacting the same motions and words night after night struck me as dismal, far more conducive to self-destruction than a melancholy disposition. I wondered how any intelligent adult could endure the boredom of playing in a long-running production and pitied the lot of the actor for having to rely on the applause of strangers for his chief stimulus and reward. While writing was lonelier than acting, it offered a more enduring sense of achievement.

The decision came in the wake of an encounter with George Cukor who, on hearing I had recently completed a play, asked to see it. I sent him my one-act farce about a dentist and his patient, which was largely inspired by all the ordeals I had experienced in the hands of dentists from the age of fourteen when I mangled my front teeth while playing football on the street. Having been subjected to Cukor's imperial directorial style, I nervously awaited his verdict, expecting him to find me guilty for having committed an atrocity. Instead, much to my relief, he expressed enthusiasm for the quality of the dialogue, which reminded him of a Broadway comedy hit, *March Hares.* "I can't say much for the plot, but your dialogue is very amusing." After expressing surprise that I had never heard of *March Hares,* he advised me to read as much as possible, get a good liberal arts education, and get in touch with him after that. (For reasons beyond my ken, I never got in touch with Cukor.) He was only ten years older than I, but, listening to his advice, I felt as if Moses himself were dictating a special commandment for my exclusive benefit.

Cukor's encouragement came at the right time. That fall, as the newly elected head of the *Clarion,* I plunged into the editorship with great relish and unaccustomed self-confidence, radically changing the publication's format and the writing style, to resemble that of *Time,* the weekly I had been admiring ever since its inception a few years earlier. My boldness paid off. Within a few months, the *Clarion* was awarded a silver trophy for excellence at Cornell University's annual contest for high school publications. Even more exhilarating was the congratulatory letter from Henry R. Luce, one of the founders of *Time*. "Of course," wrote Luce, "the contents of your magazine make as much sense to us as *Time* would to a Hottentot. There is, however, a great difference: no Hottentot reads *Time;* about half of *Time*'s editorial staff have now become ardent readers of the *Clarion.*" The letter concluded with the hope that he would see me "sometime in the near future."

In my state of bliss I interpreted the letter as a clear invitation to join the *Time* staff as quickly as possible. I promptly informed Luce that my services would be at his disposal in June on the day after I got my high school diploma, and then began reveling in the possibility of using *Time* as a convenient escape hatch from Rochester without incurring the expense and effort of a college education. The reply from *Time* dashed all such wishful thinking. There were no openings on the staff; however, since I seemed determined to be a professional journalist, I was advised to get a college education first.

That was more easily said than done; there were two obstacles immediately confronting me: a lack of tuition money and, what appeared to be more insurmountable, miserable grades in mathematics which precluded admission into the University of Rochester, the university my parents assumed I would be attending, if only for reasons of economy. The tuition I could acquire by working full time until I had saved enough money, but would my parents permit me to leave home for an out-of-town university that would admit me?

A good Sicilian son was expected to remain with his family; he left home only to be married; even then, he continued to live close by his parents. By leaving I would be violating a basic tenet of their philosophy. Yet to remain among my relatives, steeped in their past, was to deny myself the chance of finding out whether I could be an American without feeling like an impostor.

By now I had become all too aware that the wide gulf

between my Sicilian and American worlds went beyond differences of custom and language. There was a basic difference of philosophy. Ingrained in the Sicilian soul by centuries of poverty and oppression were strong elements of fatalism which my relatives called *Destino*. In their minds *Destino*, the willingness to resign oneself to misfortune, was the key to survival; to refuse to believe that an almighty force predetermined the fate of all people was to court disaster.

In his thunderings against our teachers my father must have sensed that the philosophy they drummed into us was diametrically opposed to that of his people. There was nothing fatalistic about it; constantly our teachers talked of freedom, free enterprise, free will, and stressed the ability of the individual to change and improve his situation. My need to leave my relatives was buttressed by the conviction that my teachers must be right. Although at the age of eighteen I could sound as dogmatic as the Pope when I argued with my father, I could not let him know how radically our philosophies differed. Nor did I dare correct my mother's impression that since I could not be admitted to the local university, I would be applying to colleges within commuting distance.

The week after high school graduation I landed a full-time job at twenty dollars a week, dictating sales correspondence into the mouth of a dictaphone in behalf of the Samson Cutlery Company. *"Destino,"* said my mother who, prudently, believed in crediting Destiny with happy events as well as disasters. For six days a week, eight hours a day, I sang out the praises of Samson-produced stainless steel kitchen utensils. Whenever I tired of my false enthusiasm I would sneak downstairs to chat with the shipping clerk, who was an avid reader and a poet. Philip worked as a standup comic in small nightclubs on weekends and dreamed of getting into the big time. We were a comfort to each other. To no one else in the plant did I confide my plan for getting a college degree: quitting my post as soon as I had enough money for the first year's tuition, then financing the rest of my education with summer jobs and whatever part-time work I could pick up around a campus. On less optimistic days when I would observe how much easier it might be for me to develop a career in stainless steel, Philip, who was only five years older than I, would scold me with the earnestness of a concerned parent.

After nine months I had saved enough money and been admitted to Syracuse University, despite my weakness in mathematics, for the semester that started in February 1928. Not until I had dictated my last sales letter could I summon the courage to let my parents know that Syracuse was the nearest university that would admit me. To my surprise, neither of them objected. I had underestimated their love for me, their willingness to let me judge what was best for my future. My mother wept a little at the prospect of my leaving home; then, with her instinctive pragmatism and sense of tradition, made me promise I would take courses that would qualify me as a teacher, a profession she considered more honorable than that of a writer. Among our relatives she immediately began spreading the word that my heart was set on becoming a *professore.*

Except for my parents and my uncles Peppino and Stefano, my Sicilian relatives were disturbed that I had enrolled in an out-of-town university. With their customary candor, they wondered aloud whether I had turned into a calloused *Americano,* a heretic who had lost respect for family traditions, another Uncle Peppino. From their viewpoint there was no intelligent alternative to living among those who were sure to love you since they were of your own flesh and blood. In the long run, they said, your close relatives were the only ones you could trust, and you left them only when it became absolutely necessary, or when you were taken away in a coffin.

Had I argued with this attitude I would have strengthened their suspicion that I had become a disrespectful *Americano.* Yet I could not help suggesting that traveling to Syracuse was not nearly as drastic an action as the one they had taken when they left close relatives behind in Sicily to travel three thousand miles to a foreign country. I added that the distance between

Rochester and Syracuse was as short as that between their home province, Agrigento, and Palermo, less than two hours away by train. That cheered them a little, but did not prevent them from cursing America as a land that encourages bad practices among the young, with the same invectives I had heard all through childhood.

When they saw me off at the station, they carried on as though I might never return.

TWO

Kingdom on the Hill

When I arrived in the winter of 1928 Syracuse University
was just beginning to recover its respectability as an institution
of higher learning after the calamitous reign of a chancellor
named James Roscoe Day, who conducted himself more like a
brigand than an educator.° Under his aegis the university
achieved renown for its victorious football teams of salaried
jocks and some notoriety for pandering to special business
interests at the expense of scholarly considerations.

Happily, I knew nothing then of its scandalous past. As I first
beheld the university, through a curtain of soft snowflakes,
situated on the plateau of a long hill, it struck me as a noble
kingdom directed by sages who, in their wisdom, had seen fit to
admit me. I was especially taken by a nineteenth-century castle
of red stone which, situated on a hill of its own, towered above
the other campus buildings. The sagest of all the university

° A pillar of the Methodist Church, Day was chancellor of Syracuse
University from 1893 to 1922. During his administration the student body was
increased from eight hundred to more than five thousand. The unsavory
aspects of his regime are described in Upton Sinclair's book *The Goose Step—
A Study in American Education* (1923).

35

sages must be ensconced in that castle, I imagined, and later
learned that was a good guess. She was the only recognized
genius on the faculty, a tiny and withered spinster named
Sargent who lectured on the history of Italian art in a wildly
impressionistic style that was at odds with her decrepitude.
Legend had it that her brain was willed to science.

If my initial view of the campus evoked mythic visions, my
first reaction to my campus living quarters was one of despair.
Everywhere I looked I saw Italian faces. Ironically, I who had
taken my first giant step to escape my Italian environment had
landed in an all-Italian fraternity house. A few days before one
of its members, in the presence of my father, had used this
insidious sales pitch: "You won't have to join if you don't want
to. Just come and use the place until you decide where you
want to live." With my father nodding his approval, I dared
not say no.

Most of my relatives I could enjoy, but not these fraternity
brothers. There was not a poet or philosopher among them.
They constituted a miniature ghetto gathered under one roof
for the same reason their immigrant forebears had banded
together in one neighborhood: to fortify themselves against the
fear of being surrounded by a hostile people. The fears of their
parents had become their fears. Except for some of the girls
they dated, they avoided associating with non-Italians and were
puzzled by my refusal to follow their example.

It offended them when I accepted an invitation to dine at a
Jewish fraternity house, and when I compounded this indiscretion by permitting myself to be courted by another fraternity
house, one composed largely of Catholic Irish, they reacted as
though I had committed treason. Although I was determined to
part with them as soon as I could find a legitimate excuse, they
seemed eager to make me one of them, feeling perhaps that
every fraternity house should have a token oddball like me who
preferred reading books to playing bridge. They may also have
been impressed by my Cyrano-like talent for lining up blind

dates for them on the telephone, a talent I seemed unable to exercise in my own behalf.

The Catholic Irish fraternity began wooing me as soon as I joined the staff of the *Daily Orange,* the campus newspaper, which was edited by the fraternity's president. After a number of free meals, the courtship was climaxed by a two-part Saturday-afternoon ritual that was evidently intended to demonstrate the fraternity's attachment to both the sacred and the profane. First I was taken to a rowdy burlesque show, then hustled to the nearest Catholic church for confession. When I rejected the opportunity to confess and, later, to join the fraternity, I was gently warned that as a nonfraternity man my chances of winning a top position in any campus activity were nil. I was reminded that Stephen Crane himself, in the single year he spent at Syracuse on a baseball scholarship, had deemed it wise to become a fraternity man.

All this threatened my hope of becoming the chief editor of the *Daily Orange,* but the more I learned of fraternity life the more determined I became not to join one. I deplored their cliquishness, their barbaric hazing practices, and their control of extracurricular activities. Most of all perhaps I was offended by their bourgeois view of life. At the age of eighteen "bourgeois" was the dirtiest word in my vocabulary, the word I wanted to scream in the faces of the men whose house I shared. I never did. Even then I was aware of the limits of my courage; whatever screaming I was to do would be mostly done on my typewriter.

I left the Italian fraternity house for the Victorian home of my French professor where, in exchange for doing chores around the house and grounds, I was to receive room and board. The only inhabitants of the huge house were the bachelor professor, his elderly parents, and his younger brother. They were a Mayflower-descended family, gentle and quiet and somewhat anemic. I liked them, but I felt uncomfortable in the presence of the brother who was effeminate in voice and

movement. He had just become engaged to a chunky woman of
masculine demeanor whose sparse black moustache contrasted
nicely with his sparse blond one.

Except for the burden of the chores, which included shoveling snow off the interminable sidewalks bordering the corner
house, I was treated like a member of the family. Every Sunday
we would all pile into a seven-passenger aged Cadillac and ride
through the delightful countryside around Syracuse, stopping at
the same elegant restaurant each time for a dinner of southern
fried chicken served by black waiters wearing white gloves. On
most Sundays, especially when the woman with the moustache
accompanied us, there would also be visits to family relatives
who lived in small tree-lined villages that were as quiet as
funeral parlors. We would sit in small and gloomy rooms where
the sun was permitted to penetrate only when there was
company, on staid Victorian chairs and horsehair divans
adorned with crocheted doilies, sipping tea or lemonade and
munching cookies. The conversation would be as stiff as the
furniture, a measured exchange of clichés so familiar as to be
devoid of meaning.

Apart from these excursions, there was little conversation
among the family members. It was as if they had long ago run
out of things to say to one another. At the dinner table their
silences hung over the meal like an ominous shroud. I, who
longed for silence when I was among my relatives, now began
to feel smothered by it. Adding to my uneasiness were the
impromptu visits to my room the professor's brother began
making, usually while I was preparing for bed or bathing.
There was never anything improper about what he said or did
on such occasions, but since we rarely had anything to say to
each other, they became an intrusion, a further incentive to
change my situation.

Although my weekly letters to my family avoided complaints,
they must have reflected my discontent for, without prompting,
my brother Frank began sending me part of his wages every

week (usually a five-dollar money order), a practice he was to continue the rest of my college days. This income, along with a part-time job I found in the university library, freed me of the oppressive silences, the effeminate brother, and many hours of snow shoveling.

I felt further liberated when I moved into an apartment occupied by a blithe spirit, a senior named Kenneth Langford, who was the editor of the campus literary magazine. Langford, a diabetic, lived with his widowed mother. Theirs was a reluctant menage dictated by the seriousness of his affliction, which required a specially prepared diet. The responsibility of having to make her son follow the doctor's rules had turned Mrs. Langford, a dour woman by nature, into a nagging worrywart, for although his face and body were blotched with diabetic sores and he had already lost the full use of one arm, Langford refused to have his illness interfere with his zest for living, which was largely centered around girls and literature. He must have realized how close he was to death, but he never spoke of his illness nor would he permit his mother to mention it when there were others present.

Yet there was nothing spurious about his cheerfulness. He was by far the warmest and most openhearted Anglo-Saxon American I had ever known, and we soon became fast friends. He talked to me freely about everything except his illness, including the gonorrhea he had recently contracted from a girl he had been seeing in New York. He told me that on questioning her, the girl had readily admitted sleeping with another man. My Sicilian sensibilities were confounded when I realized he was neither angry with the girl nor about to give her up.

"Why should I?" he countered. "She's a grand girl, a healthy specimen who needs more sex than I can give her from this distance. So if I want her—and I certainly do—I'll just have to share her with others."

Would he be willing to marry such a girl?

"Sure. If she'd have me, I'd marry her tomorrow."

"Even though she sleeps with other men?"

"She's the kind of girl who'll be faithful to the man she marries," he replied.

"What makes you so sure?"

He laughed and called me "a suspicious Sicilian." I hardly ever discussed my background with him, but this time I told him about the rigid sexual mores of my relatives, their intolerance of unfaithful wives, and the heavy premium they placed on the virginity of the girls they marry. I mentioned the tidbit about the Sicilian father who had bitten off the ear of a boy who was secretly dating his daughter.

"Holy cow," exclaimed Langford. "They sound even worse than my Puritan ancestors."

Inevitably, I became infected with Langford's carefree spirit and, following his example, began to concentrate only on the courses I enjoyed; the others I muddled through. One immediate advantage of this policy was that it left me with more time and energy for my *Daily Orange* assignments, which I took more seriously than those from my teachers. Determined to impress my editors, I began to dream up assignments of my own, which included interviews with prominent writers who came to Syracuse.

The first was with Edna St. Vincent Millay, then regarded as America's most successful woman poet since Emily Dickinson. The interview itself was a failure, but by writing of the circumstances attending it in a way that poked fun at myself I produced a story which the editors liked well enough to put on the front page. It began when, on learning belatedly that Millay was in the city to give a poetry reading that evening, I telephoned her hotel for an appointment only to be told by her Belgian husband that his wife was bathing; he doubted there would be time for an interview since they were due to dine with some people within forty minutes. Stimulated perhaps by the image of the poet in the bathtub, I disregarded the second part of the husband's statement and rushed to the hotel where I wrote her a note which I thought was in keeping with her Greenwich Village reputation for scorning convention. It read: "Have you dried out from your bath by now? May I please see you for a few moments?" Before I could have second thoughts, I thrust the note and a coin in a bellboy's hand and asked him to deliver it to Millay's room. While I waited I had a number of second thoughts, all depressing, but they vanished as soon as the bellboy returned with the astonishing news that I was to go up to the poet's room.

As I entered, I was greeted by a curious tableau: the husband was on his knees slipping one of Millay's feet into a golden evening slipper. "So you're the one who wrote that note!" were her first words. "I couldn't imagine what kind of a person would write such a note." Her features were plain, but her thin lips and high cheekbones gave her face classical contours. Watching her smile as she studied me, I decided it was one of the most beautiful faces I had ever seen. "As you gather," she said, nodding toward her husband who remained on his knees, "we're in a terrible hurry. I'm afraid I have time for only one question. Just one."

Of the dozens of questions that had occurred to me on the way to the hotel the only one that now presented itself concerned one of my English teachers who liked to brag of his influence on Millay when she was a student at Vassar. This was shortly before she was to publish *Renascence,* the slim volume of verse that brought her immediate fame. "At Vassar," I began, "one of your English teachers was Dr. Burges Johnson. Would you please tell me if he influenced your writing?"

Without hesitating, she replied: "He did not."

It was the end of the interview. In my ignorance of the art of interviewing, I had stupidly asked a question that could be answered with a single word or phrase. My dejection must have been all too apparent, for as I mumbled my thanks and shuffled toward the door, Millay took pity on me. Asking me to wait a moment, she wrote her name in one of the books on a desk, and handed it to me. It was her latest work, *The King's Henchman,*

a play in verse which she had written without using a single
Latin-derived word. She was smiling as she apologized for not
giving me more time and sent me on my way.

The gift changed everything. What had been a disaster now
struck me as an amusing happening. Except for omitting Burges
Johnson's name, I described it exactly as it had taken place.
When the story was published the next morning, it drew a
number of compliments, including one from the chief editor
who urged me to interview more visiting writers. After that I
tried to get an audience with every prominent writer who came
to Syracuse, not only because I enjoyed the sight of my byline
but also because part of me secretly believed that by osmosis
some of their talent might seep into me.

Among those I interviewed were G. K. Chesterton, Carl
Sandburg, Stephen Leacock, Zona Gale, Thornton Wilder, John
Cowper Powys, and Louis Untermeyer. Sandburg, more than
the others, had a personality that matched his writings. He
obviously liked people, and his talk was simple but cryptic. At
the dinner party in his honor, he and I were the only ones not
in formal dress. His sloppy blue suit was spattered with cigar
ashes and food stains; he looked like some poorly paid functionary of a minor left-wing party, but he was more at ease than
anyone else there.

Louis Untermeyer was so addicted to punning that, after
hearing him perform in conversation and on the lecture platform, I tried to refrain from punning, afraid I might become as
jarringly compulsive. Thornton Wilder, who had just become
famous with *The Bridge of San Luis Rey*, triggered a mysterious
impulse in me to mock him at every turn, so much so that he
began referring to me as his "gadfly." Yet we liked each other,
and he invited me to accompany him to a cocktail party in his
honor. When the hostess gushingly complimented him on the
accuracy with which he described the bridge at San Luis Rey,
which she had recently visited, and spoke scornfully of writers
who relied on their imaginations rather than on firsthand

observation, Wilder turned to me as soon as she was out of earshot to whisper that he had never set eyes on the bridge.

The most memorable of them was John Cowper Powys, the British novelist, whose leonine profile and penetrating eyes evoked images of high grass and thick forest; he may well have been, in a previous incarnation, some kingly primeval beast. His words, as much as the fine nostrils of his arrowhead nose, bespoke a wizard's intuition which became increasingly lucid with each cup of tea he drank. He imbibed the stuff with the avidness of a dipsomaniac, all the while hypnotizing me with talk. Long before our two-hour session was over, I knew I was in the presence of a remarkable sage.

Powys had more questions to ask of me than I of him. On learning I was full-blooded Sicilian with parents from the ancient province of Agrigento, he chided me for not using my baptismal name of Gerlando, then discoursed eloquently about the glories of Sicilian civilization which, I learned for the first time, antedated that of Rome by two thousand years. Yet he was no mere pundit; he was also a poet, a connoisseur of the humanities. His magnetism made it difficult for me to part with him. When I finally did, I longed to ask him to become my friend, but I was too much in awe to do anything more than ask that he sign my copy of his most recent book, *The Meaning of Culture.* He inscribed it to Gerlando Mangione.

In my heated quest for added prestige and new friends, I ignored my studies further and plunged into the task of resurrecting the campus literary magazine, *The Chap Book,* which had expired soon after its editor, my friend Langford, was graduated. Not attracting enough advertisers, the magazine was about to expire again when Burges Johnson, the same Johnson whose influence Edna St. Vincent Millay had denied, came to its rescue by persuading the university to purchase from me all unsold copies of future issues I edited.

Johnson had adopted me as his protégé. He was a middle-aged Vermonter, all curmudgeon, with a demeanor more like that of a hard-boiled city editor than an academic. In an earlier period, he had been a widely published essayist, a sort of Lamb with cat claws, best known for an essay defending the art of swearing. Now and then he talked of his past (though no longer of Millay); he had known Mark Twain, Hamlin Garland, and William Dean Howells, and roomed with (to the confusion of their mutual friends) Gelett Burgess,° who when asked how he and Burges Johnson were faring as roommates replied: "Extremely well. We never speak to each other."

The university planned to distribute the surplus copies it bought of *The Chap Book* to alumni and students applying for admission, but there were no unsold copies of the second issue, which contained a heretofore unknown short story by Stephen Crane that I had discovered in the magazine files of the university library,† as well as a brief article I wrote describing Crane's unpublished letters to Nellie Jane Crouse, a girl who had caught his fancy at a New York tea party.‡ This second item was another unexpected bonanza, which fell in my lap when I learned by chance that a Rochester bookstore had recently acquired the correspondence. The bookstore was reluctant to give me permission to read the letters, but finally agreed with the stipulation that I was not to take any notes.

° Gelett Burgess became one of America's most quoted humorists with these four lines of nonsense verse:

> I never saw a purple cow
> I never hope to see one
> But this I'll say and say right now
> I'd rather see than be one.

† *Chap Book*, May 1930, Syracuse Univeristy. "The Cry of the Huckleberry Pudding" had first appeared in an 1892 issue of the *University Herald* while Crane was a student at Syracuse. It was republished in Syracuse campus literary publications in 1897 and 1909.

‡ *Stephen Crane's Unpublished Letters*, ibid. Published in book form in 1954 (*Stephen Crane's Love Letters to Nellie Crouse*, Syracuse University Press), its editors described one of the letters as "the longest, the most intimately self-probing, and perhaps the most important of all his letters."

Since the letters were impounded by the Crane estate shortly afterward, the article was to remain the sole source of information about them for more than two decades. But it was the short story, "The Cry of the Huckleberry Pudding," one of Crane's poorer efforts, that created the greatest stir, especially after an Associated Press dispatch informed the nation about it. There were congratulatory letters from many strangers, and an angry note from the chagrined publisher who had recently issued what he thought was Stephen Crane's "complete" works.

Burges Johnson came to my rescue again at the end of my junior year when, to my bitter disappointment, the editorship of the *Daily Orange*, which I believed I had clearly earned, went to someone else. Just as I had been warned in my freshman year, the job was awarded to a fraternity man. The decision affected my pocketbook as well as my pride since the job paid fifteen dollars a week. When it appeared that I was going to be left out in the cold, Johnson interceded to persuade the *Daily Orange*'s governing board to create a new staff job for me, one that had not existed before and would not exist again, at eight dollars a week. As part of the compromise, I was told I could write whatever I pleased without being responsible to anyone on the staff.

Once I got over the feeling of being cheated, I rejoiced in my freedom and initiated a daily column called "Muse-ings" in which I wrote on any subject that struck my fancy. The column produced a surprising number of fringe benefits, such as free tickets to movies, plays, and concerts, dates with girls who would have ignored me ordinarily, and, most unexpected of all, better grades than I deserved from teachers who were persuaded by the column that I must be brighter than my performance in their classes indicated.

If Burges Johnson catered to my journalistic ambitions, another member of the English department, Leonard Brown, who was closer to me in age and temperament, helped to nurture and refine my literary aspirations. This soft-spoken Nebraskan was a radical of sorts for, unlike the rest of his colleagues, he dared discuss living writers in the classroom at a time when only dead writers appeared on the reading lists which college English teachers assigned to their students. Brown became a friend as well as a teacher. When the Langfords returned to their hometown in upstate Pennsylvania, where Kenneth Langford was to spend his few remaining years operating a small chain of gas stations, Leonard Brown found me living quarters in a cellar room of the apartment house where he and his family lived. In exchange for giving English lessons to the building's janitor, a recent German immigrant, I got the room rent free.

Brown and Helene Hartley, a widowed professor in the school of education, became my closest faculty friends. Both were anxious that on leaving the university I try to develop my literary talents rather than be "trapped into teaching." When Brown learned from Helene Hartley that I was taking education courses only because my parents wanted me to qualify for a teaching certificate, he dropped his usual mild manner and passionately enjoined me to avoid teaching at all costs. "What your parents expect of you is less important than what you expect of yourself," he said. Teaching, he added, drained a person of energy and emotion to the point where he could only produce writings of a cerebral nature. His bitterness reflected his own sense of entrapment—he longed to leave academia for the world of letters—but I could not imagine a happier trap than the one he occupied. He had a beautiful wife, a charming infant daughter, and an apartment filled with books and literary artifacts; there was even a spinet around which he and his friends gathered to sing English ballads and German lieder. I, who had never known such a cultured atmosphere outside of museums and in Hollywood movies, was puzzled that anyone in such circumstances could want anything more.

My cellar room had bars on the window, but it was an incubator of dreams. Lying on my cot I could look up at the open sky and stars and dream of a wife and apartment as enticing as Brown's. Lying on the same cot on weekend nights was another matter; then my libido would become inflamed by the activity in the bedroom next to my room which was only a paper-thin partition away. The bedroom was part of a large basement apartment inhabited by two graduate students, one of whom (an accounting student) had a different lover every weekend. With his pug nose and thick glasses he seemed an unlikely Don Juan, but his success with women was phenomenal. They were chiefly schoolteachers from nearby small towns. The lovemaking would start on a Friday night and continue steadily until Monday morning, always to the accompaniment of hot jazz. Above the beat of the music I could clearly hear the women moaning and exclaiming; I felt bereft for still being a virgin.

Don Juan's roommate was a student of the piano with a poetic face not unlike the mask of John Keats, and a skinny body six-and-a-half-feet tall. He was in the throes of his first love affair with a married Jewess from Manhattan ten years his senior, who barely came up to his navel. They had met on a blind date while she was visiting relatives in Syracuse and they had been together ever since. Every Saturday night Dora would phone her husband in New York to give him a full report on the status of her affair. One night, when I was attending a noisy party in the basement apartment, Dora asked me to help her find a public phone booth where, at her insistence, she sat on my lap while telling her husband how much she loved him, how much she hoped he was getting plenty of sex, and what a splendid lover the piano student was getting to be.

Until then, she had not appealed to me sexually, but listening to her report inspired an erection, which in turn inspired the hope that a woman so liberated from convention would have no objection liberating me from my virginity then and there. But when the phone conversation was over and I tried to keep her on my lap, she gently released herself, kissed me lightly on the lips, and said it was time to return to the party.

Despite my lack of technique and self-assurance for seducing girls, I could not keep away from them. Three of them occupied most of my college spare time. The first was a petite Italian brunette whom I dated until my sophomore year when I learned, in the nick of time, that her Neapolitan father was expecting me to marry her. She was succeeded by a sultry earth mother with an English name and a New Jersey twang. The senior year was mostly taken up with an Irish Catholic coed from Massachusetts who was literary, witty, and passionate, but was as firmly determined to preserve her virginity for the man she married as were all the other coeds I ever dated.

There was less time for male companionship. After Langford left Syracuse, my closest friends became an Anglo-Saxon with an Italian name and a Marxist-minded Jew, neither of whom had any use for the other. Ted Colombo was a tall blond Apollo from Long Island who was Italian only by remote ancestry. Benny Birlowitz was a runty but charismatic product of the Syracuse slums, with a shrill voice, a small chin, and a mass of kinky red hair. Birlowitz was a Communist, Colombo a snob; the only thing they had in common, besides my friendship, was a loathing for most of their college courses.

Colombo spent a great deal of time writing poetry, listening to George Gershwin's music (especially *Rhapsody in Blue)*, and drinking bootleg gin. His parents were of modest means; his mother worked as a telephone operator, so she could provide him (her only child) with a generous allowance. Colombo preferred to give the impression he was the scion of a wealthy family. In the winter months he sported a huge black bearskin coat which, contrasting theatrically with his fair skin and blond hair, sometimes provoked the sneers and jeers of strangers, particularly in slum neighborhoods. Occasionally, when he had drunk too much, he would don the coat and parade in the same neighborhoods, hoping someone would insult him so that he could give vent to the anger he felt but could not express when sober.

Colombo was my introduction to the world of avant-garde
writing. It was he who lent me a copy of Joyce's *Ulysses*
smuggled into the country for him by his friend Paul Bowles,
who was frequenting Gertrude Stein's Paris salon regularly and
making a name for himself in the arts. Bowles, though no older
than either of us, had in the span of a few months published a
poem in *transition*, exhibited an oil painting at the Metropolitan Museum, and composed a chamber piece that was performed in a Manhattan concert. At Colombo's instigation,
Bowles and I corresponded frequently for almost a year before
we met, he in a prose which sounded as if it had been written
by Gertrude Stein, I in my own imitation of Stein. When finally
we came face to face while he was visiting Colombo one
weekend, we both sensed that each of us had been pretending
to be what he was not. As much as I admired this son of a
dentist who, emulating Poe, had dropped out of the University
of Virginia, I could not reconcile his flesh-and-blood personality
with the one he projected in his letters. He must have had the
same difficulty with me. Whatever hope Colombo entertained
that Bowles and I would become intimate friends ended when,
like some Philistine, I flatly refused to join the two in an ether
party Colombo was arranging with some nurses he knew. After
that weekend, we never communicated again.

My encounter with Bowles caused me to realize that I no
longer embraced the art-for-art's-sake cult, as I had tended to
do in high school. The shock of the Sacco and Vanzetti
executions, along with Mussolini's increasing stranglehold on
Italy, made me feel that no writer worth his salt could turn his
back on social injustice. Although I could be titillated by the
esoterica of a Bowles or Colombo, even to the extent of trying
my hand at it, I found myself resentful of their attitude that the
evils promulgated by fascism and the excesses of capitalism
were of no concern to them.

As much as I deplored certain aspects of Benny Birlowitz,
such as his amoral attitude toward women, his Marxist-Leninist

gospel with its stress on the welfare of the working class, a class with which I could easily identify, struck a responsive chord in me. Except for the shrillness of his personality and his soap-box style of speech, Benny fascinated me from the first time I encountered him in Burges Johnson's class. He lived at home, in a slum area, with his immigrant parents, his four brothers, and a sister, all of whom considered him a genius. Although Benny periodically proclaimed to them his contempt for American higher education, which he considered part of the capitalist conspiracy for brainwashing the youth of America, his family was determined to provide him with a college education. To me, Benny maintained that had his family not been so insistent on sending him to college, he would have become a successful criminal. (He boasted of having been a member of the Syracuse underworld for two years.) "Only the criminals of this country have it within their power to bring about the downfall of capitalism without a bloody revolution."

Revolution was not his only obsession. The other two were to become the American Dostoievsky and to seduce as many women as possible, regardless of their age, size, or looks. The latter obsession included his own sister, a recent high school graduate with limpid brown eyes and a lusciously rounded figure who worked as a file clerk to help finance Benny's education. "So what's wrong with a little incest?" Benny asked. "Just so long as I don't knock her up." He giggled as he said that and I thought he must surely be joking, but about a week later he reported he had fed his sister a dose of Spanish fly in a glass of wine and would have had her in bed had it not been for the unexpected arrival of an uncle. His sister must have suspected his intentions for I never heard any more talk about seducing her.

Once he adopted me as his friend, Benny felt obliged to take my sexual education in hand. He registered disgust when I admitted that the various coeds I had been dating would do nothing more than neck. "Come the revolution," he announced, "all such cockteasers will be liquidated." So far the extent of my sexual experience consisted of a few minutes with a whore. One night I had accompanied a group of students on their regular Saturday-night visits to the city's redlight district and been introduced to their favorite whore who, on learning I was a virgin, had treated me with more compassion than passion. Disappointed, I resolved that rather than visit a whorehouse again, I would bide my time until a desirable and willing girl came along.

Benny, who regarded all brothels as "cesspools of capitalist exploitation," promised to find me such a girl, then telephoned a few days later to inform me that he had fixed me up with "the best lay in town." He said she was a housewife who usually charged one dollar, but since I was his friend I had only to pay her fifty cents. "How come she charges so little?" I asked suspiciously. "Because she likes to fuck—that's why," replied Benny.

The address he gave me was in a squalid neighborhood. As I walked up to the door I noticed three young children in tattered clothes playing in the front yard. The woman who came to the door wore a sloppy kimona and had no front teeth. "I was afraid you was the welfare man," she said after I explained that Benny had sent me. "You kids go on playing," she yelled at the children. As I entered the living room, the stench of poverty assailed my senses. She was about to lead me into a bedroom but the stench, as much as the image of the children, was too much for me. I hastily thrust a dollar in her hand, mumbled that I was late for an appointment, and fled.

"Well, I guess she wasn't your type," was Benny's comment when I told him what had happened. "Next time I'll line up something special for you, and it won't cost you a dime."

The "something special" materialized into a mousy Irish Catholic named Kathleen whom Benny had seduced several months before. When he had first met her—he had picked her up at a trolley stop—Kathleen was in her last months of high school and was planning to become a nun. "It was an intellectual challenge I couldn't resist," Benny explained, and described how he went about transforming her from a devout Catholic into an amoral wench who was prepared "to man the barricades in the coming revolution." He attributed his success partly to his powers of persuasion, but also to three authors whose works he insisted she read: Nietzsche, Omar Khayyám, and Anatole France.

Benny was confident that by now Kathleen had reached a level of "intellectual development" that would permit her to offer her body to anyone he designated. "You won't have any trouble," he said. He wrote down a telephone number and urged me to lose no time calling her.

I dismissed the whole thing as a product of Benny's bizarre imagination undoubtedly calculated to impress me. Benny must have read my mind, for a few nights later a girl with a hesitant voice telephoned to say that Benny had asked her to call. It was Kathleen. My blood raced at the alacrity with which she accepted my invitation to a play and raised my hopes to the point where I checked my wallet to make certain it still contained the condom I had placed there some months before. I became less hopeful when, on calling for Kathleen, I met her father, a giant twice my size who kept glaring at me as though he knew what was on my mind and in my wallet.

Kathleen was no beauty, but she had a graceful figure and eyes like emerald lakes. All evening the eyes regarded me gravely with little change of expression. She had sensuous lips which seldom moved. Except to tell me, during intermission, that she was nineteen and employed as a typist in an insurance agency and that her father was a plumber by profession, she had little more to say. We stopped at a soda fountain after the play and again I tried to engage her in conversation, this time introducing Benny's name and asking her what good books she had read recently. None of this elicited anything more than some vague smiles and a few clichés.

Convinced by now that Benny had made me the dupe of one of his tall tales, I was prepared to deposit Kathleen at her door and take my leave. But when we reached her house, she asked me in, explaining in a sudden burst of eloquence that her parents retired early and slept soundly. Within minutes we were embracing on the living-room couch and removing each other's clothes. Kathleen, who had been so tongue-tied all evening, now overwhelmed me with her lack of inhibition. Once I became adjusted to the transformation, everything went beautifully for both of us. Ours were the finest five minutes I had ever experienced. Yet a little later, while withdrawing, my elation turned into horror as I noticed that the condom I had used was badly torn.

There followed a grueling period of despair dominated by the nightmare that Kathleen would become pregnant and I would be obliged to marry her. Nothing could distract me from my anxiety. I kept closely in touch with Kathleen by telephone, hoping against hope that she had resumed menstruating, but did not dare to go near her house. When Benny learned what had happened, his first reaction was to crow over his power as Kathleen's Svengali. "Didn't I tell you she would damn well do as I told her?" In his exultation he seemed unaware of my torment. "The next time," he said, "just make sure you use a fresh condom." I replied I was too worried to think of a next time. "That's absurd," he said. "If she is pregnant, fucking won't make her any more pregnant. So why deprive yourself?"

But my worry had asphyxiated any further desire for Kathleen. In my imagination there paraded the menace of Kathleen's plumber father, shotgun in hand, demanding I marry his pregnant daughter. Even more intimidating was the sorrow of my parents on learning that I had thrown away their hopes for my future in exchange for a few minutes of pleasure. There would be nothing I could say in my defense. I could not very well let them know that it was the sense of morality they had injected in me, which took precedence over all the sophistication I had encountered in books and associates, that made me feel obliged to marry Kathleen if she were pregnant.

Fortunately, the nightmare came to a close. Two weeks after it had begun Kathleen was menstruating again. Benny provided an unsavory denouement of the affair. In the course of congratulating me, he said that he too should be congratulated. I then learned that he had been bedding Kathleen regularly, sometimes without a condom, so that if she became pregnant no one could say who the father was. He giggled, proud of his ingenuity, waiting for me to compliment him, but it was all I could do to conceal my revulsion. "When are you seeing her again?" he asked, then added: "She asks about you all the time. You know, I think she loves the idea of being screwed by both of us." I told Benny I would phone Kathleen after the midterm exams, but even as I spoke I knew I never would.

Ruefully, with a fresh condom in my wallet, I went back to dating the virgin coed I had been neglecting of late, comforting myself with the thought that even if I did not succeed in seducing her I could at least communicate with her. To make up for my neglect, I invited the coed to an upcoming senior prom; then, recalling my sister Assunta's love of dancing and my father's continued refusal to let her accept dates, I contrived a slightly dishonorable scheme that would liberate her for a weekend in Syracuse that would include the senior prom. Without mentioning my intention to take someone else to it, I got my father's permission to have Assunta attend the dance, then arranged a blind date for her with a handsome Italian-American student by means of a recent snapshot which only hinted at her stunning beauty.

It proved to be one of the most felicitous blind dates in history. Assunta and Vincenzo fell in love at first sight and within a few months were engaged to be married with the permission of both sets of parents. By a happy fluke, which my mother ascribed to Destiny, Vincenzo turned out to be her favorite kind of Italian: a native-born Sicilian.

The betrothal did a great deal to improve my image among my Sicilian relatives. I emerged as the thoughtful, matchmaking brother who, as the eldest son of the family, had fulfilled his responsibility in looking after the happiness and welfare of his sister. They were relieved that college had not transformed me into a careless *Americano* indifferent to traditional family duties. Although matchmaking had not crossed my mind when I arranged the blind date, I did not deny any of it. Whether I wished it or not, I was still a product of my Sicilian upbringing. Despite my new American friends and habits, the university had not changed that.

THREE

Manhattan Miasma

Except for the haunting aftermath of the Kathleen episode
and a bad tumble down the Faculty Club cellar stairway while
earning my board, the spring of 1931 struck me as the most
promising of all my Syracuse seasons. The air was seductively
pure; the skies beamed with an innocence that belied any
connection with the recent ravages of snow and ice.

In that terminal semester there was, to be sure, the gnawing
apprehension that final examinations invariably evoked, along
with the recurrent nightmare of suddenly realizing that commencement was next week and I had not been attending
classes. Actually the atmosphere in the classrooms was as
tranquilizing as the springtime. Not from the professors was
there the faintest suggestion that beyond the boundaries of the
campus kingdom raged a miasmal Depression that was devas-
tating the country. Two years had passed since the stock
market debacle. Yet the faculty and the university's administrators carried on as if nothing untoward had happened.

Their indifference may have been encouraged by the White
House's publicity campaign against "unjustified fear." Or it may
have stemmed from the faculty's reluctance to endanger their

58   AN ETHNIC AT LARGE

jobs by speaking their minds (the university had shown itself quick to fire professors of an antiestablishment frame of mind). Or it may have simply been that at all times, good and bad, scholars habitually bury their heads in the sands of their particular field.

A combination of all these factors may have created the silence about the Depression omnipresent in all my classrooms, including Economics I. Not even at the graduation ceremonies were there any references to it. The commencement speaker was a white-haired attorney, George Woodward Wickersham, aged seventy-four, who unburdened himself of an interminable report he and his commission had taken two years to prepare at the request of President Hoover. In tedious detail its message was that the federal government was failing to enforce criminal law and the Prohibition Act as effectively as it might. Not one word of the address was related to interests of the graduating class. For my classmates and me the address marked the commencement of the Depression, the first blunt indication that no one, aside from close friends and relatives, gave a damn about us.

Millions of other Americans were making the same discovery in that first year of the new decade but not perhaps with the same degree of shock as experienced by those innocents who, after four years in the softening sanctuary of campus life, were plummeted without preparation into an alien world where mere survival became the primary objective. For many college graduates of that year it was a time of searing anger—anger that no one had bothered to point out the gulf between knowledge and experience, no one had remembered to impress on us that freedom of choice, however desirable, had little or no meaning in a disintegrating economy.

On the surface my own situation appeared to be an enviable one. In the last few weeks of my senior year, I had been offered a job in New York on the editorial staff of *Time*. Burges Johnson, who had sponsored me for the post, was elated. My well-wishers regarded the job as an accolade I had earned by my energetic activities on campus as a reporter, columnist, and editor. How lucky I was, they exclaimed, that, unlike so many of my classmates, I would be earning my living doing what I liked to do best. The congratulations were so genuine that I could not bring myself to disenchant them with the information that I had been assigned to a department on *Time* in which I had no interest and, worse, no knowledge.

Whatever bright hopes I had entertained about the *Time* offer were dashed in an interview with Henry Luce who, after listening politely to my recital of the liberal arts courses I had studied, informed me in his stuttering voice that I was to join the magazine's Business and Finance editorial staff. His decision, as much as the stutter, astonished me. "But Mr. Luce," I protested, "I don't know a thing about business or finance," not adding that the words themselves went against my grain. He beamed, as if I had said exactly what he wanted to hear, then explained that from his viewpoint the less a writer knew about a subject, the more interestingly he could write about it for others.

Even at the age of twenty-one, the theory struck me as unduly optimistic, but I was too timid to argue with him. After all, if I was to realize my dream of leaving Rochester and living in New York, I needed the job; no one else had offered me one. But my doubts about Luce's theory increased when he recommended that as preparation for the world of business and finance I read Dreiser's *The Financier* and John Winkler's biography of John D. Rockefeller, *A Portrait in Oils*. At that point it seemed indiscreet to reveal that I had already read both books and could not imagine what possible help they would be to me.

After Luce had consigned me to the purgatory of Business and Finance I never saw him again. Had my infatuation for *Time* remained as intense as it had been in high school, I might have overcome the obstacle of writing on a subject that went against my grain. As it developed, I suffered even more than I had imagined possible, rewriting each story a half-dozen times

in a frenzy of sweat and despair, never certain which version
made sense. At the end of the first month, I became convinced
that my supervisory editor, Washington Dodge III, tolerated
me only out of kindness; I must have evoked in him the kind of
pity he might have for any lost and melancholy creature, be it a
dog or a newly hired hand.

He and my research assistant were the only staff members
who would speak to me. The others generally ignored my
presence, except when they mistook me for the office boy and
barked orders in my direction, which I pretended not to hear.
It was a blow to my ego that I, who had been something of a
campus celebrity, should suddenly be reduced to being a
nonentity without friends and, even worse, without writing
material in which I could take some pride. In my dejected
state, I decided that while I might in time become accustomed
to my antisocial colleagues, I could not go on pretending that
my job made any sense to me.

My court of appeals was the managing editor, John Martin, a
one-armed extrovert who was a whiz both as a golfer and a
caption writer. While I spoke my piece, he flung his empty
shirt sleeve in various directions, as was his habit when talking
with anyone, and finally flinging it in my direction, interrupted
me to comment that all the reports he had received about my
work were not unfavorable, regardless of my feelings about it.
Moreover, he added as he flung the empty sleeve toward the
ceiling, there were no openings in any of the departments. But
my dissatisfaction made me a ramrod of perseverance, and
when it became apparent that he would either have to fire me
or assign me to other work, he relegated me to the lowest spot
on the *Time* editorial totem pole, writing Milestones. I was to
remain there until an opening developed in one of the other
departments.

"Anything but Business and Finance would suit me fine," I
assured Martin. "Even Religion," I heard myself saying.

"We'll see," said Martin, waving me toward the door with

his empty sleeve. "Meantime, do the best you can with Milestones."

I promised I would, but my best was not good enough. The Princeton snob who reviewed my first copy for Milestones icily informed me that I had committed the "serious error" of referring to a prominent Jew as a "socialite." "No Jew is ever a socialite," he intoned. "Certainly not in the pages of *Time.*"

A few weeks later I was guilty of another error, this one so horrendous as to warrant a summons from John Martin himself, who while swinging his sleeveless arm, tongue-lashed me for revealing my ignorance of the painting "September Morn" in an obituary I had composed of the press agent who made it famous in the United States. Anyone who did not know anything about "September Morn," he ranted, did not know much of anything.

My retort that "September Morn" might be known to his generation but unknown to mine so enraged him that for a few moments he forgot his armless sleeve and could only glare at me. I thought he would surely fire me as soon as he regained his composure, but instead he offered me the choice of either continuing to write Milestones indefinitely, with no hope of being transferred to another department, or leaving at once with a month's severance pay. Without considering the consequences of becoming jobless in one of the most depressed of the Depression years, I allowed my pride to make the choice, and left.

It is one thing to know there is widespread unemployment but quite another to be one of the unemployed, to experience several times a day the indignity of being told there is no work for you. The flattering letters of introduction I had to editors and publishers produced a dozen interviews and a few book review assignments, but no job or prospect of one. After exhausting all my leads, I began making the rounds of the employment agencies. Since my severance pay was nearing the end, I now abandoned the idea of finding a job that matched my aspirations and resolved to take any work that came along, however lowly. But I soon learned that my university degree put me to a disadvantage; personnel managers saw no point hiring college graduates for work that could be done by cheaper and less educated help. Not until I began pretending that I had never gone beyond high school were employment agencies willing to receive my applications.

Before long I encountered still another hurdle—one impossible to overcome—my Mediterranean features, which were proof to some of the hiring agents that I was a Jew posing as a Gentile. I would be told that although a job was available, I could not qualify for it since it was the firm's policy not to employ Jews. Once, while protesting that I was not Jewish, the interviewer regarded me with disgust. "You should be ashamed of yourself for denying what you are," he said. Another interviewer insisted I was a Spanish Jew. To my statement that my parents were Italian, she responded: "What difference does that make? A Jew is a Jew." Only the fear of having her summon the police prevented me from asking, "Madam, would you like to examine my uncircumcised penis?"

My family knew nothing of my plight. Certain that they would demand my return to Rochester once they learned I was unemployed, I pretended in my weekly letters home that all was going well for me at *Time*. To preserve the fiction, I continued slipping a few dollars into each letter, as I had been doing ever since my arrival in Manhattan, intending to inform them of the *Time* fiasco as soon as I was employed again.

While I had no compunction concealing my situation from my parents, I felt obliged to let Burges Johnson know what had happened. He promptly replied with a letter that called me a "damn fool" for not sticking out the *Time* job, but enclosed a guest card to the Players, where he was certain I would find my next employer. "Contacts are very important when you are job hunting," he wrote. "Some of New York's leading editors and publishers belong to the Players. I urge you to take full advantage of this two-week guest card, visit the club as often as possible, make all the contacts you can. If you persist, someone is bound to recognize your good qualities and give you a job. . . ."

Johnson, who did most of the talking when we were together, could not have realized how painful it was for me to approach strangers without having some specific reason for doing so. I had no gift for small talk, especially with my morale at its pitch-bottom point. But the prospect of returning to Rochester draped in defeat made me smother my reservations about the guest card. To my daily rounds of employment agencies, I added a midday visit to the Players.

Its name was misleading. From the start I was overwhelmed by the club's heavy aura of dignity. It seemed to me that its dark ponderous furniture alone bespoke a formidable reserve that no stranger, unless he be a madman, dared ignore. The sullen doorman who studied my guest card and made a notation in his notebook (a demerit of some kind, I assumed) let me understand, without saying a word, that I had better watch my step. In vain I looked around for a contemporary, but all I saw were middle-aged and ancient faces. Wandering from one room to another, with the distinct impression I was invisible, I found the library where I imagined I would be considered less of an intruder than elsewhere.

The opulence of the decor was overwhelming: rich oriental rugs, deep leather chairs, the golden glare of the picture frames on the walls. Only in the movies had I seen anything as oppressively elegant. As I surveyed the room the only human sounds I could hear, other than the beating of my heart, were disgruntled snorts from faces behind newspapers and the clearing of throats. In my vast storehouse of fears occurred still another: suppose Henry Luce or John Martin were members of the club and were to see me there? I snatched a newspaper from a table and hid my face behind it.

Although this sharply reduced my chances of making contacts, I could now peep at what was going on without fear of recognition. A few men meandered in and out of the library;

nothing else happened. Some of the faces looked familiar, but that was probably because I had seen press photographs of them somewhere. Once I was galvanized by the sight of a bewhiskered Player bearing down on me as if he had something to say, but as soon as he got close and I let him see my full face, he veered sharply in another direction.

Every day, during the lunch hour when the building was filled with Players, I would take up my post in the library for an hour or so until my arms ached from holding the newspaper I pretended to be reading. But nothing happened. At the end of the first week I decided that since a library is, by definition, a place for reading, not for talking, I was wasting my time; I would try one of the other rooms where Players were more likely to converse. Unfortunately, I could not afford the dining room, and the bar, where strangers were most likely to drift into conversation, was presided over by a burly redhead who, on my only foray into his domain, addressed me as "sonny" and refused to serve me on the grounds that I was not old enough. Rather than argue the point and create added embarrassment for myself, I slunk away. I finally settled on the billiard room and for several days observed the players while trying to learn their game, expecting that one of them would eventually deign to take notice of me and start a conversation. No one ever did.

Time was running out and except for my brief exchange with the bartender, I had yet to communicate with anyone in the club. Not even the doorman. Ignoring his deadpan inspection of me each time I arrived at the club, I would make it a point to greet him, and he would make it a point to respond with a barely audible grunt. I tried to persuade myself that the grunt was not as hostile in the second week as it had been in the first, but I dared not gamble on that. One day as I was leaving, I imagined him to say, "Good afternoon, sir," but when I returned the next day he was as stonefaced as ever, and I concluded that I had either been mistaken or he had momentarily become absentminded.

One rainy day, as I sloshed toward Gramercy Park and the

Players, I examined my guest card closely and realized that my deadline was at hand. This would be my last chance to fulfill Burges Johnson's faith in me. A few days before he had written to ask what progress I was making at the club, and I had replied with a noncommittal letter that revealed considerable familiarity with the club's furniture, rugs, portraits, and books, but made no mention of contact with a living person. Now I was determined that somehow on this last day I would make a contact. By the time I got to the Players, I was steaming with resolution. No more procrastination, no more sitting or standing around waiting for opportunities that never developed. Forthright action was the only solution.

I swept by the doorman, without greeting him or listening for his grunt, and made a beeline for the first person I saw who was by himself. Before he could move out of my way, I stuck out my hand and in a voice that sounded shriller than mine declared: "I am Jerre Mangione." The gray head remained monumentally calm. A hand emerged and clasped mine firmly, and while the eyes gazed at me with the remoteness of a glacier, a doomsday voice answered, "I am Edgar Lee Masters."

The three-masted name, awesomely familiar to me as the author of *Spoon River Anthology*, pricked the bubble of my courage. In the graveyard stillness that followed I tried desperately to think of something to say but, unable to think at all, I turned and fled.

Although I had spent my *Time* severance pay like a miser, I was almost broke. My only income came from book reviews, but they paid poorly. Moreover, there were so many impoverished writers competing with one another for books to review that I could not count on reviewing as a steady source of income. My first review came from Malcolm Cowley who, on the strength of my Italian name assigned me Alberto Moravia's first novel, *The Indifferent Ones*. The review was to be only three hundred words long, but I labored over it as though the assignment called for three thousand words, and my literary career depended on it. When I called on Cowley for

another assignment and was told there was none available, I
assumed the worst. "Did I do so badly with the Moravia
novel?" I blurted. In the painful dialogue that followed Cowley
tried to assure me that the review was fine, but the more he
tried the less successful he felt, and the more impelled I
became to convince him that I understood perfectly. The
dialogue had reached a point of near hysteria when Cowley
mercifully put an end to it by abruptly suggesting that I return
the following week.

The act of soliciting a book-review assignment invariably
made me feel like a beggar vying with other beggars. Because
Cowley was more kindhearted than most book-review editors, I
found myself visiting the offices of *The New Republic* more
often than any other. The waiting room there, crowded with
known and unknown writers, was a silent purgatory of anxiety.
After a writer emerged from Cowley's office, all eyes in the
waiting room would be fixed on him, each of us trying to guess
whether or not he had been favored with a review assignment.
It was not always easy to tell, but in such an atmosphere it was
easy to be unreasonable: to feel pity for a writer without an
assignment and resentment for the writer with one.

Although I had no desire to become a professional critic,
book reviewing was to become my chief literary activity for the
next half-dozen years, my lifeline between me and my writing
aspirations. I feared that if I relinquished it, I might lose sight
of the goal I cherished above all others—to be an author. Yet
the art of book reviewing did not appeal to me. It was too
severe for my temperament, too demanding of a discipline
which sharpened the wits but braked the imagination. It also
induced a false sense of superiority. I was astonished at first that
I, a young man of twenty-one who had never experienced the
arduous task of writing a book, should be asked to pass
judgment on the work of my elders. With the natural arrogance
of youth I soon overcame that reservation and developed into
an overly sharp appraiser who tended to impose impossibly
high literary standards on whatever book was assigned to me,
regardless of the author's reputation or lack of it.

Later, in an effort to escape book reviewing I was to try my hand at other kinds of writing that might earn me some money. A children's story, which utilized fantasy to explain why weeping willows weep, brought me a twenty-five-dollar check from a Kansas woman's magazine and a few days of euphoria. But when I attempted to duplicate this achievement by concocting other unnatural explications of nature, the stories were rejected.

The rumor that *True Confessions* was paying one hundred dollars for each manuscript it accepted, with no questions asked about its veracity, prompted me to invent a grim odyssey about the tribulations of a young woman who, on arriving in Manhattan, is seduced and abandoned. I rewrote the manuscript several times until I was certain that her confession would excite the compassion of the most hard-boiled reader, and confidently sent it off. Two days later it bounded back with a penciled note from the editor that read: "Sorry, we don't use satire."

After two jobless months, my departure from New York seemed imminent. With some misgiving, I recalled how vehemently I had argued with my relatives on the subject of Destiny. Predestination, I had insisted, was an obsolete concept that belonged on the junk heap of history. To live without the exercise of free will was to make a mockery of life. I asked my uncle Stefano, the most intellectual of my relatives, how he could consider himself part of the twentieth century and still believe in that nonsense. He smiled and took a pinch of snuff. "My dear nephew," he said, "I don't claim to belong to the twentieth century. You can have it."

I could already hear my relatives saying to one another that it was my Destiny to rejoin my family, where I belonged. With barely enough money left for a bus ticket to Rochester, I was about to put aside my pride and let my parents know I would be returning when my luck suddenly changed. I ran into a student I had known at Syracuse, Gordon Cole, who was about to quit his job as an assistant bookkeeper in an uptown garage that also sold automobile parts, and return to the sanctuary of

the university to resume his studies. He was certain he could
persuade his employer to hire me in his place. When I told him
that math had always been my worst subject and that I knew
nothing about bookkeeping, he brushed aside these objections
with a jauntiness that recalled Henry Luce disposing of my
protest that I knew nothing of Business and Finance. The more
difficult work, he said, was done by the head bookkeeper; the
rest was a "cinch," which I could do with "a small fraction" of
my brain.

The word "fraction" gave me further pause, for it was
especially in that area of math that my mind refused to
function, but Gordon convinced me that the job was tailored
for my needs: not only did it require little mental energy but
the hours were ideal for a writer, from two in the afternoon to
ten in the evening, which would leave me the whole morning
to devote to my muse. I never learned what set of qualifications
he fabricated in my behalf, but minutes after I presented myself
for an interview I was hired at twenty dollars a week, and
asked to report for work the following afternoon.

That evening, after a few celebration drinks with Gordon, I
heard myself confessing to what I had expected to keep secret
from him: worse than being ignorant about bookkeeping, I
knew nothing whatsoever about automobiles. Never having
learned to drive (I have not to this day), I had no knowledge
about the anatomy of a car; I could not tell one automobile
part from another. How would I be able to supply the garage
mechanics with the parts they requested? They could not
identify them for me since they worked on an upper floor and
used a telephone to tell me what parts to send up by
dumbwaiter.

My friend roared throughout the confession and went on
laughing after I was finished. At that point I joined in, but
rather nervously since I could not be sure whether his hilarity
was induced by his sense of humor or by hysteria. He never did
answer my question.

The fact that my career as an assistant bookkeeper lasted a

few more months than my stint on *Time* could not be attributed to any fitness I developed for the job—never did an assistant bookkeeper prove to be more dismally inept—but simply to the compassion of the head bookkeeper who, against his better judgment, could not bring himself to let the garage owners know what a dud they had hired.

The bookkeeper's initial error was to pity me for my obvious lack of experience and to try to help me as I committed one error after another, both in arithmetic and in identifying auto parts. From the first he carefully concealed my errors and did most of my work as well as his own, in the belief I was bound to improve. By the time he realized I never would, it was too late for him to get rid of me: he had become trapped by the friendship that grew between us.

George was a blue-eyed, black-haired ex-actor of Irish-English ancestry in his early thirties. We shared a love for good writing and enjoyed the same kind of humor, but our attitude toward life differed. George, who was an alcoholic, lived for the present, I for the future. It was enough for him to survive from day to day. His obsessive need for alcohol did not interfere with his office duties. No matter how badly hung over he was, he would manage to get to the office on time. At two in the afternoon, when I reported for work, the ravages of the night before would still be inscribed under his eyes and in the sagging lines around his mouth. Yet he would manage to remain alert the rest of the day.

Alcohol transformed his personality. In the office he was gentle and quiet, almost diffident, but at night after a few drinks he became an aggressive boulevardier who prowled the streets picking up women. Occasionally, when I would join him in a late evening stroll, George would suddenly dart away and sidle up to some girl he had spotted walking alone. By some remarkable technique of language and charm, which I never understood and deeply envied, he would soon evoke a smiling response from the girl and off they would go together.

Sometimes alcohol made him vicious, especially toward the

beggars we were likely to encounter on our nocturnal walks.
They seemed harmless enough to me, but George would turn
on them with a violence he never displayed at any other time
and pelt the poor creatures with obscenities. Some of the
beggars were men who towered over us, but regardless of size,
he would explode with the same thunderous fury. They would
hurry off as if they were afraid of him.

"How can you turn on them?" I once asked during one of his
more sober evenings. "Don't you feel sorry for them?"

"Feel sorry for them?" he sputtered. "Those sons of bitches.
Hell, no, why should I?" Then, surprisingly, he let slip the fact
that at one time he had been one himself. He did not elaborate,
but I surmised that his anger might stem from his fear of
becoming a beggar again.

As our friendship grew stronger, George's criticism of my
work became more outspoken. "This job is lousy enough
without you coming along with all your goddamn mistakes and
making it lousier," he would fume. Then, afraid he may have
hurt my feelings, he would blame his "lousy mood" on a bad
hangover. He would also beg me to find another job. "Hell, you
deserve something better than this. And so do I," he would add
in a wretched voice.

I had long before resumed my job-hunting campaign. Those
morning hours, which I had expected to devote to my muse,
were spent visiting employment agencies and pursuing every
possible lead. To provide George with some ray of hope that he
would be rid of me, I began presenting him with a daily report
of my job hunting, being careful, however, to say nothing about
my visits to book-review editors for fear he might think I was
giving more attention to my literary pursuits than to the search
for a job.

Eventually it was the book reviewing that made it possible
for me to escape the garage job. On the strength of my
published reviews, an executive at the Cooper Union Institute
offered me the post of assistant librarian at fifteen hundred

dollars a year, with the understanding that I would augment my meager library experience with courses at Columbia.

Elated, I promptly phoned George to break the good news. "Well, it's about time," he said grumpily. "I was beginning to think you wanted to make bookkeeping a lifelong career. When do you start?" I explained that the librarian had wanted me to start in the morning, but I had persuaded him to wait a week so that the garage would have time to replace me. "Listen, kid," George said with great earnestness, "let's not take any chances. Forget the garage. Tell them you'll be there in the morning."

"But isn't the boss going to get sore if I leave without any notice?"

"You leave him to me," he commanded. "Hell, I'll tell him you eloped with an heiress. He'll probably send you a wedding present. . . ."

I apologized for all the extra work I had caused him and confessed I didn't know how I could have managed without him.

"I don't either," he laughed. "Well, I better get the hell back to work and fix all those stupid mistakes you made yesterday. See you around, kid. . . ."

I never saw him again.

FOUR

In the House of Genius

Until now the cliché expectation of friends that as a would-be writer I was bound to live in Greenwich Village had kept me away from that area. But one night, without quite knowing how I got there, I found lodgings in a rooming house near the Cooper Union Library, and discovered it was close to the heart of the Village, on Washington Square South, at an address which the press, recalling such former tenants as Stephen Crane, Theodore Dreiser, and Eugene O'Neill,° had dubbed "The House of Genius." My blundering into so literary an establishment struck me as a happy omen.

My own room, located in the rear of the attic under a cubistic jumble of rafters, had been occupied by the poet soldier Alan Seeger, whose best known poem "I Have a Rendezvous With Death" was published shortly before he was killed in battle. The room was barely large enough for a cot, a

---

° O'Neill lived there for a few months shortly before his second marriage in 1918. Unable to pay the rent he owed, he left behind as security a trunk said to contain a number of his manuscripts. In 1923, a Manhattan newspaper reported that the basement where the trunk was stored became flooded and the trunk's contents turned into an undecipherable mess.

small chest of drawers, a chair, and a typewriter table, which
could only be fitted under the lowest rafter. Once, rising too
quickly from my typewriter in a moment of exasperation, I
suffered a minor concussion.

James Oppenheim and his wife lived in the front of the attic.
Oppenheim was the Whitmanesque poet who had founded and
edited the magazine *Seven Arts*, which flourished until Oppenheim's pacifistic stand in World War I conflicted with his
backer's support of the war. Mrs. Oppenheim was a shadowy
blond beauty who always dressed in purple. Facing Washington
Square, their quarters commanded a fine view of the recently
erected Empire State Building. The sloping ceilings of their two
rooms, as much as their frugal decor, recalled the Paris garret
setting in *La Bohème*, an impression that grew as I learned that
the Oppenheims, like Puccini's characters, were destitute.

My information about them came from our garrulous, six-foot
landlady, Madame Branchard, who would complain that they
owed her more money than any of the other tenants; they had
not paid rent for more than a year. Because I went to a job
every day and paid the rent on time, she had me pegged as a
fellow bourgeois who could empathize with her trials as a
landlady. She regarded the writers in her house as "Grenvich
Veelage boms" since they stayed home all day, drank all night,
and seldom paid their rent on time. The Oppenheims were not
"boms," she had to admit, but her patience with them was at
an end, she kept repeating, and very soon she would order
them to leave. But I detected a lack of conviction in her threat.
She may already have known what I did not learn until the
next year when Oppenheim died: he was in the last stages of
tuberculosis.

What must have been evidence of his fatal disease—the pale
face, thin body, and fervent voice—I mistook as identifying
features of a poet. On my return from work every weekday
afternoon, promptly at five-thirty, he would appear at my door
bearing his own drink, a goblet of gin and water, the same gin
he concocted once a week in the bathtub shared by the attic

dwellers. He would discourse on two or three topics uppermost in his mind, and I would act as his sounding board until his wife summoned him for their evening meal which, in violation of Madame Branchard's strictest house rule, Mrs. Oppenheim prepared on an electric plate. Oppenheim's topics were as varied as newspaper headlines, but invariably he would funnel them into a single common denominator: Carl Jung, the oracle he revered above all other men. To hear Oppenheim talk of Jung's writings, one would have thought that they had long ago rendered the teachings of Freud, Marx, and the Bible obsolete.

In our conversations the only indication Oppenheim gave of his poverty was when he described his futile attempts to earn some money writing for all types of magazines, including some that dealt with astrology. Out of puzzlement rather than self-pity he reported that no matter how much he tried to adjust his style and material to that of a particular publication, his manuscripts came back with a printed rejection slip. As a would-be writer, it appalled me that a poet of Oppenheim's stature should be reduced to hack writing and, worse, that he should be rejected as perfunctorily as the rankest amateur.

When I ventured the explanation that a man's integrity, his inability to compromise, can be as hard a habit to break as that of a drug addict, Oppenheim smiled forlornly and replied there had been a number of lapses in his integrity. He recalled an evening when he and his wife, both dedicated liberals, had attended a fund-raising ball to further the cause of equal rights for Negroes. "I've been a lifelong champion of that cause," Oppenheim said. Yet when he saw his wife on the dance floor in the arms of a Negro, he was so horrified that he rushed onto the dance floor to stop their dance, on the pretext of expecting a long-distance phone call at home, then he left the party with his wife. "It was a reprehensible thing to do," he said unhappily, still tormented by the episode, though it had happened several years before. "I still feel strongly about equal rights for Negroes and I always shall, but how can I have a clear conscience about it?"

For all of his poignancy, Oppenheim was good for my morale. Until I moved into Madame Branchard's establishment, I had been enveloped in the miasma of such intense loneliness that, out of hunger for the sounds of friends and lovers, I sometimes found myself eavesdropping on strolling couples. Thanks to Oppenheim and to William Rollins, Jr., a novelist in his thirties whose rapid-fire talk bristled with sharp and funny nuances, my loneliness abated almost as soon as I became part of the Menagerie (Rollins' name for the rooming house). I began to lose the fear that, away from the gregarious life of my Rochester relatives and the easy sociability of campus life, I could only exist as an onlooker.

Of all the residents in the Menagerie, Rollins came closest to Madame Branchard's definition of a "bom," since he drank more heavily than the others and was broke more often. Yet she was fond of him, partly because he could speak with her in French and also because she had a penchant for handsome men. If she distrusted him, it was mainly because he was a writer and, by her lights, a useless member of society.

Rollins had already published two novels (*The Obelisk* and *Midnight Treasure*) and was working on a third, but, unable to subsist on publishers' royalties, he spent most of his time writing pulp fiction, mainly mystery tales for *Black Mask*, which were published alongside those of his friend Dashiell Hammett. At first I had the impression that I had already met him in Hemingway's writings. He was an idealist with a sardonic sense of humor, a refugee from a comfortable middle-class home near Boston, an ex-newspaper man. He had done a stint in the French Foreign Legion, and during World War I he served the French in the American Ambulance Corps along with Hemingway, Malcolm Cowley, E. E. Cummings, Slater Brown, and John Dos Passos, who was to have a powerful influence on his writings and who, until they were separated by political differences, became a close friend. Although his facade was that of a sophisticated man of the world, he was the most compassionate of men. One day when he was broke he had long way uptown to borrow ten dollars from a friend only to give most of it away to the panhandlers he encountered on his way back to Madame Branchard's.

What added to the Hemingway impression was my meeting, through Rollins, two of the people Hemingway had converted into leading characters for *The Sun Also Rises:* Harold Loeb, one of Rollins' best friends, who, flattened nose and all, became the model for Robert Cohn, and a tall, gangly English blonde with a fatuous personality who was Hemingway's inspiration for Lady Brett. Perhaps Rollins' most Hemingway trait was his humor, which bore a remarkable resemblance to that of Bill Gorton, Jake's fishing companion in *The Sun Also Rises.* It combined a stringent turn of mind with a sense of the absurd. ("Christ! To think that I went to bed with the likes of you," groaned Rollins one morning on seeing himself in a mirror while in the throes of a bad hangover.) Later, through Rollins, I was to meet other writers of his generation whose humor was of the same cloth, but at the time I marveled that it could exist outside the pages of fiction.

The Hemingway image began to fade as I realized that Rollins, despite the anarchism implied in his ironic view of life, was a dedicated Marxist who was earnestly concerned about the exploitation of the poor. He was convinced that only through socialism could democracy be achieved for all Americans, and that only the Communists had the leadership to bring about the necessary changes. On the other hand, he could not relinquish his individuality to submit to the discipline of the Communist party any more than he could resist exercising his sense of humor.

Through his mischievous eyes, Madame Branchard and her Menagerie became an Alice-in-Wonderland treasure trove of surprises, with Madame as the biggest surprise of all. Contrary to my initial impression, only a small segment of her energies was spent gossiping. On any morning she could be observed bearing on her septuagenarian back a divan or some other weighty piece of furniture that she was transferring from one room to another. A tenant's furniture would shift in accordance with Madame's current opinion of him. Only the dust on the furniture remained constant. Disliking dusting more than any other household chore, she usually let each roomer be the judge of how much cleanliness he required by leaving the dusting to him.

The dustiest part of the house was Madame's own living quarters, an enormous room on the first floor whose walls were crowded with oil paintings by her late husband. Obsessed with the life of George Washington, he had painted nothing else. The father of our country was presented in dozens of poses: on horseback, in a rowboat, leading his troops, signing presidential orders, with and without Martha. Madame Branchard treasured them as though they were all Rembrandts; no visitor entering the room could escape her conducted tour of the collection. Although they were hardly of museum caliber, Madame managed to suggest that the Metropolitan could hardly wait to lay its hands on the paintings. She accomplished this by letting it be known that one of her tenants (an elderly man whose room contained the coffin he had selected for his burial) was an employee of the Metropolitan, the inference being that the museum was so fearful of letting the paintings out of its sight that it had planted a staff member in her house to make certain no harm would befall them.

Madame Branchard made no mention of her more valid connection with the art world: her fifty-year-old son, a former truck driver, who had become a successful primitive painter. "Baby," as Madame called Emile, was installed in the lower regions of the house. In the semidarkness of his basement studio, he painted all day, producing the vivid landscapes that so delighted the New York critics. The "Truckdriver Painter," they named him as they sang his praises. The rich ladies who collected his work were no less appreciative. They tried to lionize him with parties in his honor, but before long news of Emile's scandalous behavior at such affairs got bandied about, and the parties stopped. Not only would Emile get roaring drunk and insult the hostess, but he would also make indecent proposals to any young women present and, when he was very drunk, to the older ones as well. On several occasions he had become so persistent about his proposals that he had to be forcibly ejected, at least twice by the police.

The tales of his misconduct did no damage to his prestige as a painter. Leading art critics continued to discuss his work at considerable length. Emile, who could barely read, was indifferent to what they wrote of him. He measured his fame with a ruler. "Twenty inches. Not bad, huh?," was his comment when I showed him a *New York Times* review that lauded his most recent exhibit. He gave me back the review and asked about my health. "But don't you want to know what the *Times* says about you?" I asked. "Nah," he said. "What the hell do those guys know about painting?"

Emile had been married twice but, thanks to his mother, both marriages had ended in divorce. She had long made it clear to him that as long as he chose to live in her house, he would remain a bachelor. Each time that Emile brought home a wife, Madame had pretended to be delighted with the girl, but as soon as she sensed the honeymoon period was over, she had launched a campaign to undermine the marriage. In each instance there had been a climactic scene in which Emile was given the choice of leaving the house with his wife, or remaining without her. Each time Emile had stormed and screamed at his mother for a couple of days but finally, unable to give up the basement studio which he associated with his success as a painter, had sent his wife away.

The epilogue that ensued in both instances defied all rules of logic, except those of Madame Branchard's. As soon as the divorce proceedings were over, Madame would assiduously court her former daughter-in-law until she became her bosom companion. Whether she acted out of a sense of guilt, which seemed out of character, or whether she did it to provide Emile with the opportunity of sleeping with his ex-wives without the responsibilities of marriage only Madame Branchard knew. The

80 AN ETHNIC AT LARGE

fact remained that the old woman's social life consisted mainly
of playing cards or going to the movies with her ex-daughters-
in-law, who visited her (and Emile) separately at least once a
week. I once caught a glimpse of the second Mrs. Emile
Branchard, arm in arm with her ex-mother-in-law. She was a
platinum blonde with a luscious Renoir figure. They had just
left the rooming house and were probably on their way to a
movie. The young woman was gazing up at Madame Branchard
with the unstinted affection of a devoted daughter.

Madame's refusal to have her son bring a wife to her house
may have been based on nothing more than her aversion to
living under the same roof with other women. Mrs. Oppenheim
was the only female tenant, and it was clear from the old
woman's attitude toward her own sex that she intended to keep
things that way. "Vomen make trouble," was one of her
favorite remarks. When Rollins once suggested to her face that
she wanted all the men in the house to herself, she giggled like
a young wench and, poking him in the ribs, screeched: *"Ah,
Monsieur Rollins, vous savez trop!"*

Only once during my residence did Madame permit a second
woman to move in. This happened when one of her rooms had
been vacant for more than a month, and she could not resist
renting it to a woman who said she wanted it only for six
weeks. The news that we were to have an unattached female in
our midst did not create much of a stir since the roomers
assumed that she would be aged or homely, or both. To
everyone's surprise, she turned out to be a rather comely
brunette in her late thirties. Her figure was copious, but she
had a sensual face and, to match it, a low and lingering voice
that lent intimacy to her most mundane utterances.

On the assumption that the new roomer must be lonely,
Rollins, whose room adjoined hers, gave a small cocktail party
for her, to meet some of the other tenants. We learned that her
name was Irma Gardner—*Miss* Gardner, she emphasized—and
that she had recently arrived from Indianapolis to work as a
secretary for a local Christian Science organization. The party

progressed pleasantly enough until Madame Branchard poked her face through the opened door, muttered the word "bom" as soon as she spotted Miss Gardner, then quickly withdrew.

The next day Miss Gardner, an optimist, tried to make friends with the old lady, but her overtures were rejected with a scolding for drinking with the men in the house. The following week Rollins included his neighbor in another one of his cocktail sessions. I thought that Rollins had exaggerated her loneliness until Miss Gardner surveyed the assembled guests, whom she had seen only once before, and murmured, "It is so good to be with old friends again." When Madame learned that Rollins had invited her to a second cocktail party, she demanded he pay his overdue rent then and there, shouting that since he obviously had money enough to buy gin for that "bom" of a Miss Gardner, he had enough to pay the rent he owed her. To all this, Rollins responded with a barrage of snarling French, which only Madame could follow. She understood him so well that she turned scarlet and for a few moments, long enough for Rollins to slam his door in her face, was speechless. As soon as she had recovered, she burst into Miss Gardner's room to remind her that she was to leave in two weeks.

A few days before her scheduled departure, Miss Gardner suddenly took to her bed with a mysterious ailment. No doctor came; no one could learn what was wrong with her. Madame Branchard, the only one in the house who had access to her room, refused to reveal the nature of her malady. When I asked why no doctor had been summoned, she explained that Miss Gardner was a Christian Scientist and intended to be cured by prayer. Presumably, the ladies bearing black books who called on Miss Gardner daily were ministering the gospel of Mary Baker Eddy. All of her other needs were ministered to by Madame Branchard since the patient had no friends or relatives in the city. Three times a day, all the way from the basement, where the kitchen was located, to the second floor, the old woman kept carrying trays of food to her room. For more than two weeks Madame Branchard diligently performed the role of good Samaritan, while we all marveled at her patience and goodness. All, except Rollins, who predicted that Madame's dislike of Miss Branchard was bound to assert itself in some volcanic fashion.

He obviously knew Madame better than the rest of us. Her eruption was preceded by several days of ominous rumblings. As the indignity of waiting hand and foot on a woman she despised overcame her sense of Christian charity, Madame could be heard muttering obscenities as she shuttled between the basement and the sick room. Although she still maintained a rigid silence when any of us tried to learn what was wrong with Miss Gardner, her muttering became more audible, her obscenities more obscene. The Menagerie was now of the unanimous opinion that it was simply a matter of time before her fury would burst through the narrow confines of her patience.

When the explosion finally came, no stage director could have found fault with either its timing or effectiveness. It happened on a hot summer evening when the house was filled with roomers. Because of the heat, nearly all their doors were open, everyone could hear what went on in the hallways. Madame was in the patient's room serving her supper when the public pay telephone on the second-floor landing began ringing. Apparently none of the tenants was expecting a call; no one made a move to answer it. After a half-dozen rings, Madame Branchard came out of the sick room and picked up the receiver.

"Hullo," she bellowed. She was one of those people who used the telephone as a megaphone.

"Who?"

She repeated the question several times, her voice rising in an angrier crescendo each time. She finally understood. "Miss Gardner," she roared. "You vant to talk to Miss Gardner?"

The menace in her voice caused a number of us to stick our heads out of our doors so that we might better hear what she would say next. I saw her looking around quickly, as if to make certain of her audience, then heard the exultation in her voice as it rose to the situation. Into the telephone and to the world at large she announced: "You cannot speak to Miss Gardner. Miss Gardner is having a miscarriage!"

The emphasis on "miscarriage" was that of a consummate performer. I half expected her to take a bow, but instead her lips fell into a self-satisfied smile and, holding herself more erect than usual, she descended the stairway with the slow majesty of royalty, all sweetened with revenge.

The explosion probably saved Miss Gardner's life, for that same evening a group of us took matters in our own hands and summoned a doctor. Within minutes after his arrival, she was rushed to a hospital in an ambulance. The next afternoon, when I came home from the library, I learned that the doctor had telephoned in the morning to report that Miss Gardner was in dire need of blood transfusions. Rollins, who told me the news, said it had taken him nearly all day to summon enough courage to be one of the blood donors only to learn at the hospital that he could not qualify. "Too much gin," was his shamefaced explanation.

None of us ever saw Miss Gardner again. After she returned to Indianapolis, she wrote Rollins a note expressing her gratitude to all the roomers who had given blood for her. "They are all part of me now." She also expressed the hope that she would meet with all of us again, "if not in this life, perhaps in the next." In the same mail there was also a letter addressed in her handwriting to Madame Branchard, but the old woman never revealed its contents. Except for the sly grin that crossed her face whenever Miss Gardner's name was mentioned in her presence, she gave no sign that she had ever known such a person.

Although I was enjoying life at Madame Branchard's, especially after it began to include frequent rendezvous with a dancer who had become my mistress, I was developing an intense dislike for my Cooper Union post. Out of fear that with the slightest encouragement I would resign and be among the unemployed again, I said nothing about it to my friends. At the core of my dissatisfaction was the repugnance I felt for the head librarian. I did not mind so much that he was a lazy administrator who disregarded major library problems that cried for attention and squandered his time on inconsequential details, but I was offended by his bigotry, which he advertised loudly and frequently. He despised "foreigners," and when a colleague told him I was of Italian origin, he recounted a smutty story about "a dago whore." He referred to Negroes as "niggers" and "spades," and was fond of bragging that where he came from (Georgia) "niggers" were kept in their place. But even more aggravating was his treatment of the library's clientele. Among the patrons were a number of mad scholars, such as the Irish old man who was writing a tome in Gaelic to prove that Napoleon was born in Dublin, but most of them were Bowery derelicts who, in the winter months, came into the place to keep warm. On them the librarian vented his most sadistic impulses. If a patron did not give a convincing performance of someone reading, or if he dozed off, a husky guard would hustle him out of the premises with a warning not to return. The librarian spent a great deal of time supervising the actions of the guard, upbraiding him if he thought the guard had ejected a patron too gently.

The librarian justified his harsh treatment of the derelicts on the grounds that the library was intended for "decent people," not "bums," an unrelenting attitude which had a contaminating effect on the staff members. Either out of a craven desire to please their chief or because they could not help but be influenced by the example he set, they vied with one another in demonstrating their contempt for the derelicts. This is not to suggest that I myself was not repelled by them. More than the long breadlines or the ragged men and women using the subway as a flophouse at night, the daily spectacle of so many human dregs gathering in the library was a smelly and disgusting reminder of a disintegrating society. Every morning as I climbed the stairway of the Cooper Union Institute to the library on the second floor, I would find some of them strewn across the steps like the wounded bodies in the film *Potemkin,* or leaning against the walls swilling booze or shaving lotion. The stairs were littered with empty bottles.

Not all the library patrons from the Bowery were alcoholics. Sometimes I would look into eyes which were neither stuporous nor bleary, or hear voices with a lilt. They usually belonged to men on their uppers who were using the Bowery as a temporary haven and would soon be pushing on. But the majority of the patrons were life-wrecked creatures with nowhere to go. They moved as if in a daze, with no other hope than to survive from one day to the next without becoming too cold, too hungry, or too sober. The pity I felt for them soon got me into trouble with the head librarian for ignoring one of his most strictly enforced rules: unless a patron was able to request, in his own handwriting, the specific name of the book, magazine, or newspaper he wished, he could not remain in the library. Twice the librarian had caught me writing out a request slip for some confused derelict who was in no condition to think. Both times he had reprimanded me severely in the presence of colleagues. The last time he had asked me to bear in mind that I was on probation for a year, a fact I had not known until then, and might find myself without a job if I persisted in breaking the rules. I longed to spit out my hatred of him, to tell him to go to hell, but instead heard myself apologizing.

I made no mention of the derelicts in my letters to Rochester since that might detract from my parents' illusion that I was employed by a prestigious cultural institution. My mother was disappointed that I had not found a teaching job, but the sound of my present title gave her some comfort, especially when translated into Italian: Chief Assistant to the Head Librarian. She and my father took it for granted that, despite the Depression and the head librarian's prejudice against foreigners and their offspring, which I felt impelled to mention in preparation for the day when I might be fired, I would in due time rise to an even more imposing title and commensurate pay.

Although living three hundred miles from Rochester had relieved me of the sensation that I was living a double life, I was still quite aware of my parents' authority over me and fearful that if they knew of my precarious situation at the library, they would order me back to Rochester. My letters assiduously avoided speaking of any new developments in my life that might stimulate their anxiety over my welfare. Of my mistress I naturally said nothing. Had they had any inkling I was involved with a married dancer ten years my senior they would have been horrified. My father, whose penchant for attractive women was his Achilles' heel, might have eventually understood and secretly forgiven me. But my mother would have thought I had lost my senses, and assumed I would most certainly be murdered by the dancer's avenging husband. And if I had tried to assuage this typically Sicilian assumption by explaining that the affair, in its initial stages at least, had the full sanction of the husband, she would have concluded that the wife must be a harlot, the husband her pimp, and her beloved son the naive victim of their combined evil spell.

It would have been futile trying to explain that nothing could have been further from the truth. On the other hand, I might have had difficulty describing the truth since throughout the entire affair I felt like a fictional lover in a second-rate Boccaccio tale. It began mundanely enough, at a party the Doyles gave in their 14th Street loft, which served both as their living quarters and dance studio. At the time the Doyles had been wed and faithful to each other for twelve years, and their fervent goal in life was to win recognition for Melissa's talents as a modern dancer and choreographer. To this end, her husband, Michael, had forfeited his stage aspirations to devote all his time promoting her career. Not only was he her manager, producer, and press agent, but also her housekeeper. To allow her more time for her art and also to preserve the smoothness of her hands, he did nearly all of the housework. A tall and heavy black-haired Irishman, Michael sometimes struck me as a clumsy bear who, having made a pet out of a wild bird, was now at a loss as to how to cope with it.

The invitation to the Doyles' party came from Melissa's younger sister Amy, a writer of unpublished fairy tales who had been my classmate at Syracuse. It was hard to think of the two women as sisters. Amy was a blonde with an awkward figure and a painfully shy personality; her eyes habitually bore the agonized expression of an animal at bay. Melissa, who had been a Rockette, was as brown and slim as Pocahontas, all poise and grace. "What is even more enticing than her physical beauty," I rhapsodized in my diary the next day, "is the laughter of her eyes, the caress of her smile, and the music of her voice."

Smitten as soon as we were introduced, I suffered such an acute attack of shyness that all I could do the rest of the evening was watch Melissa's every move and long for the courage to talk or dance with her. Only toward the end of the party, after Amy had gone to bed and Melissa's husband was out of the studio escorting a female guest to the subway and the only remaining guests were myself and a drunken ex-football player with lechery on his mind, did my shyness vanish. It suddenly happened when the ex-football player announced he wanted to be left alone with Melissa and ordered me to leave.

"If Mrs. Doyle wants me to leave, I'll leave," I replied, determined to protect her until her husband returned. "Other-wise . . ."

"Otherwise, my ass," he said. "You're getting the hell out of here right now." As he took a step toward me, Melissa, who barely came up to my shoulders, stepped between us to be my shield. "Don't you dare lay a finger on him, Tom Coolahan," she cried. "You're the one who had better go home."

"So that's the way it is," he leered. "In that case I will beat the shit out of him." Melissa placed herself closer to me. "But first," he added, "I'm going to have myself another drink."

He was guzzling whiskey straight from a bottle when Michael returned. Coolahan left soon afterward. I was about to follow suit, but Melissa, certain he was outside waiting for me, insisted I remain and have some scrambled eggs with her and her husband.

So began my friendship with the Doyles. Although adultery was not in my thoughts, I used every possible ruse to be near Melissa, or Wisp, as I began to call her when we were alone. To ingratiate myself with Michael, I helped him with the publicity for her oncoming recital, which the Doyles regarded as the most important of her career, and ran some of his errands when he was busy at the studio. Several evenings a week, when Michael was moonlighting as stage manager for a small repertory company in Brooklyn, Wisp and I took long walks or sat in Italian restaurants sipping *puncini* out of coffee cups. The ten-year age difference between us never interfered with the enjoyment we found in each other's company. Except for her political attitudes, which were far to the right of mine, she seemed more in tune with my thinking and temperament than any girl I had known. She, in turn, found me "mature far beyond my years," a condition she gravely attributed to my Old World genes. Aside from politics, there was only one other subject we carefully avoided: our feelings for each other. Only once, when I had drunk too many *puncini*, did I touch on the subject, impulsively expressing the wish that I could have known her before she married. The burst of laughter with which she greeted the remark seared my soul until she observed that at the time of her marriage I was but nine years old.

From the amount of time that Wisp was willing to spend with me, I gradually began to suspect that all was not well with her marriage. Yet I could not bring myself to say or do anything that might suggest a betrayal of Michael, who trusted us implicitly. By now my yearning to make love to her tormented me to such a degree that I considered bowing out of the Doyles' life and dating other women. Before I could persuade myself that I had no other alternative, Wisp experienced a crushing disappointment in her career which changed everything.

The dance recital, which she and Michael had counted on to establish her as one of New York's leading dancers, turned out to be a disaster. The studio was packed for the performance, but only one critic showed up, John Martin of the *New York Times,* and he demoralized Wisp and her company by walking out at the end of the first number. On the next day neither the *Times* nor any other newspaper carried any mention of the recital.

For nearly twenty-four hours Wisp locked herself in a bedroom, refusing to speak with anyone. Then, while Michael was out, she packed a bag and left New York to visit her parents in the upstate mountain village where she had grown up. The note she left for Michael said she needed some time to think for herself. When she returned after a week, I received separate phone calls from her and from Michael, each one asking me to drop by the studio that evening.

Wisp did most of the talking at first. In a voice that struck me as falsely enthusiastic she described the charms of her hometown and spoke of a teaching offer made to her by the local superintendent of schools. Michael, who did not appear to be listening, finally interrupted to suggest that the three of us go for a walk. He explained he had "something important" to discuss with us and he did not want to be disturbed by unexpected visitors or phone calls. After we had walked for several blocks in silence, Michael asked that I move to his right because he had poor hearing on his left ear. Then, as we continued to stroll with his wife on one side of him and I on the other, he turned to me and asked if I loved Melissa.

I was too stunned by the question to do anything more than nod.

"I thought you did," Michael said, "but I had to make sure." He took a deep breath as though to acquire strength to say more, and added: "I want you to forget that I'm married to Melissa. At least for a while. I want you to be together. Do I make myself clear?"

Not knowing what to say, I nodded again.

"I'm not insane," he continued. "I want you to be with Melissa because I love her and want her to be happy."

Wisp, who had apparently anticipated her husband's proposal, said nothing until I asked her how she felt about it. Her amber eyes regarded me candidly. "If what Michael is suggesting appeals to you, it appeals to me too," she said. "But I'm not making any promises about the future to either of you. . . ."

"All I ask," said Michael gruffly, "is that you continue to live at the studio. And come home nights."

The next afternoon, under the rafters of my room at Madame Branchard's, Wisp and I became lovers.

I had no illusions about the arrangement. For Wisp, in the beginning, it represented an interlude for recovering from the trauma of her failed recital; for Michael it was a last-ditch attempt to save his marriage. In my eagerness to make love to Wisp these practical aspects of our triangle did not dampen my ardor, even after Wisp admitted in an unguarded moment that had she not found me a satisfactory lover, she would have thrown me over for the upstate teaching job. Of our compatibility in bed neither of us could have any doubts; Wisp kept marveling at the new intensity of her sexuality, and I could hardly wait for each workday to end so that I could provide her with further evidence of it.

Michael had obviously hoped that within a few months Wisp would become bored with her young lover and cheerfully resume her place as his wife. But instead of diminishing, our affinity for each other grew stronger. So did our guilt feelings. In deference to Michael's pride, I stopped going to the studio when he was likely to be there, and when I escorted Wisp home from our rendezvous, I would go only as far as her door. We also agreed to keep our liaison a secret from our friends, and Wisp made it a point not to speak of me in Michael's presence. Yet all such precautions could not conceal from him the fact that our affair was flourishing. Wisp looked better than she had for months and was again involved with her dance projects. There was another factor that was beyond our control: Wisp's habit of talking in her sleep, which was to cancel all our precautions.

There came the inevitable night when she used my name in an explicitly amorous context, and Michael, who was a light sleeper, heard her. Enraged, he leaped out of bed—they occupied twin beds—woke her up, and demanded that she stop seeing me. He then put on some clothes and rushed out of the studio to a bar. The next day, after he had sobered up, he repeated his demand and as an afterthought promised that as soon as she gave me up, he would buy her a new refrigerator, something she had been wanting for years.

We laughed when she told me about the refrigerator, but the prospect of losing Wisp filled me with such dread that I proposed then and there, that she divorce Michael and marry me. Then almost at once I began worrying how I could support her and how my parents would feel about a daughter-in-law who was ten years my senior and a divorcee. Wisp, who was not lacking in perception, must have sensed that for all the "maturity" she credited me with, I was not ready for marriage. Except to characterize my proposal as "tempting," she was noncommittal about it, saying that it was too soon to contemplate a step as serious as marriage. As for Michael's demand, she assured me she had no intention of ending our relationship just because Michael had ordered her to do so.

Now that we were obliged to meet secretly and less frequently, I appreciated her merits more than ever. She had become my lover, friend, and, without ever making me feel like a student, my teacher; from her I learned the art and rewards of reciprocity in bed. I also came to realize that our rendezvous, clandestine though they were, gave my life a comforting sense of order and, despite the harassing atmosphere of the Cooper Union job, a feeling of hope for my future. Had I been less of a Sicilian, I would have thrown caution to the winds and persuaded Wisp to marry me.

Whether or not she had sex with Michael during this secret phase of our affair she never told me and I was afraid to ask. I suspected she did, for I began to notice changes in our relationship. While our lovemaking continued to be as pleasurable as ever, outside the bed she was less patient with me, irritable to the point where it became apparent she was having trouble living peaceably with Michael while continuing to see me. The serenity that had prevailed during our meetings began to wane. As if to promote a gulf between us, she mentioned our age difference more and more; she also insisted on discussing political topics, a practice we had been avoiding in the interests of harmony. To provoke me further, she voiced anti-Semitic views, which I had previously attributed only to Michael, and when I responded to them, she would argue that my attitudes were those of the Communists. For the first time, we began to quarrel.

One afternoon after a session of torrid lovemaking, Wisp propped herself on an elbow and broke the fateful news that she and Michael had decided to leave Manhattan and live in Brooklyn, where they expected to make a fresh start with her marriage and her dancing career. She said she loved me, but that she also loved Michael; she had decided it would be best for all of us if she returned to him.

The news came as no surprise, but I felt miserable. "What about the refrigerator?" I asked, trying to conceal my unhappiness. "Are you getting a new refrigerator?"

Wisp laughed. "Of course I am," she said. "It's being delivered next week. The latest model." I laughed with her, and then we made love again for the last time.

The separation from Wisp accelerated my departure from Cooper Union. For the first time I found myself disagreeing with the head librarian openly, sometimes with a Sicilian fervor that left no doubt about my dislike of him. Some of my anger came from the awareness that, by some subtle process of time, I was beginning to treat the derelicts with the same spirit of contempt that the head librarian had engendered among the other staff members.

Inasmuch as my conscience would not permit me to quit the job, my subconscious did what was necessary to achieve my dismissal. I, who for almost a year had been unfailingly punctual, began arriving later and later every morning until, finally, I was arriving around lunchtime. On top of this, I had taken no steps to enroll for library courses at Columbia, as I had agreed to do when hired. These derelictions the head librarian reported to the executive director of Cooper Union, with the result that one wintry morning I was formally informed that my services were no longer required.

FIVE

A Good Time for the Blues

Franklin D. Roosevelt first became President of the United States about the time I rejoined the ranks of the unemployed. Casting my first vote, I was among the millions of Americans who brought Roosevelt into the White House by a landslide. Like most voters, I knew little about the man that would qualify him to take charge of an almost bankrupt nation, but I was certain I wanted no more of the incumbent Herbert Hoover, the ex-engineer, who, a few weeks before the election, was quoted as saying: "Perhaps what this country needs is a great poem. Something to lift people out of fear and selfishness. Sometimes a great poem can do more than legislation. . . ."

The brutal evidence was everywhere that much more than a faith in poetry was required if the nation was to survive. Most of the nation's press was glossing over the evidence; not so a roving reporter named Oscar Ameringer who, after traveling through some twenty states, testified before a House Committee on Unemployment in February 1932. Ameringer reported that the forest fires which had been raging in the state of Washington all summer and fall were set by jobless lumber workers and impoverished farmers in an effort to earn a few dollars as fire fighters. In Oregon he learned that the local sheep raisers were slaughtering thousands of ewes because they did not bring enough in the market to pay for their shipping expenses. Everywhere he noted the paradox that while Americans were going hungry, vast quantities of food were being permitted to rot in the fields because of low market prices that hardly paid the harvesting costs.

Wherever he drove, Ameringer found the roads crowded with starving hitchhikers—men, women, and children hoping to find a place where they could work, eat, and sleep. In Arkansas he picked up a family whose mother was hugging a dead chicken under her ragged coat. She explained she had found it dead on the road, then added wryly: "They promised me a chicken in the pot, and now I got mine . . ." °

Ameringer concluded his testimony with a neat summary of the nation's economic dilemma: "The farmers are being pauperized by the poverty of the industrial populations and the industrial populations are being pauperized by the poverty of the farmers. Neither has the money to buy the produce of the other; hence we have overproduction and underconsumption at the same time in the same country."

In Manhattan the pauperizing effects of the Depression were everywhere in evidence. Night and day men and women dug into trash and garbage pails, scavenging for anything that could be eaten or sold. There were breadlines, often lined four abreast by men who kept their heads down. In all boroughs of the city the landscape was blighted with "Hoovervilles"—rows of small, mangy shacks built by the homeless out of egg crates, packing cases, and tar paper. Periodically the police demolished the shacks with the legal excuse there were not sufficient water and toilet facilities nearby, and periodically they were rebuilt. But perhaps the most prevalent reminders of the Depression were the hangdog expressions on the faces of men and women as

---

° "A chicken in every pot and a car in every garage" was the slogan of the Republican party during Herbert Hoover's first campaign for the presidency.

they walked the streets of New York with no jobs and little hope of finding any.

Not knowing how long I would be unemployed, I moved from Madame Branchard's to a cheaper room on East Ninth Street. The lugubrious atmosphere of the new quarters, together with the difficulty of finding a job discouraged me so much that, in a weak moment, I let my family know of my unemployment. Immediately my brother Frank, now a factory foreman for Samson Cutlery Company, my former employer, spoke to one of the owners and determined I could have my old job again.

The prospect of going back in time and place five years appalled me. I intensified my job-hunting effort, but nothing turned up. My money was almost gone and I was trying to decide whether it would be better to starve in New York or be employed in Rochester when I again ran into an ex-schoolmate who was able to provide an answer. This time it was an athletic girl I had known in high school who, luckily for me, had recently become the mistress of a store executive at Barnes and Noble, the bookdealers. On her recommendation, her lover hired me for a month's work at fifteen dollars a week. The executive, a middle-aged and quiet man by the name of Wilbur Pearce, apologized for the paltry pay, explaining that his firm had originally thought a teen-ager could do the job.

A fifth grader would have done as well. The job was so idiotically simple that I thought Pearce must be joking when he first described it to me. Apparently it was based on the premise that while Barnes and Noble customers were book readers, they were not readers of signs. Eight hours a day, six days a week, I was to stand in front of the lower Fifth Avenue building the firm had recently vacated and simply make sure their customers read a large signboard which plainly announced that Barnes and Noble was now located in a store four blocks north.

"Is that all I do?" I asked.

"That's all." Pearce apologized again, this time for the lowly nature of the job. "Are you sure you want it?"

"I'm positive."

The morning I started was the snowiest New York had known that winter, reminding me of the high drifts of snow in the long winter months of childhood when I would keep my shoulders hunched up to my ears while hating the cold and damning my relatives for not having migrated to some region of the country where the weather approximated that of Sicily. To keep warm on that first morning, I stayed inside as much as possible, my face glued to the door, on the lookout for Barnes and Noble customers. As soon as I spotted one, I would dart out into the snow and direct his attention to the signboard with the new address. Sometimes I made the mistake of addressing myself to persons who had never heard of Barnes and Noble, and they would recoil from me, as if from a madman.

For the first few days I wondered what Burges Johnson and all my other teachers who had such high hopes for me would think if they saw what moronic use I was making of my intelligence. When that got me nowhere, I tried to amuse myself by paying close attention to the remarks I overheard about Barnes and Noble in the course of doing my job. It then occurred to me that some of the customers' comments might be useful to the firm's management, and I began typing one-page daily summaries of them, and passing them on to Pearce. He, in turn, sent them to J. B. Barnes, one of the firm's partners, who wrote me a note expressing appreciation for the reports. "Please keep on writing them. They can do a great deal to help us understand the psychology of our customers." Encouraged, I adopted more aggressive techniques; instead of simply eavesdropping, I deliberately began engaging customers in conversation, eliciting their opinions of the firm and its services. In short, I became an amateur market researcher. Although I tried to make the reports sound factual, I kept them as readable as possible. The results were gratifying. Before long Barnes was mimeographing each report as it came in and distributing copies to his staff with the admonition to study it carefully. When the sign-reading stint was over at the end of the month,

Barnes hired me as a sales clerk in the new store at a salary increase of five dollars.

My career as a book clerk came to an end when a back injury I sustained in college began causing me such excruciating pain that it was no longer possible for me to be on my feet all day. All the doctors I visited—orthopedists, X-ray specialists, and an Amazonic osteopath—recommended I find a job that would permit me to sit most of the day. They seemed unaware of the scarcity of jobs, sitting or standing. The corset prescribed by an orthopedist, which I was to wear daily for the next ten years, provided some relief but not enough. I finally let Barnes know that unless he could change my job from a standing one to a sitting one, I would be obliged to return to Rochester where there was a sitting job waiting for me. Barnes spent several minutes talking about the charms of Rochester, but promised he would try to assign me a desk job. A few days later I was ensconced in the semidarkness of the store's balcony where all day long I poured over publishers' catalogues looking up the prices of books. The monotony of the work and the darkness around me taxed both my morale and my eyesight.

In retrospect the job as well as my private life made it one of the blackest periods I would ever know. For several months I had been living with a depressed Austrian girl and seeing the world through her fear-haunted eyes. At first I knew little more about her than I could deduce from the melancholy tone of her Garbo voice as it struggled with English. The voice as well as her facial resemblance to Garbo, coupled with the theatrical nature of our first encounter, made me feel like an actor who has been thrust into a role which his conscience compels him to pursue to its end. Not for the next two gloomy years was I to know what that ending would be.

It began one morning as I was leaving my room to go to work. In the hallway I noticed a girl picking up a bottle of milk in front of a closed door. I assumed it was her door and her milk until she became aware of my presence and her guilty eyes met mine. She hastily put the bottle down and rushed down the hallway to another door, not far from my own, which she opened and slammed behind her.

All day long I worried about the girl and reproached myself for frightening her off. That evening, driven by the memory of her eyes and the suspicion she might be hungry, I knocked on her door and, without mentioning the morning encounter, introduced myself as her neighbor. She stared at me with dark luminous eyes, not speaking yet not rebuffing me. Pretending it was my birthday, I suggested she help me celebrate with dinner at a nearby Italian restaurant. Then afraid she might say no, I quickly added that we were probably of the same age, twenty-three, all the more reason for joining me on my birthday. The amendment evoked a smile, followed by the shy correction that she was a year older, and acceptance.

As I was to learn much later, the "birthday" meal was the first food Freya had had in two days. There was little I knew about her after that first evening other than the fact she had been without a job for several months. Her reluctance to speak about herself was to continue throughout our relationship. At first I did not pry into her past; I was only concerned with the plight of her present. She reminded me of all the helpless heroines I had encountered in books, and I must have fancied myself her rescuing hero. Her beauty contributed to my romantic view of our situation; so did the impression that she was even lonelier than I.

Before long Freya and I were taking all of our evening meals together. When she learned what a small salary I earned, she ruled out restaurants and insisted on cooking for both of us on the single-jet gas stove in her room. By the end of the month we were living together in a one-room apartment on West Third Street which was equipped with a three-jet gas stove and a private bathroom, a luxury neither of us had before enjoyed in New York. The rent was low because the building was next to the Sixth Avenue El, which thundered by every ten minutes, causing our walls to quiver and the dishes to rattle.

Despite Freya's frugal habits, my salary barely covered the costs of food and rent. My book-review earnings made an

occasional movie or play possible, but there was never enough
money for new clothes. When I saw that Freya badly needed a
warm winter coat to replace the miserably thin jacket she wore
on the coldest days, I decided to buy her a coat on the
installment plan, which, I explained to her, was the American
and patriotic thing to do, the poor man's contribution to the
Gross National Product. Freya was not amused, protesting it
would mean incurring a debt that would take many months to
pay off. I argued that was better than having her catch
pneumonia, which would get us further into debt, but withheld
from her my secret reasons for incurring the debt. One was to
convince her I had no intention of abandoning her; the other
was to assure myself of the same thing.

Already I had developed serious reservations about the
"experiment," as we called our menage. For all the affection
we felt toward each other our life was steeped in depression.
Freya, I soon discovered, was subject to frequent bouts of
Weltschmerz, as she referred to her fits of melancholia, and I
could not help becoming infected by them. She never spoke of
suicide, but I suspected it was in her thoughts. There were
times when I would come home from work to an empty
apartment, and find her new winter coat hanging in the closet
like an ominous clue. Since she seldom went outdoors, especially at that hour, I would assume the worst and start
combing the neighborhood while praying I could get to her in
time. Although I never succeeded in finding her, she would
invariably return in a few hours with a vague explanation that
she had felt like walking, and apologize for causing me to
worry. As intimate as we were, I was unable to let her know
that with each of her disappearances I would relive the
agonizingly anxious hours of my childhood when my father
would fail to appear at dinnertime and my mother, surrounded
by her children, would silently wait for him at the front
window of our house, where we might see him the moment he
turned into our street, all the while suppressing the terror that,
like his father, he had drowned himself.

Although Freya may have considered suicide only when she

was severely depressed, the fear that she might try to take her own life constantly preyed on me. What was also alarming was her total dependency on my company. As far as I could tell, she had no friends of her own and made no effort to acquire any. While she was unfailingly gracious to my friends—she was especially responsive to Bill Rollins—she generally showed little interest in what they did or said. The only acquaintance of hers I ever encountered was a middle-aged blond Russian with a goatee and false teeth which kept slipping whenever he spoke. He appeared at our door one evening, explaining he had loaned Freya five dollars nearly a year ago and was badly in need of it. I gave him the money while Freya apologized for not repaying sooner, but she neither asked him in nor showed any other signs of friendship. When I questioned her, she would only say that he was a sculptor who had once been her neighbor.

Despite her reluctance to speak of her past, I had by now gleaned enough facts from her to confirm the impression that she was a badly mauled victim of circumstances. When she was four years old, shortly before the outbreak of World War I, her parents deposited her with a relative in Graz, Austria, while they visited the United States. The war began before they could get back to Austria, and Freya grew up without parents. She was passed from one relative to another; no one seemed inclined to take full charge of her. Two uncles became extremely fond of her, more so than their wives, but they were drafted into the army and she never saw them again.

When the war ended and communication with her parents was resumed, money began to arrive for her support and she fared better. Freya kept expecting them to return, but finally they informed her they had decided to live in the United States and would send for her as soon as they had saved enough money for her trip. Then Freya's mother became pregnant and gave birth to her second child, a boy. By the time the parents decided they could afford her voyage and an apartment large enough for four, the war had been over for seven years, and Freya was seventeen years old.

The reunion was not a happy one. After so long a separation the parents expected their daughter to be demonstrably affectionate toward them, but for Freya the man and woman who identified themselves as her father and mother were part of a past she had long forgotten. She experienced none of the filial love expected of her. "My mother said I was cold like a stranger, not as a daughter should be. But I felt like a stranger, and I could not pretend to love them just because they expected me to. . . . I tell you, *liebling*, it was a terrible situation and it became more terrible."

Freya's room was next to that of her parents and late at night, when they thought she was asleep, she would sometimes overhear them discussing her. In this way she learned that while her father felt some degree of guilt for having abandoned her for so many years, her mother persisted in regarding Freya as a heartless daughter who lacked the proper respect for her parents. In an obvious attempt to win her affection, the father began paying more attention to her. While his wife remained at home with their young son, he went to the movies with Freya, showed her the sights of New York, and on one occasion took her dancing at a nightclub.

Through the bedroom walls Freya began hearing her mother berate her father for lavishing so much attention on her. After each of their excursions, the mother's nagging became sharper, her resentment of Freya cruder. One night her scolding crescendoed into the blunt accusation that his feelings for Freya had become incestuous. Freya could bear no more. She waited until they had stopped quarreling and fallen asleep, then slipped out of the apartment and, with no money and only a smattering of English, out of their lives.

I never learned what happened to Freya in the five years that passed from the time she left her parents to the time we met. Once she began talking of a job she had with a traveling circus but thought better of it and would not continue. Knowing how innocent and gullible she was by nature, I could easily imagine how often she must have been hurt and betrayed by strangers she trusted, and I was resolved not to join their company. For better or worse, until she acquired enough self-confidence to be on her own, I was bound to her not only out of compassion but also because I could not help feeling responsible for her welfare.

Her lack of self-confidence translated itself into apathy. Apart from some desultory reading and writing—mostly poems in German that were never completed—Freya seldom acted on her own initiative. To force her out of the apartment at least once a day, I insisted she prepare some sandwiches for both of us each morning and join me for lunch at Madison Square Park, which was near the bookstore. When the weather was too cool for outdoor eating, we repaired to a cafeteria where we could eat our sandwiches with the purchase of two cups of tea. She claimed to enjoy these daily excursions, but after lunch she would head straight home, unwilling to go anywhere without me.

Her *Weltschmerz* might abate, she agreed, if she had some work to do that would take her out of the apartment and herself. Since job hunting was too difficult an ordeal for her, I prepared, with her consent, a letter for her signature that stressed her thorough knowledge of German, and sent it to a list of potential employers. The only response came from a writer who said he was engaged in a lengthy scholarly project and needed a research assistant with a knowledge of German. Freya did not like the handwriting. "I don't trust a man with that kind of handwriting," she said, but at my urging she telephoned and arranged an appointment for the next afternoon.

On her return from the interview I found her upset and on the verge of tears. Except for reporting that she had not qualified for the job, she would say nothing more. Later on, in bed, she told me what had happened. Her would-be employer had been satisfied with her qualifications and had hired her on the spot. But as she was leaving his office, he had made a pass at her and made it quite clear that if she expected to work for him, he would expect her "to make me happy now and then." I could feel Freya's tears on my face as she clung to me. "Oh, *liebling*," she moaned, "it has always been like that for me."

For all of her depression, Freya rarely wept, at least not in my presence. Only once had I seen her cry without restraint, and that was because of a canary named Mozart which I had given her as a birthday present. Freya had learned everything there was to know about the care and feeding of canaries, but one night I came home to find her in tears with Mozart's corpse cupped in her hands, blaming herself for his sudden death, lamenting that she always brought "bad luck to everything." I promised to buy her another canary but she would not hear of it, wailing that it too would die. As I tried unsuccessfully to comfort her, I fathomed how much her loveless childhood must have been spent in tears, and I too began to cry. As soon as that happened, she regained her composure.

If there was little joy in our life, this was not true of the other unmarried and impoverished couples I knew in the Village. For most of them life was a celebration, not an ordeal. As devoted to each other as the happiest of legally wed couples, they found cheer in being together. Other than the worry of making ends meet, their only other personal concern was keeping their liaison secret from their parents. Often they were courageous men and women who, for the sake of their principles, willingly risked arrest or being trampled on by police horses at left-wing demonstrations, but a single letter from a parent announcing a forthcoming visit to New York would transform them into abject cowards.

Compromising furniture, especially that in the bedroom, was hastily stored elsewhere. Clothes in closets and bureau drawers were reviewed and reduced to those of a single occupant and sex, and temporary quarters were found for the dislodged mate. Despite all precautions, a parental visit was liable to be attended by a variety of gaffes. One girl absentmindedly found herself telling her lover's father that his son John sometimes kept her awake at night with his snoring. Another girl forgot to check the household's soiled laundry before her parents arrived, and there was hell to pay when the mother's sharp eyes detected male socks and shorts comingling with her daughter's underwear.

Fortunately for us, my parents were too poor to make trips to New York, but that did not spare me from my own manifestations of cowardice, especially at Christmas, which Sicilians consider the most sacrosanct of all family holidays. "As long as your parents are alive," my mother had drummed into her children, "you must always spend Christmas at home." I was no more capable of disobeying that edict than I was of letting my parents know that I had acquired a common-law wife. Although I asked Freya to accompany me, I was relieved when she refused for it would have meant telling my family too many lies about our relationship and, also, subjecting her to a barrage of questions about her past. In an attempt to assuage my feelings of guilt over leaving her behind, Freya insisted that being alone was far more preferable to spending several days in a household full of noisy Sicilians whose language she did not understand.

The first of the unmarried couples I knew in the Village were Warren Spawn and Rebecca Ginzberg who lived in a sloppy tenement building on Cornelia Street whose halls constantly smelled of urine. Once you got past the stench and into their place, you had the exhilarating sensation of suddenly being in an immaculately clean museum. Everywhere (even in the kitchen) was a profusion of medieval art and artifacts purchased in the twenties when Warren had been an affluent attorney living with a socialite wife in a Park Avenue apartment. With the crash, Warren lost his affluence, his clients, and his wife. Unable to earn money, he grew a beard and, along with his medieval collection, moved into the cheapest tenement flat he could find in the Village. A little later he was found by Rebecca, who had a talent for picking up men. She took him in tow and, after she had moved into his apartment, persuaded him to put aside his "petty bourgeois Republican attitudes," and apply for relief. She also succeeded in charming the social worker sent to investigate the extent of his poverty, with the result that the social worker certified Warren for the relief rolls without reporting that he owned an art collection worth a small fortune.

The contrast between Warren and Rebecca was as striking as that between the raucously Italian atmosphere of Cornelia Street and the churchlike dignity of their apartment. With his Anglo-Saxon reserve and neatly trimmed auburn beard, Warren resembled a humorless Edwardian bishop. Rebecca, on the other hand, was warm, ribald, and flamboyantly clever. Only a few of her friends knew that her parents were Russian Orthodox Jews, whom she dutifully visited every Friday night. Warren spent most of his time reading scholarly tomes on medieval art and visiting museums. Rebecca's chief interest was the left-wing movement. She marched in picket lines, participated in anti-Fascist demonstrations, and when I first met her at the John Reed Club she was active in the newly formed Writers Union, which was demanding that the government create jobs for unemployed writers.

In her leisure time Rebecca wrote unpublishable short stories and kept the apartment spotless. Her favorite recreation was picking up men who struck her fancy (I was one of the many) and taking them to her apartment for platonic bouts of conversation and wine. Whenever anyone tried to make love to her, she would back away, explaining she had taken a vow to be faithful to Warren. To Warren's complaint that she was asking for trouble by bringing strangers home, her reply was that it was safer than going to their apartments. "Besides," she would add, "who the hell would dare rape me with all those saints on the walls?" When asked what she had in common with Warren, she replied that he was a genius in bed. Medievalists, she maintained, knew more about sex than anybody else.

Through Rebecca I met the Malmbergs, who became lifelong friends. They lived in an adjoining tenement and, like Warren and Rebecca, were able to rise above the squalor of the building. Carl was a second-generation Danish-American from Montana with a Latin temperament; Elizabeth was a quiet and willowy New Englander, who seemed embarrassed to be a Mayflower descendant. She spoke so little that almost everything she said sounded sagacious. Carl was an eloquent rebel who discoursed angrily on the miserable state of the union, the capitalist system's lack of system, and the destructive ways of Trotskyites. The Malmbergs were bone poor, but Carl would not apply for relief, chiefly out of pride. He was industrious by nature. At the time we met he was operating a one-man fiction factory from his apartment, writing a new full-length novel about once a month, for which a publisher paid him a weekly wage of twenty dollars. The novels were romances, mysteries, and adventure stories—Carl used a different pseudonym for each genre—written for rental-library customers with a tapeworm appetite for escapist literature. Apart from being a prolific novelist, Carl was also a gourmet cook, a handyman, and an artist. The first modern paintings I ever saw in the flesh were Malmberg impressions of Cornelia Street.

Near the Malmbergs lived Tom Coolahan, the same Coolahan who had once threatened to throw me out of Wisp's studio. Both of us pretended we had never met when we were introduced. Coolahan lived with a girl named Mary who supported their menage with a secretarial job, while he spent most of his days trying to be a sculptor.

Coolahan, who liked to be the center of attention, often bragged of his sex life with Mary. His favorite topic of conversation was the home therapy prescribed for both of them by his analyst: copulation several times a day. Whenever his libido demanded it, he would summon Mary home for lunch and they would partake of sex and sandwiches in bed until it was time for her to return to her office. At his analyst's suggestion, he kept a large chart next to their bed on which he recorded each of their orgasms. "Bring me that fucking chart," he would bellow at Mary, eager to show it off to some visitor.

The most talented artist on Cornelia Street was the artist Alice Neel, a friend of the Malmbergs and Rebecca, who was to wait thirty years before the portraits she was then painting would bring her fame. While her friends admired the quality of her work, they had nothing but criticism for her judgment in choosing lovers. The Cuban she married in the twenties absconded with their fifteen-month-old daughter and returned to Cuba. Unable to find them, Alice suffered a nervous breakdown that was climaxed by a suicide attempt. Her next mate was an intellectual sailor named Kenneth Doolittle who was a drug addict with a propensity for violence and impulsiveness. At a party in their Cornelia Street apartment Doolittle fascinated some twenty guests by trying to have sex with an artist in their presence. Alice reacted to her lover's conduct with the indulgence of an affectionate parent, but found it difficult to put up with the violent temper tantrums he staged whenever she paid attention to other men. When I first met them, they had been together for three years and Alice, a free spirit, was beginning to be courted by a wealthy Harvard graduate who tempted her with gourmet restaurant meals and luxurious weekends in the country. Matters came to a head when Doolittle, in a jealous rage, slashed sixty of her canvases, ripped most of her clothes, and set fire to her studio. Barely escaping with her life, Alice took refuge in the apartment of the Harvard graduate. But easy living proved to be too tame for her temperament, and she left him, for a while, to have an affair and her first son with a Puerto Rican singer in Spanish Harlem. There were other lovers and traumas but, regardless of what was happening to her, there was always her fierce dedication to art.

If Alice had the makings of a living legend, Joe Gould, another of Rebecca's friends, had already become one. Gould was a bald and skinny graduate of Harvard with a stringy goatee and long forehead which made him look like a cartoon of an intellectual. For his habit of flapping his arms to simulate a flying gull after he had imbibed, he was also known as Dr. Seagull. He was then engaged in what purported to be the most ambitious one-man literary project of all times, an oral history of the world. Gould subsisted largely on whatever food, drink, and dimes he could cadge; occasionally he earned a little money book reviewing for *The New Republic*, where I would catch glimpses of him, huddled in a corner of the reception room, furtively shunning all the other reviewers waiting their turn to see Malcolm Cowley, as though afraid one of them might shoo him away.°

The Gould at *The New Republic* was unlike the one I encountered at Rebecca's parties. He usually arrived drunk and obstreperous, determined to be the center of attention. At one party he removed all of his clothes, demanded a ruler, then challenged each male guest to compare the length of his penis with "this magnificent one of mine." When no one took up the challenge, he called them a gang of "cock-sucking cuckolds" and offered to screw any woman present looking for a genuine male. This scene may have been the one that inspired Alice Neel's portrait of Gould, a comic masterpiece of surrealism titled "Variations of an Old Theme on the Source of Russian Architecture," which could not be shown in public legally until almost three decades later. Except for his rimless spectacles, Gould is depicted in the nude with three sets of genitalia. He is seated with his legs spread apart and a hand resting on each knee, like a wrestler eagerly set for action. To the left and right of him are profiles of his pot-bellied torso, each with the usual. number of genitalia. The mischief in his eyes and mouth recalls my favorite Joe Gould quip: "I have delusions of grandeur. I sometimes think I am Joe Gould."

° Among the reviewers I encountered in *The New Republic* waiting room were Hamilton Basso, Alfred Kazin, James T. Farrell, and Otis Ferguson, who was to become a full-time staff member of the magazine. Ferguson, a bachelor, lived in the same Cornelia Street tenement occupied by the Malmbergs. Like all the other apartments in the building, Ferguson's was unheated. To keep warm at night, he pitched a tent on the kitchen floor in front of a coal stove, and used the tent as his bedroom. Ferguson was killed by enemy fire during World War II, while a crewman on a merchant-marine ship.

The only Village personage who rivaled Gould in notoriety was Maxwell Bodenheim, the poet and novelist. In the twenties he had become the personification of Village scandals, the author of risqué novels which advocated uninhibited free love. Many a girl with sexual fantasies, who was rebelling against her middle-class background, tried to attach herself to Bodenheim, and a surprising number of them succeeded. The Bodenheim legend incorporated lurid tales of the sexual extremes to which the girls went to demonstrate to the world, with the novelist's collaboration, what free spirits they were. One of his mistresses enjoyed being paraded at the end of his leash up and down lower Fifth Avenue. Bill Rollins caught a glimpse of them one early evening as the girl strolled in front of Bodenheim in a tight-fitting tiger-skin dress, wearing around her neck an iron collar to which was attached the leather leash which Bodenheim would jerk from time to time.

By the time I knew Bodenheim in the early thirties, he had renounced all such shenanigans and embraced as a religion, with all the fervor of a penitent convert, the class struggle against capitalism as ordained by Marx and Lenin. He was never without some young and beautiful girl for a mistress, but instead of free love he now preached the gospel of communism, mainly through his poetry which he recited *con brio*, with his eyes tightly shut, as though he were experiencing then and there the agony of the oppressed masses. The poems were usually cliché ridden, inferior to those he had produced in his sybarite days, but the clichés were obscured by the clenched eyelids and the feverish inflection.

When Bodenheim turned Communist, he gave up his sado-masochistic ways, at least in public, as well as the girls in his entourage who catered to them. One of his ex-mistresses was the disowned daughter of Jewish Orthodox parents, a fiery brunette with piercing green eyes and disheveled hair. Marilyn, as I shall call her here, eventually took up with a Village poet who, fancying himself the reincarnation of François Villon, had no compunction exploiting the girl's infatuation for him. To augment his welfare checks, he encouraged Marilyn to steal, beg, and whore, convincing her that every time she did so she was helping to undermine the capitalistic system. If she did not bring home enough money, her lover would beat her and send her out on the street again. Marilyn maintained that it was a pleasure to be beaten by America's greatest living poet; the only thing that mattered to her was that he permit her to continue being his woman.

Ten minutes after Bill Rollins had introduced me to Marilyn she was tapping on my door to propose having sex together. For three dollars she would be mine for an hour; for ten she would spend the whole night with me and fix my breakfast. I turned her down, not because she lacked sex appeal, but because she looked dirty and I had already heard of her promiscuous whoring and was afraid she was diseased. The next time I saw her was from the top of a Fifth Avenue bus. As soon as she spotted me from the sidewalk, she boarded the bus, climbed to the upper deck and, in a scolding voice which implied I owed her money, demanded fifty cents. I gave her the coin and she was off the bus before the conductor could collect her fare.

Our final encounter took place one night in Stewart's Cafeteria on Sheridan Square. Marilyn came to my table and, explaining that her lover had locked her out for the night as punishment for failing to wash his socks, asked that she spend the night with me. She became incensed when I told her the bed wasn't large enough to hold two and threatened that if I did not take her in or give her some money, she would spread the word that I was a fairy. I shrugged, and she went off cursing me. About a week later Bill Rollins reported that Marilyn had told him she was certain I was a homosexual. Rollins said he had thanked her for the information and promised to break the news to the girl I was bedding.

Despite such characters, the Village atmosphere of the thirties struck me as sober. The tourists, who were drawn there by what they had read of its wild and wicked ways, must have been disappointed. For a time a few professional Villagers, still imbued with the bohemian spirit of the twenties, frequented Stewart's Cafeteria and the tourists flocked there to watch them. After a while the bohemians tired of being objects of curiosity and abandoned the place; but until its demise the tourists continued to come and stare, though never certain whether they were staring at bohemians or at other tourists.

To capitalize on the tourist trade there were several abortive attempts to provide entertainment that matched the average tourist's preconceived image of Village life. One cellar cafe featured the poet Eli Siegel reading Vachel Lindsay's *The Congo* while breaking furniture as he read, presumably because customers expected Village life to be melodramatic. The resident Villagers diligently avoided all places where tourists were likely to go. For diversion they attended free lectures (some at the John Reed Club headquarters on Sixth Avenue), visited the newly opened Whitney Museum of Art on Eighth Street, or frequented Eva Le Gallienne's Fourteenth Street Civic Repertory Theater, a huge auditorium with plenty of low-priced seats where Freya and I saw our first Chekhov plays and such star performers as Joseph Schildkraut, Josephine Hutchinson, and Le Gallienne herself.

For musical excitement the Villagers listened to Dixieland jazz as performed at Nick's, on lower Seventh Avenue, by Pee Wee Russell and his group. Since Freya and I could not afford the prices of that establishment, we listened to the group while standing outdoors pretending to be immersed in the window display of the next-door haberdashery.* To hear some of the great black jazz artists, we would travel by subway to Harlem's Savoy Ballroom where Louis Armstrong, Ella Fitzgerald, and Chick Webb were entrancing audiences long before they were permitted into white territory.

On those rare occasions when we dined out, we would look

---

* I was introduced to the pleasure of jazz by the late Charles Edward Smith, the first critic to write of jazz as a serious art form. Smith mastered the language of jazzmen and was on good terms with nearly all of the great performers of the twenties and thirties. His exploration of their lives and music is recorded in the book *Jazzmen* (1939), written in collaboration with Frederic Ramsey, Jr.

for an Italian restaurant where the clientele was mainly Italian, for it was axiomatic that as soon as the clientele became mainly non-Italian the quality of the food went down and the prices went up. One reason for this may have been the hostility that the Italians had for their fellow Villagers. For the sake of their businesses, the Italian restaurant and store owners carefully concealed it behind a facade of cordiality. But beneath the facade was a severe distrust for the life style and mores of the Villagers, which were shocking to the Italians. As a sociologist of the thirties aptly put it, "To the Italians, living among the Villagers was almost like living in a large-scale disorderly house." °

Apart from making certain their daughters kept away from Villagers, the public stance of the Italians was to pretend that how the Villagers chose to live was of no concern to them. In reality, they were deeply concerned that their children might be influenced by them and, like my relatives in Rochester, tried to make the children comply to the strict code of behavior they had brought with them from Italy.

I became acquainted with some of them in Washington Square, which they utilized as they might have the *piazza* of their native villages. On Sundays the Italians paraded around the square dressed in their best churchgoing clothes, screaming at their children when they got out of hand. Sometimes they rested on the park benches and gossiped in their native dialect. In the evenings, when the weather was warm enough, the older men would sit in clusters chewing on their crooked DiNobile stogies, while they played checkers and kibitzed. A surprising number of them were Sicilian, and I would sometimes wander from one cluster to another listening to the poetry of their speech and thinking fondly of my Rochester relatives.

My Sunday morning visits to the square, without Freya, became a habit for a while, an intermission for reflecting on where I had come from and where I might be going. The old

° Caroline Ware, *Greenwich Village* (1934).

men would ignore my presence until I dropped some remark in Sicilian. At that point they would express astonishment that I was not an "American," and eagerly make room for me to sit with them.

Their first question was usually about my parents and the names of the Sicilian towns they hailed from. After that, they would ask why I was not with them. Without paying much attention to my reply, they would start bemoaning the fate of all Italian parents with American-born progeny, complaining how difficult it was to raise well-mannered sons and daughters in this *terra maledetta,* where children are systematically encouraged not to respect their elders. The phrases expressing these sentiments, as well as their vehemence, were almost identical to those of my relatives. I did not mind; it was like being home. We covered a variety of topics, including the Villagers, whom they regarded as *butani* and *curnuti* (whores and pimps), but ultimately wound up discussing politics.

Like most of my relatives, they were dismally conservative and pro-Fascist. Mussolini, they believed, would bring increasing glory to Italy and respect to all Italians, even to those in the United States. Futilely I would argue with them. Mussolini, I predicted, could bring only ruin to Italy; like all tyrants, he could not survive without dragging the Italians into war. I quoted my father's definition of Il Duce as "a big-mouthed braggart with an insatiable appetite for power," but they quoted me passages from *Il Progresso,* the Italian New York daily, their Bible, which constantly presented Mussolini as Italy's greatest hero. A genuine Italian hero, I told them, was Giuseppe Garibaldi, a champion of freedom, in whose honor they and the other Italians in New York had erected a statue in Washington Square, only a few yards away from us; he would have been the first to oppose Mussolini's dictatorship. "You're young, you're wrong, and you're crazy," one of the old men retorted. "Garibaldi would have gladly traded his red shirt for a black one."

Fascismo was only a word to them. Its anatomy was beyond

their understanding and would remain so as long as the Italian and American press kept promoting Mussolini as a great leader who was putting Italy on its feet—mostly, one gathered from the *New York Times,* by making its trains run on time. By now the old Sicilians were too blinded by their nostalgia for Italy to see beyond Il Duce's rhetoric. After a while I got tired of arguing with the old men and stopped visiting them. It was too painful for me to be reminded every Sunday that even in a country like the United States, where the press was uncensored, it was easy to fool people into championing fascism.

Later on I was to know Carlo Tresca, Gaetano Salvemini, Gaspare Nicotri, and other Italians who spoke powerfully against fascism, but at the time the only Italian anti-Fascist I knew was my father. Though he had little education, he had enough political acumen to realize that Mussolini's dictatorship spelled disaster. His juicy invectives against Il Duce's policies were music to me. When one of our pro-Fascist relatives declared that Mussolini had "eight million bayonets ready for any emergency," my father replied: "Where does he have them? Stuck up his ass?"

At about this time my father's stand against fascism gave me the courage to take a stand against his somewhat fascistic policy toward the courtship of my sister Assunta and her fiancé, Vincenzo. Although they had been engaged for almost three years, and there was no doubt about Vincenzo's honorable intentions, my father would not permit the couple to be together without a chaperone. In a letter I wrote him, with all the tact I could command in my broken Italian, I protested that he was endangering the betrothal and hinted that, unless he permitted the couple more freedom, I would feel compelled to take an action which we would all regret. Whether it was the ominous vagueness of the threat or the realization that he was being unduly Sicilian, I never found out. There was no reply to my letter, a fact which cost me some sleepless nights, but before long my father stopped interfering with the courtship. Assunta and Vincenzo were married six months later.

There was no satisfaction in having my father comply with my demand. On the contrary, it saddened me to have reduced, in however slight a degree, his authority as a Sicilian father. For I loved him enough to worry about the state of his pride. In the blackest moments of my life with Freya, I seriously considered proving my love by returning to the sanctuary of my family.

SIX

The Left-Winged Whirl

In the circumscribed world of the Villagers, the anxiety generated by the general acceptance of Mussolini's dictatorship and the rise of new demagogues (Hitler in Germany, Huey Long in the United States) hovered over them like a bomber about to drop its load. The ravages of the Depression sharpened their fear that the United States was tending toward fascism, and drew them toward left-wing ideologies, particularly toward the Communist party line that the only hope for the nation's salvation was to break with bourgeois tradition, as developed under capitalism, and support the revolutionary aspirations of the American working class. For reasons that might be more apparent to a psychologist than to a political analyst, this theme, bolstered by the optimism held out for the Soviet Union's future, gripped the imagination of many American intellectuals in the early thirties and entrapped it for nearly a decade.

The popularity of the Marxist-Leninist doctrine in the early thirties was no sudden development; its seeds had long been sown by the success of the Bolshevik Revolution, the rise of fascism in Italy, and the steady disparagement of American

119

middle-class values, some of it, curiously, expressed by the vociferous anti-Marxist H. L. Mencken, whose influential *American Mercury* of the twenties relentlessly promoted the impression that the worst aspects of American capitalism could be equated with the bourgeois ("booboisie" was his concoction) standards of middle America.

The collapse of the economy was, of course, the major factor that persuaded thousands of American intellectuals to move quickly into the left-wing orbit. In their vanguard were the writers who were producing proletarian literature—novels, poems, articles, and manifestos—all of which in varying degrees espoused the political goals of the American Communist party. In September 1932, two months before the presidential election, fifty-three American writers and artists (among them Edmund Wilson, John Dos Passos, Malcolm Cowley, Sidney Hook, and Waldo Frank) signed their names to a pamphlet which denounced the Democratic and Republican parties as hopelessly corrupt, rejected the Socialist party as a "do nothing group," and declared their support for the Communist party on the grounds that it alone presented a viable program for fighting fascism and eliminating poverty. They further declared that under capitalism the United States was "like a house rotting away: the roof leaks, the sills and rafters are crumbling." Citing the paradox of mass privation and potential plenty, they deplored the waste of talent in a country that had "never been able to provide its population with a sufficiently large body of trained intellectuals to satisfy its cultural needs."

While I could subscribe to most of the statements in the pamphlet, their implication that a successful American revolution, led by the Communist party, was a genuine possibility struck me as juvenile. Yet I could not help but be impressed by the forceful style of the Communist party leadership, and gradually became convinced that the party had the capability of pressuring the New Deal to move further to the left, to a position that would increase the strength of the working class and induce the nation to take an aggressively anti-Fascist stand.

On the other hand, I could not bring myself to join the Communist party. Some inner warning system, created perhaps by the wariness that Sicilians have developed through centuries of foreign invasions, made me chary of affiliating myself with a political organization that, like the Catholic Church I had rejected, handed down dogmas and orders which its membership was blindly expected to accept.

I became instead a "fellow traveler," the label pinned on intellectual sympathizers of the Communist party who were either unwilling or unable to become party members. It happened in 1932, the year when the Communist party hierarchy, which had been generally disdainful of intellectuals until then, decided it was important to enlist "all friendly intellectuals into the ranks of the revolution." On his return from Kharkov, where the decision was reached, the Communist American writer Mike Gold proclaimed: "Every door must be opened wide to fellow travelers. We need them. We must not fear they will corrupt us with their bourgeois ideas."

For me the opening of doors meant I would be welcomed as a contributor to left-wing periodicals at a time when few publications were accepting the work of new writers; it also meant fraternizing with writers who were already well established. These were no small considerations for any young anti-Fascist anxious to make his mark in the literary world, and I happily began attending the meetings of the Communist-controlled John Reed Club, which provided a forum for discussions of Marxist-Leninist doctrine as it applied to literature and art.

My introduction to the group was to have been formally made by the novelist Edward Dahlberg, whom I had met through Malcolm Cowley; but it never took place, for within five minutes after we had entered the club's meeting hall Dahlberg became involved in a ferocious argument with the chairman which sent him stomping out of the place in a rage, leaving me behind to fend for myself.

Argumentation, as I soon discovered, was the John Reed

Club's chief activity. The debates usually centered on differences of Marxist interpretation as precipitated by recently
published books and articles. As one who had found Marx and
Engels unreadable, except for their *Communist Manifesto*, I
could not follow most of the discussions, but I was fascinated by
the forensic style of such participants as Philip Rahv and Alfred
Hayes, who sounded more like trial lawyers than men of letters.
The oral fluency of the John Reeders belied my theory that men
and women become writers because they have difficulty expressing themselves in conversation.

Not everyone had the gift of gab. Kenneth Fearing, who was
producing electrifying poems about the Depression, had a low-
voltage personality that seldom made itself heard. On those few
occasions when he addressed the group his slow and laconic
speech provided a refreshing contrast to the customary oratory.
Nelson Algren, who was visiting from Chicago, could barely
speak. When asked to comment about his recently published
first novel, *Somebody in Boots*, Algren, ill at ease and groping
for words, simply reported that hardly anyone had either
reviewed the book or bought it, and sat down amid a funereal
hush. For the first time I understood through my viscera the
anguish of publishing a book that is ignored.

Now and then the organization's leadership saw to it that its
members got down to the business of promoting the revolution.
I shied away from such chores as distributing leaflets and
performing on public soapboxes, but took part in several anti-
Fascist demonstrations in Union Square, one of which proved to
be so brutal that to this day I cannot look at a policeman on
horseback without fearing I might be trampled on or struck by
a billy. Much easier was the course in book reviewing I
volunteered to teach in the club's writing program, which was
designed to attract young intellectuals with left-wing inclinations. I gave it up after two weeks, suddenly embarrassed by
the presumption such teaching implied.

As part of its strategy to project a strong cultural image, the
John Reed Club also conducted a series of free lectures and, in
1934, launched *The Partisan Review*. The new literary publica-

tion was edited by Philip Rahv and William Phillips, known to John Reeders as "The Bobbsey Twins" because of the closeness of their friendship and their thinking ° The first issue consisted entirely of contributions by John Reeders, including myself.

For almost two years I sporadically attended the club's meetings and lectures, drawn by the companionship of writers, yet often feeling like an impostor for not becoming convinced that revolution, as prescribed by Marxian catechism, was my cup of tea. Sometimes, becoming bored by the oratory, I amused myself by trying to guess which were the hard-core Communists and which the fellow travelers. My tendency was to categorize the most voluble and passionate speakers as the Communists, but I could never be sure. Adding to the uncertainty was the extensive use of aliases both on the part of Communists and non-Communists.† During the McCarthy era, when I was asked by the House Un-American Activities Committee whether certain writers I had known at the John Reed Club were Communists, I could truthfully reply that I could not positively identify anyone as a Communist; no one had ever shown me documentary proof of his party membership or invited me to join the party.

The John Reed Club died in 1934 when, in preparation for the Communist party's popular-front strategy, the party leadership decided to liquidate the thirty John Reed clubs operating from coast to coast. The plan was to replace them with a single organization of national scope to be known as the League of American Writers, with the expectation that it would attract

° Rahv and Phillips developed *The Partisan Review* into a lifelong project. After they broke with the Communist party in 1937, they established the magazine as an independent enterprise. It still continues with William Phillips as its editor. Rahv was its coeditor until his death in 1974.

†Although I used my own name at the John Reed Club, I adopted two pseudonyms for the fiction and reviews I published in left-wing publications: Mario Michele and Jay Gerlando. In the same period Kyle Crichton, a highly successful staff writer on *Collier's*, signed his *New Masses* articles "Robert Forsyth." A pseudonym acted as a safeguard against being fired by your capitalist employer. Its other advantage was that, like a mask worn at a carnival, it made you feel less inhibited.

prominent writers who were reluctant to be associated with a group as obviously leftist as a John Reed Club. With Machiavellian nicety, the party's hierarchy arranged to have the clubs preside over their own demise by asking them to issue a "Call for an American Writers' Congress," whose main business would be to create their successor. The "Call" was addressed to "all writers who have achieved some standing in their respective fields, who have clearly indicated their sympathy to the revolutionary cause, who do not need to be convinced of the decay of capitalism or the inevitability of revolution."

Some John Reeders became indignant at the party's decision to terminate the clubs and refused to sign the call. Richard Wright, who was then secretary of the John Reed Club in Chicago, asked what was to become of all the young writers in the clubs who were not considered "important" enough to join the League of American Writers. The question went unanswered. In New York, Leon Dennen, another John Reeder, protested that to disband the clubs without first consulting its twelve hundred members was "undemocratic." In a response that brooked no argument, a Communist party functionary told him that "first we must carry out the decisions of the party and then speak of 'democracy' and what not." For me, however, the end of the John Reed Club came as a distinct relief. The constant hair-splitting dialectical jousting at the meetings made me feel more and more out of place; the general atmosphere struck me as grossly sectarian. The concept of a league of American writers, with popular-front goals to draw left wingers of all sects, appealed both to my sense of political reality and to my sense of prudence. My only concern was that I might not be considered important enough to be admitted into its membership.

From some of the statements made at the Writers' Congress, which was attended by more than four thousand writers, would-be writers, and sundry left-wing sympathizers, one might have deduced that the Communist party, the organizers of the congress, had indeed finally embarked on a nonsectarian course. "We must dig deep into the treasures of our national tradition and cultural heritage without succumbing to narrow chauvinism," said Earl Browder, the executive secretary of the party, in his opening address. He was roundly applauded when he added that the party wanted "writers to be good writers, not bad strike leaders." Taking Browder at his word, Waldo Frank, the non-Communist chairman of the congress, lambasted left-wing writers for taking orders from Communist leaders and turning out propaganda instead of "deep revolutionary art." James T. Farrell, who lectured on the short story, followed suit by charging that so-called proletarian fiction was riddled with Communist clichés and stereotypes. But while dissident opinions like those of Frank and Farrell were permitted to be heard, the organizers of the congress made certain they were in the minority. The cumulative impression of the proceedings was that while writers might differ on the distinctions between literature and propaganda, the old slogan of the John Reed clubs—"Art is a class weapon"—was still good enough for the party leadership. Despite the popular-front stance, with its common denominator of antifascism, the Communist hierarchy was not about to abandon its policy of placing ideological considerations ahead of literary quality.

The truth of this was brought home to me by the book-review editor of the *New Masses*, who had assigned me Ignazio Silone's first novel, *Fontamara*. The editor readily published my favorable appraisal of it, but as soon as it appeared some of his colleagues demanded to know why I would praise the work of a writer who was a "Trotskyite." On being informed that I had no previous knowledge of Silone's political views, they forgave me for my ignorance. But when I maintained that *Fontamara* deserved all the praise I had given it, regardless of the author's political affiliation, one of the editors turned away from me as though I were a dirty heretic. Another smiled at me benevolently, with pity in his eyes.°

° The Communist party's antagonism to Ignazio Silone was publicly demonstrated in 1935 by a conspicuous act of omission. When the left-wing Theater Union produced a stage adaptation of *Fontamara*, titled *Bitter Stream*, the program carried no mention of either the novel or the author.

A few months later when Clifford Odets rocketed to fame with the production of three plays, I displeased the strict party liners again with a *Daily Worker* review of *Paradise Lost* that found it inferior to Odets' *Awake and Sing.* This time no one spoke to me about my review, but shortly after its publication, the *Daily Worker* published a second review of the play which praised it lavishly. To make certain the second review would have the effect of canceling out the first, the review was assigned to a writer of the theater who was far better known than I, the playwright John Howard Lawson. Apparently, the party did not want to risk alienating as successful a left-wing playwright as Odets.

It was the last review I wrote for the *Daily Worker.* But for several years I continued writing for the *New Masses,* using it as a vehicle for expressing my anti-Fascist sentiments while appeasing my need as a writer to see my writing in print. Despite the strict party liners on the staff, none of the editors ever tampered with my prose or withheld publication of any manuscript I submitted. There was no pay for what I wrote, except a free subscription to the magazine and the satisfaction of writing as I pleased. Now and then some of the editors went out of their way to compliment me, as happened when I tried my hand writing satire about an imaginary Italian-American named Francesco who becomes a worshiper of Benito Mussolini and a self-appointed Aryan.° Encouraged by the number of compliments it received, I wrote a second sketch about Francesco which describes his adventures as he allies himself with a Nazi fräulein in the Bronx.†

One of my anti-Fascist pieces for the *New Masses* was an interview with Luigi Pirandello, who had recently been awarded the Nobel Prize for literature and was visiting the United States for the first time. As much as I admired his

---

° "Francesco's an Aryan" by Mario Michele, *New Masses,* December 18, 1938.

† "Francesco Becomes a Lion" by Mario Michele, *New Masses,* April 25, 1939.

writings, I had recently published a review in *The New Republic* that sharply took him to task for having accepted Italian fascism without a word of public protest. In this respect he did not differ from nearly all other Italian writers who went along with the Fascist regime. But I had expected more of Pirandello since I supposed that his worldwide fame would have protected him from recrimination were he to have expressed his disapproval of the Fascists. By his silence he had, deliberately or not, allied himself with the dictatorship.

Actually, there was no trace of Fascist propaganda in Pirandello's writings. However, by repeatedly expressing the concept that people waste their lives by searching for a reality which cannot be distinguished from illusion, nearly all of his major plays projected a vision of life that was nicely compatible with the Fascist version of government. The Fascists were astute enough to realize that if the Italians could accept Pirandello's philosophy, they would have no difficulty accepting fascism and all the illusions its propaganda fed them.

Eager to hear Pirandello's own view of Mussolini's dictatorship (my naiveté was boundless in those days), I telephoned his hotel room and introduced myself to his male secretary as a writer of Sicilian parentage who would be honored to interview the playwright, stressing the fact that my father had also been born in Porto Empedocle (Pirandello's native town) and had, in fact, known the Pirandello family in his youth. Prudently I did not explain that my father's only connection with the family was that of a young errand boy who used to deliver the coffee and pastries they ordered from the Porto Empedocle cafe that employed him; nor did I make any mention either of the *New Masses* or *The New Republic*. The secretary said I could have an hour of Pirandello's time if I came immediately.

Pirandello, who was then sixty-seven and would be dead in two years, already looked like a man who has completed his work and is resigned to death. His eyes had already begun the process of withdrawal; the rest of him emitted an aura of fatigue. His large head was already familiar; I had seen many photographs of it, with its white goatee and ovally bald pate. As he came forward to greet me, I was surprised that such a head should be set on so short and squat a body. The voice was more alive than the rest of him, and I could not help responding to its warmth. Since he knew no English, we spoke in Italian, I with a mishmash of Sicilian dialect and a smattering of college-learned grammar. As he questioned me about his *paesani,* my father and mother, my awe of him as a literary genius and as the first Sicilian intellectual I had ever encountered rapidly evaporated.

When I told him about my father's boyhood deliveries to the sumptuous Pirandello residence (his father was the proprietor of a sulphur mine) he smiled and affirmed the truth of my father's boast that Castiglione of Porto Empedocle, the cafe where my father had learned the art of pastry making, produced the best *cannoli* in all of Sicily. He would have been content chatting indefinitely about the Sicily he had long ago left behind, but I was anxious to start questioning him about his relationship to the Fascist regime.

Until now the secretary had been sitting at a desk in the room talking into a telephone in a language that sounded like Hungarian (at one point I was astonished to hear him enunciate the name of Greta Garbo), but as soon as I began asking Pirandello about the Fascist government's policy toward writers, the secretary ended his telephone conversation and interrupted Pirandello with a question in French that seemed to involve the name of Garbo and the appointment calendar.

When I repeated my question to Pirandello, the secretary intervened in a peremptory voice to inform me that Signore Pirandello had not come to the United States to discuss "political matters." I rephrased the question, trying to prune it of political implications, but as soon as Pirandello began replying the secretary found another pretext for interrupting us. Before long he gave up all pretense of being occupied at his desk; it became clear that one of his chief functions was that of censor. As long as we discussed noncontroversial matters, he said nothing, but as soon as we touched on areas that might reveal Pirandello's attitude toward the Fascist regime, he would promptly intrude.

At first it disturbed me to note with what acquiescence an author of Pirandello's stature accepted the secretary's censorship. Then it occurred to me that the secretary might simply be carrying out Pirandello's own instructions. The secretary's final interruption was to let me know that my time had expired. When I tried to ignore him, he went to the door and opened it for me. "I am sorry," he said, without sounding sorry, "but an important person is waiting to see Signore Pirandello." Those were his actual words. Pirandello raised his eyebrows, as though he understood enough English to realize I was being insulted.

Possibly to compensate for his secretary's bad manners, Pirandello's good-bye was effusively warm. He urged me to visit the island of our ancestors and asked me to convey his personal regards to my father, then asked me to look him up when I came to Rome.

As I left, I looked around in the corridor and lobby for a tall and beautiful woman with a wide-brimmed slouch hat that usually covered half her face, for it occurred to me that Pirandello's next caller might well be the star of my dream life, Greta Garbo, whom I had recently seen in the motion-picture version of Pirandello's play *As You Desire Me*. But there was no one I saw who bore the slightest resemblance to Garbo. So I went home and made love to Freya, who did resemble her.

Living with Freya accentuated the meaning of aloneness. For her it was a desirable barrier against the outside world; for me it thickened the gloom into which we were locked. Freya clung to her shyness as if it were a shield; I secretly longed to be rid of mine, to start being gregarious like my Sicilian relatives, who held that to be alone is to invite despair. The only friend we saw regularly was Bill Rollins with whom Freya had felt at ease from the moment they met. The few acquaintances I had brought home from the John Reed Club did not appeal to her.

She claimed they lacked imagination and were too serious. Bill
was also serious, but he preferred to be amusing, and for that
she was grateful. He would arrive with a bottle of wine and
juicy morsels of gossip about Madame Branchard's Menagerie,
and Freya would reciprocate by cooking spaghetti and a
tomato sauce flavored with Italian sausage, a cheap meat that
did wonders for the sauce.

Bill kept inviting us to parties at Madame Branchard's, but
Freya would invariably think of some excuse for not going and,
often as not, I would choose to stay home with her. Finally, in
a determined effort to dislodge us from our apartment, Bill,
remembering with what nostalgia Freya talked of the green
woods and farmlands she had known as a child in Austria, asked
his friend Peggy Cowley to include us in a weekend house
party she was giving in her summer place near Pawling.
Predictably, Freya begged off but, realizing how eager I was to
meet more of Bill's friends, persuaded me to go.

The house guests were all ten to fifteen years older than I
and, like Bill, a hard-drinking, literary, and highly diverting lot.
Bill had associated with some of them in Paris after World War
I when the French capital became a magnet for American
writers who, disdaining the Philistine values of their native
country, settled there to write fiction and poetry, edit avant-
garde little magazines, and issue virulent manifestoes on aes-
thetic issues. As Kay Boyle and Robert McAlmon put it in the
title of a combined memoir: "Being Geniuses Together."

The crash of 1929 abruptly stopped the flow of checks from
their families, and most of them were obliged to return to the
land they had scorned. Either because they were older and
presumably wiser or because distance had endowed them with
a fresh perspective for appreciation, a number of them lost
their contempt for the United States. Before long they were
writing respectfully of the American character and embracing
traditional American values with an ardor which suggested that
the nation was ripe for a spiritual reawakening.

Entertainment, not ideology, was the crux of Peggy Cowley's house party, with applejack providing the main stimulant. The guests shuttled between Peggy Cowley's home and the neighboring home of Slater Brown, whom E. E. Cummings had immortalized in *The Enormous Room* as his bosom internment companion, "B." Brown, who was then writing a novel about his Pawling neighbors, fascinated me with his steady barrage of persiflage which, even through the barrier of his stuttering, emerged with stunning clarity. The drinking was so prodigal as to include guzzling hens and roosters, who preferred beer to applejack. I instinctively became an observer, too dazzled by the crossfires of wit to open my mouth. Yet afterward it was not the humor that I retained, but the talk I heard about writers I had read.

From our hostess we heard her firsthand account of how her intimate friend Hart Crane had died in April of that year while they were traveling together on a ship from Mexico. She and Crane were standing and chatting near the ship's rail when the poet, who was in the throes of a nasty hangover, suddenly jumped on the rail and dived into the Caribbean. According to her, he had no intention of killing himself; it was simply a dramatic bid for attention that was frustrated by the unexpected presence of sharks. One of the sharks got him before he could be pulled out of the sea. Her report had the impact of a horror story until she began describing the pained astonishment that came over Crane's face as he saw the murderous shark approaching him, at which point it became a satiric portraiture of the poet, another morsel of absurdity for the entertainment of the guests.°

° Peggy Cowley's description of Hart Crane's death, as told to her guests, differs markedly from the definitive account of it in John Unterecker's biography of Crane, *Voyager* (1969). In that version Peggy Cowley, by her own admission, was elsewhere on the ship when Crane leaped to his death. Moreover, Unterecker makes no mention of sharks and leaves no doubt of Crane's intention to commit suicide.

Peggy Cowley was a veritable cornucopia of gossip about the numerous writers she knew, but her habit of using only their first names made it difficult for me to identify them. Only when she spoke of "Ernest" was I certain whom she meant, and I listened avidly as she described Hemingway's "abominable behavior" while a weekend guest in the same house where we were gathered. In the dead of night, when he assumed everyone had gone to bed, she had caught him red-handed perusing the personal letters she kept in her desk, "looking for material he could use in his stories."

They all gossiped as freely about themselves as they did of others, not even sparing their hostess. It amused them to point out that Peggy Cowley's current lover, a young rustic of the area, bore a striking resemblance both to Hart Crane and to her estranged husband, Malcolm Cowley; they accused her of living in the past. One of the guests told of the night when she had wandered outdoors and been bitten by a presumably poisonous snake. A sober neighbor had rushed her by automobile at breakneck speed over treacherous country roads to the nearest hospital several miles away only to discover that Peggy was never in any serious danger: the great amount of alcohol in her system immunized her from any snake poison.

Their talent for entertaining one another made most of my left-wing acquaintances in New York seem prematurely old and grim by comparison. Gertrude Stein may have considered them "lost," but to me they were far more self-assured than my contemporaries, despite their heavy drinking and their propensity for adultery. From the sound of their laughter and the astuteness of their wit I could sense how much they had benefited from growing up in an era when the United States was the most ambitious and optimistic nation on earth, in a time when there was almost no warfare. They were also fortunate to have had parents whose roots were deeply imbedded in American soil and who spoke the native language. They had no identity problems, none of the conflicts that gnawed at the psyche of every son and daughter of immigrant parents to whom English was a foreign tongue. No matter how much they might rail or rebel against the nation's mores and political system, no one could dispute their status as Americans.

Although their cordiality toward me was evident enough, I felt like an outsider, a foreigner invading their privacy. Except for Bill Rollins, a proven friend, I could not help suspect them of condescension. At the same time I sensed I was probably as much a victim of stereotype thinking as they were; that I must, in order to avoid the anxieties of paranoia, learn to accept individuals on their own merit, without regard as to who their ancestors were, as I had done with such nonethnic friends as Kenneth Langford, Leonard Brown, and Bill Rollins.

It had taken me a longer time to arrive at that point of wisdom with Ed Havill, the high school companion whom I once considered too arrogantly Anglo-Saxon to become a friend. But now at last our friendship was on a firm footing. It had taken several years, but now all the remnants of the affectations we once sported as members of the Conceit Club were gone; there was no more need for posing. And we had both outgrown our awe of Richard Haney, who had exerted a stronger influence on us than we realized. By now I had also come to understand that what I took for arrogance was nothing more than a facade for shyness.

Our lives had taken drastically different directions, but we still had in common our obsession to become writers. Forgoing a college education in his impatience to start writing fiction, Ed had built, with his own hands, a cabin on a piece of land overlooking Lake Keuka, a high school graduation present from his parents. There he was living a more Thoreau existence than Thoreau himself had led, residing in the cabin all year around, even during the murderous winters of upstate New York, and supporting himself without being harnessed to a job. In the warm months he did handyman chores for families in and around Penn Yan, the nearest village; in the fall he picked grapes in the Keuka vineyards. Between jobs and in the winter months, he pounded out his first publishable fiction.

For a long time he went it alone, but one day he wrote he had taken a wife, a cellist recently graduated from the Eastman School of Music, and invited Freya and me to spend my one-week vacation with them. Freya, to my surprise, agreed to make the trip, even though we had no travel money and would have to hitchhike both ways, some six hundred miles altogether. Except for the disagreeable experience of being picked up by a salesman who made an overt pass at Freya, it was an easy journey to Keuka; we arrived in a day and a half.

In the years since my departure from Rochester, Ed and I had exchanged letters now and then, and occasionally we saw each other on my visits home (he and my father enjoyed a great rapport, especially on the subject of homemade wine). But not until I observed him on his Keuka homestead did I grasp how much he had changed since our *Clarion* days. While I had been moving outwardly, groping for an understanding of my relationship with people of various backgrounds, Ed, though as fully city-bred as I, had been moving inwardly toward nature, until now there was something almost holy about him. It was as if the anchorite years he had spent coping with the rigors of nature had endowed him with a religion he could embrace. They had also provided him with manual skills, which I would have thought were beyond his capacity. Now he was a farmer par excellence, the master of a garden that supplied him and his wife with far more than they could consume; he had also developed into an expert handyman. Without assistance, he had expanded a one-room cabin into a solid and commodious home. All in all, he had become self-sufficient, an escapee from the nine-to-five straitjacket, unfettered by luxuries, and devoutly appreciative of the simple pleasures, such as the colors of dawn and the taste of spring water.

Aside from our literary ambitions, we had little in common. Politically we had no connection. As long as government did not interfere unduly with his own life, it was of no concern to him. The extent to which I worried that fascism might come to America and that Germany and Italy might engage the world in another world war seemed to puzzle him. The more we talked the more apparent it became that predominant in his thinking were the verities of nature and his resolve to come to terms with them as a man and a writer. For the first time I understood that friendship can be based on nothing more than mutual respect and affection.

And memories. We laughed at ourselves for having proclaimed, along with other members of the Conceit Club, that the world would recognize us as literary geniuses by the time we were twenty-one. Actually, Ed and I were the only ones of the group who were writing and publishing. Mitch Rappaport, who had become a high school English teacher and was preparing for a doctoral degree in psychology, had recently died from an attack of pneumonia that killed him within forty-eight hours. His heartbroken young wife, blaming herself for the tragedy, took her own life a few days after his burial. Also dead was Eugene Rimington who had died of a congenital brain disease. Jerry Joroslow had given up his ambition to be a composer as soon as he discovered he was tone deaf. He was now a law-enforcement agent for the Treasury Department and, rumor had it, one of its best marksmen. Surprisingly, Richard Haney had married the girl he seduced in the astronomical laboratory when he learned she was pregnant. He was now a freshman English teacher in a small Pennsylvania college. For intellectual exercise, he composed miniature chess problems, some of which got into print.

Freya agreed with me that Ed had fared better than any of us. He was at ease with his environment and free of all grubby obligations. Freya particularly admired his ability to put the clutter and noise of city life permanently behind him. For her, as for Ed, nature was an easy source of strength, a sanctuary from the trials of the secular world. A few days of the Keuka countryside intensified her dislike of Manhattan. Here, with the sun, woods, and clear air acting like a powerful tonic on her, she was in her element. I had never seen her so cheerful.

Encouraged by Ed (his wife remained noncommittal), we

toyed with the notion of leaving the city and living near the
Havills, embracing the good and simple life under Ed's tutelage. We went so far as to investigate a small house for sale
situated on a hilltop that commanded a superb view of the lake
and the surrounding hills. Yet even as we reveled in our
Utopian prospect, I knew how hopeless it was. I had neither
any of Ed's manual skills nor a back strong enough to work a
garden. Nor the true desire to live in isolation; the city, with all
of its ugliness, was my fount of nourishment, my main hope for
survival.°

Nonetheless, the visit to the Havills became a turning point
in our lives. In the clarity of the Keuka sunlight came the
awareness that we could not go on infecting each other with
gloom, as we had been doing for two years. Since (without
saying so) Freya needed the security of marriage, we must
either marry or try to lead separate lives. I could not persuade
myself that a wedding certificate would do anything more than
institutionalize our gloom. But if I did not love her enough to
marry her, I loved her too much to abandon her.

On the hunch that the trinity of sea, sun, and sky might
overcome Freya's *Weltschmerz,* as Keuka had, as soon as we
returned to the city we moved into a spacious furnished room
close to the beach at Far Rockaway. For me it meant two hours
of train travel six days a week, but it proved to be worth the
trouble. The rooming house was filled with bright young men
and women, mostly Jewish New Yorkers who were either
vacationing or, like myself, commuting to city jobs. The com-

---

° Doris Havill left her husband two years later because she could no longer
endure their isolated life, and moved to New York City. Some years later Ed
married a girl who had been reared on a Montana sheep ranch. It was a
happy marriage, and they had three sons. As soon as the oldest one reached
college age, Ed became a full-time staff member of the *Penn Yan Chronicle
Express,* so that he could finance his sons' education. He was one of the
newspaper's executive editors when he died in 1964, at the age of fifty-six.
During his lifetime he published four novels, which were lyrical statements of
his close bonds to nature, as well as a number of short stories.

munal kitchen forced Freya to leave our room while I was at work; for the first time since we had been together, without any urging from me, she began to meet people on her own and make friends. Within a few weeks she developed a genuine rapport with a young schoolteacher named Susan Klingman.

Susan, a warm and perceptive soul, was quickly able to penetrate Freya's defenses and discover the poetry in the darkness within her. She also grasped the dilemma of Freya's relationship with me and divined that it could only be resolved by Freya's willingness to develop enough self-esteem to participate in the world. During the long summer days they spent together Susan must have encouraged Freya to look beyond the boundaries of our relationship and appraise herself as an individual, for by the end of the summer she had accomplished what I had failed to do in all the time we had been together.

Not until we returned to New York in September did I appreciate the extent of Freya's metamorphosis. At her suggestion, we abandoned the Village and took a small apartment in the Murray Hill section of the city, not far from the apartment house where Susan lived with a bachelor brother. A few days after we had moved in, my father became seriously ill and I went to Rochester for four days until he was out of danger. In the past my trips to my family had always had a saddening effect on Freya, but on my return I found her in fine spirits, bubbling over with the news that a friend of Susan's, the manager of a large midtown bookstore, had hired her as a clerk. On questioning her, I learned that she had met Susan's friend at a party she attended with Susan and her brother. I also learned that on the day following the party the four of them had gone to the theater together.

My immediate Sicilian reaction to all this was unadulterated jealousy. It must have surfaced, for while I was interrogating Freya for further details, she cut me short and throwing her arms around me, thoroughly delighted, exclaimed: "How wonderful, *liebling!* You think I have done something with some other man?" I would not admit it. "But supposing you did," I said, trying not to sound miserable, "what right would I have to object? After all, we're not married. . . ."

"You think we should be?"

I said I wasn't sure.

She became quiet and I was afraid she might cry. "I don't think we should be," she finally said. "We are too much the same. My *Weltschermz* brings out yours. We should be married but to different kinds of people. Yes?"

"Is this what Susan Klingman has been telling you?" I asked, suddenly becoming suspicious.

"No, *liebling*, it is what I have been telling myself."

We talked until we were too tired to say anything more, then fell asleep in each other's arms. When we talked again, all of the next evening, we agreed it would be best for both of us if we separated. Ten days later we had our last hours together. By that time Freya had tried her bookstore job and liked it; she had also arranged to room with a college classmate of Susan's who had a large apartment in the same building where Susan and her brother lived.

We had our final meal together in a Lebanese restaurant on Lexington Avenue and splurged with a bottle of rosé. After-ward we walked to Central Park and sat on a park bench holding hands like recently met lovers. We were both feeling miserable and sorry for ourselves and for each other, and I thought I must be a damn fool to give up a beautiful girl to whom I was so closely attached. I asked her to promise she would come back to me if the new arrangement did not work out to her satisfaction, and she asked me to promise that I would give my bad back plenty of rest, eat regularly in restaurants that served decent food, change my socks every day, and never give up trying to be a writer.

On the way home, riding on top of a double-decker Fifth Avenue bus, we clung to each other without speaking. When we entered the apartment and saw her luggage in the middle of the floor, Freya burst into tears, and I cried to see her crying. We stopped the tears with love-making. The next evening I accompanied her to her new quarters. Her new roommate was waiting for her, very cheerful and hospitable. I felt like an intruder. As I kissed Freya, I remembered the envelope in my pocket containing some money I had recently received for an article. I thrust it into her hands and quickly left.

For the next couple of months I phoned her two or three times a week to make sure she was all right. After a while our conversations began to take on the stilted quality of old acquaintances who have somehow lost track of what the other is like. She was not always home when I called, and I would speak with her cheerful roommate instead. From all indications, Freya was having a far easier time than I. My main trouble was coming home to an empty apartment every evening. I kept thinking she might return, and at night when I tried to fall asleep I would hear her soft pronunciation of *liebling* and long to be with her. When I realized she would never return, I gave up the apartment and moved back to the Village where I could be closer to cheap restaurants and the noisy distractions of the left-wing world.

SEVEN

Out of the Woods . . .

In the belief that boredom can be the most destructive of all human afflictions, my only 1934 New Year resolution was to find a job that would not be a daily insult to my intelligence. Three months later, by dint of bluff and luck, I became an editor in a book-publishing house. In the same auspicious month of March, on my twenty-fifth birthday, I began sharing an apartment with a young and jolly blonde of Polish ancestry and left-wing leanings, who was employed by the Dupont Corporation as a filing clerk. I had met her at a benefit dance for the Scottsboro boys. But before any of this happened, Benny Birlowitz, with whom I had been corresponding sporadically, came to New York and once again, by simply being himself, injected a period of misery into my life.

Our previous encounter had been on the Syracuse campus four years before when Benny had informed me, with the nonchalance of a noncomformist, that he would not be graduating with the rest of his class since he had refused to take a course in chemistry required for his degree. "Who the hell needs it?" he asked. "The revolution will be here in no time." One summer he teamed up with two Syracuse friends, a would-be artist and a would-be concert pianist, and the trio left for Los Angeles. "We figure," wrote Benny on a penny postal bearing a photograph of Charlie Chaplin, "that the only way to beat the Depression is to live in a city filled with so many quacks that anything can happen." But all that happened was that within two months they ran out of money, and despite Benny's valiant efforts to ingratiate himself with their ancient landlady by having sex with her, they were ejected for not paying their rent.

Benny tried panhandling for a while (his two friends would watch him begging from a distance, pretending not to know him), but his wild and tattered appearance, which suggested that of an escaped lunatic, frightened off most of the people he approached. Finally came the day when, desperate for food and shelter, they were obliged to wire their families for bus fares home. Benny's siblings, who took his word that he was writing the great American novel, promised to support him indefinitely, provided he wrote at home so that their widowed mother would not be alone during the day. Before long Benny tired of her company and chicken soup and, on the pretext of seeing a publisher about his manuscript, took off for New York.

He came directly to my minuscule one-room establishment without advance warning, full of exuberance and epic intentions, asking that I put him up for a few days while he put the finishing touches on a section of his novel. He was confident that the first publisher who read it would offer him a contract and a fat advance, which he vowed to share with me so that I could quit my job and become a full-time writer. Touched by his generous spirit, I told him he could stay for a while if he supplied his own cot. Benny promptly borrowed some money from me (I never saw it again) and went out to buy the cot.

I regretted letting him stay as soon as he began congratulating me for "getting rid" of Freya. Women, he said, were a hindrance to all writers, except for purposes of fucking. When I insisted that my separation from Freya was by mutual consent,

he replied that I must learn to overcome my romantic bourgeois tendencies if I expected to be in the vanguard of the
coming revolution. "What revolution?" I asked. "There isn't
going to be a revolution." This shocked him and convinced him
that Freya must have been "a corrupting influence" on me.
When I accused him of thinking in left-wing clichés, he simply
giggled and began a long monologue about his lecherous
adventures in California.

There was no doubt about his talent as a storyteller. In a few
days it became apparent that he liked telling stories better than
he liked writing them. His manuscript remained packed in his
suitcase. On my return from work each day, he would start
talking and continue into the night until I would be obliged to
remind him that I had a job to go to in the morning; he was
always asleep when I left. From his monologues I gathered that
he spent a great deal of time roaming the streets, trying to pick
up women.

Whenever I asked about his manuscript, he would give the
same reply: he was undergoing a period of "gestation" that was
bound to pay off any day. After two weeks had passed and he
was still gestating, I suggested that since he was not writing in
New York, it might be wise to return to Syracuse. He reacted
as if I had punched him, his whole face wincing in pain at the
indignity of my suggestion. "Are you serious?" he asked. On
being assured that I was, he promised to start work on his
manuscript the next morning. But he never got any further than
unpacking the manuscript, for that was the day he discovered
Union Square and the pleasures of feeding pigeons while
listening to soapbox orators.

Benny pronounced Union Square the most fascinating forum
in America, the only place where you could learn what
Americans were really thinking, "a far more reliable source of
information than those crappy capitalistic rags you read." (It
irked him that I perused the *New York Times* every day).
Although the Square was nearby I seldom visited it but a few

days later, spurred by Benny's enthusiasm, I did on my lunch hour. There, to my astonishment, was Benny surrounded by an attentive crowd of some thirty men. Since nearly everyone in his audience was taller than he, I could not see him, but his shrill Savonarola voice expounding on the sins of capitalism was unmistakable even from a distance.

Although his rhetoric was laced with esoteric words which only a pundit could understand, its eloquence had the audience spellbound. There was a long silence when he finished; only as he was walking away did some of the men come out of their trance and shout compliments in his direction. Benny, headed for the public toilet, did not bother acknowledging them.

That evening when I told him I had heard most of his speech and was impressed by his oratory, he blushed like a schoolboy caught masturbating. Without saying that he was probably a better orator than a writer, I suggested he should consider working for some labor union or left-wing party as a professional proselytizer. He said he would think about it, then abruptly changed the subject by telling me about a married woman with big breasts he had picked up in the Forty-second Street public library that afternoon.

By now Benny had been in my place for more than a month. His prolonged stay was interfering with my writing, my sleep, and my love life. My repeated insinuation that he was wasting his time and mine by remaining in New York was ignored. With his brothers sending him enough money for his meals and laundry, he was content following his daily pattern of rising late in the morning, orating in Union Square at midday when it was crowded, and trying to pick up women the rest of the time. There was no more talk of his novel.

Finding it increasingly difficult to be civil to Benny, I contrived to spend most evenings away from my room (without ever mentioning my Polish blonde), all the while chiding myself for lacking the courage to kick him out. My exasperation at Benny's indifference to the situation was reaching the boiling point when a solution from an unexpected source suddenly presented itself. In the middle of the night I woke with the sensation I was being attacked by an army of crawling creatures. Putting on the light, I saw masses of bedbugs all over me and Benny, and everywhere else in the room.

In the face of such a full-fledged invasion, I decided that the bedbugs were entitled to the place. The next morning I found temporary living quarters in a cheap hotel not far from the bookstore, and that evening I broke the news to Benny that I was moving out at once. When he rebuked me for my unfriendly attitude toward bedbugs, whom he characterized as "the proletariat of the insect world," I replied he was welcome to live with them until the end of the month since the rent was paid until then. He appeared to be quite grateful for this and helped me carry my bags to a taxi. His final words were: "See you on the barricades, pal."

Through a mutual friend I later learned that shortly after his return to Syracuse Benny became a paid functionary of the local Communist party organization. The next year, using his party pseudonym, he ran for the office of mayor on the Communist ticket.

Once I was free of Benny my luck began to change. On learning that the head of a book publishing firm, Robert M. McBride, was looking for a male secretary who knew something about contemporary literature, I applied for the job, despite my ignorance of shorthand and my inability to change a typewriter ribbon. Thanks to an interview with McBride's buxom office manager, a blond Italophile with a Calabrian lover, I was hired for a two-week probationary period. Since I was uncertain how far the office manager's love of Italians would stretch, I lied about my ability to take shorthand, then frantically tried to memorize the contents of a speedwriting textbook in the two weeks that remained before I assumed my new post.

The little I learned proved to be more of a hindrance than a help. Until McBride called my bluff, the first few days of pretending I could take his dictation were a nightmare. The letters I typed bore little or no resemblance to those he dictated. When I presented them for his signature, I would put on my best poker face. He did the same and would readily sign the letters as though they were faithful transcriptions. We played this game for almost a week, then he suddenly tired of it. One morning as I poised my pencil over a stenographic pad, I felt his icy blue eyes piercing mine. "Now whom do you think you're kidding, Mr. Mangione?" he asked. "You're certainly no stenographer. I've known that from the first letter I dictated to you."

A tall, lean Scotsman with thin lips and a bald head, he bore a discomforting resemblance to an elementary school principal who had once whipped me. While there was no likelihood I would get the strap this time, I worried that McBride might give me the ax. As I started to mutter an apology for my bluffing, he cut me short. "Luckily," he said with the suggestion of a smile, "you write pretty good letters. But let's stop pretending they are my letters. From now on, I'll just give you the gist of what I want said and you go on writing the letters in your own words."

In the ensuing three years that he was my employer I was to hear a number of disparaging stories about McBride, and contribute some of my own, but with this incident etched in my memory, I could not share in the wholesale dislike of him prevalent in the office. A little later I had still another reason to be beholden to him. McBride, a confirmed bachelor in his fifties, tried to kiss one of his editors, a confirmed spinster in her thirties, and when she slapped his face and quit, he promoted me to her job.

My wage, thirty dollars a week, was hardly commensurate with my highfalutin new title—book editor and publicity director—but I gloried in finally having a post which transcended the grubby goal of economic survival. As an ex-English major and aspiring writer, I could not imagine earning my livelihood in a more stimulating atmosphere than a book-publishing house. It was to take me awhile to perceive that an editorial job in a publishing firm is more likely to ruin an incipient writing career than launch it. But in that promising spring, after all the absurd jobs that had battered my ego, my situation delighted me. It made me feel that at last I was emerging out of the dark woods through which I had been traveling since my arrival in Manhattan.

My elation was soon put to the test by the squelching reality of having to deal, almost exclusively, with writers whose chances of publication were either dim or nonexistent. As the youngest member of the staff, it fell on me to read all unsolicited manuscripts and to talk to all writers who came to deliver their manuscripts under the misapprehension that a conversation about their work with an editor might make it more publishable. The latter included a fanatical middle-aged woman who held my hand while she assured me that her manuscript was bound to have a tremendous sale because it had been written, word for word, by God Himself. She disclaimed being its author, describing herself as an intermediary who, heeding His call, had sat at a typewriter while His words passed through her fingertips on to the machine. She pressed my hand and stared into my eyes, as if trying to hypnotize me, and added: "I am confident that you will find this manuscript the greatest masterpiece since the Bible. Every American who believes in God will read it." Hoping for a miracle, I sat down to read it, but the manuscript was gibberish from start to finish.

Most of my visitors were harmless, but a scowling, red-bearded giant who arrived with a sheaf of poems gave me a few bad moments. In a manner that reeked of violence he thrust the manuscript at me and demanded, then and there, an opinion of his poetry. His huge figure hovered over me menacingly while I glanced at some of the poems. They were of miserable quality, but how to tell him without being punched? "Well, what do you think of them?" he snarled, obviously suspecting I was stalling for time. As I handed back his manuscript, I measured the distance between me and a door that might serve as an escape hatch; then, in as firm a voice as could be mustered, I informed him that the poems were not publishable.

The next few seconds were pure astonishment. "Well, that's okay," the giant proclaimed with the broadest of smiles. "How about some nice cuff links instead?" And with that he whipped out a box from an overcoat pocket and opened it with a flourish. The links were too garish for my taste, but in the vastness of my relief they seemed to be exactly what I wanted.

The consistently dreadful quality of the unsolicited manuscripts I examined was a puzzlement; it was difficult to understand how so many of their authors could delude themselves for several hundred pages that what they wrote could possibly interest anyone but a few devoted friends. At first I conscientiously read every manuscript from start to finish, but when I could no longer keep up with the flood of submissions, I followed the example of the senior editor who, insisting that he didn't have to eat all of an egg to know it was bad, refused to read beyond the first few chapters of a manuscript unless it held his attention. Of the hundreds of unsolicited manuscripts that crossed my desk during my McBride years only three seemed good enough to publish—a mystery, a Western, and a newspaperman's Thoreau-ish account of his meanderings along the tributary rivers of the Midwest, *Sycamore Shores* by Clark Barnaby Firestone (1936), which the *New York Times Book Review* featured on its front page.

Although the manuscripts submitted through literary agents were generally superior to those sent in directly by writers, chances were that by the time they reached us they had already been rejected by a number of other publishers. For the house of McBride no longer enjoyed the prestige it once had had in the twenties when James Branch Cabell had been its most famous and most lucrative author. In those years McBride spent most of his time on Wall Street playing the stock market, content to leave the operations of his flourishing publishing firm in the hands of a topnotch editorial staff. The stock-market crash changed all that. McBride, retreating from Wall Street, fired his most expensive editors and assumed command of the firm's editorial policies. By the time I joined the firm it had ceased to be a first-rate publishing house.

Now and then a distinguished book landed on the McBride list, but it was usually in spite of its president's literary obtuseness. I recall the author with stricken eyes who had just emerged from an editorial conference with McBride. He was holding both sides of his head, as though trying to contain his sanity, and groaning, "Jesus, God, was he really talking about my book?" McBride's lack of literary perception was matched by his ignorance of the world outside the Park Avenue set with whom he socialized. After the firm had accepted Edward Newhouse's novel of the Depression, *You Can't Sleep Here,* and it was already in galley-proof form, McBride changed his mind about publishing it because the novel's main character, who slept on a park bench for lack of money, struck him as "unbelievable"; he held that "no American who is not afraid of hard work need go without food or a bed."

One of the few fine novels that McBride permitted to be published was Bill Rollins' *The Shadow Before,* which, by coincidence, was issued on the same day I joined the editorial staff. Edmund Wilson had recommended the manuscript to his friend Coburn Gilman, the editor of McBride's only money-making enterprise, *Travel* magazine. Gilman, sharing Wilson's enthusiasm for the novel, had persuaded McBride to publish it. Had McBride read it he probably would have rejected it since the novel, based on a famous strike of textile workers in Gastonia, Georgia, was infused with a strongly prolabor theme. True to Gilman's prediction, *The Shadow Before* received rave notices and was hailed by several critics as one of the best proletarian novels ever written by an American. Comparing Rollins to John Dos Passos in an enthusiastic *New York Times* review, Louis Kronenberger noted similarities of technique but added: "From the standpoint of drama and readability, I think Rollins has beaten Dos Passos out. From the standpoint of lucidity and pace, I know he has."

Like most proletarian novels of the thirties, *The Shadow Before* sold less than two thousand copies and netted Bill only five hundred dollars, the advance paid to him on royalties. There were, however, some unexpected fringe benefits. In the Soviet Union the Russian translation of the novel created such a sensation that the authorities sent Bill enough Moscow gold to pay for his travel to and from their country, along with the invitation to remain there as long as he wished.° The most immediate fringe benefit was a job in Hollywood for a few weeks at two hundred dollars per week, the lowest salary, according to Bill, ever paid to a Hollywood writer.

Until the scriptwriting job materialized, Bill accepted a slew of invitations from lionizing hostesses, in order to avail himself of free drinks and sandwiches (he was living on borrowed money then). The parties offended him; invariably he would come away from them with the impression of having been a supernumerary. "They talk about my book as if I weren't present, as if the novel had been written by some extraordinary writer that I hadn't yet met," he complained. He reported that at one party, where he had drunk too much, he had become so affected by this attitude that he found himself talking about himself in the third person.

Bill's disgust with McBride for his unwillingness to advertise *The Shadow Before* led him to break his contract with the firm and sign up with Knopf for his next novel. The cavalier attitude of both authors and publishers toward contractual commitments

---

° Accepting the invitation, Bill Rollins spent more than a year in the Soviet Union, living on the fat of his Russian royalties. He could have remained indefinitely, except that he became bored with his easy life and nostalgic for cheap American cigars, his favorite smoke, and the *New York Times,* to which he was addicted. Before returning, he used some of his Soviet royalties to import an American friend to whom he owed some money, and put him up in style for several months.

came as a surprise and, on one occasion, thrust me in the middle of a painful charade of frustration. It began with my discovery that Ignazio Silone, the author of *Fontamara,* was without an American publisher, no longer committed to Random House, which had recently forfeited all claim to his future work by rejecting a collection of his short stories. Despite McBride's excessively cautious nature, I managed to convince him that it would be a good investment to publish the short stories, even at a loss, since it would give us first crack at Silone's novel, which might well be a winner.

Inasmuch as short-story collections rarely sell well, it came as no surprise that Silone's collection, *Mr. Aristotle,* although reviewed and praised extensively, sold less than five hundred copies. A little later, I received from Silone, who was living in Zurich as an anti-Fascist exile, the first half of his new novel *Bread and Wine.* I read it with a sense of mounting excitement, finding it more substantial than *Fontamara,* yet infused with the same dramatic atmosphere and ironic understatement that had made the first novel so successful. The manuscript was then submitted to two experts in modern Italian literature whose enthusiasm for the chapters even exceeded mine.

Armed with their reports, I had expected McBride to take my advice and sign a contract with Silone at once. Though impressed by the reports, McBride told me there was no hurry about the contract since we were legally entitled to see all of the manuscript before arriving at a final decision. In an effort to change his mind, I translated for him part of a letter from Silone in which he said he wanted a contract now because he was badly in need of money. McBride's reply to this was that Silone's financial situation was his own problem, not ours. Heartsick, I returned the manuscript to Silone's agent in New York, with a note that tried to assure him that Silone would get his contract as soon as he delivered the rest of the chapters.

Within a few days my worst premonition was realized. Whit Burnett at Harper's had read the early chapters and promptly signed a contract to publish the completed novel. McBride became enraged when I broke the news to him, and threatened to sue the agent, Silone, and Harper's, but in the end he did nothing about it. The galling denouement to the whole affair came in the form of a Book-of-the-Month circular which announced that the club's forthcoming selection was *Bread and Wine*. In the margin of the circular was penciled this note to me from McBride: "Don't we have the darndest luck?"

McBride's lack of literary taste was not always a liability. On a trip to England he purchased outright from Warwick Deeping, for a small sum of money, a boxful of old novels Deeping had published before producing his big best seller, *Sorrel and Son*. A discriminating editor would have summarily rejected the lot for their cloying sentimentality and antediluvian plots, but McBride sensed that they could be republished at a profit. Once a year it became my chore to select the least obnoxious novel of the group and make it more presentable by giving it a new title and updating the text. When, for example, the heroine would note with alarm that the hero was driving his car at thirty miles an hour, I would double the speed. My final embellishment would be to write a jacket blurb which invariably compared the novel favorably with *Sorrel and Son*.

For reasons which no one (including McBride) claimed to understand, these antiquated Deepings, which were published each year on Washington's Birthday, never failed to sell at least ten thousand copies, a large sale for those days. Their popularity infuriated the publisher of Deeping's new novels, which seldom sold more than half that number, and embarrassed the author who, unsuccessfully, begged McBride to allow him to buy back the rest of his old novels, apparently with the hope of setting a match to them.

The enterprise was not without its humorous aspects. In an era when bookstores strictly observed publishers' publication dates, a letter arrived from a woman in California who had somehow managed to read our latest Deeping offering two weeks before its official release and who, in praising the novel, passionately and repeatedly declared that it had produced "a change of life" in her. When I shared the letter with my colleague Coburn Gilman at a luncheon which included too many martinis, we were inspired to reply with the following telegram: MANY THANKS FOR YOUR APPRECIATION OF NEW DEEP- ING BUT PLEASE POSTPONE CHANGE OF LIFE TO PUBLICATION DATE, FEBRUARY 22ND.

Perhaps because Gilman, for all of his erudition and editorial skills, was not above acts of juvenilia like this one, I regarded him as the happiest of my McBride fringe benefits. With his square, portly figure, his high-laced shoes, and sturdy cane, Gilman looked more like an English country squire than a man of letters. His heavy drinking, on which he relied to overcome his shyness, had no discernible effect on his prodigious capacity for work. With a tiny budget and no other assistance than a secretary who was hopelessly in love with him, he produced, monthly, McBride's only successful enterprise, *Travel.* More closely in touch with the literary scene than anyone else on the staff, he also served as the book department's chief talent scout.

Yet he and McBride could barely tolerate each other. Usu- ally, Gilman managed to keep his low opinion of the publisher to himself, but one afternoon while McBride was in Europe, Gilman, filled with gin and havoc, began passing his hat among the employees, intoning that every penny collected would be used to send McBride through high school. He sounded like W. C. Fields playing the role of a snake-oil artist. "Bear in mind, my friends, that a McBride who can read is the kind of McBride we need. So open up your hearts and purse strings and give generously to this wonderful cause." After collecting sev- eral dollars, he adjourned to his office and with the same W. C. Fields inflection began telephoning some of the firm's creditors to inform them that the house of McBride was enjoying such great prosperity that there was absolutely no need for them to pay their bills. Only his secretary's SOS call to Gilman's mistress (the two women were on the friendliest terms), which brought her lickety-split to the office, prevented any further shenanigans.

McBride, appreciating Gilman's value to the firm, prudently refrained from voicing any criticism of him. But one afternoon while I was conferring with him, he observed Gilman reeling into his office after a three-hour luncheon, and, turning to me, sputtered: "The gall of that man. He drinks and he carries a stick—and on his salary!"

For all of their differences of taste and temperament, McBride relied heavily on Gilman's judgment. On his recommendation, McBride acquired the part-time services of Jacques LeClercq, the brilliant translator of Rabelais and professor of French literature at Queens College, not suspecting then that LeClercq was an old drinking crony of Gilman's and, also, carried a cane. Dapper and witty, sporting a trim moustache which made him resemble Ronald Colman, LeClercq, drunk or sober, exuded the suavity of a boulevardier. He impressed me as the most sophisticated human being I had ever known, the perfect boon companion for Gilman.

Appropriately enough, the first product of their McBride teamwork was an early Rabelaisian novel of Jules Romains titled *Les Copains* (The Pals), which Gilman procured and LeClercq translated into English as *The Boys in the Back Room.* Romains was then at the top of his career as the author of one of the most ambitious novel cycles in literary history, *Men of Good Will,* which eventually was to encompass twenty-seven volumes. When Gilman informed us that Romains would be in New York shortly to write some articles for a Paris newspaper, LeClercq saw it as an opportunity to persuade the Frenchman to let us publish more of his work and proposed a luncheon in his honor to be attended by Gilman, himself, and me. Ever the penny pincher, McBride tried to discourage it by allotting only ten dollars toward its expense. Undaunted, LeClercq arranged to have the luncheon at a Fifth Avenue Italian restaurant where Gilman's credit was good.

From the point of view of cultivating Romains' good will, the luncheon proved to be a disaster, mainly because the French writer made the mistake of bringing his beautiful secretary with him. As soon as the three of us set eyes on the ravishing black-eyed brunette, we lost all sight of the luncheon's purpose. Simultaneously, we all tried to woo her, while ignoring Romains. The novelist tried valiantly to interject himself into the conversation, but got nowhere. The secretary's vivacious response to our advances, combined with the euphoric effect of the martinis, spurred us to vie with one another for her attention. Finally, Romains, unable to take any more of it, abruptly rose from the table and in a resolute voice announced: "We must go to the Brooklyn Bridge—at once!" With that, he seized his startled queen bee by the hand and, flinging a barely audible *au revoir* to us over his shoulder, fled with her to the nearest taxi.

By now the bill had long ago exceeded McBride's ten-dollar allotment and we had yet to order lunch. Gilman called for another round of martinis, this time to toast "the charms of the most adorable damsel out of Paris, our dearly departed." I left soon afterward, aware that one more martini would make me sick. Gilman and LeClercq, I learned later, kept on imbibing all afternoon and evening until the restaurant closed. Both men were absent from the office the next day.

"How did the luncheon with Romains go?" McBride asked me.

"Very well," I replied. "Romains might do an article about the Brooklyn Bridge for *Travel.*"

"And where is Mr. Gilman today?"

"Probably discussing the article with Romains . . ."

"And Mr. LeClercq?" persisted McBride suspiciously.

"Mr. LeClercq is probably acting as Mr. Gilman's interpreter," I said. "His French is perfect, you know."

McBride grunted noncommittally and I escaped, afraid I could improvise no more.

The elder statesman of the McBride staff was Richard Glaenzer, who, although amused by the office high jinks, did not

156

participate in them. He was the quintessence of Victorian elegance with his high celluloid collar, pince-nez glasses, and Old World manners. Glaenzer's refined sensibility naturally cast him in the role of editor for James Branch Cabell, once McBride's most acclaimed author. The stock-market crash had relegated Cabell's ironic concoctions to the junk heap of literary history; after that he was damned by the critics as a writer of escapist novels. Cabell, who was in the habit of producing a book every year, acknowledged his loss of favor by cutting down, not his output but his name, which became simply Branch Cabell.

This Depression-minded economy restored neither his prestige nor his sales, but the McBride office continued to treat him with all the respect he commanded in the twenties. Actually, his connection with McBride began in 1915 when his first novel, *The Rivet in Grandfather's Neck*, after being rejected by a dozen publishers, struck the fancy of a young McBride editor, Guy Holt, then only twenty-three years old, thirteen years younger than Cabell. The age difference fazed neither of them. Cabell found him "an affably sadistic editor," and until 1927, when Holt departed from McBride, regarded him as his "collaborator." As he wrote in a book of memoirs, "I felt forlornly as to every book completed after 1927 that it could have been improved if only his [Holt's] tonic carpings could have helped, as he phrased matters, 'to spank it into existence.'"

Glaenzer, who succeeded Holt as Cabell's editor, was no spanker. The minor editorial suggestions he addressed to Cabell were couched in a diplomatic style which became the norm for all office communications with the novelist. My own dealings with him consisted of turning out an occasional blurb for a new work and acting as his agent in matters of publicity and subsidiary rights. It irked me to be deferential to an author whose work reflected not the slightest interest in such major concerns as poverty, race prejudice, and the growth of fascism; who, despite the ravages of the Depression, remained committed to the mores and narrow perspective of his aristocratic ivory tower in Richmond, Virginia, which he called home. Yet though I felt hypocritical, my letters to Cabell managed to maintain a cordial enough tone to elicit responses in kind.

I soon found that Cabell was not above the use of flattery to gain his ends. When, in his behalf, I discovered the top fee he could get from a reprint publisher interested in his first novel, he was pleased to find that "to your other virtues you add the accomplishment of being a first-rate and quick-fire sleuth," then suggested that in writing the reprint publisher "you have but to pass naturally from your role of Sherlock to that of Shylock." To my request for an autobiographical sketch which *Arts and Decoration* (another McBride magazine) was willing to publish with a photograph of him by Carl Van Vechten, Cabell replied that "since nothing brilliant and superb" had occurred to him, he "had best leave the entire production to you and Van Vechten, and sit by simply to applaud."

Until I left McBride's, my relationship with Cabell remained an epistolary one, despite occasional trips he made to New York. When given the opportunity to make his acquaintance, I bypassed it. By that time I had discovered that authors were usually less appealing in the flesh than they were in their writings. I also observed that authors who tend to sound disparaging about their work are often better writers than those who brag about it. The exception to all this was William Saroyan, a congenital but appealing braggart, who achieved instant fame with his first book of stories, *The Daring Young Man on the Flying Trapeze.*

The stories were the first in the Depression to break the hard gloom of proletarian literature. In some respects they were as fanciful and escapist as Cabell's concoctions, but their characters and situations bore enough resemblance to reality to give them an aura of truth. All of Saroyan's characters had a sad time or a happy time; there were no strikes or unions, and no one was clubbed by a policeman. John Steinbeck was to turn on

the same kind of California sunshine the next year with the
happy-go-lucky characters of *Tortilla Flat*, but 1934 belonged
to Saroyan. He was supremely aware of the fact, as was almost
everyone else who came within speaking distance of him.

In a week when the Manhattan literary firmament was filled
with bursting rockets sent up by the critics to proclaim their
new star, Saroyan ambled into the McBride office and informed
Bridget Cassidy, our tough-minded, redheaded receptionist, that
he wished to see me. The partition between the reception room
and my cubicle was so flimsy I could hear every word of their
dialogue. It went something like this:

"Would you ask Jerre Mangione if I could see him?"

"Who shall I say is calling, sir?"

"William Saroyan."

"What firm do you represent, Mr. Saroyan?"

"I guess you didn't hear me. I'm William Saroyan."

"I heard you the first time, Mr. Saroyan. Now will you please
tell me what agency or firm you represent?"

"You mean to tell me you don't know who I am?"

"That's right."

"Listen. I'm William Saroyan. The author. You must have
been reading about me."

"No."

"You're kidding."

"Mr. Saroyan, will you tell me what you want to see Mr.
Mangione about?"

The rising inflection in Cassidy's voice signaled a loud
explosion. I rushed out to the reception room, in time to save
Saroyan from her Irish temper. In my office he fretted about
Cassidy's lack of response to his name and wanted to know if
she ever read anything. Warwick Deeping was her favorite
novelist, I said, and asked what I could do for him. He
explained that a mutual friend had suggested my introducing
him to the editor of *Travel*; since he was planning a trip to
Armenia, he wanted to write an article or two about it for the
magazine. I led him to Coby Gilman and introduced them. No

sooner had I left Gilman's office than I heard Saroyan complaining, "Say, what kind of a receptionist do you have in this joint? She claims she's never heard of me. . . ."

Encountering him at a number of gatherings after that, I marveled at his cocky promotion of himself; he was as uninhibited as a pushcart huckster yelling out his wares above the din of a crowded market. Whether he actually believed all the praises he bellowed of his literary prowess or whether he was simply playing a publicity role that might increase his sales, I could never be certain, but after all the shy writers I had met, it was refreshing to watch this son of Armenian immigrants, an ethnic like myself, acting as though the world were his oyster; and I envied him, not only for his success but also for his extroverted personality. Although his childhood had been a cruel nightmare, it had left no discernible scars. He had the self-assurance of a steel magnate.

Tess Slesinger hosted one of the parties given for Saroyan. She was a young and beautiful woman who herself had recently moved into the orbit of fame with a best-selling first novel about New York sophisticates called *The Unpossessed.** I had never met her but came to the party at Saroyan's invitation, arriving late after a great deal of liquor had been consumed. At the door Tess Slesinger greeted me with the salutation: "Come right in, sir. Will you have me? Or would you prefer a martini?" Saroyan might have been able to come up with a suitable rejoinder; I could only gulp and blush, and settle for a drink.

She ushered me into a room filled with writers, editors, and critics, among them Fred Marsh, a frequent reviewer for the *New York Times Book Review,* who was intensely engaged in a drunken conversation with Saroyan. Marsh was doing most of the talking, propounding the thesis that Saroyan was nothing

* Published in 1934, *The Unpossessed* was followed the next year by a volume of short stories, *Time: The Present.* Tess Slesinger died in 1945 at the age of forty.

less than a genius. Saroyan, when he could get a word in edgewise, was arguing that he was no such thing. At first I thought that Saroyan must be ill not to acknowledge that Marsh was absolutely right, but the longer I listened the more modest he sounded. The only conclusion I could draw was that under the influence of alcohol, Saroyan had lost sight of his flamboyant public personality and reverted to what may have been his own private self.

As much as I would like to have become his friend, Saroyan's obsession with himself precluded any genuine rapport between us. Only once did he express the slightest interest in what I was doing, while we were drinking coffee after having attended together a session of the American Writers' Congress. How wonderful it must be, he said of my situation, not to be burdened with literary ambition and to be working as an editor in a publishing house where one earned "a decent living" and associated with "decent people." I tried to explain that my salary was far from "decent," my job was not as idyllic as he made it out to be, and that I too was "burdened" with literary ambition. Although he observed the amenities of the attentive listener, I doubt that he heard much of what I said. He had been romanticizing, or rather Saroyanizing, about my circumstances and could not help but reject any facts that interfered with his fantasy.

Whatever ambition I may have had to earn a decent salary by becoming McBride's editor in chief was squelched as soon as I observed with what dispatch McBride fired the men he hired for the post. Robert Ballou, the ablest of them, was fired after a few months, presumably for having failed to find the magical manuscript that would become a best seller and restore the firm's declining fortunes. Ballou arrived at McBride's with the dubious distinction of having been one of the unluckiest publishers of the thirties. One of the first to have faith in John Steinbeck's literary talent, he had spent most of his money publishing such early Steinbeck fiction as *Pastures of Heaven* and *To a God Unknown*, both of which received few reviews

FAMILY

Jerre Mangione's parents, Gaspare and Giuseppina, on their wedding day in Rochester, New York, April 1908.

Below: The Mangione family and their first car, in 1920. Missing is brother Frank, age ten, who took the photograph.

The wedding of Mangione's sister Assunta (Sue) and James D'Amico. They met on a blind date. Mangione is behind the bride; his brother Frank is on extreme left, his sister Rita on extreme right.

Giuseppina Mangione and her iconoclastic brother, Uncle Peppino.

Mangione with his parents in the mid-forties.

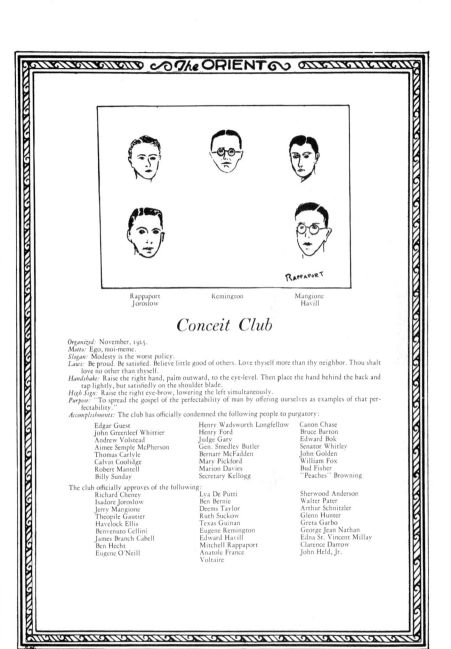

Rappaport   Remington   Mangione
Joroslow   Havill

Conceit Club

Organized: November, 1925.
Motto: Ego, moi-meme.
Slogan: Modesty is the worst policy.
Laws: Be proud. Be satisfied. Believe little good of others. Love thyself more than thy neighbor. Thou shalt love no other than thyself.
Handshake: Raise the right hand, palm outward, to the eye-level. Then place the hand behind the back and tap lightly, but satisfiedly on the shoulder blade.
High Sign: Raise the right eye-brow, lowering the left simultaneously.
Purpose: "To spread the gospel of the perfectability of man by offering ourselves as examples of that perfectability."
Accomplishments: The club has officially condemned the following people to purgatory:

Edgar Guest	Henry Wadsworth Longfellow	Canon Chase
John Greenleaf Whittier	Henry Ford	Bruce Barton
Andrew Volstead	Judge Gary	Edward Bok
Aimee Semple McPherson	Gen. Smedley Butler	Senator Whitley
Thomas Carlyle	Bernarr McFadden	John Golden
Calvin Coolidge	Mary Pickford	William Fox
Robert Mantell	Marion Davies	Bud Fisher
Billy Sunday	Secretary Kellogg	"Peaches" Browning

The club officially approves of the following:

Richard Cheney	Lya De Putti	Sherwood Anderson
Isadore Joroslow	Ben Bernie	Walter Pater
Jerry Mangione	Deems Taylor	Arthur Schnitzler
Theopile Gautier	Ruth Suckow	Glenn Hunter
Havelock Ellis	Texas Guinan	Greta Garbo
Benvenuto Cellini	Eugene Remington	George Jean Nathan
James Branch Cabell	Edward Havill	Edna St. Vincent Millay
Ben Hecht	Mitchell Rappaport	Clarence Darrow
Eugene O'Neill	Anatole France	John Held, Jr.
	Voltaire	

The Conceit Club manifesto, from the Rochester East High School yearbook.

Mangione with his widowed aunt Rosina and her spinster daughter Concetta in Realmonte, his mother's native village.

Great-uncle Calogero of Agrigento who, like Aunt Rosina, lived to be a nonagenarian.

Mangione (with pipe) with some local intellectuals, off the shore of Porto Empedocle, his father's native town.

Henry G. Alsberg, the national director of the Federal Writers' Project, was a powerhouse of tenacity.

Mangione, while living on Kenneth Burke's literary farm at Andover, New Jersey, in 1940.

Vardis Fisher, novelist and state director of the Idaho Writers' Project. He advocated more suicides.

YADDO

Guests of Yaddo, September 1939. Director Elizabeth Ames is at right end of first row. Next to her, right to left, Nathan Asch, Marjorie Peabody Waite, Mangione. Behind him, left to right, Josephine Herbst, Eleanor Clark, David Diamond, Delmore Schwartz. Third row, left to right, Newton Arvin, Arthur Arent, Rudolf Von Ripper, and Richard Bermann, who died at Yaddo a few hours after the Nazi invasion of Poland.

Mangione in a Yaddo bedroom.

INTERNMENT CAMPS

Mangione (second from right) with the Santa Fe camp commander, Lloyd H. Jensen (to his left). Behind them are the Border Patrolmen in charge of the camp's security.

A group from Latin America is brought to the Immigration Service's Santa Fe camp for internment. U.S. Border Patrolmen in front row.

German aliens in the mess hall at the Kenedy internment camp in Texas. Japanese prisoners ate in a separate mess hall.

Theatricals were a favorite entertainment at the Santa Fe camp. Actors playing female roles were exempted from camp duties that might roughen their hands.

A German-born Catholic priest from Central America, interned at Camp Kenedy, painted one entire wall of the camp's improvised chapel with scenes from the life of Christ.

Below: The outdoor stage at the Santa Fe camp was constructed by the aliens interned there.

Ivan Williams, camp commander of several internment camps, whose exploits made him a legend among interned aliens.

Earl G. Harrison, the compassionate commissioner of the Immigration Service, custodian agency for the government's quasi-secret internment of German, Italian, and Japanese aliens.

The chain fence and guard towers at camps like Kenedy and Fort Lincoln, North Dakota, accentuated the bleakness of the landscape around them.

PERSONALITIES

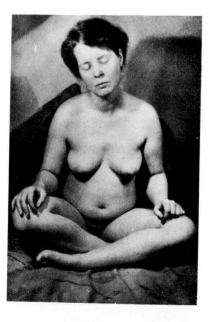

Edna St. Vincent Millay, the most successful woman poet of her day, had a reputation for scorning convention.

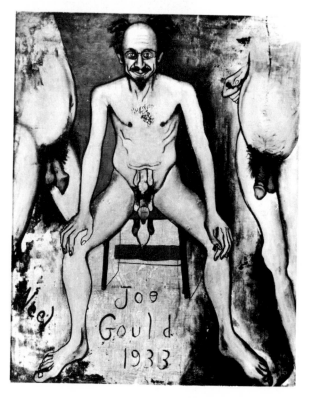

Above left: Alice Neel was to wait more than thirty years before the portraits she painted in the early thirties would bring her fame.

Left: Alice Neel's portrait of Joe Gould, a Greenwich Village eccentric, is titled: "Variations of an Old Theme on the source of Russian architecture."

Mangione with his boyhood friend Edward Havill, a novelist who lived a more Thoreau-like existence than Thoreau himself did.

Right: William Rollins, Jr. His highly acclaimed proletariat novel, The Shadow Before, *inspired the Soviets to send him Moscow gold for a long Russian sojourn.*

Coburn Gillman. For all his brilliance as an editor and literary talent scout, he was given to buffoonery.

William Saroyan achieved instant fame in 1934 with his first book. Under the influence of cocktails, he denied being a genius.

Luigi Pirandello's plays projected a vision of life that was nicely compatible with the Fascist version of government.

Ignazio Silone, the left-wing author of Bread and Wine. In Fascist Italy no writer would admit knowing his name or work. (Credit: Maywald)

Carlo Tresca, who was murdered by an unknown assassin in 1943, is shown in a New York courtroom. He was probably the most arrested labor leader in American history. (UPI)

Right: Kenneth Burke, "the Aristotle of the twentieth century," with his second wife, Elizabeth, and their two young sons, in the early forties.

Richard Wright, who got his start on the Federal Writers' Project, claimed in the thirties that he could never marry a white woman, but eventually he did.

Paul Corey, the novelist, and his wife, the poet Ruth Lechlitner, outside their home near Cold Spring -on-the- Hudson, New York. Corey constructed the house with his own hands, trading eggs from his chickens for building materials.

Jelly Roll Morton, a father of jazz, at a recording session in 1938. In Washington, D.C., he operated a firetrap nightclub which featured a juggler performing with lighted kerosene lamps. (Credit: Ramsey Archive)

Charles Edward Smith, the pioneer jazz critic. While in Washington, D.C., he put his mistress on a rigid schedule.

(Credit: Frederic Ramsey, Jr.)

Below: U.S. Attorney General Francis Biddle. He freed 600,000 Italian-Americans from the category of "alien enemies."

Corrado di Niscemi, the part-time Sicilian prince who spent half the year at his Palermo palace and the other half in his Philadelphia apartment.

John Frederick Lewis, Jr., the Philadelphia millionaire who was embarrassed by his wealth.

and sales, and gone into bankruptcy. Steinbeck's next novel, *Tortilla Flat*, which Ballou would have published had he remained solvent a few months longer, put the author on the road to fame and big royalties.

From the outset of my friendship with him, Ballou struck me as a frustrated saint, a modern-day mystic who would suffer from stomach ulcers as part of his penance for being alive in a world filled with scorpions in different guises. He belonged to no particular church but was a serious student of all religious sects. His fascination for esoteric religions matched that of my uncle Peppino, who by now had become a zealous member of the Holy Rollers. It was Ballou who introduced me to the world of Father Divine, whom thousands of followers regarded as God in the flesh.

His worshipers, also known as "angels," adopted such names as Glorious Illumination, Heavenly Dove, and Pleasing Joy. They practiced celibacy and, eschewing public welfare, lived in the dozen or so "Heavens" Father Divine had established in Harlem where, for fifteen cents, anyone could partake of a meat dish served with vegetables, bread, and a beverage. "The real God," read a Father Divine edict, "is the God that feeds us."

The "Heaven" to which Ballou took me, along with two of his woman friends, was in a stadiumlike meeting hall where we sat among several hundred spectators, black and white, and concentrated on the scene below: Some one hundred of Father Divine's angels, mostly black, sat around a long rectangle of banquet tables consuming fried chicken while they listened to one another testify to the power and goodness of their God. Presiding over the banquet was the squat, bald-headed figure of Father Divine, who seemed far too engrossed in his food to hear what was being said of him.

The meal and testimonials proceeded peacefully enough until a young mulatto girl, as though suddenly possessed, dropped the chicken leg she was chewing and, leaping on the table barefooted, silently dashed from one end of the long rectangle to the other, clearing water glasses, bread baskets, and serving dishes without touching any of them. No one applauded the girl's singular stunt but an old black man next to me tugged at my sleeve and whispered: "See that? She didn't spill a thing. She sure has God inside her."

The girl's action marked the beginning of disorder. The angels became increasingly hysterical as they told of their salvation from sin through the intercession of their God. They shouted and screeched and their speech became gibberish while their bodies writhed convulsively in the rhythms of copulation. Abandoning their meal, more and more of the angels rose from the table to join the orgy. One of Ballou's friends, sickened by the scene, begged us to get her out of the hall, but the doors were barricaded and the angel guards had strict orders not to open them until Father Divine gave the word.

When the Father finally stopped eating and rose to speak, we breathed more easily, figuring he would put an end to the hysteria. But it was a false assumption. His opening comments were reasonably clear, but he became more emotional and less intelligible as he continued until his speech made no sense at all. It made no difference to the angels; they needed only the sound of his voice to excite them further. They screamed and groaned and rolled on the floor while their God went on orating, the garbled words rolling out of his mouth with an imperial accent that directed the frenzied worshipers as surely as a conductor's baton. Only when he abruptly came to a stop and walked away from the scene, as though tired of the whole affair, did the pandemonium end.

We left as soon as the doors were opened, and fled into the Harlem night.

My McBride job afforded me entry to social and political areas which my John Reed Club friends would have considered enemy territory. In the sumptuous East Side apartment of Harold Strauss (a publisher's editor with an affluent wife) I met two of their enemies: George Sokolsky, the Buddha-shaped Hearst columnist and professional anti-Communist, and Lewis

Corey, a Marxist economist who, under his original name of Louis Fraina, had been a founder of the American Communist party. Corey was now being damned as a deviationist by ex-comrades who had become Stalinists.

The two men were so diametrically opposed in their political views that the Strausses and their guests expected verbal fireworks as soon as they came face to face. But what may have been intended as the highlight of the evening never came off. Despite repeated efforts to incite argument, the two men paid no attention to each other, much to everyone's disappointment. Later I learned there was a "capitalistic" reason for their behavior. Sokolsky and Corey had just signed a contract with a lecture agency that was sending them on a nationwide tour to stage debates on the subject of Marxism. In refusing to be baited into an argument at the Strauss party they had exercised the prerogative of professional lecturers to abstain from performing without a fee.

Through Coby Gilman I became friendly with the radical Carlo Tresca, who also was anathema to my Stalinist acquaintances. I had long admired Tresca from afar as a militant labor leader and anti-Fascist. At the time we met he was still editor and publisher of *Il Martello*, the Italian-language weekly he founded in 1919, which kept hammering away at the same themes that had obsessed Tresca from the time he became a teen-age revolutionist in his native Abruzzi: social injustice, exploitation of the working classes, and totalitarianism in any form. His parents had been wealthy landowners, but the hard life of the Abruzzi peasants (the same peasants that Silone was to write about) had made him a socialist agitator and, later, the publisher of a revolutionary journal, *Il Germe*. When the journal exposed corruption among high government officials, Tresca was arrested and convicted of libel. Faced with the choice of going to jail or into exile, at the age of twenty-four he fled to Switzerland where he met other exiled Italian radicals, among them a loud-mouthed young socialist named Benito Mussolini, whom he regarded as a charlatan and a crook

(Tresca was to tell me that during a brief period when he and the future dictator of Italy shared the same sleeping quarters, Mussolini filched his watch).

On learning how Italian immigrants were being badly exploited by American capitalists, Tresca came to the United States in 1904, and soon became a labor agitator among the steel workers and coal miners of Pennsylvania. From then on, he figured in many of the nation's great strikes, including the 1912 and 1913 strikes of textile workers in Lawrence, Massachusetts, and Paterson, New Jersey, and the Mesabi Iron Range Strike of 1916. As Max Eastman wrote of Tresca's career, "There is hardly a major industrial conflict, a genuine revolt of workers in the first quarter of the century in which Carlo Tresca did not join the vanguard and stand in the front line under fire."

Tresca may well have been one of the most-arrested labor agitators in history. By the time we met in the mid-thirties, he had been arrested more than thirty times. Some of the "crimes" with which he was charged were as trivial as shouting "Viva Socialismo" in the face of a policeman, some as serious as first-degree murder. In the early twenties, when Tresca began his attacks against Mussolini's regime, the Italian embassy in Washington managed to get him convicted for sending "obscene matter" through the mails. This consisted of a four-line advertisement in Il Martello which announced a book about birth control by Margaret Sanger. He was sentenced to a year in jail, but President Coolidge commuted the sentence to four months.

Both his friends and enemies were aware of his beguiling personality. One of my favorite Tresca stories tells of his encounter with Coolidge soon after he had been released from the Atlanta penitentiary. Stopping off in Washington for some sightseeing, Tresca was passing the White House grounds when he got into conversation with a group of young children playing near the entrance gate. The big black-bearded man, with his broken English and alluring smile, entranced the children and they pulled him along until they were inside the White House. Mistaking him for a relative of the children, President Coolidge shook hands with him as well as the children. Tresca, of course, did not identify himself, but as he left several reporters immediately recognized him. When he would not answer their questions, they invented their own interpretation of his meeting with the President. One front-page headline read: TRESCA AT WHITE HOUSE; CRIMINAL ANARCHIST RELEASED FROM ATLANTA MAKES HIS PEACE WITH PRESIDENT.

Throughout the thirties Tresca concentrated his efforts on preventing Italian fascism from getting a foothold in New York. He and some of his husky supporters, adopting some of the Fascists' own techniques, conducted a relentless campaign of guerrilla warfare against Mussolini's sympathizers, one which eventually was to cost Tresca his life. Whenever pro-Fascists gathered for a meeting, Tresca and his friends would be on hand to disrupt it. If heckling did not do the trick, they would initiate a general brawl, in the course of which a patrol wagon and ambulance (both summoned by Tresca's lieutenants) would arrive and, except for those who were too slow or too injured to disperse, the meeting hall would be abandoned. The American press, which kept praising the Fascist regime for its efficiency, took a dim view of Tresca's tactics. One Manhattan tabloid called him "an unmitigated political gangster who derives perverse pleasure from trying to be the proverbial fly in Il Duce's ointment." Oblivious to such criticism, Tresca continued his warfare until few Italian Americans in New York City dared set foot in a pro-Mussolini meeting.

My introduction to Tresca came about when Gilman, unable to accompany Tresca to an anti-Fascist lecture by Count Carlo Sforza, who had been Italy's Prime Minister just before Mussolini came to power, arranged with Tresca to have me go in his place. Ten minutes later I was in the offices of *Il Martello*, located in a dingy building at Fifteenth Street and Fifth Avenue, a short distance from the spot where Tresca would one night be struck down by the bullet of an unknown assassin.*

---

* The search for Tresca's assassin became a major fictional theme in my novel *Night Search* (Crown, 1966).

The bare reception room was bleakly lighted by a single electric bulb dangling from a high ceiling; the only sounds came from the hissing and rattling of decrepit radiators. There was no one in sight. After a while a young Italian badly in need of a shave emerged from a side door behind a long counter, and in broken English asked me my business. Before I had finished explaining, he stuck out his lower lip, shook his head, and told me that Tresca had left. I insisted he must be mistaken (Gilman had telephoned Tresca, in my presence, to tell him I was on my way), but he kept showing me his lower lip and shaking his head. Soon he was joined by an older Italian wearing a battered felt hat and smoking a black Toscano. He jerked a thumb toward the exit and ordered me to leave.

I said I would wait for Tresca. When the two men began moving toward me to throw me out, I shouted at the top of my lungs, "Mangione is my name. I want to see Carlo Tresca." Seconds later, the enormous presence of Tresca was upon me with outstretched arms, thundering a roar of welcome. After embracing me as though I were a long-lost son, he informed the men in Italian that he and I were going uptown to Columbia University to hear Count Sforza's lecture. The older man said it would be best if one of them came along. "But I don't need a bodyguard today," Tresca answered. "I have Mangione." With that, he looked down at me and smiled brightly. Weighing less than 130 pounds then and feeling no more able to protect him than a poodle can protect a lion, I barely managed to return the smile. The men followed him as he went back to his office to get his hat and coat; I could hear them remonstrating with him, then being cut short with a severe "No."

On the street Tresca became furtive and quiet. He led me down a subway entrance and went from one corridor to another through a dizzy complex of sharp turns, sweaty walls, and split stairways. We finally went up a long stairway and into broad daylight. I followed him into a taxi, expecting that now he would relax, but after we had gone three blocks he ordered the driver to let us out. While we waited for another cab, he simply explained he had not liked the cab driver's looks. The next cab driver's face was no more reassuring, but Tresca seemed no longer worried. During the long drive uptown he asked me questions in Italian about my work at McBride and showed great interest in the fact that we had just published a book of short stories by Ignazio Silone, a fellow *Abruzzese.* He recalled that as a young man he had organized a union in the same Abruzzi town that Silone called "Fontamara."

Inside the auditorium where the lecture was to be given Tresca carried himself with the aplomb of a monarch. From all sides he was greeted with cries of "Allo, Carlo," *"Come si va, Carlo?," "Saluti, Carlo."* He acknowledged each one with a smile or a nod but occasionally, to let me know that the greeting was not from a friend, he would bend down to my ear and hiss: "Fascista sonafabeetch." We sat in the last row of the packed auditorium, with a view of the whole assemblage. Throughout the hall Tresca's presence created considerable excitement; people kept nudging one another, pointing their chins in our direction, twisting their necks to get a good look at him. Count Sforza received a standing ovation when he came out on the platform, but after the audience wearied of trying to follow his scholarly rhetoric, understandable only to the few who were as educated as Sforza, their attention wandered back to Tresca.

Tresca himself paid little attention to the speaker. His eyes kept darting to different sections of the auditorium like those of a cat alerting itself to every possibility of danger. It occurred to me that he had come not to listen but to let the assemblage know that anyone who threatened the safety of the speaker would have to account to Tresca. The situation was potentially dangerous since the Casa Italiana, a part of Columbia University, was suspected of functioning as a distribution center for Fascist propaganda. That Sforza would dare speak on enemy territory must have antagonized the Mussolini sympathizers on the campus. But there was only one brief manifestation of that and it was quickly squelched. Toward the end of the lecture, a man near the center of the hall suddenly stood up and began denouncing Sforza with a fierce barrage of Italian. Tresca was on his feet instantly, outshouting the heckler with his powerful voice, ordering him to shut up or get out. There was a solid round of applause as the heckler hurriedly left the hall.

When the lecture was over, the chairman of the meeting thanked Tresca for dealing with the heckler, then offered to introduce him to Count Sforza. Tresca politely declined. As he later explained to me, although he and Sforza were enemies of Mussolini and his regime, they had nothing else in common. In Tresca's view, Sforza still represented the Italian establishment he had attacked long before the arrival of fascism.

Before anyone else could approach him, Tresca hurried toward the nearest exit. Outdoors, he became furtive again, moving along quickly and often glancing over his shoulder. He suddenly pulled me off the sidewalk and into the doorway of a store, muttering that we were being followed. "I see him," he whispered. "When he comes, let me do all the talking." Moments later he stepped out of the doorway directly in the path of an Italian I had noted in the lecture hall, a few rows away from us. To my surprise, the confrontation was without drama. Tresca simply shook hands with the man and spoke to him in Italian in a friendly way. The Italian was no less cordial. He was much younger than Tresca and almost as tall; his face was scarred as though it had once been ripped by a dull knife. They chatted amiably on the sidewalk for a while, telling each other how dull the lecture had been, then we all proceeded to the subway station together and got on the same downtown train. Tresca never introduced us. During the ride the Italian tried to say something to me in broken English, but Tresca quickly interrupted him and held his attention the rest of the way.

We all left the train at the Fourteenth Street station, where the Italian shook hands with both of us before he went on his way. Tresca kept his eyes on him until he was out of sight, then led me in the opposite direction. After another confounding series of twists and turns, we went up a stairway to the street. I wanted to ask Tresca about the Italian, but his mind was now on other matters, mainly his worry over a publisher's contract he had signed for his autobiography. The contract was almost a year old, but so far he had produced only one chapter; he found that he had neither the time nor the patience to go on with it. When I commented that it would be a pity not to write it, he proposed we become collaborators; he would tell me his life story in Italian and I would write it in English.

Although Tresca appealed to me, his proposal did not. For some complicated ego reason, which I was later to regret, I wanted my first book to be my own. He must have sensed my reluctance for he hastily added that I need not make up my mind: "Just let me know if you decide you'd like to do it." I never did, and the autobiography was never written. The only noteworthy biographical material published of Tresca in his lifetime was a brief chapter in Max Eastman's *Heroes I Have Known*. Eastman deleted the chapter in a subsequent edition of the book. This happened after Eastman, the erstwhile radical, had become a successful establishment writer, no longer willing to acknowledge as a hero a man who never capitulated to the establishment. It was also after Tresca had been murdered by an unknown assassin who, in my imagination, became the scar-faced Italian that had followed us after the Count Sforza lecture.

Tresca, the man of action, provided a sharp contrast to the left-wing aesthetes I kept meeting at cocktail parties, mostly at the home of Charles Studin who, ordered by his doctor, following a heart attack, to see people as often as possible without exerting himself unduly, became Manhattan's most prolific party giver. A retired and wealthy attorney, Studin hosted as many as five or six cocktail parties a week. Nearly all of his guests were writers, artists, editors, composers, and dancers; the only lawyers and businessmen he invited were patrons of the arts. With their therapeutic aspect in mind, Studin began the parties at five and ended them promptly at seven. If anyone dared stay overtime, he was hustled toward the door by a butler who doubled as a bouncer. Because of the strictly enforced schedule, Studin's guests were said to imbibe their martinis (the only drink ever served) at a faster rate than anywhere else in the world.

The parties were Studin's full-time occupation. With the assistance of an all-day secretary, he maintained a huge rotating file of the guests to be invited and memorized the name and achievements of every guest who ever set foot in his home. Although the parties were usually jammed, he not only managed to greet each arriving guest personally, but also saw to it that he was introduced to the guest of honor (often the author of a recently published book or the artist whose exhibit had just opened) as well as to every guest whom it might benefit him to meet. He had a strong sense of philanthropy.

He was a fatherly person with brown, friendly eyes that emitted more empathy than the banality of his party remarks could ever suggest. Although he was the personification of geniality, his comments sounded like those of a robot that had been programmed to say nothing that might start an argument. His closest friends knew that he was far more intelligent than he appeared to be at his parties; what guests often mistook for dullness was actually the neutral posture of a host who wanted to continue inviting Stalinists, Trotskyites, Socialists, anarchists, Democrats, and Republicans to the same parties. Certainly, nowhere else in New York could men and women of such diverse political faiths congregate without being at one another's throats; Studin's nonpolitical stance created the aura of a truce.

Probably no Studin guest was ever converted from one political faith to another, but the two-hour drinking sessions in a neutral zone, where all dogma was suspended in favor of congeniality, could not help but promote some degree of tolerance for all ideologies. The young Communist firebrand who had never talked with a wealthy capitalist would find

himself face to face with a rich patron of the arts who bore no
resemblance to the monstrous capitalists stereotyped in the left-
wing media. By the same token, Studin's wealthy friends were
bound to modify their wild notions of what radicals were like.
At any Studin party the class struggle was likely to suffer a
setback of sorts.

Unlike most other party invitations issued in those days,
Studin's entailed no financial obligation and no espousal of a
cause. At only one Studin party of my recollection were the
guests tapped for donations, much to the distress of the host.
The instigator was the guest of honor himself, John Lomax, a
Mississippian who was one of the pioneer collectors of American folk songs and literature. Lomax had brought with him a
black singer he had recently sprung out of a southern jail, the
superb but then unknown Leadbelly. Lomax antagonized the
guests from the start by introducing Leadbelly with the condescension of an antebellum plantation owner praising the fine
points of a slave on the block. After Leadbelly had performed
for a while, Lomax offended us further by submitting the great
black singer to what his audience interpreted as an act of
public humiliation: passing the hat. When he instructed Leadbelly to do so, I noticed Studin take a step toward Lomax, as if
he were about to object, then suddenly change his mind. It was
the only time I had ever seen Studin looking unhappy at one of
his parties.

Studin's living room became an oasis for every kind of dream
and deal. Despite the prevalence of insipid party chatter,
anything could happen there. You might meet an editor who
could get you a better job, or a published author or critic who
might take an interest in your writing, or an attractive girl who
might go to bed with you. (The guest I mooned over most—
from too discreet a distance—was Mary McCarthy, who looked
more like a movie starlet than the caustic woman of letters she
was in print.) Whether or not anything happened, being at a
Studin party made you feel privileged, on the brink of new

opportunities, and if by chance Studin and his secretary skipped over your name for more than a couple of weeks, you worried about it and all the opportunities you might be losing.

I became friendly enough with Studin so that on one occasion he let me bring a guest of my own to one of his parties. She was a young and unpublished writer who bore an enticing resemblance to Marlene Dietrich (I was still of an age when I judged the beauty of women by their physical similarities to my favorite Hollywood actresses). In the brief time I had known her I had sensed her fascination for the company of published writers, which seemed based on the belief that the more time she could spend with them the sooner would her own literary talent bloom.° I had mixed motives in inviting her; one was to impress her with the literary company I kept; another was to express my gratitude for an extraordinary favor she had recently done my family.

I had first heard of her when she telephoned me at McBride's and, introducing herself as the New York correspondent for a Rochester newspaper, asked to interview me. At our luncheon we discovered, to our mutual astonishment, that her father was the same shoe factory executive who, only the week before, had fired my father for his participation in a sitdown strike, one of the first of its kind in the nation. Although the workers had won the strike, my father, as punishment for having been one of the ringleaders, was dismissed. He had been a satisfactory employee of the factory for many years, but the union was not strong enough to insist that he be retained. Now, at this crisis period when my father was facing the nightmare of prolonged unemployment, Providence—or, to use my relatives' word *Destino*— had thoughtfully arranged to bring me together with the daughter of the man who could, if he wished, rehire him.

° Edna Manley put this belief to the supreme test by marrying, a few years later, Ludwig Lewisohn, a much-married author who was forty years her senior. But nothing bloomed, except their feelings of incompatability. The marriage lasted a few months.

I made the most of the opportunity. By the time our luncheon was over, I had succeeded in thoroughly arousing her compassion for my family's economic plight. She promised to telephone her father that very evening. Before the week was over, my father was restored to his job.

EIGHT

Afraid in Fascist Italy

Unexpectedly, my five years of New York had strengthened rather than weakened my bond with my Sicilian relatives. None of the new friends had their warm and easy acceptance of life, their talent for celebrating it. Now I found myself admiring my relatives for some of the same qualities I had once found intolerable. There were still vestiges of my childhood resentments, but on the whole I felt lucky to be one of them. It gave me a root feeling, a connection with a substantial past that made the uncertain present more bearable. It was shocking to realize that more than once I had thought of cutting myself off from such a natural source of strength.

My relatives must have sensed my change of attitude. "When are you coming back?" they asked on my visits to Rochester, with more persistence than ever. In my rusty Sicilian I cited reasons for remaining in New York they might understand; the other reasons I kept to myself. It would have been beyond their ken to be told that I was more responsive than ever to the Horatio Alger syndrome implanted by my public-school teachers, or that the promises proffered in the demonic Manhattan landscape, though often based on quicksand premises, held me enthralled. Nor could I tell that for all of its precariousness, I preferred the unpredictability of my new world to their tightly programmed old one.

Yet for all my faith in the American Way of Life and the Lucky Break, the Sicilian Way began to obsess me as it never had before. Sicily became an irresistible magnet which I needed to explore and fathom. At first I tried learning about it through books, but too many of them were written by travel writers who stuffed their scant information of the island with obese language. The historians were more illuminating; they made it clear that Sicily had been one of the mainsprings of Western civilization, providing ample proof that the glory of ancient Greece had been lavishly spread throughout the island, especially in Siracusa and in Agrigento, the province of my ancestors.

But how to reconcile Sicilian history with the American melting-pot concept that had been drummed into every school-child of my generation? Particularly hard to swallow was the arrogant assumption of politicians and some sociologists that American civilization, though still in its adolescence, should take precedence over the older civilizations of its latter-day immigrants. I began to ask myself such questions: Was it in the chemistry of human nature or in the interest of the national welfare for my relatives (and for all other immigrants from Mediterranean and eastern European nations) to become Anglo-Saxonized? Was there any substantial difference between assimilation and extinction? In other words, wasn't the application of the melting-pot concept an insidious kind of genocide?

Out of such unanswered questions was born the urgent desire to explore my ethnic identity in Sicily itself. But there was a major obstacle to making such a journey: fascism was firmly entrenched in all parts of Italy, and I was clearly on record, with my published articles, as an anti-Fascist. Bill Rollins warned that it was no time for me to be going to Italy. The recent conquest of Ethiopia by the Italians had incited the Fascist regime to behave as if it had the world by the tail. Only recently the *Times*'s Rome correspondent had reported that two more young Italian-Americans traveling in Italy had been seized by the Fascists for induction into the Italian army. It won't happen to me, I argued, since I would be posing, with Coby Gilman's approval, as a correspondent for *Travel* magazine. As for my anti-Fascist articles, I was confident, foolishly so, that the Fascist authorities would never suspect that Gerlando Mangione, the baptismal name that appeared on my passport, and Jerre Mangione, the anti-Fascist writer, were one and the same person.

Possibly suspecting that I might be underestimating the efficiency of the Fascist police and needed additional camouflage, Gilman equipped me with a letter of introduction from the head of the Italian Tourist Bureau in New York addressed to the Minister of Propaganda in Rome. The letter identified me as Gerlando Mangione, a correspondent for *Travel*, "who comes to Italy with the intention of refreshing his ideas about our nation from the political-economic point of view but, above all, from that of the tourist." It closed with the greeting "*Saluti Fascisti*" and the name of G. Panteleoni who, I was to discover, was a *pezzo grosso*, a big shot, in the Fascist party.

With three hundred dollars borrowed from the Mutual Aid Society (a group that loaned money without interest to persons engaged in "worthy causes"), I booked round-trip passage on the *Conte di Savoia* and the *Rex*, then asked my father to let our relatives in Sicily know I was on my way. My parents had mixed feelings about the trip. They knew enough about my political attitudes to fear I might get into trouble with the Fascists; on the other hand, they were elated that I should want to visit their native land; it was further proof of my devotion to them. They bragged about it as if it were a milestone of success and began inviting relatives to the *buon viaggio* celebration I was to attend on the eve of my journey.

On the same day I was to travel to Rochester, Carlo Tresca gave what Coby Gilman facetiously called "a farewell lunch" for me. Tresca and the driver of a battered jalopy picked me up at my apartment, then spent the next half hour on a dizzy course through dozens of Village streets, apparently to confound anyone trying to follow us. We finally came to a stop at a basement Italian restaurant without a sign, which I was never able to find again.

To my dismay the restaurant was filled to capacity with guests of Tresca, some thirty of them, and I worried that with so many persons knowing of my journey the Fascists were bound to find out that Mangione, a friend of Mussolini's old enemy Carlo Tresca, was about to leave for Italy. Tresca had no such worry. He took me on a tour of the tables and made sure I was introduced to everyone. Except for Coby Gilman and his inamorata Dawn Powell,° they were all strangers, but it was somewhat reassuring to recognize some of their names, such as A. J. Muste, the pacifist; Harry Kelly, the philosophical anarchist; Arturo Giovannitti, the poet and labor leader. Tresca, an enormous man, had ordered a huge repast that rivaled the banquets of my relatives in quantity and culinary diversity. The chianti flowed generously. Seated nearby, Tresca kept toasting me every time he refilled his wine glass.

Three hours after the luncheon started, the guests were only halfway through the menu. As the guest of honor, it embarrassed me to be the first to leave, but with my parents expecting me that evening I could not do otherwise. Tresca accompanied me to the door. He embraced me, kissed me on both cheeks, then raising his voice to a stentorian level, so that all could hear, advised: "If Mussolini bringa you trouble, you let Carlo know rightaway."

It sounded like bad advice. If the Fascists knew I was a

° A prolific novelist and, occasionally, a Hollywood scriptwriter. Reviewing *Turn, Magic Wheel* (1936) for *The New Republic,* I commented on her rich talent for social comedy, unsurpassed by any of her American contemporaries, but also noted that now and then she lapsed into sentimentality. The review concluded: "It is only when Dawn Powell is completely unserious that she becomes a serious writer." Her response to all this was a postcard message from Martha's Vineyard where she was vacationing: "Sleeping under blankets. Wish it were you."

friend of Tresca, the avowed enemy of Mussolini, who was said to be high on Il Duce's list of anti-Fascists to be assassinated, I would surely get into deep trouble. That Tresca should not have figured that one out for himself disturbed me until I recalled the large quantity of chianti he had consumed.

A houseful of relatives was waiting for me when I got to Rochester. I had not seen so many of them together since my sister Assunta's wedding. They drank my father's oldest wine, ate his pastries, and marveled that I, not they, was going to Sicily. One by one they pelted me with messages and addresses of relatives and friends scattered throughout the island. To visit all of them would have taken at least a year. A number of them asked me to make sure I talked with my father's first cousin, Vincenzo Fiorentino, who had left Rochester a few years before to return to Sicily; they were eager to find out how he was faring. Behind this request was their dream of living in Sicily again.

A great-uncle, who was well in his eighties and still working every day as a blacksmith, precipitated a hot political argument when he urged me to visit Marsala as a tribute to his favorite hero Garibaldi, who had landed there with one thousand volunteers to liberate the Italians from foreign rule. "Keep away from Marsala," my uncle Peppino warned. "The Fascists have no use for Garibaldi." The Mussolini lovers at the party vehemently disagreed. "Both Garibaldi and Mussolini are heroes in Italy," one of them insisted, "because Garibaldi, like Il Duce, wanted the same thing for Italy: the respect of other nations." Uncle Stefano's rebuttal to all this was that his only hero was Dante. As far as he was concerned, all politicians, particularly Mussolini, should be boiled in oil and fed to the vultures.

On the way to the train station my father expressed his worry that I might be drafted into the Italian army as a reprisal for his having escaped army service by migrating to the States. "Don't stray too far from cities where there are American consuls to protect you," he warned. My mother was the last one to embrace me before I got on the train. "As a favor to me, when you feel like expressing a political opinion, don't do it," she said. "And tell your Zia Rosina [her septuagenarian sister who had nursed her after the death of their mother] how I long to see her again. May Christ and the Virgin Mary watch over you."

In a few weeks I was to become almost paranoid in my fear that the Fascist authorities would forcefully induct me into the Italian army and ship me to Ethiopia, and would wonder how much weight my mother's prayers for my safety could have. But in my first Italian hours, aboard the small ship taking me from Naples to Palermo overnight, I experienced a miracle of sorts that left me euphoric. In the twilight I unexpectedly overheard some of the crew members conversing among themselves in the dialect that was my first language, rich as ever in nuance and unflawed by Italo-American barbarisms, and my senses were overwhelmed with the emotion of being a full-blooded Sicilian in direct touch with his life source. A lapse into sentimentality, I tried to tell myself, but at dawn there was the same surge of joy as I beheld the port of Palermo on a blue horizon gradually materializing into a pink and rosy pleasure dome.

Yet once I landed the exultation became a submerged memory, despite the seductive heirlooms of Palermo's architectural past. My critical self took complete charge and I became the wary foreigner comparing what I saw and felt with what my Rochester relatives had led me to expect. They had spoken of Sicily's poverty, but I had never imagined it could be as wretched as it was in the slums of Palermo. The other surprise was the cruelty of the summer landscape, as it revealed itself from the window of the train taking me to Agrigento. Instead of the undulating hills and lush vegetation I had heard described all through my childhood, I saw sun-scorched fields and towering naked mountains and precipices, endlessly menacing, some in the shape of monsters. The mythologists who placed the gates of Hades in Sicily were certainly more reliable than the memories of my Rochester relatives.

The scenery became friendlier as we approached Agrigento and the sea. There were patches of vegetation, groves of lemon, almond, and olive trees, and much more sky. Then, like the sun emerging from a dark cloud, the Mediterranean burst into view. Moments before we began to descend into Agrigento, I saw the Valley of the Temples and beyond this ancient Greek spectacle the pier of Porto Empedocle constructed from the ruins of a dismantled Greek temple on the orders of a bigoted Catholic bishop.

A large committee of relatives was at the station to greet me. I kissed and let myself be kissed, assuming that each person must belong to my mother's or father's family for they all looked a little like me. But the only one I could positively identify was my great-uncle Calogero, who had looked after my father when he was left an orphan. One relative, who was six feet tall, sensed that I did not know who he was. With tears in his eyes, he caught me up in his arms a second time. "Don't you really know me?" he cried, hurt. "I am your uncle Giuseppe, your father's brother."

I looked for Vincenzo Fiorentino, the relative I had known in my childhood who had returned to Sicily when he became a widower, but he was not among them. My uncle informed me he was visiting a sick relative in Trapani and was expected to return in a few days.

Even before we left the station my relatives began to quarrel as to where I should stay; each relative threatened to become offended if I rejected his hospitality. They were appalled by my suggestion that I stay at a hotel. Finally, they agreed I was to take turns staying with each of them, first with my great-uncle because he was the oldest, then with Uncle Giuseppe, after that ... I interrupted to explain I could not spend all of my time in Sicily since I had been commissioned to write some magazine articles about other places in Italy. They listened in disbelief.

They had known me less than twenty minutes and were depressed that I could bear to leave them. Only when I produced the letter addressed to the Minister of Propaganda in Rome did they concede I could not spend all my time with them. The letter made a deep impression; all during my stay they introduced me as the "son of Gasparino Mangione and Peppina Polizzi who has a letter of introduction to the Minister of Propaganda."

I was astonished how quickly they accepted me as one deserving of their affection and loyalty simply because we were closely related. As one whose habit it is to judge a person by his individual traits, I felt guilty for not being able to respond in kind. But if they were aware of this American peculiarity, there was no sign of it. In their eagerness to demonstrate how much they loved me, they swamped me with their hospitality, especially at mealtimes. I would insist I had eaten more than enough; they would reply I had hardly begun and pile my dish high with food again. "*Mangia, mangia,*" they would order. "Eat it without bread but eat it," they would finally cry in despair. In a culture where bread is literally the staff of life, this is a Sicilian's most generous gesture. None of the families was affluent enough to afford the quantities and varieties of dishes served to me, yet each one swore the meal was nothing but a snack and that I must be bent on starving myself to eat so little.

I tried several times to buy provisions for some of the poorer families but only succeeded in insulting them; only because I was an American and did not know any better was I forgiven. Their pride was even greater than their poverty. The only ones with steady incomes were the civil-service employees and their pay was so paltry that it mystified me how they could make ends meet. The majority of my relatives were masons and carpenters who were often unemployed; they earned far less than the civil-service workers.

The family I got to know best was that of my great-uncle Calogero, who lived with his wife and his son's family. Giugiu (the nickname for Gerlando), the son, was the breadwinner for the whole family. He had been a carpenter but lost part of an arm while working an electric saw; for his membership in the Fascist party he was given a civil-service post. As much as they loved me, my lack of enthusiasm for Mussolini disturbed Giugiu and his two young children, and they pummeled me with Fascist propaganda until I was provoked into arguing with them. "If fascism is so wonderful why is there so much poverty in Sicily?" I asked. "There was more poverty before Mussolini took charge of the country," Giugiu replied, and regarded me with pitying eyes for my inability to appreciate Il Duce's genius.

The poverty in Agrigento was nothing compared to that of my mother's birthplace, Realmonte, which was less than five miles away. I had only to sniff the village's putrid air to understand why there were more people from Realmonte in Rochester than remained in Realmonte. There were no sewers or pavements; the nearest water supply was seven miles away. Although on a hill, with the Mediterranean less than a mile away and plainly visible, Realmonte's beautiful situation seemed to have no connection with its residents.

My Zia Rosina's house, no better or worse than the others, consisted of two small rooms and an alcove just large enough to hold a stove. There were no toilet facilities either in the house or in its immediate vicinity. The roughly cemented walls of the rooms were plastered with Fascist propaganda posters proclaiming Mussolini's promise to restore Italy to the glories of the Roman Empire. My aunt, who lived with a spinster daughter and a middle-aged bachelor son, did not share their approbation of the Fascist regime; but her notions of "government" were badly confused for she made a sharp distinction between it and its head, whom she regarded as a great leader.

Zia Rosina's ignorance of government was due to a lack of information, not of intelligence. She was a sparkling reservoir of wisdom, undefeated by the ugliness that had surrounded her all her life. She had my mother's gift of insight and her brother's

(Uncle Peppino's) sharp sense of humor. Having fallen in love with her, it pained me to see her continuously dressed in black. When I asked why she wore mourning five years after the death of her husband, she blamed the stupidity of the villagers. A widow was expected to wear mourning to her grave. If she dared do otherwise, the villagers spread malicious gossip about her. "One thing I hold against my husband, *bonarma*, is that he would never consent to moving to a more civilized place."

On my last evening in Realmonte I sat on the village piazza with some of the men in the village. Among them was an ex-American who had recently been deported to Italy, for what crime I never learned. To the annoyance of the others, he spoke to me only in English, undoubtedly out of a sense of caution. "This town stinks, the whole country stinks. If you ask me, their system of government stinks. But none of these guys know it. They been here all their lives; that's all they know, they don't know no better." He confided he was working on a scheme to bribe his way back to the States. "It's gonna cost a lot, but believe me, I'd rather be dying in Brooklyn than living in this friggin' country."

The villagers were reluctant to discuss politics at first, and when they did they repeated the Fascist party line as recorded in the controlled press. A postal clerk who had lost a leg in World War I gloated over the Ethiopian victory: "It won't be long before our armies will be showing the world that the French are an effeminate race who can't fight and the English a bunch of bastards who are expert only in the art of betrayal." When I asked him what he meant by "betrayal," he reminded me that it was the British who had persuaded the League of Nations to impose economic sanctions on Italy as punishment for conquering Ethiopia.

"Before long," said an unemployed carpenter, "we'll all be migrating to Ethiopia where we can live like kings. That's where our future is."

"I hope you're right because there is no future in Realmonte," a young man said. "The only reason people stay here is because there is nowhere to go now."

The ex-American caught my eye and winked.

The next afternoon I kissed Zia Rosina good-bye, and left Realmonte on a train that was a half hour late.

Despite Uncle Giuseppe's reputation as the gloomiest man in Porto Empedocle (his occupation as a coffinmaker may have contributed to it), I found him in excellent spirits. He had just completed arrangements for the marriage of his eldest son (also named Gerlando, after our mutual grandfather who drowned himself in the Mediterranean) to the daughter of the local bandmaster. Since bandmasters rated higher on the local social scale than coffinmakers, he was as pleased as a businessman who had just swung a profitable deal. He seemed amused when I expressed astonishment on learning that Gerlando, who was stationed in Rome as a Department of Justice agent, had yet to set eyes on his future bride. All he had was her photograph and his father's assurance that the marriage would be a good one.

With the wedding arrangements almost completed, my uncle and the family of the prospective bride were already treating one another with the easy familiarity of relatives. At a dinner for me hosted by the bandmaster and his wife, I met Maria, Gerlando's betrothed. She was a plump, rosy-cheeked brunette who, having been told I bore a striking resemblance to her future husband, kept scrutinizing me all evening with nervous eyes. At one point she produced a photograph of Gerlando and compared his facial features with mine, while shaking her head and saying she could not see much of a resemblance. It was hard to tell whether she was relieved or disappointed.

Uncle Giuseppe kept me in Porto Empedocle as long as he dared, then hastily drove me to Agrigento where my great-uncle was impatiently waiting for me with a gang of relatives who wanted to make my acquaintance. On the way, my uncle advised me about marriage. "Your best bet would be to marry a Sicilian girl who lives in Sicily and hasn't been spoiled by crazy

American ideas." I reminded him that I would be leaving Sicily in a few days. "That doesn't matter," he replied. "I can always mail you photographs. If the idea appeals to you, just let me know. I know just the schoolteacher who would make you a good wife." He stopped the car just in time to avoid hitting a goat. "If the idea appeals to you," he repeated, "just let me know. Think of the joy you would give your parents if you became betrothed to a girl from Porto Empedocle." I promised him I would think about it.

As we were approaching Agrigento he gave me another piece of advice. "Whatever you do, don't entangle yourself with a woman while you're in Italy. You can get into a great deal of trouble that way. If you feel that you need a woman, go to a brothel. It's safer and healthier and, in the long run, much cheaper."

Vincenzo Fiorentino was one of the relatives waiting for me at my great-uncle's house. The sick cousin he had been visiting in Trapani died and he had been obliged to remain much longer than he had planned. He wept as he embraced me, sobbing how good it was to see an old friend from Rochester. He had aged considerably since our last meeting five years earlier, but later I noticed that he still wore a smart black hat cocked to one side, as he had ever since the death of his lachrymose wife.

The next morning, so that we could talk without being interrupted, we packed a luncheon of bread, cheese, and wine and took a bus to the Valley of the Temples. There, with our backs resting against a column of the Temple of Concordia and our eyes on the sea, we ate and conversed. I had remembered Zio Vincenzo (I called him uncle in deference to his age) as a reticent man, probably silenced by his wife's endless lamentations, but there was nothing reticent about him now as he talked of his years in Rochester. He asked about his old friends there and wanted to know if Uncle Stefano was still talking of returning to Sicily. I told him it was still his dream; in Rochester he could never stop feeling like a foreigner.

"I used to feel that way there," he said. "But actually I feel much more foreign here. Tell Stefano to stay where he is. Things have changed here. There is still beauty, of course, especially in the spring when this valley is filled with wild-flowers, but I find that beauty is not enough for me. The neighborhood in Rochester where I lived is far from beautiful, but I would rather be there. There is a blight on all of Italy and it seems to be getting worse. The newspapers claim there won't be another war, but I don't believe it. I can see it coming closer all the time, the biggest war the world has ever known, and I curse the day when I decided to come back to this benighted land."

To my suggestion that he return to Rochester, he replied that it was too late, he was too old; and he doubted that the Fascist authorities would permit him to leave the country. "Living here is like being in a prison. But at my age (he was in his sixties) it no longer matters. I might as well be buried where I was born. . . ."

Notwithstanding Zio Vincenzo's nostalgia for his American past, all my Sicilian observations pointed to the conclusion that there was essentially little difference between my relatives in Rochester and those in Sicily.° The champions of the American melting-pot theory were wrong. Despite three decades of American residence, my Rochester relatives remained Sicilian to the core. If Zio Vincenzo missed his life in Rochester it was not because he had become "Americanized" there. What he missed were his old cronies and the American prerogative of speaking one's mind without fear of being reported to the authorities as a subversive.

Everywhere in Sicily I was aware of that fear. People were careful how they worded a political opinion; they rarely said anything that might be construed as a criticism of the regime unless they were with relatives or with friends they trusted. But

---

° A fuller account of this first Sicilian journey may be found in the final chapters of my first book, *Mount Allegro* (1943).

sometimes, in the heat of emotion, they would forget to be careful. In a Porto Empedocle barbershop, while waiting my turn, I listened to a pudgy government clerk pontificating on the duty of every Italian to "tighten his belt in order to keep our country strong," then watched a fisherman jump out of the barber's chair and shout into the clerk's face: *"Porca miseria!* How much tighter do you think we can tighten our belts? They're so damn tight now we can't breathe. I tell you if we don't make ourselves heard soon, this government is going to squeeze us to death. . . ." Abruptly, he stopped, aware he had said too much. The stillness that followed was harrowing.

On balance, my Rochester relatives were a more contented lot than their Sicilian counterparts. For despite the Depression, their poverty was not nearly as desperate, and because their children were getting more education than they had, they tended to be far more hopeful about the future. As far as I could make out, the Sicilians had only two major hopes: that Ethiopia turn out to be a land of plenty, and that there be no more war.

I stopped in Palermo a few days before proceeding to Rome, and then began the nightmare that was to plague me the rest of my journey. When I went to the American Express office to pick up my mail, I was horrified to discover that every envelope had been opened and crudely resealed. I showed the resealed envelopes to a cousin accompanying me and asked whether it was customary for the Italian post office to examine foreign mail. He doubted it. "Perhaps," he suggested, "they think you are an American spy." I told him I was not, but I was not sure he believed me.

The letters inside the envelopes did nothing for my peace of mind. Although none expressed anti-Fascist sentiments, some expressed the hope I was maintaining a discreet silence about my political opinions, and one of them mentioned the lunch Carlo Tresca gave for me. I bitterly pictured myself answering the letters from a Fascist jail cell. For a while I considered reporting the matter to the American consulate but, with Italian-American relations at their lowest ebb, I decided it would be a waste of time.°

Noticing my distress, my cousin tried to assure me there was no cause for worry. "If they wanted to nab you, they would have by now. They must have decided you aren't a spy." I worried anyway and began counting the number of days that remained before I could embark from Genoa on the *Rex*. I thought of canceling my itinerary and returning on the earliest available ship but was reluctant to forgo the magazine assignments I had undertaken. Nor would my pride permit me to be frightened off so quickly.

The opened letters were not my only concern. I was also upset by the frequency with which Italians mistook me for a native. In the fever of my anxiety I began to feel I was gradually losing my identity as an American. The most shattering of these experiences took place in the Palermo train station when an elderly, well-dressed traveler, to whom I had turned for assistance in unraveling the mysteries of the timetable for Rome, began berating me for trying to make a fool of him by pretending I was a foreigner. In vain, I tried to explain that I was an American unaccustomed to the Italian railroad time system. With blazing eyes and flailing arms, he kept scolding me until I felt obliged to prove, with my American passport, that I was indeed a foreigner. He left without apologizing, still angry, declaring at the top of his voice that Americans had no business being in Italy.

After that I made certain that my Italian was so broken that no one could doubt I was a foreigner. I also wore my loudest neckwear, hoping it would contribute to my identity as an

° The Fascist press was then attacking the United States almost daily for its role in persuading the League of Nations to impose economic sanctions on Italy. The old Fascist party slogan *Mi ne frego* (I don't give a damn) had been resurrected and was being displayed in store windows to advertise the contempt of Italians for those who had the gall to object to their Ethiopian conquest.

American. But of my physical features, which were undeniably Italian, I could do nothing. Although I hungrily sought the company of American tourists as a means of asserting my birthright, at times they only emphasized my sensation of not really being one of them. On the way to Rome an American girl, trying to open a recalcitrant window, asked for my assistance in broken Italian. When, after opening the window, I commented in English on the universal stubbornness of train windows, she and her companions expressed amazement that I spoke English so well. Not until we had an extended conversation were they convinced I was a native American.

At the train station in Rome I was met by Uncle Giuseppe's son Gerlando, who had taken time off from his regular duties as Edda Mussolini's personal guard. Gerlando had never been a coffinmaker, but he had his father's gloomy temperament. Moments after we embraced he began complaining about his health and the dangers of bacterial infection, an obsession which I soon discovered compelled him to wash his hands several times each hour. I aggravated his dolefulness when I rejected the invitation to share his one-room apartment and informed him I had made hotel reservations. "But I am your cousin," he kept protesting. "Why should you go to a hotel? They will only rob you."

On the way to the hotel we stopped at a sidewalk cafe. The most pressing subject on Gerlando's mind was the girl his father had selected to be his wife. Contrary to the impression he had given Uncle Giuseppe, he was by no means confident of his father's taste in such matters, although as a dutiful Sicilian son he was prepared to spend the rest of his life with the girl. He was bursting with curiosity to know what she was like. His first questions were about Maria's anatomy. Did she have good legs? Was she fatter than a woman should be? What about her breasts—were they really as large as they seemed to be in her photograph? Had I noticed the size of her feet? He kept firing such questions at me while pointing to women passing by and asking me to compare them with his prospective wife. When he

had finished with Maria's anatomy, he began asking me questions about her disposition.

I finally changed the subject by asking him, with as much
casualness as I could fake, whether it was the Italian government's policy to open letters addressed to foreign visitors. He
immediately wanted to know why I would ask such a question.
When I explained, he looked deeply disturbed and stared at me
without saying anything for a while. Then, speaking almost in a
whisper, he asked if I had published anything that might be
interpreted as being unfriendly to the Italian government. I
admitted to some articles the Fascists might not like, among
them reviews of books by Alberto Moravia, Ignazio Silone, and
Luigi Pirandello. The only one of these names he recognized
was that of Pirandello.

"Why in the world would you want to criticize the work of
such an important writer?" he hissed. "Don't you know that he
won the Nobel Prize?" I tried to explain that my criticism of
Pirandello was not based on his work, which I admired, but on
his willingness to be touted as a champion of the Fascist
regime. "And what is wrong with that?" Gerlando replied. He
was plainly alarmed that I would dare find fault with the
establishment. From subsequent encounters I was to learn that
although he was no Fascist zealot, he staunchly believed that
any government establishment, regardless of its nature, should
be supported.

The letter to the Minister of Propaganda, which I now
produced, had a calming effect on him until he began worrying
that since we shared the same name, there was the possibility
that my anti-Fascist views might be attributed to him. He was
relieved to learn that my writings were signed "Jerre Mangione," though not to the extent of persisting in his demand
that I share his apartment.

At the hotel he urged me not to mention the opened letters
to anyone; if there were any others, I was to let him know, not
by telephone but in person. As for the letter to the Minister of
Propaganda, I was to present it as soon as possible since the

authorities would know by morning, through the hotel registration, that I had arrived in Rome. He was anxious to spend the evening with me, but I explained I had a dinner date with an American girl I had met on the train. "If you want a woman," Gerlando said, "it would be better if you went to a bordello," repeating almost verbatim his father's advice to me in Sicily. "It's her company I want, not her body," I replied, and he looked at me as though he were certain by now that I was insane.

The next morning, half expecting to be arrested, I set out to deliver my letter to the Minister of Propaganda. The governmental building housing his offices bristled with armed guards. When challenged by one of them, I showed him the envelope of my letter with the Minister's name and was promptly escorted to an elevator reserved for the use of the Minister and his chief officials. At my destination a black-shirted receptionist greeted me with a single word: *"Dica"* (Speak). In my most broken Italian I explained the purpose of my visit. Without saying a word, he disappeared into another room and was gone for an agonizingly long time. On his return he guided me through a long winding corridor to a palatial room dominated by a gigantic photo portrait of Il Duce, then left me alone. Not until I heard the command *"Dica"* did I note that under the portrait, seated at a desk, was a slim young man in Fascist garb.

Intimidated by the severity of the voice, I advanced and, without speaking, handed him my letter of introduction. The hardness vanished as soon as he was finished reading it; he seemed genuinely sorry to inform me that the Minister was not in Rome and would not return for ten days. Was there anything he himself could do for me in the meantime? Or would I prefer to wait until the Minister got back? There was no need for me to speak to the Minister personally, I replied; all I required for now were some photographs of Sicily which might be of interest to readers of *Travel.*

His manner became even more affable as he summoned a clerk and instructed him to take me to his office and supply me with whatever I needed. Within minutes, the clerk assembled a great batch of photographs; an unduly large number of them depicted scenes from classic Greek tragedies performed in recent years in the ancient amphitheaters of Siracusa and Taormina. In order to lighten my load, I tried to return some of them, but the clerk insisted I take them all, maintaining that all Americans have a passionate love for Greek tragedy. In my jittery state, I was not disposed to disagree; nor did I resist when he pressed on me several thick pamphlets extolling the achievements of the Fascist regime.

As I was about to leave, a corner of my eye caught sight of my letter of introduction lying near the edge of the clerk's desk. I considered pocketing it in his presence, letting him assume it belonged to me but, out of fear that he might make an issue of its ownership, I decided there was nothing else to do but steal it. With this in mind, I told the clerk that I had almost forgotten I needed a photograph of Luigi Pirandello. Then, while he went to the files, I slipped the letter into a pants pocket. The clerk returned with two photographs—one of Pirandello, the other of his mistress, the actress Marta Alba. I now began worrying that he might notice the absence of the letter from his desk but, to my relief, as his final gesture of hospitality, the clerk offered to accompany me to the elevator.

At dinner that evening Gerlando was unimpressed by my account of the friendly treatment I had been accorded at the Minister's office. Government bureaucracy being slow, he darkly observed, it meant that the Minister's office had not yet been alerted by the officials who opened my mail. "If you're lucky," he added, "you'll be out of Italy before the word about you gets around." In view of his mood, I said nothing of the two letters I had picked up at the American Express office that afternoon which, like the others, had been opened and resealed. It was beginning to occur to me that, because of his association with the Department of Justice, I should never have mentioned the subject to him.

In an effort to be cheerful, I asked Gerlando what it was like to be the personal bodyguard of Mussolini's daughter, but he refused to discuss the subject. "How do I know," he asked, "that you wouldn't write about it?" Then, for the first time, I saw the suggestion of a smile on his face.

We were leaving the *trattoria* when a vast throng, such as one might see after the close of a big sporting event, came streaming toward us from the nearby Piazza del Popolo. When I asked for an explanation of the throng, Gerlando blandly replied that Mussolini must have just finished speaking from the balcony of his headquarters. I became angry and demanded to know why he hadn't let me know about the speech in time; surely, he must have realized that I would have wanted to watch Mussolini in action. Gerlando listened to me in surprise. "I had no idea you'd be interested," he said. "Why would you want to listen to him if you have no use for his philosophy of government?" Resisting the impulse to call him an imbecile, I tried to explain that my abhorrence of Mussolini's policies did not diminish my interest in him as a historical phenomenon. Only later did I realize that Gerlando would not have wished to run the risk of compromising himself by being seen in my company at a rally that was bound to be well attended by Fascist informers.

By now I had developed a sense of caution that sometimes veered on paranoia. When, a few days later, a British correspondent to whom I had a letter of introduction, offered to arrange private interviews with Mussolini and Pope Pius, I instantly invented excuses for turning down the offer. Though tempted by the opportunity of getting a close view of Il Duce, I rationalized that only by keeping a low profile could I escape being arrested and/or inducted in the Italian army. The prospect of having an interview with the Pope was easier to resist, although it would have given my mother something to brag about. I could not respect him for having capitulated to the Fascist regime. The idea of symbolically capitulating to him by kissing his ring (a gesture which I assumed was *de rigueur* in a private audience) was too distasteful.

Before leaving Rome I delivered two more letters of introduction, one to a leading Italian literary critic, Massimo
Bontempelli, who acknowledged that literary creativity under
the Fascist regime was at a low ebb; most of the books being
published in Italy were translations of standard foreign works.
However, when I asked him how much Fascist censorship had
to do with this state of affairs, Bontempelli said: "What
censorship?"

Without revealing that my source of information was the
Italian novelist Alberto Moravia, with whom I had recently
spent three days in New York, I told Bontempelli I had heard it
on good authority that Fascist officials required writers to
submit their manuscripts for approval before publication. There
was no such rule, Bontempelli maintained, though he admitted
that most Italian authors followed that practice "to avoid
misunderstandings."

In New York Moravia had informed me that his first novel,
The Indifferent Ones, had been withdrawn shortly after its
publication. "Unlike Hitler," Moravia had said, "Mussolini
doesn't burn books; he just quietly suppresses them."

Remembering this, I asked Bontempelli whether it was the
practice of the Fascist regime to withdraw from publication
books which they regarded with disfavor. Bontempelli denied
there was such a practice but acknowledged that writers who
did not submit their manuscripts for approval were "making
life more difficult for themselves."

Before I left, I asked his opinion of Ignazio Silone, explaining
that in the States he was regarded as Italy's most gifted fiction
writer. "Silone?" asked Bontempelli. "Never heard of him.
What has he written?" Pretending to be surprised by such
ignorance, I spoke enthusiastically of *Fontamara, Bread and
Wine,* and *Mr. Aristotle,* without revealing that their anti-
Fascist point of view precluded their publication in Mussolini's
Italy; I also skipped over the fact that Silone was living in Swiss
exile as an avowed enemy of the Fascist regime. "I'll look him
up," Bontempelli said and wrote Silone's name in a notebook.

Spreading the news of Silone among the Fascist writers I encountered fulfilled some need in me to identify myself as an anti-Fascist without actually admitting it. I could not understand what good it did but I kept on doing it, hoping perhaps that one of the writers might reveal himself to me as a secret admirer of Silone and his anti-Fascist stand.

My last letter of introduction was to the celebrated poet Fillipo Tommaso Marinetti, the founder of the Futurist movement and, later, one of the first members of the Fascist party. Though not yet sixty, he looked ancient and frail, a ghost of the vigorous figure he must have once been. Listening to the sepulchral inflection of his voice in the chiaroscuro of his heavily draped apartment, I recalled a couple of sentences from his writings that told of his enthusiasm for war. "We go into war singing and dancing," and "I glorify violent death as the crowning achievement of youth." ·

What manner of a poet could exult in the slaughter of men? It was this question that had brought me to his apartment. Through a welter of amenities I strained for clues to perversity, trying to take into account my antipathy to violence and to all the other arrogant aspects of the Fascist mystique that Marinetti championed. Was his love of war and violent death simply the expression of a surrealistic sensibility not to be judged by ordinary standards? Or was it the blatant nihilism of a rotting soul? I could reach no conclusion.

After we had run out of conversation, I indulged myself in the Ignazio Silone ploy. Hearing no new responses, I bade Marinetti good morning and hurriedly went out into the sunshine.

As in a Kafka situation, a pair of carabiniere came to the hotel one morning and asked me to accompany them to the nearby headquarters of the *Publica Sicurezza*. Their only explanation was that the commissioner wished to ask me some questions; they could not tell me how long it would take. In my frightened state, which I did my best to conceal, my first thought was to let Gerlando know what was happening. On asking if I could make a phone call, I was told I could telephone from the commissioner's office. On our way I changed my mind—Gerlando was not important enough to help me; I would only be compromising him. I would call the office of the American ambassador instead. But at the station I was immediately ushered into a room where the commissioner and an assistant were waiting to interrogate me; at that point the notion of insisting on making a phone call seemed indiscreet, if not actually incriminating. I decided to put it off until I learned the charges against me.

At first the questions were routine: where had I been since landing at Naples, how long did I intend to stay in Rome, where would I be going next. The commissioner, whose poker face revealed nothing more than a faint air of disdain, kept referring to a file which, I suspected, contained all the information being asked of me. Suddenly, without a change of expression, he sprung the question I had hoped would never be asked: Was I related to a certain Jerre Mangione?

The question was intended to trap me, I imagined, to tempt me into denying any connection with Jerre Mangione, so as to provide the authorities with incontrovertible evidence of my deceit; surely by now they must know, from the letters sent to me, the answer to the question. My best bet, I decided, was to tell the truth.

"Jerre" and "Gerlando" Mangione, I told the commissioner, were one and the same person, myself; "Jerre" was the Americanized version of my baptismal name "Gerlando."

"Gerlando," the commissioner observed in his monotonous voice, "is a Sicilian name."

My parents were both born in Sicily, I explained, in the province of Agrigento where Gerlandus, a Norman bishop of the twelfth century, had achieved the status of a saint. They had met in Rochester shortly after their migration there, and I was their firstborn. To emphasize my American birth and United States citizenship, I showed the commissioner my passport, which he had not yet asked to see.

He and his assistant glanced at it perfunctorily, as if it was of no importance, but kept it. Next the commissioner wanted to know the "purpose" of my trip. I was tempted to answer the question by producing my letter to the Minister of Propaganda, but was afraid that the commissioner might be aware of its theft. After I had described my journalistic mission, the commissioner wanted to know why I was making the journey at this particular time. I replied that it was the only time I could get off from my duties at the publishing house that employed me. I had said too much for now he was asking what kind of books McBride published. That line of questioning, which might involve a discussion about Ignazio Silone (although Italian writers did not seem to know about him, I was certain the police did), alarmed me to such a degree that I decided I had better produce the letter to the Minister of Propaganda after all.

As I watched for some change of expression in the commissioner's silvery face while he read the letter, I saw his eyebrows go up and the corners of his mouth go down. He passed the letter to the assistant, then made a notation in the file. After the assistant had read it, the two men conferred in whispers for a while. Then the commissioner, clearing his throat, handed me both the letter and my passport, and with a smile that struck me as sinister thanked me for answering his questions and bade me good day.

The suspicion that a foolproof trap was being prepared for me persisted, and I decided to leave Rome two days earlier than I had planned. Gerlando, who knew nothing of my session with the commissioner, was still worried about my safety, which he undoubtedly linked with his own. On our way to the train that was to take me to Florence, he begged me to stop writing anti-Fascist articles. "It is a foolish thing to do and it will get you nowhere. You can't afford to oppose a leader as powerful as Il Duce." I did not argue with him. As we embraced, I wished him a happy marriage with his Maria and asked him to let me know when it would happen so that I could send a gift. The train was pulling out of the station when he remembered to ask me when I would be returning to Italy.

"After the war," I replied.

He was not sure he had heard right. "What war?"

In the flesh the beauty of Florence exceeded my greatest expectations. I spent most of the first day in and around Il Duomo, fascinated by the vibrancy of Giotto's colors and moved by the exquisite simplicity of the cathedral's interior which, after the gaudy rococo of the Mezzogiorno churches, inspired a depth of serenity I had never before experienced in a religious place. Yet I could not sustain the serenity for long. In my anxious state I worried that it might, like a tranquilizing drug, blunt whatever wits I needed to survive my days in Italy.

My sense of apprehension mounted the next evening when I witnessed the spectacle of a Fascist militia, armed to the teeth, striding through the darkness with blazing torches while singing lustily of Italy's military might. I remembered then that Florence, once the fountainhead of humanism, had long been a stronghold of fascism, one of the first cities to support Mussolini during his drive for black-shirted power in the early twenties. In such a city, I thought, the chances of surviving another session with the police would be nil, and I cut my stay in half.

On the last day I climbed to the top of Giotto's tower for a comprehensive view of the city. On the way up the long and lonely stairway, strangely devoid of tourists, I stopped at each landing to inspect the clutter of damaged and abandoned statuary, which had apparently been placed there for storage. The statues lay about in surrealistic disarray—at one landing Saint Peter was cozily ensconced in the arms of the Madonna— with their plaster surfaces offering an open invitation to passing graffito writers.

I noticed scribblings of names, dates, declarations of love and even bits of poetry, but nowhere could I find a single slogan or sentiment of an anti-Fascist nature. I had already known the same disappointment in the other cities on my itinerary. Except for occasional news items in the *Paris Herald* reporting the arrest of some anti-Fascists, one might have thought that there were no Italians opposing the Mussolini regime.

The dazzling panorama from the top of the tower could not dispel the bitterness of this reflection. On my way down, I reexamined the grafitti more carefully, hoping I had overlooked some expression of antifascism, but found nothing. Had Matteoti, the Roselli brothers, Arturo di Lorentis and all the other Italian heroes who had died in the cause of antifascism been completely forgotten? It seemed incredible that Mussolini's power had become so pervasive as to have inhibited all graffiti writers who had ever visited the tower. On the final landing, in a burst of daring, I quickly wrote the words *Abbasso Mussolini* (Down with Mussolini) across the torso of a female saint with a broken nose, then fled, my heart pounding as though I had just provided the Italian police with their final nail for my coffin.

Venice, except for the last few hours there, was far less worrisome, mainly because I was able to lose myself in the fantasy of the city. On the third day, hungry for conversation, I became acquainted with a solemn dark-eyed girl who looked enough like me to be a cousin. I had spotted her while part of a group that was watching at high noon two robot blackamoors above the cathedral clock as they took turns swinging their hammers against a huge bronze bell to toll the hour of the day. She noticed me watching her and smiled; moments later I was by her side, and we were chatting away like old acquaintances. She had plain features and her body was small and thin, but she was warm and personable and, as I had guessed, a Sicilian. Her native town was Morreale, on the outskirts of Palermo. What was a Sicilian *signorina* doing so far from her family? I inquired. Venice, she replied, was preferable to the other cities where she had worked. When I asked about the nature of her work, she seemed abashed. "Don't you really know?" she asked shyly. Then I knew: she was a prostitute.

That I had not identified her as one sooner pleased Carmela. She could not have been more than nineteen, but she had been in the profession for three years, previously in Palermo, Naples, Bologna, and Rome. Venice suited her best; as the farthest city from Sicily, there was less likelihood of encountering any of her relatives; also, only in Venice could she operate without a license and without being attached to a bordello, as the law required. She disliked brothels: the work was too hard; she was obliged to take on anyone who wanted her. As a free-lancer, she could more or less choose her customers and work as much or as little as she pleased. The lack of a license created a problem with the police now and then, but since prostitution was one of the city's major tourist attractions, the authorities tended to be lenient.

Carmela did nothing for my libido, but I was reluctant to part with her and suggested we lunch at some restaurant of her own choosing, preferably one not frequented by tourists. Carmela said she would take me to a *trattoria* where she and her friends ate regularly and cheaply. "If you're lucky," she smiled, "we'll find my roommate, Zina, there. She is a real beauty." On the way I learned more about Carmela's past. Her father had thrown her out when he learned she was pregnant by a lover who had disappeared. With the secret assistance of an aunt, she found sanctuary in a Palermo convent, but as soon as her son was born she was presented with the alternative of either giving him up and taking the veil or leaving the convent with him. She left the next day and arranged to board the infant with a spinster friend of the aunt's; a few hours later she turned to prostitution as the only means available for supporting herself and the child. "One day when my son is old enough to understand the tragedy of life, we'll be together. For the present I do the best I can and pray to the Blessed Virgin."

In the slums of the Rialto Carmela led me down a crooked alley to her *trattoria*. As we entered, there were greetings shouted at Carmela from all directions of the crowded room. A woman demanded to know who I was. Carmela ignored her and made a beeline for a table which was occupied by an apple-cheeked man, small enough to be a jockey, and a stunning blonde with vivacious green eyes, Carmela's roommate, Zina. Carmela introduced me as a relative from New York, and I was immediately made to feel part of the group. Pino, the small man, showed me and Carmela a heavy gold watch he had stolen that morning from a German tourist, saying it was "always a pleasure to steal from those Nazi pigs."

He asked me to decipher the inscription engraved on the watch, but I did not know enough German to understand it. Zina, who was seated next to me, said: "Had Pino known you were going to be here, he would have stolen a watch with an English inscription on it. He's the best pickpocket in Venice."

I found it difficult to keep my eyes off her. She was tastefully dressed in a simple black satin suit which seemed incongruous in the restaurant's rowdy atmosphere, and she was as lively as she was beautiful. That she enjoyed her calling was obvious from her eager flow of shop talk. Apropos of the stolen watch, she told of having to say no that morning to a rich German businessman who had offered to pay three times her customary fee. "Every time I refused, he would raise the fee. Finally, I had to tell him the reason: I had just begun to have my period. Isn't that the damndest luck?"

Pino said he could not sympathize with her. "There are a hundred ways of satisfying a man, especially a rich man. I don't have to tell you that. . . ."

Zina retorted that with a perfect stranger there could only be one way for her. "It's a different matter, of course, if I get to know and like him. . . ." She smiled at me, as though sensing how much she appealed to me, then turned to Carmela. "I'm terribly sorry, *cara*. We could have used all that money."

Carmela told her to stop worrying; they had no unpaid bills.

Zina declared Carmela the best roommate in the world, then described a special service she had performed for her in their

apartment when she (Zina) had come home one night with a
pezzo grosso from Milan. In bed she found that she had no
appetite for him. "He was too old and I was too tired." Before
the Milanese could become aware of her feelings, she went into
Carmela's bedroom, on the pretext of having to go to the
bathroom, and enlisted her roommate's help. While Zina
waited in her bed, Carmela, unidentifiable in the dark, slipped
into bed with the Milanese. After she had successfully screwed
him and he had fallen asleep, the two girls changed beds again.
"The old fool never knew the difference," Zina laughed.
"When he left, he gave me a big tip and said I was the best lay
he had ever had in Venice."

While we were all having espresso and cognac, some of the
other diners, curious about Carmela's American friend, came to
our table. One was a thief, a friend of Pino's, who showed us a
box of old silverware and two diamond rings he was taking to a
fence. We were also visited by a homosexual pimp who
complained to Zina that one of his girls, who owed him money,
had just run off with a student. Zina, who knew the girl and the
student, was amused. "Wasn't that the same student you've
been living with?" she asked. He admitted it was, adding that
the student also owed him money. "Come to think of it," he
said, "I've not only been cheated but also cuckolded," and
everyone laughed.

Addressing himself to me, the pimp said that he had heard
that prostitution was no longer a lucrative business in the
States, the reason being that American men could get all the
sex they wanted since nearly all American women were promiscuous. *Did I agree with that?* I replied that he should not
believe everything he heard. When the pimp began arguing
with me, Carmela called him an idiot and contended that if
prostitution wasn't thriving in the States it was simply because
American women, unlike those in Italy, could find better ways
of making a living.

"But what better way is there?" Zina commented and

pressed her thigh against mine. Moments later, to my great disappointment, she left with Pino, saying they had a business appointment and would see us later.

Our final visitors were a Neapolitan couple, a pretty brunette in her twenties and her middle-aged husband who, Carmela told me later, was also her pimp. He claimed to be "fascinated" that I was from New York and asked if I knew any of his Brooklyn relatives. I had heard the same question throughout my journey and had a pat answer for it—I had been in Brooklyn so few times that I did not even know my own relatives there. He then wanted to know what had brought me to Italy, initiating a series of questions that were disconcertingly similar to those asked by the Roman police commissioner. As the interrogation continued, I could see Carmela becoming increasingly annoyed. Finally, in the middle of one of the questions, her patience snapped. Pushing back her chair, she announced that we had an urgent appointment to keep. "*Peccato,*" the Neapolitan said as we shook hands. "Perhaps we can see you later."

When I asked for the check, I was informed that Pino had taken care of it. As soon as we were outdoors, Carmela told me about the Neapolitan couple and said they could not be trusted. She and her friends suspected them of being informers and were always careful of what was said in their presence. "No matter how innocent a foreigner may be," Carmela added, "those two can cause him all kinds of trouble. I hope you didn't mind my interrupting. . . ."

Carmela dropped the subject to tell me that she was on her way to a hotel where she had an appointment with a "client," then asked how long I planned to stay in Venice; she was certain I had made a hit with her roommate and that, if I wished to spend some time with Zina in a couple of days, she would be glad to arrange it. But what she had told me about the Neapolitans had flooded my mind with worry, and Zina now seemed like a luxury I could do without. I wasn't certain how long I could stay in Venice, I told Carmela, and suggested that she and I have lunch on the following day, this time at a restaurant where we could be alone. Carmela squeezed my hand and said she would meet me at noon in front of the cathedral clock.

I never saw Carmela again. Her comments about the Neapolitan couple plunged me more deeply into the icy abyss of my fear; I spent a sleepless night imagining the couple had already gone to the local police and soon they could come to fetch me for another interrogation. By now the authorities may have collated all their incriminating information, including my friendship with Carlo Tresca, who was undoubtedly near the top of Il Duce's assassination list, and my letter to the Minister would now carry no more weight than my American passport had so far. I decried my stupidity for having allowed Carlo to give me a send-off luncheon on my departure, convinced by now that there had been a Fascist informer at the restaurant. Even if I were being unduly pessimistic, I told myself, there was the possibility that the police might detain me long enough to miss my ship, due to sail from Genoa in four days. I was determined to be on it, safely returning home. By dawn I had decided I could not remain in Venice, and an hour later I was on my way to Genoa.

As the train pulled out of the station, Venice was enveloped in a sullen gray mist that matched my mood. During most of the trip I kept picturing Carmela waiting for me past the hour of our appointment, puzzled perhaps at first, then sadly relegating me to the large category of men in her past who could not be trusted. I wished I could have written her an explanation but I knew neither her surname nor address and had failed to note the name of the *trattoria* where we had lunched.

In Genoa I checked into a cheap hotel on the waterfront and got a room that afforded me a clear view of the pier where the *Rex* was to leave for New York. While I waited for it to dock, I prowled around the slums of the port district and found them even more miserable than those in Palermo. It was my only sightseeing. For as long as I could remember, my uncle Stefano had been urging me to visit the cemetery of Genoa, which he considered the most beautiful sight in Italy, but I lacked the courage to venture beyond the hotel area. After the *Rex* pulled into port, I remained in my room as much as possible, subsisting largely on bread, cheese and fruit washed down with a local wine, while keeping an eye on the ship. For two days my chief activity was reading newspapers. From the *Paris Herald* I learned that an American correspondent in Venice had been given twelve hours to leave Italy for having reported the arrest of eight anti-Fascists.

On the morning that the *Rex* began receiving passengers, I was among the first to board it.

NINE

Into the New Deal

Two unexpected developments, one international, the other personal, occurred simultaneously while the *Rex* was taking me toward New York and Anna, the Polish girl I had been living with for two years. Both were to affect the course of my life.

The international development, which began three days after we left Genoa, was presented to the passengers in such Fascist-garbled bulletins that not until I had access to the New York press did it become clear that the rebel forces of Generalissimo Francisco Franco, with the support of Hitler and Mussolini, had launched their attempt to overthrow the legal government of the Spanish Republic. The personal development, which I found far more astonishing, was suddenly falling in love and wanting to marry a thin blond American named Ellen Ingram, who had boarded the ship at Gibraltar after having spent a year in Spain painting landscapes.

I tried to talk myself out of love, reasoning that aside from our physical attraction for each other and our mutual interest in art, we had little else in common. There was also the alarming consideration that Ellen was, in spite of her artistic sensibility, a hopelessly rock-ribbed Methodist who, while admitting her attraction to me, refused to kiss, dance, or hold hands. But my reasoning powers were of no avail; I remained convinced that this was the girl with whom I would willingly spend the rest of my life.

At first it puzzled me that my ardor for Ellen seemed to increase with each fresh revelation of her old-fashioned virtues, which included the vow to preserve her virginity for the man she married. Only months later, when I had regained some of my wits, did it dawn on me that many of her values were the same ones I had derided in my Sicilian relatives, and what was even more absurd, were still a part of me. Apparently, the miracle of discovering Sicilian values lodged in an unmistakably American girl, the blond personification of my bicultural yearnings, was more than my American-Sicilian psyche could resist.

On the night before our arrival, as we were examining the stars at the prow of the ship, I asked her to become my wife. Ellen promptly turned me down, explaining she was already betrothed to a Methodist minister whom she would marry in a month's time. With all the desperate eloquence of one deeply enamored I tried to persuade her that as an artist she would be happier with me than with a minister. Although she was not encouraging, I pleaded with her all of the next morning. Even while the ship was docking and she was waving to her minister on the pier, who sedately waved back, I was begging her to marry me instead. It was no use. The prospect of becoming a minister's wife and producing a flock of newborn Methodists was far more appealing to her than being married to a struggling writer who was not a Methodist. When we parted, she let me kiss her for the first time but would not give me her address.

Whatever passion had existed between Anna and me had long run its course by the time I left for Italy. Yet we were still sufficiently attuned to each other for her to resent the change in me. For a few days she attributed my depressed state to returning to a job that no longer interested me, but when I showed little inclination to resume our sex life, she guessed what had happened and began questioning me, gently but relentlessly, until the whole story was out, including my futile efforts to reach Ellen by telephone with no other hope than to hear her voice again.

Anna, a devoted left winger, was outraged that I should think of marrying "a reactionary Methodist." She interpreted it as "obvious proof" of my eagerness to bring our relationship to an end and declared she would not live with a man who was in love with someone else. Having expected, naively, compassion instead of anger, I made no effort to dissuade her. That evening I moved out and took up residence with Wilbur Pearce (the Barnes and Noble store manager who had once before befriended me), whose young mistress had recently left him for a Communist labor organizer.

I envied Pearce's ability to be philosophical about his situation. "She's young and needs to have a fling now and then," he said. "But she'll be back." True enough, she returned within a month but only long enough to recuperate from an abortion she had while her lover was in the South organizing sharecroppers. Pearce cheerfully provided the sanctuary she needed. As soon as she was well, she borrowed some money from him and went South to join her lover. "She'll be back," he repeated.

In my attempt to forget Ellen I persuaded a girl in Chicago with whom I had been corresponding to come to Manhattan, and had a brief affair with her. The correspondence began several months before when, on a bet, I had replied to her advertisement in the "Personal Column" of the *Saturday Review of Literature*: "Bright young woman wants to correspond with bright young man interested in literature, music, and love." By the time I invited Mona to visit me in New York, our letters dealt almost exclusively with love. From the first encounter, there was no question of the sexual excitement we aroused in each other, but after a few days I began to feel like an imposter, an actor playing the role of the lover. I was still obsessed with the memory of Ellen and could not fully match the intensity of Mona's rapture. Accusing me of not being in love with her, she began striking out with the sharp points of her hurt until I felt impelled to admit my love for someone else. We remained friends, but it troubled me that I had encouraged her to travel all the way from Chicago for a love affair with no future. Before she returned home, however, I inadvertently made it up to her by bringing her to a fund-raising party for Loyalist Spain where she met the son of a philosophical anarchist who was to become her husband and eventually the father of their four children.

By now the Spanish Civil War had become the concern of every New York liberal and radical with an anti-Fascist bone in his body. The spirit of antifascism was reaching its zenith as it became increasingly clear that the success of the Franco-Hitler-Mussolini coalition in Spain was bound to stimulate Fascist activity throughout Europe and strengthen the burgeoning Fascist movement in the United States. But this was a minority point of view, held chiefly by the nation's intelligentsia. The rest of the population was either indifferent to the developments in Germany, Italy, and Spain or was inclined to believe the propaganda of right wingers that Hitler, Mussolini, and Franco were waging a holy war against the forces of communism. As far as the popular press and the general public were concerned, all anti-Fascists were either Communists or Communist sympathizers.°

Despite their minority status, the nation's anti-Fascists had taken for granted that Franklin D. Roosevelt would soon come to the rescue of the beleaguered Spanish Republic, or at least permit it to buy American arms for its fight against the Franco usurpers. But they had overestimated Roosevelt's sense of idealism. Roosevelt the politician prevailed over Roosevelt the anti-Fascist. Intent on piling up as large a vote as possible in the approaching presidential election of November 1936, he

° The Federal Bureau of Investigation held to this point of view even after the United States was at war with Germany and Italy. Suspected Communists or sympathizers were described in its files as having been "premature anti-Fascists."

shocked his anti-Fascist constituents and delighted the nation's right-wing elements by adopting a strict "hands off" policy of neutrality, which virtually assured the Franco forces of victory and undoubtedly hastened the advent of World War II.

In the same month that Roosevelt was reelected by one of the country's greatest landslide votes, the Franco forces, amply implemented with men and armaments from Mussolini and Hitler, were within striking distance of the gates of Madrid, and the Republic appeared to be doomed. At that point, as in an old-fashioned movie when the Marines arrive in the nick of time to disperse and slaughter the villains, anti-Fascist military units consisting of volunteers from the free countries of Europe began rushing to the assistance of the Loyalist defenders. The news that Franco's army was now being effectively repelled had an exhilarating effect on anti-Fascists everywhere. In the States it accelerated American help for Loyalist Spain, and it stimulated the creation of a volunteer military unit known as the Abraham Lincoln Brigade.

While Pope Pius was blessing additional troops that Mussolini was sending to join Franco's forces, the first group of American volunteers, pretending to be tourists, were crossing the Atlantic on the *Normandy*. By February 1937, more than three thousand members of the Lincoln Brigade had smuggled themselves across the French-Spanish border, some crawling on their hands and knees for hours to escape detection, and joined the battle for the defense of the Valencia road to Madrid.

My former roommate, Benny Birlowitz, whom I had not seen since I had left him with a room full of bedbugs, was among the first to volunteer in the Lincoln Brigade. He reappeared in New York at a party I attended for a group of volunteers about to leave for Spain. When I did not at once realize that he was one of the departing volunteers, he became offended. "What's the matter?" he demanded. "Don't you think I have the guts to be a soldier?" I could not let on that with his diminutive body and poor eyesight he struck me as the most unlikely of soldiers. Trying to imagine Benny on the battlefield brought home to me, more tellingly than anything else, how desperate the military situation of the Spanish Republic must be.

He spoke of becoming a mighty warrior with the same self-assurance he had once described his plan to write the great American novel. After a few more drinks, he wanted to know when I would be joining him in Spain. I made some excuse about my bad back which, five years after its injury, still compelled me to wear a corset most of the time. Had he been more sober, I would have added that even with a stronger back it was doubtful that I had the stomach for killing anyone. As I was leaving, he caught me by the arm and asked me again when I was going to Spain. Without waiting for an answer, he glared at me and intoned: "Any guy who won't fight for the Loyalists is no friend of mine." Then he stopped glaring and, at the doorway, gave me a bear hug.°

While I could not go to Spain I could, it developed, go to Washington and become an "information specialist" for the Resettlement Administration, one of the New Deal's more radical enterprises. Curiously enough, the war in Spain was responsible for this change in my life. The job had been awarded to Alvah Bessie, the author, but he had suddenly decided to fight with the Lincoln Brigade instead, and his agent, my friend Elizabeth Nowell, had urged me to apply for it. I went after the job as if my life depended on it, partly because I was bored with my work at McBride's, and partly because my emotional involvement with the left-wing movement made me anxious to join the New Deal and work for that benighted third of the nation who, in Roosevelt's phrase, were "ill-housed, ill-clad, ill-nourished."

In January 1937, in the same month that the Resettlement Administration's name was changed to the Farm Security Administration (a name that struck as much fear in me as

° Approximately half of the Americans who served in the Lincoln Brigade lost their lives, but Benny Birlowitz was not one of them. On noting his ineptness as a soldier, his comrades kept him out of combat by electing him to be their librarian.

"Business and Finance" once had), the agency's director of information wrote to say that of the fifty-two candidates he had interviewed for the job, I was the one he had decided to hire. "We shall be very happy to have you here and I think the whole matter will work out well. . . ."

Yet I was already beginning to question my ability to cope with the job. I marveled at my audacity in applying for it. What did I know about the problems of destitute farmers, the main business of the agency? The batch of pamphlets the director had sent me as samples of the kind of writing I would be doing were both impressive and intimidating. "The Source of our Wealth is Our Land, and Our Civilization and National Well-being Rest on it," one of them proclaimed. The pamphlets told how farm foreclosures, bankruptcies, and unprecedented low prices for agricultural products had forced more than a million farm families to go on relief rolls. "They were victims of trends which had manifested themselves over a long period of years. . . ."

To start reversing the trends, the Roosevelt administration, in 1935, created the Resettlement Administration in the Department of Agriculture which was headed by Dr. Rexford Guy Tugwell, one of the most messianic of the original New Deal brain trusters. In a program of remarkable magnitude that evoked Tugwell's famous slogan "Make America Over," the new agency launched a multipronged program to benefit both the nation's destitute farmers and the land they could not profitably farm because it had suffered either from erosion or overcultivation.

One of the agency's most socialistic activities was to establish new communities for some of the farmers who had been made landless by the severe droughts, dust storms, and floods that devastated large areas of the nation in 1930, 1934, and early in 1936. In these "resettlement" communities, indigent farmers could make a fresh start with government loans and communally shared agricultural equipment, which no single farmer could afford by himself.

The pamphlets admitted that the Resettlement Administration could reach only a fraction of the indigent farmers in need of help. And although the agency had begun acquiring some ten million acres of substandard acreage with the intention of restoring some of it to its original grassland state, and reforesting or converting the rest of the acquired land into parks and refuges for wild animals and birds, it did not expect to solve in the foreseeable future land problems which had been completely ignored for decades. Actually, the problems that faced the agency were far more serious than any of the pamphlets suggested. None of the literature evoked the grimness of a more recently published report by the President's Committee on Tenancy, which detailed the horrifying living conditions of 25 percent of the nation's farm families.

Despite my apprehension about dealing with matters which, except for a few childhood months as a fruit picker on farms around Rochester, were alien to me, there was satisfaction in the prospect of joining a government agency that was so zealously dedicated to the needs of one of the nation's largest group of disadvantaged Americans. That some of the New Deal critics were damning its programs as "socialistic" and its head, Rexford G. Tugwell, as a "revolutionary" confirmed my positive feelings about the agency. What I did not know at the time was that, as a concession to the more conservative elements of the Democratic party, Tugwell was being pushed out of the New Deal just as I was coming into it.

The title "information specialist," I was soon relieved to learn, had no formidable connotation. It was simply a civil-service euphemism for government employees producing material which, outside of government, would have gone by the name of publicity. My writing consisted chiefly of news releases and articles bylined by the agency's top-echelon officials. It was no more difficult than turning out book blurbs, often easier since it was unnecessary to strain for the extravagant claims encouraged by Robert McBride. After a few weeks I stopped worrying about my inability to cope with the job, and began worrying that I might tire of it unless I was given something more challenging to do. I longed to ghostwrite impassioned speeches that would please the liberals and infuriate the reactionaries, or create original films, such as Pare Lorentz's Whitmanesque *The Plough that Broke the Plains* and *The River* (both produced under the agency's auspices), or work with my colleague Roy Stryker, who was documenting the plight of American farmers and farmlands with a staff of the nation's most gifted photographers. But with my superficial awareness of farm problems it hardly seemed likely that I would be asked to be anything more than a skillful hack.

I might have gradually become reconciled to that fate had it not been for the accident of sharing a house with three other men, two of whom were top executives of the WPA Federal Writers' Project: Henry G. Alsberg, its national director, and Clair Laning, one of his chief assistants. Along with a friend I had originally known in New York, Wallace Krimont, the four of us lived in comparative luxury with an old black woman who cooked and laundered for us and wistfully reminisced of the years when she had been a servant of "important people," the rich and socially elite McLeans, whose former mansion on Dupont Circle now housed the national staff of the Federal Writers' Project.

Listening to Henry Alsberg's incessant shop talk at the dinner table drastically altered my impressions of the Federal Writers' Project which, like those of the general public, were based on the lurid newspaper accounts of the strikes, demonstrations, and scandals rampant in the Project's New York City office, recently described as a "hotbed of left-wing shenanigans." One unforgettable episode involved the director of that office, the one-legged poet Orrick Johns, who had been beaten into an unconscious state and set on fire by a sailor whose girlfriend (a Project staff member) the poet had been bedding. From Alsberg and his colleagues I soon learned that although it was true the New

York City Project was a maelstrom of conflicting personalities and ideologies, the forty-eight state projects, though beset by the same severe obstacles of periodic firings and administrative blunders, were working assiduously to produce the hundreds of volumes in the American Guide Series that would eventually provide the nation with its first detailed self-portrait.

The story of the Federal Writers' Project began to excite me. An unprecedented adventure in collective culture, it was one of four nationwide arts projects for destitute artists, musicians, and actors operating under the aegis of the Works Progress Administration. The four arts projects, launched in the fall of 1935, immediately absorbed some forty thousand men and women from the relief rolls and gave them the opportunity to exercise their talents while earning a subsistence wage which varied in the states from $100 to $50 a month.° That the federal government would dare put persons of that ilk on its own payroll outraged most of the American press and the anti-New Deal politicians when the projects began. Harry Hopkins, the WPA overlord, had a neat retort for them: "Hell, they've got to eat just like other people."

The Writers' Project was currently under heavy attack in the press and in Congress because, unlike its three sister projects which had already piled up an impressive record of achievement, the writers had nothing more to show than a few skinny pamphlets. Alsberg, in his public statements, patiently tried to explain that it takes a longer time to prepare a book than it does to paint a mural, produce a play, or stage a concert, but the attacks continued. At the dinner table Alsberg would occasionally ask my advice about some of the publishing problems that were preventing the Project from issuing its material more rapidly. When I suggested he augment his

---

° A comprehensive history of the Writers' Project is available in my book *The Dream and the Deal: the Federal Writers' Project, 1935–1943*, Little, Brown, 1972; Avon Books, paperback edition, 1974, Banyan Books library edition, 1976.

Washington staff with someone who had experience in the publishing world, he promptly offered me the job.

As fascinated as I was by the Writers' Project, my first inclination was to reject the offer. Lining up sponsors for publishable manuscripts and negotiating contracts with publishers was a job for an extrovert, I told myself; it meant being a salesman, not with my typewriter but with the most gauche part of my anatomy, my tongue. Not realizing the nature of my reservations, Alsberg said it would be "insane" of me to refuse a job with so important a title as "national coordinating editor," especially as I could have it without taking any cut in my current salary. (It was this sort of specious logic that endeared him to his friends.) What about the destitute farmers and their problems? I asked him. How could I abandon them and my boss, M. E. Gilfond, who had selected me out of fifty-two applicants?

"Easily," responded Alsberg, who was as full of pronouncements as an Old Testament prophet. "Let some yokel worry about the destitute farmers. You'll do better worrying about destitute writers."

Eager though I was to work for the Writers' Project, it took me more than two weeks to summon enough courage to let Gilfond know I had been offered a job that had greater appeal for me than my present one. He was a man with a steel-trap brain, but he failed to realize how much I wanted the Project job. My apologetic tone must have given him the impression that I had not quite made up my mind. He appealed to my sense of caution: the job I had was far more secure than the one on the Writers' Project since it was part of the Department of Agriculture which, unlike the WPA, was a permanent agency. He pointed out that the Project job, unlike my present one, was excluded from civil-service benefits and might not survive the next WPA appropriation.

When Gilfond realized he was making no headway with these arguments (after all the job insecurity I had experienced, I considered it a normal state), he proposed sending me on a

ten-day tour of some southern states where I would get a
firsthand view of some of the agency's projects in action. He
was confident that once I was able to relate to the reality of the
agency's work in the field, I would return to Washington with a
surge of enthusiasm that would preclude taking any other job.
"If the trip doesn't do that for you," he promised, "then I'll
release you to the Writers' Project."

Although I could not imagine changing my mind, my conscience would not permit me to reject his proposition. Three
days later I was heading south in an old Buick with two of my
colleagues, a field supervisor in his forties by the name of John
Sperry, and Philip Brown, a young writer who had been reared
on an upstate New York farm that neighbored Rex Tugwell's.
The titular commander of the expedition and the owner of the
Buick was Sperry, but Brown did all the driving. During most
of the journey Sperry sat in the back seat sipping bourbon and
becoming increasingly congenial. Brown and I made the most
of the situation by varying the planned itinerary to make stops
that were unrelated to the business of the Resettlement Administration, such as Jefferson's home in Monticello, the spring-
blooming gardens of Charlottesville, and several coastal
beaches, including one where Brown narrowly missed being
shot by riflemen using the area as a target range. Our commander seldom interfered, though at one point he imperiously
ordered a twenty-three-mile retreat into a county that sold
liquor as soon as he discovered we were traveling through a
county that did not.

In Richmond, our first nonscheduled stop, I called on James
Branch Cabell, with whom I had corresponded during my
McBride years but never met. In the stillness of his study, away
from his wife and son, I tried to penetrate the mask he wore of
the proper Virginia gentleman. Aware that the New Deal and
its radical programs were abhorrent to him, I looked for some
slippage of the mask as I described, with more enthusiasm than
I felt, my contribution to the Resettlement Administration's

program for succoring impoverished farmers and exhausted land. Although he had invited my remarks by inquiring about the nature of my job, the subject, so alien to this gracious southern atmosphere, must have struck him as a gross intrusion on his life style which had long ago successfully divided the world into two separate and distinct spheres: the titillating but orderly fantasies of a make-believe world that were the stuff of *Jurgen* and his other famous novels, and his day-by-day existence as a Virginia Brahmin faithfully conforming to all the restrictions of respectability.

As we chatted, the mask revealed nothing new, least of all the supreme irony of Cabell's life that had come to my attention the moment I set foot in his home. The author of the novels that had captivated critics and readers with their scintillating ironical nuances was the father of the feebleminded lad who, with his half-witted smile, had taken charge of my wraps at the door.

We traveled nearly two thousand miles through Virginia, North Carolina, Tennessee, Georgia, and South Carolina, meeting with county agents in the employ of our agency and talking with their farmer clients. A few of the farmers looked vigorous and optimistic; they and their families had not known poverty long enough to have been broken by it, and it appeared that with government assistance they could earn a decent living again. There were many more of the others, farm families that had never known anything but poverty at the rock-bottom level and hoped for nothing more than continued survival. Every variety of erosion afflicted them: poor housing, inadequate food, bad health, and chronic despair.

Not since the slums of Sicily and Genoa had I beheld such overwhelming poverty. But here, without the presence of Italian bravura, it seemed to me to be far more abject. The houses were rickety shacks with leaking roofs and gaps in the walls that let in rain and wind. Some had no windows and doors, no running water, no indoor toilets. Large families were jammęd into two- or three-room shacks. Among them was a family with thirteen children and only three beds. The youngest of the children, thin and pale, grouped themselves around the mother like a gang of hungry suckling puppies. The same family kept a cow in a pen that fitted as snugly as a glove, but the cow was too emaciated to give milk. Like the other families we visited, this one was getting some government help, but it was obviously too little.

The field supervisor accompanying us said that 80 percent of the families who applied to him for governmental assistance were turned down, either for lack of funds or because they were not judged promising enough for rehabilitation. Although all the supervisors we encountered were experts in their work, I noted a wide disparity in their intelligence and compassion. The best of them knew how to deal with indigent farmers without hurting their pride; others were tight-lipped and blunt, plainly contemptuous of their clients for being poor. Their treatment of us expressed a certain degree of deference because we were from Washington, but some of the supervisors could not conceal their resentment at being obliged to answer our questions. Only after they had gradually realized we were not there to spy on them but to educate ourselves about their work did they show any friendliness. Whether we met with supervisors or clients, an omnipresent problem was trying to overcome their innate hostility for Northerners.

Before long we learned that one of the standard procedures among southern men for achieving some degree of cordiality with strangers was to urinate together. As soon as introductions had been made, someone in the group would unbutton his fly and take out his penis, and the others would immediately follow suit. Dogs have a similar protocol, except that they line up in order to urinate on the same spot. The men, on the other hand, urinated more or less in unison and chose their own watering places.

However, no amount of group urinating could dispel the prejudice that the Italian sound of my name instantly inspired among the Southerners we met. As soon as they heard it and took into account my Latin features, they literally turned their backs to me. From their viewpoint, I rated far worse than a damnyankee: I was some goddamned foreigner who had no business being in the United States government and even less business asking questions about their work. After a few days of this, Brown and Sperry, disgusted with such blatant bigotry and not knowing how else to cope with it, began introducing me as Smith instead of Mangione. That solved the problem. As "Jerry Smith" I became as socially acceptable as Brown and Sperry.

Only once, while traveling in Tennessee, did the change of name create confusion. Toward evening, after seven hours of travel over bumpy roads that were originally intended for mule-driven wagons, we arrived at Penderlea, a recently established homestead settlement, with the hope of spending the night there. As soon as we drove into the place, the manager of the settlement ordered us to leave. Regulations, he claimed, made it illegal for outsiders to remain there overnight. Sperry, suspecting that the manager's anxiety to be rid of us involved something more than a lack of hospitality, argued that he had never heard of such regulations, that we were not "outsiders," that, in any case, he could not eject us without written authorization from Washington. The manager was furious. "I'll have you out of here in less than an hour," he yelled and disappeared into his office.

Confident that it was too late in the day for the manager to reach our Washington office, we wandered around the settlement until we found a young couple who were willing to put us up for the night. Before retiring, we learned from them what it was that the manager had hoped to conceal from us: the residents of the settlement, thoroughly dissatisfied with his undemocratic policies, were in the process of organizing a general strike as a means of letting Washington know they wanted a new manager.

The next morning Gilfond sent the manager the authorization he had requested. The telegram read: "Okay for Sperry

and Brown to leave, but who the hell is Jerry Smith and what
the hell has happened to Jerry Mangione?"

A few miles out of Penderlea, still chortling over Gilfond's
telegram, we telephoned to tell him about the impending strike
and to dispel the mystery of Jerry Smith.

Throughout the journey we saw enough evidence of land and
human erosion to convince us that only the government was in
a position to rehabilitate the barren land and the people who
could no longer eke a living from it. Near Chattanooga we
passed through a ten-mile stretch of unmitigated devastation
that was beyond recovery and outside the province of governmental intercession. The land, which had been poisoned to
death by the chemical fumes of neighboring copper mines, was
like a huge layer of ash, a gigantic cadaver. Yet in this blighted
expanse where the atmosphere was putrid, where one would
not expect the lowliest animals to survive, stood the community
of Duckworth, a company town with rows of gray houses where
the miners and their families lived. Nothing I had ever seen
proclaimed more loudly man's willingness to subject himself to
danger and ugliness in his search for a livelihood; it also
advertised the extent to which management, in the name of
free enterprise and profits, is willing to ignore human misery.

Tennessee provided other surprises. While we were admiring
the lilting landscape around Dayton, Brown brought the Buick
to an abrupt stop and pointed to a sign with an arrow that read
"William Jennings Bryan University." Curiosity impelled us to
follow the arrow until we came upon a bleak, treeless campus
with a desultory group of buildings that looked as though they
had been ravaged by fire or bombs. Accenting the desolation of
the scene was an out-of-tune rendering on the cornet of
"Onward Christian Soldiers." The performer was a pimply
faced student, the only person in sight, who informed us that
there had been no destruction. The campus buildings had been
partially constructed, then abandoned for lack of funds. The
university, nonetheless, continued with some sixty students and
nine faculty members who instructed them in intensive Bible

training and hymn music. After a four-year course the graduates went to the Belgian Congo as missionaries.

Eleven years had passed since this area achieved international fame as the setting for the "Monkey Trial," in which a
twenty-four-year-old schoolteacher by the name of John T.
Scopes had been charged with violating a recently enacted
state law forbidding the teaching of "any theory that denies the
story of the divine creation of man as taught in the Bible." But
the trial's two chief protagonists were Clarence Darrow, the
nation's most prominent champion of liberal causes and under-
dogs, who had been engaged by the American Civil Liberties
Union to defend Scopes, and William Jennings Bryan, who had
been Secretary of State and a presidential candidate in three
election campaigns. Darrow, a hero of American intellectuals,
was known to be an atheist, while Bryan was a strict Fundamentalist who insisted that the statements in Genesis be
interpreted literally. H. L. Mencken, while reporting the trial,
wrote of him:

> Once he had one leg in the White House and the nation
> trembled under his roars. Now he is a tinpot pope in the
> Coca-Cola belt and a brother to the forlorn pastors who
> belabor halfwits in galvanized iron tabernacles behind the
> railroad yards.

The "tinpot pope" won his case, temporarily at least (the
verdict against Scopes was later overturned by a technicality,
which left the issue of the trial unresolved), but Bryan was dead
in the same year, a victim perhaps of the same intense emotions
he helped to engender.

With the trial in mind, I asked the student where the library
was, and we were directed to a shambles of a building whose
only roofed room looked like a disorderly warehouse. Most of
the books were piled high in a wild disarray of stacks that
covered the huge floor. A few of the books were on shelves but
in no particular order. When I inquired of the librarian if there

was a copy of Darwin's *Origin of the Species* in the collection, she plainly indicated she had never heard of the book or its author. After I spelled Darwin's name for her, she vaguely recalled having seen the name on some books and pointed to a far corner of the room. Left to our own devices, Brown and I scoured the shelves until we found three copies of the work, each in a different place.

Two of the copies were obviously from Bryan's home library; they bore a bookplate consisting of a Latin motto *(Suaviter in Modo—Fortiter in Re)*, a photograph of Bryan among his books, and the signatures of himself and his wife, Mary J. Bryan. It was the third copy that gave me such a bibliographic thrill as to raise goose pimples up and down my spine. This, I realized, was the very copy that Bryan must have pored over while preparing his case against Darrow. Many of the pages were dogeared. Throughout the text were underlined whole paragraphs as well as individual words; any words that implied doubt such as "probably" and "apparently" were heavily underscored. Most revealing of all were the penciled marginal notes in Bryan's handwriting, which included such exclamations as "Rubbish!" and "Not so!" and such cryptic phrases as "Males select females," "Savages strong," and "Family tree."

My impulse was to steal the book, to rescue it from its almost certain fate of being unappreciated or, even worse, discarded. I tried to persuade myself that I should conceal the book in my jacket and, on our return to Washington, present it to the Library of Congress, so as to make it readily available to scholars. But I could not summon the courage to do it. In the company of relatively new friends, who did not seem to share my excitement over the find, I feared they might regard me as a thief. Sorrowfully I placed the book back on its shelf, grouping it with the other two copies, and resolutely walked away.

On our way out, I considered informing the librarian of what a scholarly treasure the shabbiest of the three copies represented, but my distrust of her as a librarian in Dayton,

Tennessee, who had never heard of Darwin caused me to reject the idea. For all I knew, I reasoned, she might be some Fundamentalist fanatic who would cheerfully destroy all three copies once she learned, from Bryan's own marginal notes, that he regarded Darwin as an advocate of the Devil.

This episode, as much as the experience of having to pretend my name was Smith, epitomized for me a world with which I could feel little relation. It was one of the American areas where, like other ethnics, I would always be regarded as a stranger and foreigner. While I could champion and even work for the success of rehabilitation projects such as those sponsored by the New Deal, the South would remain as far removed from my psyche as any distant planet. On the other hand, the problems of impoverished writers throughout the nation were so directly related to my own experience that I could easily become involved with them with genuine empathy and enthusiasm.

On our return to Washington, with all the diplomacy at my command, I told Gilfond that although the agency's field projects had made a favorable impression on me, I still preferred the job offered to me on the Writers' Project. True to his promise, he signed the release that would make my transfer possible and wished me luck.

From the start, my association with the Writers' Project acted as a powerful tonic on my spirits. There was constant confusion, but there was also the exhilaration of contributing to a significant historical event, the first of its kind. My colleagues and I were literally making history. Working long hours for the glory of the Writers' Project while Congress and the press hammered away at its inglorious record of accomplishment, we were like a gang of inspired revolutionists who, determined to give substance to a dream, recognized no obstacles. Each of us suspected that never again might we know a means of earning a livelihood that involved us as fully and selflessly.

Except for a brief but scorching affair with a brainy colleague from Arkansas who had the face of a chorus girl and the

sexual appetite of a Messalina, it was a period of deep
gratification. Although I lacked the glibness of a salesman, I
discovered to my surprise that I was able to convince publishers
that the Project's manuscripts were well worth their investment. This won me the gratitude and support of my colleagues
who realized that the continuation of the Writers' Project
depended to a great extent on the willingness of publishers to
make books of its manuscripts.

At first I worked with only one assistant, a blonde of old
American ancestry, who was a talented administrator as well as
a secretary. But with the Project operating in high gear—some
fifty thousand words of material pouring in daily from the state
offices—I acquired a second assistant. He was Charles Edward
Smith, the pioneer jazz critic who had become one of my
closest friends. As the three of us flung ourselves into the task of
lining up sponsors and publishers for the hundreds of manuscripts being completed, I was distressed to find that Smith,
whose sense of humor had always delighted me, became, almost
overnight, compulsively bureaucratic. Although he was now
earning twice the salary he had received as a relief worker on
the New York City Writers' Project, I began to think I had
done him a disservice by having him transferred to Washington
until I finally realized that his obsessive need to imprison
himself within a tightly structured routine amounted to an act
of self-preservation. Although he had never admitted it, his
divorce a few months before from Louise Hays Miller had
touched off a surge of emotional disorder which he was hoping
to dispel with a strict program of external order.

How assiduously Smith pursued this form of home therapy
became even more apparent when the girl with whom he was
currently having an affair complained to me that he would see
her twice a week and only at stipulated hours. A few days
before she had made the mistake of arriving at his apartment at
an unscheduled time. Smith, usually the kindest of men,
furiously turned her away, threatening to end their relationship
if she ever again disregarded their schedule. She asked me if his

peculiar behavior could be attributed to his unhappiness over the end of his marriage. I let her think that might well be the explanation; I could not tell her that some years before his marriage he had tried to kill himself.

My secretary, who shall be called Margaret here, did her best to keep us on a steady keel, teasing Smith into laughter when he became overly bureaucratic, and instilling some of her optimism into me when I showed signs of slipping into a blue funk. I had never known a girl as warmhearted and generous as Margaret. Eventually, after my infatuation with the Arkansas Messalina had reached its traumatic climax, our friendship turned into love.

The end of my affair with the Arkansas girl came after a colleague, pitying me for my ignorance, revealed what was apparently common knowledge among the males in the office: during my out-of-town business trips, she shared her favors with several of them and lately she had become the mistress of a high-ranking WPA official. When I accused her of all this, she coolly admitted her relationship with the official; the rest she dismissed as office scandalmongering. My anger was potent enough to unburden me of the infatuation. Within a few weeks Margaret, who was separated from her husband and lived with a young daughter, became my mistress and we settled into a relationship that was to continue monogamously and for the most part happily for the next five years.

Having come to Washington from the squalor and sky-scrapers of Manhattan, at first I had reveled in the city's magnificent trees and stretches of green, but after a few months it struck me as the dreariest of cities. It was hard to make my senses realize that here were made momentous political deci-sions that significantly affected the whole world. The sameness of the population, the preponderance of white government employees who were well clothed, well sheltered, and well fed, accentuated the unreality of the city. Every time I returned from a field trip, its trees and grass seemed more like stage props, its people further encased in a cocoon far removed from the Depression and all the other unpleasantries of the outside world. After a while I came to think of Washington as a big stage set cluttered with neatly attired robots and phony Greek architecture.

Aside from the strip-teasing fare of a burlesque house and occasional symphony concerts and road shows, the city offered little live entertainment. There were black nightclubs, but few that welcomed whites. Only one of them catered to whites. This was a second-story firetrap operated by the immortal jazzman Jelly Roll Morton, to whom I was introduced by our mutual friend Charles Edward Smith. Until I became afraid of being burned alive, I visited the nightclub frequently, usually in the company of Smith or of Alan Lomax, who was then tape-recording Jelly Roll's music for the archives of the Library of Congress.

For a while Jelly Roll was the sole attraction of the place. He smiled at everyone, revealing the diamonds imbedded in his front teeth, and several times each evening he would sit at a piano and perform some of his own compositions. Invariably, he opened the program with a pianistic flourish and the words: "Meee and Beethoven. Recorded by theee Librareee of Congress!" Between performances, he enjoyed reminiscing about his past in the sporting houses of New Orleans.

I stopped visiting the club when Jelly Roll, in a bid for more customers, added an alarming feature to the evening's activities: a juggler who, twice each evening, would lie on the floor and juggle lighted kerosene lamps with the soles of his feet. Being a heavy drinker, the juggler did not inspire confidence, and it was all too easy to imagine one of the kerosene lamps dropping to the floor and turning the whole place into a murderous inferno. During the juggling act, the only exit door in the club got more attention than the performer.

The scarcity of good restaurants in Washington served as an excuse for occasional trips to Baltimore where, after a good dinner, we would visit the various clip joints on its seamy waterfront as an antidote to the epicene atmosphere of Washington. But most of the social life took place in the privacy of homes, with out-of-town guests often being feted with all-night drinking parties. Visiting state directors of the Writers' Project often were guests of honor. The most popular of them was the novelist Lyle Saxon, a suave and witty middle-aged bachelor who directed the Louisiana Project and was known as the unofficial mayor of New Orleans. A skillful raconteur, he regaled me and my colleagues with autobiographical anecdotes, many of which dealt with his black cook, who had been in his employ for many years. Saxon attributed her artistry as a gourmet cook to the fact that she could not read and was therefore unimpeded by the restrictions of written recipes. Saxon claimed she was the best cook in New Orleans but, according to one of his stories, they did not always communicate well. One morning he informed her that six guests were coming to dinner that evening and she was to buy whatever food she needed for the occasion. Only after arriving at his office did he realize he had neglected to leave her any money for the shopping. Telephoning the cook, he directed her to come to the offices of the WPA (where the Writers' Project office was located) and pick up the money.

On returning home that evening, Saxon saw no sign of the cook nor any evidence that a meal was in preparation. He surmised she had been in an accident and was about to start telephoning the city's hospitals when she appeared, thoroughly exhausted and tearful. She explained she had gone to the offices of the WP and A (her interpretation of WPA), as he had directed her to do, and had been standing in line all day for the money she was to pick up, only to be told by the WP and A official that they could not give her any money until a social worker had investigated her circumstances. "I told the man that would be too late," she wailed. "Told him our guests would be here at seven this very evening but he paid me no mind. Mr. Saxon, I don't want to be investigated by any social worker. . . ."

The novelist Vardis Fisher, who was state director of the Idaho Writers' Project, had long infuriated the Washington staff by disregarding most of their editorial instructions; but after the appearance of *Idaho*, the first of the forty-eight state guides, which received rave reviews, Alsberg invited him to Washington and he was treated like a conquering hero. At one of the parties for him I was attracted to him by his curmudgeon temperament and salty talk. We were soon engaged in a lengthy conversation which began with literary gossip and wound up with a Fisher monologue on the positive aspects of suicide. By that time he had consumed a great quantity of bourbon but this neither impeded the flow of his words nor blurred his speech. The gist of the monologue was that it was a damn shame that Americans are conditioned to consider suicide a crime against society. He seemed convinced that were there not a social stigma attached to suicide, more Americans would take their lives, and the country would be far stronger for it.

At first I could not tell whether he was serious or pulling my leg. It is the freedom to take one's own life, he added, that distinguishes man from beast; only man has the intelligence to dispose of himself when life becomes too painful or tiresome. If Congress had any sense, it would pass a law awarding grants to the families of persons taking the suicide route. He proposed forming an organization similar to Alcoholics Anonymous whose membership would proselytize one another on the philosophical advantages of suicide and also promote and publicize painless and speedy methods of taking one's life.

Fisher finally stopped his monologue and asked, "How about it, Mangione? Are you with me? I'll organize the West. You take care of the East? We'll strike a blow for true liberty. What do you say?"

As I poured him another bourbon, I promised I would think about it and let him know my decision the next time we met. That did not happen until I visited Idaho more than thirty-four years later, a month before he died of natural causes, but by then he had lost all memory of his monologue.*

---

* Except for not remembering our 1935 conversation, Fisher, in 1969, was in fine fettle and still drinking bourbon as he described his extraordinary experiences on the Writers' Project for what proved to be his last taped interview.

The out-of-town guests who separately were frequent guests at our house were Mary Heaton Vorse, a veteran left-wing journalist and author of the novel *Strike!*, and Josephine Herbst, whose novels were rated among the best of the current proletarian crop. Although the women were casual acquaintances and there was a twelve-year-age difference between them, they had much in common. Both had become converts to the gospel of Marxian revolution while still in their twenties, both were in the vanguard of the women's liberation movement, and both, as journalists, had covered important events of international significance here and in Europe.

Mary Heaton Vorse, the older of the two, spent a week with us after she had received a slight bullet wound above one eye while covering a Detroit strike. Mary, who spoke with the cultivated inflection of a grande dame, appeared far too old, fragile, and fastidious to have ever been near a strike. Actually, she had covered most of the militant strikes of her time and was as spirited and indomitable as Joan of Arc. Her two chief concerns were social injustice, particularly as it affected the exploited working class, and her children who, though long past the age of consent, she went on supporting, even when it often meant borrowing money or taking on jobs she disliked.

When I first met Josephine she had just returned from Spain where she had been writing dispatches about the war, along with her friend Ernest Hemingway. In Madrid, they and a corps of foreign journalists had stayed at a hotel which, at one point, was badly bombed by Franco's air force. Following the bombing, Josephine and Hemingway compared notes as to what had happened and concluded that the situation and hotel residents involved in it provided rich material for a play. Since they had no wish to collaborate, they flipped a coin to determine which of them would write it, and Hemingway won the toss. The result was *The Fifth Column*, Hemingway's only excursion into dramaturgy.

At the time Josephine told me this story I was the chairman of the local branch of the League of American Writers, which was trying to raise funds for the Loyalists. Sensing that

Josephine was still eager to express some of her observations of the Spanish war in play form, I had no trouble persuading her to write a one-act script in the "living newspaper" documentary technique recently evolved by the Federal Theatre Project. My plan was to have the play cosponsored by the League and all the other Washington groups engaged in helping the Loyalist cause.

Within a few weeks, Josephine, working intensively with her intimate friend Nathan Asch, completed a script titled *The Spanish Road*. The League enthusiastically approved it and, by prearrangement, turned it over to the local Theatre Union for casting and production. Almost at once there ensued a ferocious battle of temperaments and ideologies when the Theatre Union, which was closely allied with the Communist party, decided that the script suffered from "some basic ideological flaws," and demanded that radical changes be made "to clarify the message."

The message was clear enough, the writers insisted, and they accused the producer of trying to reduce the script into "a stupid propaganda vehicle reflecting a narrow Stalinist-Communist point of view." In the heated argument that followed, Asch threw up his hands in disgust and declared he would have nothing more to do with the project. At my urging, Charles Smith relinquished his obsession with the bureaucratic paperwork of his job long enough to replace Asch as Josephine's collaborator. Smith made some changes in the play which met with Josephine's approval, but the changes were not drastic enough to suit the producer and his Theatre Union associates.

When both sides seemed to have reached a stalemate, Josephine decided that the only thing left to do was to have a heart-to-heart talk with the producer in the privacy of his home, away from the pressures of his comrades. I agreed to accompany her. On our way she explained that her hope was to convince the producer that their mutual concern for the Loyalist cause was far more important than their differences of opinion about the script. While she could not have her name associated with a play that violated her integrity as a writer, she was prepared to make one or two more changes that would probably be to his liking.

We had arrived without telephoning, but the producer did not seem to be surprised by the visit. He received us cordially, introduced Josephine to his wife and children as "a great novelist," then invited us into his study for coffee. When Josephine began talking, she sounded reasonable and in complete control of her emotions. I thought there was a good chance of winning him to her point of view. He listened carefully enough but as soon as she paused, he announced in no uncertain terms that the script would either incorporate all the changes he and his associates had requested or there would be no production.

Josephine stared at him for a moment, appalled. Then all the exasperation she had been enduring for two months erupted. "You stupid son of a bitch," she roared and slapped him hard on the face. With that, she made a beeline for the door and I followed. Outdoors, I expected her to verbalize her anger further but she became stone-faced and silent, hurrying as though she could not get out of the neighborhood fast enough. When she finally stopped, she burst into an uncontrollable fit of weeping, sobbing on my shoulder with an intensity I had not heard since the last Sicilian funeral I attended. I felt, as I tried to comfort her, that she was grieving for all the idealists thwarted by the machinations of political bureaucrats.

There was no production. The League of American Writers was able to stage other fund-raising events for the Loyalists, but tried to steer clear of orthodox Stalinists and their absurdities. The most successful event it sponsored was a talk by Ralph Bates, a British captain in the International Brigade and the author of several highly praised novels. He had just come from the battlefields of Spain.

The audience in the packed auditorium was visibly moved as Bates described in vivid detail a scene he had witnessed in a bombed-out Spanish church that was serving as a temporary hospital for the wounded and the dying. From my position on the platform (I had introduced Bates) I watched men and women reaching for handkerchiefs to wipe away tears. There was a stunned silence as the speaker came to the conclusion of the talk, followed by a standing ovation. After acknowledging the sustained applause, Bates turned to me and whispered into my ear: "How did you like it? It's the opening chapter of the novel I'm writing."

Through my League of American Writers' activities I also met Ernst Toller, the German poet and playwright, who had come to Washington to promote a plan for feeding the starving children of Spain. An exile and foe of Nazi Germany, Toller naturally favored the Loyalist cause, but the motive of his mission was humanistic, not political. He wanted to feed all hungry Spanish children, be they the children of Fascists or Loyalists.

Until our encounter, I had no knowledge of his mission. My purpose in seeking him out was to invite him to speak to the membership of the League. When I phoned his room from the Mayflower Hotel lobby, the girl who answered may have assumed I was someone else, for she asked me to come up, even before I could tell her my name. From the moment I entered the room I felt like an actor in a surrealistic dream. Toller ignored me at first. He was pacing up and down a tiny floor space in front of a bed, with a cream puff in one hand and a sheaf of papers in the other, dictating in various directions as though he were surrounded by a battery of stenographers, his sensitive face drawn tight with worry. The only other person in the room was a girl bent over a typewriter looking even more worried as she tried to type out what he was saying in his heavy accent.

When Toller finally noticed me, he put the cream puff on the bed, shook hands without hearing my name, and handed me a manuscript. "Here, read this, and please hurry. We have little time. Make sure the English is all right. Oh, what a difficult language!" The urgency of his manner made my own business seem inconsequential; I made no effort to explain it. Instead I began proofreading his statement on how it would be possible, with the aid of the Friends Service Committee, to bring food to the hungry children of Spain. I worked as fast as possible, correcting spellings and grammatical errors, and handed the corrected pages to the girl for typing. Meanwhile, Toller was running around the room, collecting pages from the floor and under the bed, moaning over and over again that the gentlemen of the press were due in a few minutes. The success of his mission depended on the press conference; it would not do to keep the journalists waiting, he told us. How were we coming along with his statement? By that time, I too was munching on a cream puff and sneaking nervous glances at the clock.

The statement was finally completed. The typist was pale with exhaustion. I handed her the box with the rest of the cream puffs, and the three of us rushed upstairs to the room where the conference was to take place. When we arrived, breathless, expecting to see a swarm of journalists, we found no one. Except for a table with a glass and a water pitcher and twenty gilded chairs, the room was bare. Toller took to floor pacing again, while I tried to assure him that newspaper people in my country are congenitally tardy. Actually, I knew nothing about their sense of punctuality, but by now Toller seemed like an old and vulnerable friend whom I must try to protect from his own anxieties. Toller, not assured, was certain no one would show up and feared his mission was "doomed" because "yours is a country where nothing can be accomplished without the help of publicity."

Twenty minutes after the appointed time, a young man with a slouch hat walked in and asked me if I was Ernst Toller. I rushed him over to Toller who greeted him effusively, as if he were the most important journalist in America, and offered him a cigarette. I lighted the cigarette and offered him a copy of the press statement and a gilded chair. But our zeal was cut short by the young man's explanation that he was not a newspaperman but a great admirer of Toller's writings. Would Mr. Toller oblige him with his autograph? I was afraid that Toller had run out of patience and would turn on the young man. But instead he smiled sadly, wrote out his name, and thanked the young man for reading his books.

The journalists began arriving a little later. Toller became a changed man in their presence. The woebegone look disappeared; he radiated charm and confidence as he concentrated on the task of interesting the audience in his food plan. They listened attentively and, judging from the questions they asked, were affected by his sincerity. When the questions and comments were over, Toller nodded in my direction and announced that his "assistant" would now give each of them a copy of his prepared statement. There were a few more questions, one of which brought out the fact that Toller had left Germany when Hitler was coming into power, in 1932, and that for the past year he had been living in New York City. Then the conference was over.

Toller and I shook hands with the reporters as they filed out of the room. When we had said good-bye to the last one, he turned to me and said, "By the way, what did you say your name was?"

Toller's plan for feeding the Spanish children, though supported by Eleanor Roosevelt, never materialized. He was unable to get the cooperation of the State Department, nor was he able to persuade enough liberal and left-wing groups to set aside their differences long enough to help him promote the plan. A few months after our encounter, in the loneliness of a New York hotel room, he hanged himself. He was then forty-eight years old. The failure of his plan for the Spanish children probably had little connection with his suicide, but it may well have contributed to the despair he must have experienced for a world where, repeatedly in the face of danger, men and women of goodwill have been unwilling to act together for their mutual benefit.

*   *   *

Although I had a cause I believed in, a mistress I cherished, and a job I enjoyed, I was unhappy for having worked so little on my own writing since arriving in Washington. To escape the social distractions of the Alsberg-Laning-Krimont menage and gain more privacy, I moved into a spacious but low-priced apartment overlooking a black slum area adjacent to the Library of Congress, and shared it with Charles Flato, an economist by profession and a gourmet cook by avocation, who also sought privacy for his own writing. Before settling down to our typewriters, we threw a big housewarming party to which friends were invited to bring household items we lacked. (John Cheever brought a recording of Midge Williams singing Langston Hughes's lyrics, "Love is Like Whisky, Love is Like Red, Red Wine; If you want to be Happy, you gotta love all the time.") I had barely begun my daily writing regime when there were several interruptions, the longest one an illness that almost took my life. Before that happened, Alsberg sent me to Chicago to attend a nationwide conference of Writers' Project supervisors.

It was a precarious time for the Federal Writers' Project. The newly formed Dies Committee was on the warpath, grabbing big headlines with unproven charges that the New York City office was a hot bed of communism, and conducting hearings which disregarded rules of evidence and due process. The fact that the committee, for all of its abuses, had the support of the press, the public, and the Congress suggested the approaching demise of the Project. The Chicago conference reflected none of this apprehension; a happy-go-lucky atmosphere prevailed as the participants congratulated one another on the increasing number of Project books being published and on the praise which the nation's leading critics were lavishing on them.

There was entertainment for the delegates every night of their week-long stay. At one of the parties I danced with Katherine Dunham, the exotic choreographer who was then studying anthropology at the University of Chicago while conducting Project studies of the Black Muslim movement and Chicago's storefront black churches. On another night we visited a dive in the black district where we watched a nude mulatto dancer named "Lovey" perform erotic gyrations on the floor while one of my colleagues, Ben Botkin, the Project's erudite national folklore editor, studiously jotted down notes on her performance. In the same dive we heard the boogie-woogie of pianists Meade Lux Lewis and Edward Ammons who, only a week later, were to introduce the same music at New York's Carnegie Hall and win instant fame.

Shortly before leaving Chicago we were treated to a captivating Federal Theatre Project production of *The Mikado* played by an all-Negro cast. The most theatrical segment of that night was to occur later at a party for some of the cast members at our hotel which I attended with Dorothy Farrell, who was recently separated from her husband, James T. Farrell. The protagonist of the real-life drama became a pretty young mulatto, a dancer in *The Mikado* chorus line, who was anxiously awaiting the arrival of her husband, a black union organizer. Apparently, his wife's presence at a hotel party had aroused his suspicions, and he kept telephoning her from the strike meeting he was attending to accuse her of being in a hotel room with another man.

Every time he called, the girl would tearfully protest that he was the only man in her life and summon Dorothy to the telephone in a futile effort to convince him there was no man with his wife. Shortly after midnight the husband, still fired with jealousy, telephoned to say that he was coming for her. When two hours passed and he had not appeared, she was certain he had been murdered by strike breakers (as had happened recently to another Chicago black union organizer). At one point she screamed that she could not live without him and ran toward an open window. We held her until she quieted down; then trying to distract her, Dorothy asked that she teach us one of the dance steps she had used in *The Mikado*. In between lessons, she kept crying that her husband was bleeding to death in some gutter, and threatening suicide.

The husband finally arrived at four in the morning, unharmed but quite stoned. As he rushed into the room, he pushed aside his wife, who was trying to throw her arms around him, and made a beeline for me, swinging his fists and shouting, "There's the lousy bastard who's trying to screw my wife." Before he could reach me, Dorothy Farrell, whom he knew, stepped between us and, luckily for me, was able to persuade him that I had no designs on his wife.

When I returned to Washington, the image of the black husband coming toward me with murder in his eyes remained with me and soon became part of a recurring nightmare in which the black husband was sometimes replaced by a white man, no less violent, whose features corresponded to those of Margaret's husband as she had described them to me. Although he and Margaret had been formally separated for more than a year, he was still demanding that she and their child return to him. Her constant fear was that he might discover my identity and try to harm me physically. I pretended to be amused by her concern, pointing out that cuckolded American husbands were not likely to behave like their Sicilian counterparts, but secretly I was afraid she might have good reason to be concerned; she had excellent judgment.

How deeply ingrained was our fear of her husband was dramatized by an episode that occurred shortly after I returned from my Chicago trip and had taken to my bed with a high temperature. For two weeks my doctor persisted in diagnosing my condition as the grippe. Margaret, suddenly distrusting him, summoned a specialist who declared I had pneumonia and phoned for an ambulance to take me to the hospital. While the hospital attendants were climbing the stairway with a stretcher, Margaret, who was waiting for them at the head of the stairwell, was horrified to recognize one of the men as a close friend of her husband's. She ran back to my bed and, though terror-stricken, began shutting the suitcase she had packed for me while hastily explaining about the attendant. Moments before the two men came into the bedroom, she fled to another part of the apartment to conceal herself.

As I was to learn later, Margaret had saved my life by summoning the second doctor in the nick of time. The hospital examination revealed I was stricken with double pneumonia of a type that could not then be treated by drugs. For what seemed like an interminable period but actually amounted to one week, I was under twenty-four-hour intensive-care treatment, only vaguely aware of the anxious faces hovering around my bedside—Margaret, my mother and father, my brother and my two sisters, the only visitors permitted at first.

The ordeal, together with the impression left by Margaret's fear of being recognized by her husband's friend, transferred me into a grisly realm dominated by a vengeful husband and the witchlike features of the old woman who, though ostensibly there to massage my body with alcohol during the night, became an obscene sorceress rubbing me to death. When I had passed the crisis, the visitors became more visible, the nightmare began to recede. The doctor sounded optimistic, but one morning the radio announced that Thomas Wolfe had just died of pneumonia at the age of thirty-eight, and I suffered a relapse that night. The old woman reappeared and I went through the same agony again.

Once I finally began to recover it was not gratitude I felt but deep anger. Anger with the doctor who had misdiagnosed my illness. Anger with Margaret's husband for dominating my nightmares. Anger with friends who sent bunches of cut flowers, which I would fling across the room as they arrived. (From early childhood I associated them mainly with funerals.) Anger with a colleague for sending me a book quoting the dying words of famous men. Anger with the dowdy woman from the WPA personnel office who, pretending to be solicitous of my health, had come to check on whether I was ill or malingering. Anger that I had almost been cheated out of a normal life span.

My bad temper alarmed my parents and Margaret who were accustomed to regarding me as congenial and generally considerate of others. But the specialist was pleased with it; it was an indication I was getting stronger. Yet it was another month before he would permit me to leave the hospital. Even then it was with the stipulation I spend at least six weeks convalescing, learning to walk again after my long stay in bed, and trying to regain the thirty pounds or so I had lost.

As if I were demoted to childhood, once more I fell into the tender but dictatorial care of my parents who for several weeks lived in my apartment ministering to my needs. Once a day, leaning on my father for support, I ventured outdoors to exercise my legs. Morning, noon, and night, at my mother's command, I drank the juice of rare roast beef on the theory it would enrich my blood and improve my color, and at lunch and dinner I was plied with my father's homemade red wine, his own specific for enriching blood. To tease my appetite, my parents took turns cooking my favorite dishes, including one I could never find in restaurants, the Sicilian dish *brusciuluna,* a happy combination of Romano cheese, salami, and moon-shaped slivers of hard-boiled eggs, which my father encased in tenderized rolls of beef firmly held together by string and toothpicks, and baptized with a rich tomato sauce. As a further demonstration of his love, he engaged in the arduous ritual of preparing his Sicilian dessert masterpiece, *cannoli.*

Margaret, at my parents' urging, was a frequent guest at these feasts. Although their scanty English made it impossible for them to communicate with her as fully as they would have liked, they approved of her. My mother marveled that Margaret was of old American stock. "For me she is just like a Sicilian girl," she confided, expressing the highest compliment she could bestow on her. I was pleased that my mother appreciated Margaret's qualities but, uncertain of what her reaction might be, I did not tell her that Margaret was married and the mother of a young daughter.

To hasten my recovery, the specialist ordered me to spend a

month at the seashore, preferably not too far from Washington so that I could get back to him quickly if I needed his help. I could not afford even a week at the lowliest seashore resort; my hospital bills had wiped out nearly all my savings. Not wanting to go into debt, my only hope was to try to trade on my small reputation as a writer of travel articles. Luckily, the only resort hotel I applied to, the newly built Cavalier at Virginia Beach, promptly offered me a free room with a view of the sea; I was to pay only for my meals.°

It being off season, the hotel was nearly empty. I had never been alone over such a long period; yet I was not lonely. For the first time, I became immersed in sunrises, sunsets, skies, tides, waves, birds, and stones. My close brush with death made me feel closer to nature than ever before, and more inclined to meditate. I could not help interpreting my illness as a warning that in the remaining years of my life—I was almost thirty—I must pay more attention to what I wanted to do most: read more extensively and write, especially, write.

It was not enough, I decided, to publish occasional stories, articles, and reviews; they were too ephemeral. A book is substantial; a good one might be read long after one's death. The need to write a book was not an unfamiliar one; it had been gnawing at me ever since my college days. But I had always pushed it aside, rationalizing I had yet to be drawn to a subject or theme significant enough to warrant lengthy treatment. Now, in the clarity of my aloneness, I finally realized that the book material for which I had been searching had been under my nose all the time. The three weeks of reunion with my parents had vividly resurrected the memory of my Sicilian life in Rochester. I could write revealingly about the subject I knew best of all: the struggles and foibles of my immigrant relatives, as seen through the eyes of an offspring (myself) who

° As a token of my gratitude, I concocted an ersatz folk tale in which the only reference to the resort was in the opening sentence: "It happened at Virginia Beach." *The Washington Post* published it but without the opening sentence.

at first feels resentful of them for the un-American culture they impose on him but who later, through the passage of time and the perspective of distance, comes to cherish them for their wisdom and their celebration of life. At last, the Sicilian immigrants, the most maligned of the Italian Americans, would be presented as I knew them to be, not as the criminals projected by the American press.

The idea for such a book was not originally mine; it had been suggested by a New York editor at Viking Press after he had read four or five magazine pieces I had published about my journey to Sicily, one of which, incidentally, struck the fancy of a writer whose poetry I admired but whose politics I deplored, Ezra Pound.* At the time the editor's suggestion had not made much of an impression; I was still filled with vaguely grandiose literary notions of what my first book should be like. But now I began jotting down notes about my relatives in preparation for the time when I could get the book under way.

I would not have to wait for long. The end of Henry Alsberg's tenure with the Writers' Project, and automatically mine, was clearly in sight. Following Alsberg's appearance before the Dies Committee, during which he tried to appease the committee by testifying as a cooperative witness, his WPA superior, Colonel F.C. Harrington, had suggested he resign his post as director. Alsberg's response was that he would not quit the Project until all of its major publications were in print; but everyone, except Alsberg, knew he was fighting a losing battle.

A month before Congress was to determine the fate of all the WPA arts projects, in May 1939, I received an invitation to have Sunday supper with Mrs. Franklin D. Roosevelt at the

---

* Ezra Pound, then living in Fascist Italy, contributed a newsletter periodically to the short-lived American magazine *Globe* (1937–38), which published two of my sketches, "Sicilian Policemen" and "A Man's Best Audience Is His Horse," which dealt with an anti-Fascist carriage driver I met in Palermo. In his correspondence to the *Globe* editors Pound praised the first sketch in three different letters, but made no comment about the second. Presumably, its anti-Fascist content offended his Fascist sensibilities.

White House. The invitation quoted her as saying that she was not certain the President could be present but that if he were, he would probably be wearing a business suit. The invitation had no connection with my government job, having been issued at the request of Mrs. Charles S. Fayerweather, an elderly writer of juvenile novels who had become my friend during my McBride years and who was a close friend of Mrs. Roosevelt's; but Alsberg regarded my visit to the White House as a providential opportunity to enlist the aid of the Roosevelts in rescuing the Writers' Project from the congressional ax. I argued that it would be futile, as well as in bad taste, for me to attempt the role of lobbyist at a purely social occasion, but even as I was donning my best business suit, Alsberg was briefing me on what I should tell the Roosevelts about the accomplishments of the Project.

At the White House there was no sign of the President as Mrs. Roosevelt introduced me to the four supper guests, who were there for the weekend, and to her husband's secretary, Marguerite LeHand, who was to join us. But as we were about to enter the dining room, a black servant thrust his head into a doorway to say that supper was "about ready," and I heard the unmistakable voice of the President shout that he was "ready too." Moments later while we were taking our places at the dinner table—I was placed next to Mrs. Roosevelt's good ear— the President was rolled down the dining-room ramp and placed at the head of the table, opposite his wife. The double shock of being in the President's presence for the first time and seeing him confined to a wheelchair was quickly mitigated by the electrifying vitality of the man which filled the room from the moment he entered.

As soon as Mrs. Roosevelt had finished introducing me to him, he began an extensive monologue which first inquired, with more than a suggestion of scorn, whether any of us had listened to a Mussolini speech broadcast a few hours before (he had not, nor had any of the guests), then went on to describe gleefully an article by the playwright George Kaufman in the current issue of the *Nation* which satirized the propensity of Washington news analysts to attach undue significance to the President's most trival remarks and actions. He quoted verbatim several paragraphs that explored the subtle meanings implicit in the fact that the President had recently said "Good morning" to his assembled secretaries while facing east. One of the paragraphs struck the supper guests as especially funny; "Why did he (the President) especially select morning of all the available periods of the day? Because it is in the morning that the sun rises. And where does it rise? In the east, of course. East is the Orient; East is Japan, and so the President's statement begins to take form and pattern. Here we have definite proof that the Presidential mind is at last concerned definitely with the Japanese-Chinese situation. . . ."

No one else, except myself, seemed to feel constrained by the President's presence. The general tenor was that of a Sunday-night family free-for-all, with the guests and hosts competing for attention. As in a family conversation, one topic followed another without logical transitions. At one point Walter Brown, Governor Lehman's press secretary, who was at the table with his wife, asked the President if there had been any repercussions to his recent directive authorizing the Navy to buy Argentine canned beef rather than the domestic variety. (At a recent press conference Roosevelt had contended that Argentine beef was far superior to ours and half as expensive, and sharply criticized an amendment pending in the Navy Appropriations bill which could compel the Navy to buy domestic beef exclusively.) Grinning at Brown's question, the President said that telegrams protesting his directive had been pouring in all weekend. Most of them, he added, sounded as if they had been inspired by the western farm associations and the Hearst press.

Sardonically, the President noted there had been no complaints from the big meat packers, most of whom operated their own packing plants in Argentina. The telegrams from cattlemen as well as the Hearst editorials were accusing him of "collusion" and "corruption," but he said that all he had in mind was that the men in the Navy eat good beef. By this time I was sufficiently relaxed to suggest that the President and his administration could always expect a certain amount of "beefing" from the Hearst press. The President laughed at the pun. (At his press conference the next day he had some verbal fun of his own with the subject. On being told by a reporter that Westerners were saying he had impugned the valor of the American cow, the President retorted that he had not meant to cast aspersions on either the virtue of the American cow or the valor of the American bull.)

Not surprisingly, the topic that commanded the most sustained attention was the Administration's foreign policy, which for the first time in New Deal history was receiving higher priority than domestic issues. The President's January 1939 message to Congress made it clear that the period of radical social reforms was drawing to a close. Requesting a national defense budget larger than the one proposed for public works, he warned that "a war which threatened to envelop the world in flames" was in the offing.

Until now I had been impressed by the President's buoyant optimism, but there was the sound of worry in his voice as he dwelled on the importance of alerting Americans to the pitfalls of isolationist thinking. Then, as if he could not do without his optimism, he expressed the belief that the New Deal's policy of providing all possible aid to anti-Fascist nations was gradually winning acceptance; he detected encouraging signs of this in various parts of the country.

"Not in Seattle!" Mrs. Roosevelt interrupted. From her recent visit there she could attest that isolationist thinking prevailed in that area.

Her personality was a surprise to me. Until that evening I had been inclined to judge it by the rather innocuous style of her newspaper column, "My Day." Actually, she had an incisive intellect and, as she demonstrated throughout the supper, a no-nonsense view of reality.

Toward the close of the supper, while Roosevelt was bemoaning the lack of confidence in the nation's economy and
wondering what it was that people were afraid of, Mrs.
Roosevelt mischievously interjected the sharpest riposte of the
evening: "Darling, they are afraid of you." The President
accepted her footnote with a grace that suggested he was
accustomed to having his wife set him right whenever the
occasion required it.

What might turn the tide of public opinion, he ruminated,
was facing up to the possibility that Nazi Germany and Italy
might join forces and win the war. (The Rome-Berlin Axis
became a fait accompli only two weeks later.) Speculating on
that hypothesis, he predicted that if England were defeated, the
Fascist groups in most of the Western Hemisphere would be
swept into power and the United States would find itself
isolated, tightly encircled by nations with an antidemocratic
ideology, a development that would certainly spell political and
economic disaster for our country. Warming up to his argument, he added that, quite apart from our traditional historical
ties with England, it was distinctly to our advantage to assist
the British in every possible way since their country was the
sole bulwark that stood between us and Hitler's ambitions; to
ignore this fact would be to ignore our own fate.

In the general discussion that followed I asked the President
if he had read Quincy Howe's recently published book, *England
Expects Every American to Do His Duty*, which expressed a
point of view contrary to his own. He simply nodded, then
went on to present the final phase of his argument, pointing out
that if Germany were to win the war, none of the defeated
nations could expect any show of mercy. He was certain that
unlike France and England, which had deeply humanistic
traditions, Germany would be a ruthless conqueror, the tough
boss state of the world.

When asked about the Soviet Union's role in Europe after
the war, Roosevelt replied that although the Soviets held the
balance of power in Europe, it was unlikely they would try to

dominate world affairs. The Soviet Union was too concerned with its domestic problems to become involved with external affairs. His final word for the Soviets was to praise them for the consistency of their foreign policy.

As the supper progressed, I found myself revising my previous concept of Roosevelt. Except for his hands-off policy on the Spanish Civil War, which was contributing to the victory of Franco's Fascist forces, I had long admired him for his sagacious statesmanship. Hearing him in this informal atmosphere, I realized how much I had idealized him. He was neither as wise nor as proud as I had supposed him to be. His glibness, his propensity for generalizations, jarred me; so did his lack of prudence, especially when he spoke of Boake Carter, a popular radio commentator who was an outspoken enemy of the New Deal.

The President made no bones of the fact that he was having Carter "thoroughly investigated," apparently by the FBI. He was quite certain that Carter—"or whatever his real name is"— had a nefarious background which, when brought to light, would put an end to his career. That Roosevelt, the statesman I had admired, should admit to such vindictiveness came as the greatest jolt of all. All during the supper I was also concerned about his unrestrained candor in the presence of a total stranger, myself; I winced at the havoc a less reliable guest could create with some of the President's pronouncements. Later, however, I realized I was overreacting, judging him by the impossibly rigid standards of a hero worshiper, and reflected that actually I should have been pleased that the President had paid his guests the supreme compliment of relaxing in their presence by thinking aloud without feeling obliged to weigh his words.

Before our hostess ended the supper, the President spoke of two other matters on his mind, first of his efforts to raise money for the rescue of Jewish refugees in Europe. He told us that his personal appeal for funds to the nation's wealthiest Jews had met with little success. "There is apt to be much bickering among very rich Jews and little sympathy for me." Now he was directing his appeal to Jews of "middle wealth" and finding them much more responsive. Next, he noted with considerable amusement that his friend Herbert Lehman, who had been considerably "miffed" by the President's decision to run for office a third time, seemed to have experienced a drastic change of heart. The last time he saw the governor everything was "hunky-dory" between them. With a grin, Roosevelt added that "Herbert's manner was almost cuddly."

The President left as soon as supper was over, explaining he had a full evening of work ahead of him. Except for Miss LeHand, the rest of us adjourned to Mrs. Roosevelt's sitting room where she chatted with us while knitting on a half-finished pullover. The conversation became even more desultory than it had been at supper. The only noteworthy exchange I recall took place between Walter Brown and our hostess. On the subject of Republicans Brown declared rather vehemently that he could never bring himself to vote for a Republican. Mrs. Roosevelt, in her most genteel voice, responded that she could not make such a statement; she thought it would be quite possible for her to make occasional exceptions, and mentioned Fiorello La Guardia as the sort of Republican for whom she could vote with a clear conscience.

As soon as the conversation began to lag, I was finally able to introduce the topic of the Federal Writers' Project and its perilous status. There was no need for me to propagandize. My hostess was fully aware both of its achievements and of the congressional enemies who were trying to kill all four of the federally sponsored arts projects. But though she spoke of the high quality of the Project books with enthusiasm and personal knowledge, she indicated that continuing federal sponsorship of the four arts projects was a lost cause. Without her actually saying so, I understood that the New Deal was turning its back on most projects unrelated to defense preparations for the oncoming war. The President himself had said as much at the supper table.

A casual remark dropped by Brown to the effect that Mrs. Roosevelt was flying to New York that evening provided the cue for my departure. "Oh, I have plenty of time," said our hostess, without missing a stitch with her knitting needles. "I have ten minutes." Five minutes later, clutching some letters the guests had asked me to mail for them in the outside world, I left the White House. All the way home the President's voice filled my head as I wondered how to tell Alsberg that a new era was definitely in store for him, for me, and for everyone else.

TEN

Nests of Literati

In the summer of 1939, when Congress put an end to the Federal Writers' Project and ordered it to be reorganized under state-by-state sponsorship, I was ensconced in the Victorian manor house of Yaddo, the estate at Saratoga Springs, New York, which serves as a retreat for working writers, artists, and composers. The WPA dismissal notice arrived just as I was struggling to start the story of my Sicilian relatives. While it disturbed me to be unemployed again, the gothic spell of Yaddo soon obliterated nearly all my apprehensions, except those related to my manuscript.

I worked at an agonizingly slow rate, full of doubts and self-consciousness. Two years before I had sworn off book reviewing in the belief that it tended to make me hypercritical of my own writing, but I still found myself throwing away nearly everything I wrote. I spent several weeks trying to hit on a style that would let me tell my story without sounding either like a sociologist or a fiction writer. When that problem was resolved, I worried about my ability to produce enough pages to make a book and took to examining the shortest volume I could find to see how short a publishable book could be. Worst of all, I began to question the validity of the project, asking myself who else besides Sicilians (few of whom could read English) could possibly be interested in reading about my relatives. Only my stubbornness and Kenneth Fearing's warning to me when the Yaddo invitation arrived—"At Yaddo you either work or you go nuts"—kept me at my typewriter.

Away from my manuscript, I was intrigued by the company of my fellow Yaddoites and by the ominously melancholy atmosphere of the place with its shadowy pines, its ghostly lakes, and the false yet plausible legend that Edgar Allan Poe had composed "The Raven" while stopping at an inn which had once been on the premises. No less haunting were the pitiful misfortunes of the Spencer Trask family, the founders of the estate. Two of the children died of diphtheria, the manor house was totally destroyed by fire, and as a crowning blow, Spencer Trask himself was accidentally killed on a train which was part of the New York Central, the same company he headed.

On the surface Yaddo suggested a somber but posh retreat as far removed from the realities of the outside world as a Trappist monastery, especially during the day when a heavy stillness hung over the grounds as the guests concentrated on communing with their muses. Actually, it was a veritable microcosm of the world, a mirror of public opinion, and also of private neuroses. Unlike the Trappists, the guests brought their personal problems with them and shared them with anyone who would listen.

One poet went so far as to bring his new bride with him, despite strict Yaddo regulations forbidding the overnight residence of spouses, concubines, cats, dogs, and other pets. He was Delmore Schwartz, a twenty-six-year-old Adonis from Brooklyn who had just published his first volume of poetry, *In Dreams Begin Responsibilities*. Unbeknown to anyone, Schwartz had concealed his young wife in the bedroom assigned to him. After a few days of confinement the girl became restive and, without consulting her husband, began wandering around the fields in broad daylight, chatting with whatever guests she happened to encounter.

The invitation to spend a month at Yaddo had arrived only a few days after Schwartz's marriage, and he had been faced with the problem of either leaving his young bride behind or saying no to the invitation. Unable to face either alternative, he had decided to take his wife with him, hoping that some solution would present itself. None had so far; he loved his wife and he loved Yaddo, and he would try to keep her a secret from Mrs. Elizabeth Ames, the director of Yaddo, as long as possible.

Meanwhile his bride was becoming increasingly miserable trying to keep out of sight and subsisting on whatever snacks Schwartz could cadge from the dining room where we all had our evening meal. Gertrude was a beguiling girl, as endearing as a woodland nymph. I could understand Schwartz's reluctance to deny himself her company, but it puzzled me that a writer of his sensitivity would be willing to subject her to such a demeaning situation. I tried to convince him that Mrs. Ames was not the martinet he imagined her to be but a considerate human being who would undoubtedly make allowances for having his bride there once she knew the circumstances; but Schwartz was not convinced.

I felt especially sorry for Gertrude after the evening meal when, as a Yaddo ritual, the guests gathered in the great living room of the mansion for coffee and conversation with Mrs. Ames and her sister Marjorie, and I would catch glimpses of the girl who, Ophelia-like, would furtively peer through the big glass wall at one end of the room. If Schwartz or any of the other guests noticed her then, they pretended not to and went on chatting until Mrs. Ames and her sister took their leave, at which time Schwartz would rush out into the night, presumably to find and possibly scold his wife.

While Schwartz could endure the situation, I could not. One evening, while darkness was falling, I again saw the young bride lurking about the big glass wall, evidently trying to muster enough courage to peer into the room. This time my impulses got the best of me. Without a word to Schwartz, I went outdoors in search of the girl. When I had found her, I took her by the hand and asked her to come with me. She

asked no questions and quietly came along. Still holding her
hand, I led her into the living room and up to Mrs. Ames.
"Elizabeth," I began "I think it's about time you met Mrs.
Delmore Schwartz."

Luckily, my hunch about Mrs. Ames's reaction to Gertrude
proved to be accurate. Neither she nor Schwartz was banished
from Yaddo. Charmed by Gertrude, Mrs. Ames arranged to
provide the girl with freedom of the grounds and regular meals
for the rest of her husband's stay.

That in such a nest of introverts I could be capable of so
extrovert an action provided me with the few euphoric moments I was to experience at Yaddo. The problems of my
manuscript troubled me, as did the political discussions at the
table, often acrimonious and all too painfully remindful of the
difficulties intellectuals have in finding a common ground at a
time of crisis. When Hitler and Stalin deepened the crisis in
August by signing a nonaggression pact, the arguments between
the Stalinists and the non-Stalinists became so violent that, by
mutual consent, a moratorium was imposed on political discussions around the dinner table.

The three anti-Nazi refugees among us had already imposed
such a ban on themselves. Two of them were the Austrian
novelists Hermann Broch, internationally famous for his trilogy
The Sleepwalkers, and his friend Richard Bermann, who was not
as gifted a literary artist as Broch but was far more personable.
The third refugee was the German artist Rudolf von Ripper, a
manic extrovert we secretly referred to as Jack the Ripper.
None of these men ever spoke to us of their experiences with
the Nazis. But rumor had it that Von Ripper, who had a gro-
tesquely damaged eye that did not function, had been badly
tortured in the Nazi concentration camp by being placed in a
burial pit in a standing position and covered with dirt up to his
nose. Only Von Ripper's ghoulish drawings of Nazis and their
atrocities, which were rendered in a delicate line that belied
the man's blunt personality, conveyed his sense of horror. Away
from his studio, he behaved like a demon on a lark.

One evening, after the customary coffee and conversation

session with Mrs. Ames and her sister, Von Ripper fastened on
me as a fishing companion. For lack of bait, he invaded a brook
in a Yaddo rock garden and captured some of its goldfish,
assuring me that fish were like people, "incapable of resisting
the lure of gold." After an hour or so of attracting nothing but
mosquito bites, he conceded that fish were not as much like
people as he had supposed, and called it quits.

I had hoped that we could then part company, but Von
Ripper had other plans for me. He insisted I accompany him to
Saratoga Springs to purchase flowers for a writer whom he
would only identify as "the most beautiful girl at Yaddo."
Originally, he had hoped to present her with a mess of fish, but
he now thought that flowers would do as well. As I had
expected, all the florist shops in town were shut tight at that
hour, but Von Ripper assured me he would soon have all the
flowers he needed. Not until we were returning to Yaddo and
approached the formal gardens of a large estate did I learn
what he had in mind. Ordering me to be his lookout man, he
darted to a large bed of gold and purple irises and, to my
horror, proceeded to pull them out of the ground, roots and all.
Now and then he would hold one up in the moonlight for me to
admire, as exultant as Perseus displaying the head of Medusa. I
became increasingly nervous and when he showed no inclination to stop, I pretended that someone was approaching. At my
signal, he quickly gathered the plants under his arms and began
sprinting toward Yaddo, while screaming at me in German to
follow.

There was no one in sight when we reached the manor
house. Von Ripper took his loot into the kitchen where he
sliced off the roots and, for lack of twine, tied the flowers
together with his shoelaces. After that he led the way to an
empty bedroom on an upper floor which was usually occupied
by the writer Eleanor Clark, and placed the flowers squarely in
the middle of her bed.

I much preferred the company of Richard Bermann, the
Austrian refugee. As often as possible, I would try to sit at the
same table with him. He was a master storyteller, a fount of

autobiographical anecdotes which he related with a singular refinement of wit and grace through fat, purplish lips that seemed totally unsuited to the subtleties that passed through them. He had no explanation for his squat body and potato-skin coloring, but the lips he facetiously ascribed to the escapades of a gadding grandmother traveling through the heart of Africa. The fascination of his stories usually stemmed from a narrative style nicely laced with irony rather than their content. But it was the content of one story that made it stick in my memory long after the others had faded away.

In Vienna, while Gestapo agents were hunting for him, Bermann found refuge in the tiny apartment of a former girlfriend who went to an office job every morning. In order to keep out of sight while the girl was at work, Bermann spent most of the day under her bed. The nights were pleasantly occupied with the girl in the bed, but after he had read what few books there were in the apartment the daylight hours under the bed seemed endless. To relieve the tedium, he hit on the idea of passing away the time by writing a novel. The manuscript was nearly completed when Bermann was suddenly obliged to find a new hiding place; in the rush of leaving the apartment before the Gestapo agents got there, he left the manuscript behind. "A pity," he commented with an impish grin. "Had I been able to complete it, it would have established a new literary category—novels written under a bed."

The story was to become an epitaph of sorts on the morning I saw his body being carried out of the mansion into a funeral limousine, leaving behind another unfinished Bermann manuscript. This happened the morning after we had listened to the fateful announcement on radio that World War II had definitely begun: the German army had invaded Poland. At the dinner table he showed no signs of being disturbed by the news, but his avoidance of the subject struck me as significant. Even while the funeral car was drawing away from the mansion I began to hear the rumor that Bermann had taken his own life, a rumor which the *New York Times* obituary story, that ascribed his death to a heart attack during the night, did little to squelch.

The day before the Polish invasion an official photograph of the Yaddoites, for the archives, had been taken on the grand stairway of the mansion. Only two of the group responded to the photographer's plea for a smile: Newton Arvin, the literary historian who had been mainly responsible for my Yaddo fellowship, and Federico Castellan, a Spanish artist, who looked younger and healthier than the rest of the group but who was to die before most of them. The rest of the faces registered a variety of expressions ranging from disdain to deep preoccupation. The most worried face belonged to Josephine Herbst who, with the exception of Bermann and the other European refugees, was better informed about the impending explosion in Europe than the rest of us.

The presence of Nathan Asch in the picture recalls a one-line drama enacted between him and his friend Josephine in a Saratoga Springs restaurant crowded with Skidmore coeds. The students witnessed a grimly determined Josephine enter the dining room and head straight for a telephone booth in the rear where, without bothering to close its door, she dialed a number, then shouted into the telephone for all the world to hear: "Nathan, if you don't do as I say, I'm going to come there and cut off your balls." She then slammed down the receiver and with her jaw still tightly set she strode toward the door, while the Skidmore girls applauded and cheered.

The only disdainful face in the photograph was that of a Midwestern woman in her late twenties who had come to Yaddo to work on her first novel. On first meeting her, most of the male writers had been delighted with her flirtatious ways and had gladly accepted the invitation to visit her studio privately. But by the time the photograph was taken all the men were avoiding her as though she had a contagious disease; they had discovered that what she wanted of them was not their bodies but their help in writing her novel. They were further put on their guard by a document she carried on her person which, signed by a Utah police captain, purported to certify that she had been raped on a certain date. She enjoyed exhibiting the document at the slightest pretext; curiously, she seemed to regard it as a means of averting further rape. When one of the writers warned her that it was dangerous for a lone woman to walk to and from town after dark, as had become her custom, she replied: "I'm not at all worried. I always carry my certificate of rape with me."

Her peculiar behavior proved to be too much even for Mrs. Ames, who in her capacity as director had long become accustomed to the varied peculiarities of Yaddo guests. After the woman had repeatedly feigned illness because she was attracted to the handsome young doctor summoned each time to her bedroom (at Yaddo expense) Mrs. Ames ran out of patience and asked her to leave. Eventually, the first novel she had been trying to write at Yaddo was duly published by a prestigious Boston house, and much to the mystification of all the writers whose assistance she had solicited, it was enthusiastically reviewed as one of the best novels of that year.

Missing from the group photograph was the composer Marc Blitzstein. Two years before, Blitzstein had become the darling of the New York intelligentsia with his opera, *The Cradle Will Rock*, a devastatingly sardonic indictment of capitalism. The weekend before Bermann's death, Blitzstein threw a clandestine cocktail party for Gypsy Rose Lee, who was then at the crest of her career as the nation's leading stripper. The secrecy of the gathering was based on Blitzstein's fear that Mrs. Ames might object to it. Nearly everyone else was present, including her sister Marjorie Waite.°

The party was staged in Blitzstein's spectacular studio, the replica of a medieval tower room, complete with moat and

---

° Marjorie Waite was the adopted daughter of George Foster Peabody, Spencer Trask's business partner. Peabody, along with Katrina Trask (Spencer Trask's widow and ultimately Peabody's wife), established Yaddo as a retreat for artists in 1922. It began functioning in 1926.

bridge, overlooking the ghostliest of the Yaddo lakes. An even more incongruous aspect of the affair was the bucolic semblance of its guest of honor who, far from suggesting a sexually teasing siren of the burlesque stage, smacked of a wholesome Iowa farming girl with her hair pulled back in a ponytail and her face glowingly pink as if it had just been scrubbed hard with soap and water. Yet there was no mistaking her libidinous allure. The only heterosexual male at the party who seemed indifferent to it was her current husband, a manufacturer of dental equipment. He went from one guest to another trying to elicit sympathy for the bad state of his ulcer, with little success.

Although our relationship was never anything more than that of casual acquaintances, it was Bermann who made the deepest impression on me at Yaddo that summer.* The only permanent record I have of him is the Yaddo group photograph which shows him seated behind Delmore Schwartz and next to Von Ripper, who is behind Eleanor Clark. Bermann is the least conspicuous figure in the photo. Everything in his face appears hidden, the eyes by a pair of thick lenses, the rest of the face by the bemused mask of a man accustomed to concealing his private thoughts.

Although there was barely any discussion of Bermann's death, it, as much as its apocalyptic timing, cast a pall on all of us at first. But within a few days, as if to convince ourselves that Bermann's death need not portend our own defeat, we were hard at work on our projects once more.

My Yaddo sojourn was rapidly drawing to a close, and once again I was faced with the problem of earning a livelihood, but for the first time there was no difficulty finding congenial work. On the recommendation of my former chief, M. E. Gilfond, I was hired by the Works Progress Administration to write the

---

* Bermann was to become my inspiration for a leading character in my novel *The Ship and the Flame* (1948), which deals with a group of refugees escaping Europe at the beginning of World War II. In the narrative the character based on Bermann (Renner) commits suicide rather than submit to capture by the Nazis.

captions for its exhibition in the 1939 New York World's Fair; on completing that stint, the Department of Commerce appointed me as a public-relations consultant to stimulate magazine publicity for the forthcoming 1940 Census. Charles Jackson, whose first novel, *The Lost Weekend*, was to make him rich and famous five years later, was hired at the same time to do similar work with the radio networks. The publicity was deemed necessary to help alleviate the anxiety of the public when it was confronted by many new and seemingly prying questions the Census Bureau was planning to ask.

Although I was on the Census Bureau's Washington payroll, my station was New York, and I had only to report to Washington twice a month. It was a joy being in Manhattan again, especially since Margaret managed to be transferred there for a year and lived with me in a Bank Street apartment I rented. Persuading magazine editors to publish articles on the 1940 Census seemed wonderfully simple after my experience as the Writers' Project literary agent, but I missed the excitement of the Project with its overlapping crises and volatile personalities. Except for Charles Jackson, my Census Bureau colleagues were typical bureaucrats, agreeable but unimaginative. Jackson, whom I invariably encountered each time I visited the Washington office, was unlike anyone I had ever met. Making friends, I soon discovered, was a mania with him. His overtures at friendship extended from the lowliest office clerk to the executive in charge of his work. He seemed to believe that if one did not become his friend, he might become his enemy. It was as if he were constantly engaged in a strategy of ingratiation by which he would avoid some awful impending disaster.

Deliberate or not, his display of vulnerability was so candid as to affect the most conventional of his colleagues. He spoke freely of his traumatic past: of his tubercular condition in earlier years when he betook himself to the same Swiss sanitarium Thomas Mann immortalized in one of Jackson's favorite novels, *The Magic Mountain;* of his years as an alcoholic, which he was about to synthesize fictionally into a single weekend, and of his marital difficulties which, to a close listener, were, like his alcoholism, related to homosexual inclinations. I envied his ability to talk uninhibitedly, to keep nothing within himself that might fester and poison; and thought how Bermann, who hid his problems behind a barricade of anecdotes, and Bill Rollins, who was gradually drinking himself to an early grave because he could speak easily of everything but his personal problems, might have been better off revealing all as Jackson did.

The Census Bureau job came to an end in April 1940, just a week before the Nazi army seized all of Denmark and the greater part of Norway. Apparently I had done my work well. Gilfond, noting the number of national magazines that had published articles on the forthcoming census at my urging, offered to finance me should I decide to become a professional literary agent; and Roscoe Wright, the Census Bureau's public-relations director, hinted that I might expect a job offer from him soon, but having saved enough money to see me through until the following fall, I had no desire to work on anything else but my book. Afraid that my savings would be spent quickly if I remained in Manhattan, I looked for a country place which would be cheaper and have fewer distractions, but one not too far from the city.

An invitation to work on my manuscript at Cold-Spring-on-Hudson came from my friends Paul Corey and his wife, Ruth Lechlitner, who lived on a small chicken farm. Paul, who detested office life, had recently quit his Writers' Project job in Albany and was completing his trilogy of Iowa farm life.* Between bouts on the typewriter, Paul, a formidable handyman, was constructing a spacious home with his own hands, often trading the eggs he got from his hens for building materials. "The house with a foundation of eggs," a friend called

---

* *Three Miles Square* (1939), *The Road Returns* (1940), and *County Seat* (1941).

it. Ruth was a published poet with a passion for cats, wild-flowers, and gardening, who kept the family solvent with her earnings as a book reviewer. There was a strong bond of affection between the three of us.

Paul was an eloquent dissenter who constantly addressed complaints to newspapers, politicians, and capitalistic enterprises. At the end of each letter he invariably wrote: "Copy to Drew Pearson." ° He was also a keen student of military problems. Unlike my friend Kenneth Burke who had written me that "the attempt to say what's going on in Europe would be like the job of a radio announcer giving a blow-by-blow description of a free-for-all while blindfolded," Paul was seldom at a loss to analyze the political and military strategy of any nation involved in the European war.

When the United States entered the war the following year, Paul promptly applied for an army commission, expecting that his great fund of military knowledge would be useful to the intelligence service. Quite certain of getting the commission but unhappy at the prospect of leaving a lonely wife behind, he waived his long-standing objection to bring children into a disaster-prone world in order that Ruth could occupy herself with their child while he was in the Army. The child, a daughter with Paul's blue eyes and blond hair, was born a few weeks before the Army notified Paul that his application for a commission was rejected.

Our friendship was of such durability that it was able to survive the emotional tennis match of a literary collaboration. Shortly after the war in Spain began, we wrote a one-act play, *The Loyalist.* It was based on Prosper Merimée's short-story masterpiece, "Matteo Falcone," in which a Corsican father executes his corruptible young son for betraying a refugee from the law. Instead of Corsica, our setting was Spain; we made our

° Drew Pearson then conducted the syndicated column "Washington Merry-Go-Round." Nowadays Paul Corey sends copies of his complaints to Pearson's successor, Jack Anderson.

protagonists Loyalists and Fascists. The play was never produced because we insisted on keeping the ending intact, as
Mérimée had written it. That a father could bring himself to
kill his own son was too grim a resolution for American tastes,
producers maintained. We got nowhere with the argument that
Americans were mature enough to accept the thesis of a father
shooting his son for the sake of a principle which was essential
to his code of honor. While nothing came of our effort, it
deepened my respect for Paul's ability to write convincingly of
characters who were totally removed from his own experience.
In a sense, this talent explained how we could have become
friends, for his Midwest Anglo-Saxon farm background bore not
the slightest resemblance to mine.

Actually, most of the literati I encountered at the Coreys' for
weekend sessions of drinking, gossiping, and arguing were of
diverse backgrounds. On one weekend I found myself sharing a
room with an old acquaintance, Richard Wright, who joked and
clowned for all of us and, in the mornings while quite sober,
would outdo the Coreys' resident rooster with a series of
exuberant crows that were difficult to distinguish from the real
thing. His happy mood may well have come from the news that
his first novel, *Native Son* (1940), had just been selected by the
Book-of-the-Month Club and was headed for the best-seller lists
even before publication. We had met while we were on the
Writers' Project, shortly after I had persuaded Henry Alsberg to
include his "Ethics of Living Jim Crow" in the Project's
anthology *American Stuff* (1937); later it became one of the
stories in Wright's first book, *Uncle Tom's Children* (1938), for
which he was awarded a Guggenheim Fellowship to write
Native Son.

In Harlem we had once attended a performance of one of the
Federal Theatre Project's biggest hits, *Macbeth*, which, set in
Haiti with an all-black cast and voodoo-practicing witches,
became popularly known as *Blackbeth*. Over a drink after the
play, apropos of writers like ourselves who could not write well
without feeling sexually close to some woman, Wright con-

fessed that although he had a number of white friends, some of them women, he could never take a Caucasian wife. A few years later when he did, after a brief first marriage to a black girl, it took me some time to understand how he could have changed his mind for he had placed a great deal of stress on the word "never." The key to the explanation may have been that his original resolution was based on the surging anger he felt toward the white race. This hatred, which provided the stimulus for expressing his literary talent, was bound to abate once he experienced the catharsis gained from writing his early short stories and *Native Son*. With the catharsis, he achieved the equilibrium he needed to distinguish between whites who would always be the enemy and whites, like the Jewess he married and his white friends, who could never be.

My fondness for the Coreys and their friends tempted me to accept their invitation to live with them while I worked on my manuscript; but, finally, the image of three writers under the same small roof vying for privacy and the same bathroom led me to make other plans. I accepted, instead, Kenneth Burke's offer to live in a barn on his farm in northern New Jersey. For one hundred dollars I could occupy two furnished rooms of his barn all summer and as far into the autumn as I could withstand the cold. The facilities were primitive: kerosene lamps, outhouse, and water that had to be carried about fifty yards, from a pump adjacent to the Burke farmhouse. The accommodations of the Burkes were equally primitive, mainly because Burke, who described himself as an Agro-Bohemian, abhorred the polluting effects of technology and considered all utilities dispensing electricity as the arch fiends of capitalistic society. True to his beliefs, he would not permit a single electric wire to run through any part of his property.

More appealing than the rustic life was the prospect of spending a few months as a close neighbor of KB (as he preferred to be called). As I knew from his writings, he was a great deal more than an Agro-Bohemian: poet, novelist, short-story writer, critic, musicologist, psychologist, philosopher, semanticist. His insights into Aristotle, St. Augustine, Marx, and Freud put him head and shoulders above most literary commentators, a fact that was not generally appreciated since his writing style was too complex for most readers. In the thirties a mutual friend estimated that the number of Americans who could fully understand Burke's writings numbered less than a thousand; and there might have been some question about them for as one critic put it: "Burke's thoughts are as elusive as shadows. Getting the gist is like trying to put salt on the tail of a brilliantly plumaged bird. Once you think you have him firmly in hand, you find yourself clutching a vivid tailfeather or two while he has gone off again."

Yet, as I knew from previous dealings with him, outside the pages of his books he was down-to-earth and quite understandable, a commoner with uncommon points of view that were not difficult to follow. When he talked, which was often, his eyes lighted up, as though a switch had been turned on inside, and his hands and arms became as gesticulatory as those of an Italian or Jew. There was nothing glib about him, either in the way he expressed himself or in the way he interpreted what was said to him. Words obsessed him too much to be taken lightly. On the other hand, he could not help frequently interrupting himself with laughter, as though to lighten the burden of his meaning.

In the late afternoons, after we had quit our typewriters for the day and were ready to discuss the latest news, as reported in the *New York Times,* we would rest on the lawn in front of his house and talk. Even as KB talked, both hands kept busy, one of them gesticulating, the other clenching a knife that rooted out the weeds in his lawn with a vehemence that suggested he was symbolically getting rid of the world's evils. I could tell how strongly he felt about a subject by the degree of passion with which he attacked the weeds. His sense of humor appealed to me as much as his seriousness; he often managed to combine both.

"Am now swamped in my material on Human Relations," he

AN ETHNIC AT LARGE

had written me shortly before my arrival. "Hoping against hope that I'll get it done while there are still some left." After a bitter feud with the editors of the *Partisan Review*, he sent me this message: "Here are some lines I whisper to the selph like a stentor, while out bumping among the trees:

Cockneys get their aitches wrong,
But if you would get yours true
Then join the ever-growing throng
That puts an aitch in P()artisan Review.

His wit spared no one, least of all himself. "When he didn't fight other people, he fought himself—and boy! could he fight dirty." And although Aristotle was a favorite mentor, he observed that "Aristotle, who believed that we think with our stomachs, died of dyspepsia." Of a mutual acquaintance, he wrote, "He had learned to be one of those simple, wholesome people who stay sane by driving other people crazy." Reflecting autobiographically one afternoon, KB noted that he might never have become a man of letters had he not, as a young child, tried to spit down a stairwell. He had leaned over too far in the effort, and landed on his head two flights below. (It was not until many years later that doctors discovered he had broken his neck.) The accident prevented him from attending school until he was eight years old, by which time he had lost his earlier hatred of books and was so eager to read well that, even before he could attend school, he carried a dictionary around the house with him.

As a voracious reader, he grew up wanting to be a writer. His first story, "La Baudelairienne," concerned a beautiful girl whose face had been disfigured by acid. To express his sympathy and show how much he loved her, her lover scarred his own face with acid. When the girl saw him, she shrieked in horror: "Get out, get out!"

After KB had finished his high school education in Pittsburgh, he attended Ohio State and Columbia University but dropped out as soon as he discovered that in order to study the courses that interested him, he was required to take courses that did not. Not wanting to waste time, and also afraid that if he pursued the regular college curriculum he would become a scholar instead of a writer, he went to his father with the following proposition: "Pay me a fraction of what you are paying Columbia and let me live in Greenwich Village and I promise I'll get my education by myself." The elder Burke agreed, and KB spent the next several years studying in the best New York libraries.

By the time we met in the early thirties, through his friend Malcolm Cowley, KB was already well known in intellectual circles both as a critic (music as well as literature) and a writer of short stories. In 1928, he had won the *Dial* award for distinguished service to American letters. In 1932, he published his first and only novel, *Towards a Better Life,* whose main character is a man losing his mind. Burke had tried to follow the conventional form of a novel but, becoming bored with all the mundane details that entailed, he wound up writing the novel as a series of perceptive essays about his characters. Burke then gave up fiction writing altogether and returned to the high cerebral polemics he had begun in 1931 with *Counter Statement,* a work whose unorthodox proposals incensed both Marxists and establishment spokesmen.

Adopting the position of when in Rome, do as the Greeks do, Burke held that the most effective way to sabotage the nation's ugly and inefficient industrial system was to encourage artists to emphasize the negative aspects of life under capitalism, such as indolence, dissipation, distrust, hypochondria, bad sportsmanship. He argued that by stressing such qualities the bourgeois, the machine, the efficiency expert, and the patrioteer can be checked. With Machiavellian finesse, he added that "a society is sound only if it can prosper on its vices, since virtues are by very definition rare and exceptional."

Left-wing critics described his views as frivolous and nihilistic and characterized his philosophy as that of "the petit

bourgeois gone mad." The Depression had brought Burke closer
to the views of the Communist party but, in the face of its
attacks, he stuck by his guns. Being called a petit bourgeois did
not offend him since he considered himself one. At the first
American Writers' Congress in 1935, he scandalized the
orthodox Communists in the audience by proposing that all
future left-wing propaganda substitute the word "people" for
"masses." He argued that words like "masses," "workers," and
"proletarians" tended to exclude some of the very elements in
society that the Communists were trying to win over. At the
end of his presentation, he acknowledged that his advice bore
"the telltale stamp of my class, the petite bourgeoisie," but
held that the allegiance of his class to the left-wing cause was
"vitally important."

For these views he was severely reprimanded in public by
such Communist bigwigs as Mike Gold and Joseph Freeman,
who gave elaborate Marxist reasons for rejecting the use of
"people." Only two months later both men were obliged to
swallow their rationales when the Comintern passed a resolution calling for a "People's Front," in which Communist parties
in all countries were urged to ally themselves with as many
liberals and bourgeois, petit and otherwise, as possible.

Burke's unorthodox education may have contributed to his
tendency to shy away from the orthodoxies of his contemporaries. In the twenties, unlike many of his intellectual friends,
he neither allied himself with left-wing groups nor did he join
the American expatriates in Paris. Deeply involved with his
reading, writing, and family life—he had married at the age of
twenty-two—he followed no direction but his own. After the
1929 crash, he moved his family to an abandoned New Jersey
farm near Andover which he and his wife had bought for a
song; but he did not abandon Manhattan. He was music critic
for the *Nation* for two years, and he lectured to university
students in the city on the practice and theory of literary
criticism. In the three hours spent on commuting back and
forth to New York, he applied his remarkable powers of

concentration to translating a number of German books by such noted writers as Oswald Spengler, Thomas Mann, and Emil Ludwig. Meanwhile, he was gathering notes for a series of books dealing with the strategy of ideas and symbols that would establish his reputation here and in England as the twentieth-century Aristotle.°

Other than the information that he was the father of three daughters and a young son, I knew little of KB's private life; but in the course of the summer I learned that the seemingly smooth rhythm of his personal life was marked by a dramatic undercurrent of Shakespearean dimension. Libby, the woman who had become his second wife seven years before, was the younger sister of KB's first wife. They had fallen in love shortly after KB's move to Andover, and after some monumental wrestling with their consciences, KB divorced his first wife and married Libby. Now the two sisters lived on the same road within a short walk of each other; the first Mrs. Burke and her three daughters were in the spacious main house of the property, while Libby and KB and their son occupied a small farmhouse. Except for the first wife, who was seldom seen, the two families lived almost as one, the daughters spending nearly as much time with KB and Libby as they did with their mother.

Observing KB and Libby together in a marriage that seemed heaven ordained, I could not imagine KB being married to anyone else, certainly not to his first wife with whom he had little in common, except for their progeny. Unlike her older sister, Libby was sparkling and imaginative and, though of independent thought, so closely attuned to her husband's complex temperament as to give the impression that she may well have understood it better than he did. I had never known a better marriage; yet the circumstances that begat it and the deep conflicts it must have stirred in the two sisters and in KB

° Kenneth Burke's most important books include *Permanence and Change* (1935), *Attitudes Toward History* (1937), *The Philosophy of Literary Form* (1941), *A Grammar of Motives* (1946), *A Rhetoric of Motives* (1950), *The Rhetoric of Religion* (1961), *Language as Symbolic Action* (1966).

struck me as mind-boggling as anything in the literature of drama which Burke, a master among modern-day critics, had ever attempted to analyze.

Except for KB's occasional bouts with dyspepsia and insomnia, there were no outward symptoms of psychological stress among any of the drama's protagonists. An atmosphere of accomplishment and conviviality prevailed. Although I followed a rigid work schedule every day, there was always time for discussions with KB on the lawn, which did me a world of good. From them I gained a more intelligent perspective on the dialectics of the thirties which, after such alarming developments as the Moscow trials, the Nazi-Soviet pact, and the Soviet's war on Finland, I sorely needed to preserve my self-respect for having championed the Soviet Union during most of the thirties.

The evenings were frequently given to entertainment. The tenants (there were a half dozen of us that summer occupying the various small buildings on the Burke property) and whatever visiting guests were about would foregather at the Burke farmhouse to drink, talk, and sing old songs to piano accompaniment provided by KB on an ancient upright.* There was also time for sports, for swimming in the Burke pond, for tennis, and most of all for croquet which sometimes had the vicious overtones of warfare and continued into the night, with flashlights and lanterns guiding the aim of the passionate players.

While I lived a paradisaical existence, with my manuscript flourishing and Margaret joining me weekends, Nazi fire power was consuming one European nation after another. By June 1940, when I arrived at Andover, the German armies had conquered Holland, Belgium, Norway, Denmark, and Luxembourg. As an advertisement of its ruthlessness, the German

---

* Among the friends of the Burkes who visited their place that summer were Peter Bloom, the painter, Malcolm and Muriel Cowley, Matthew and Hannah Josephson, and Allen Tate and his wife, Caroline Gordon.

Luftwaffe had raided the defenseless city of Rotterdam and killed thirty thousand civilians. On June 17, the French forces, under the feeble leadership of Marshal Pétain, capitulated to the Nazi, and Hitler was preparing to dance a jig in Paris. As President Roosevelt had foreseen during the White House supper I attended the year before, Great Britain now became the only hope left for the survival of democracy in Europe.

For the first time since the advent of Hitler as Germany's Führer, Congress expressed alarm over the events in Europe. Moved to a point of hysteria by the rapid conquests of the Nazi armies in their westward drive, and suddenly fearful that a "fifth column" might be forming in the United States to take over the government, Congress hurriedly passed the Smith bill (eventually known as the Alien Registration Act), which in the late summer of 1940 made it mandatory for all aliens residing in the United States to be registered and fingerprinted.

Attorney General Robert H. Jackson called the new law "a phase of our national defense program." But both he and the Solicitor General, Francis Biddle, who was to become Attorney General the following year when Jackson was elevated to the United States Supreme Court, recognized it as a neurotic reflection of congressional fears which could easily create irreparable harm by alienating the large segment of foreign-born residents who were not citizens. To prevent the law from backfiring, it had to be administered with great skill and tact; somehow, aliens had to be convinced that the Smith Act was not an expression of hostility toward them. Biddle entrusted the task to a prominent Philadelphia lawyer, Earl G. Harrison, a New Deal Republican who had worked closely with social agencies involved with the foreign born.

For his deputy Harrison chose a University of Pennsylvania classmate, Donald Perry, a Yugoslav by birth despite his name. To direct the intensive publicity program that would inform aliens of what they had to do to comply with the law, while simultaneously assuring them they would not be fitting a noose around their necks by submitting to registration and fingerprinting, Harrison selected my erstwhile chief, M. E. Gilfond, a Jew. Gilfond, in turn, decided he wanted me as his chief assistant. To what extent his choice was motivated by my Italian background I would never know, but it may well have been a primary consideration since the number of Italian aliens in the country far surpassed that of any other immigrant group.

When Gilfond's telegraphed offer arrived in Andover, my first reaction was to turn it down. I wanted to keep on writing my manuscript in the Burke barn as far into the autumn as the weather would permit, but I soon realized that in good conscience the job in Washington must take precedence over the manuscript. Sooner or later the United States was bound to be directly involved in the war. Already it was an indirect participant. With France firmly in Nazi control and Great Britain looming as Hitler's next big target, the Americans were about to sell the British fifty overage American destroyers in exchange for naval bases. It would only be a matter of months, I figured, when some major disaster, of such magnitude as the sinking of the *Lusitania* in World War I, would catapult the Americans, isolationists and all, into the fray.

Until that happened, I owed it to my anti-Fascist convictions to help Gilfond mount an informational program that would try to mitigate the nasty implications of the Smith Act. There was also the consideration that as an Italian American I perhaps understood the mentality of Italian aliens and their basic loyalty to the American government better than anyone called Biddle or Harrison, and might conceivably serve as their friend in court.

While I was sending Gilfond my telegram of acceptance, I could not help muse on the curious fact that now there would be two persons, first cousins, with the baptismal name of Gerlando Mangione working for Departments of Justice, one in Fascist Rome, the other in Washington, D.C.

ELEVEN

Washington at War

The sneak attack on Pearl Harbor was more than a year away, but the frenetic atmosphere throughout the Alien Registration Division, which had been hastily installed in an abandoned ice-skating rink, suggested that we were already at war. The rapidly assembled staff, which included twenty young lawyers imported from Philadelphia, worked feverishly in the sticky summer heat to prepare the complicated apparatus and regulations for registering and fingerprinting an undetermined number of American residents who had never acquired American citizenship.

Originally, the aliens were to have been registered and fingerprinted at police stations, but Francis Biddle and Earl Harrison, in their determination to minimize the unfriendly implications of mandatory fingerprinting, insisted that the registration take place in the nation's post offices instead. Taking his cue from them, M. E. Gilfond set the guidelines for a pre-registration publicity campaign which was designed to allay the fears of the aliens while impressing them with the need to comply with the law. My own contribution was to implement the campaign with news releases, question-and-answer pamphlets, and other information materials that would tell the aliens what to do. At the same time, the nation's social-service agencies and foreign-language press were mobilized to help the aliens in every possible way.

In a nationwide attempt to ease the minds of aliens, a number of foreign-born celebrities who were not citizens were persuaded to be registered and fingerprinted by Earl Harrison on coast-to-coast radio networks. But despite all such efforts, it was impossible to convince many of the aliens that registration would not get them into trouble. Some had reason to be afraid. Having entered the country illegally and not realizing that it might be possible to legalize their status, they equated registration with deportation. Others simply refused to believe they would not be placing themselves in jeopardy by identifying themselves as aliens. All such men and women were likely to become the prey of shyster lawyers who, as soon as the registration was announced, began to exploit their fears regardless of whether or not they were justified.°

Earl Harrison, fortunately, proved to be a perfect choice for the job. With a degree of genuine empathy which at that time of my life I found remarkable in one who called himself a Republican, he understood the fears of the aliens and did everything within his administrative powers to calm them. Through the social-service agencies and the foreign-language press he also stressed certain positive aspects of the Alien Registration Act which, in the heat of the antagonism it evoked, had been generally ignored. One of its most redeeming features, he pointed out, was that as a federal law it forestalled

° There was no law to prevent the rash of shyster-lawyer establishments that suddenly sprang up to exploit aliens fearing the registration. In Manhattan I saw my colleague Harold Lund, whose only authority was to deal with social-service agencies, put one of these establishments out of business. A master of chutzpah, he simply flashed his Department of Justice building pass, then informed the receptionist that her boss was to report to the office of the United States Attorney the next morning. When we passed the place the next day, the sign advertising "Expert Advice to Aliens" was gone; in its place was a big "For Rent" sign.

the hysterical plans of overly patriotic communities which, responding to the panic notion that every alien was either a fifth columnist or a potential one, had been contemplating their own registration and fingerprinting programs. Harrison also suggested that the factual data resulting from the registration could dispel much of the ignorance that characterized the average American's concept of aliens and provide a solid foundation for a broad Americanization program.

Harrison's social conscience and innate sense of decency were so much like Eleanor Roosevelt's that I resolved to get the two together. Mrs. Roosevelt readily agreed, especially as she was receiving a great deal of mail from distressed aliens, and invited Harrison, his wife, and me to join her at the White House for Sunday dinner.

The occasion took place on December 8, 1940, while the President was out of the country, on the first leg of a fifteen-day Caribbean cruise to investigate American and British military bases. Without Roosevelt's dynamic presence, the dinner lacked the excitement of my first visit to the White House. Except for a sharp but brief exchange between two of the guests—Eric Biddle and Henry Morgenthau—a cool aura of politeness prevailed during most of the dinner, despite the steady flow of warmth from our hostess.

The Harrisons and I were the first to arrive. An attendant ushered us into a blue room with gilded chairs, informed us that Mrs. Roosevelt would join us shortly, and showed us a diagram indicating where we were to sit at the table. From the outset it became evident to Harrison and me that the dinner could hardly serve as the proper setting for a frank discussion of alien registration problems, for the first guests to join us were a Chinese couple, members of that race which our naturalization laws had, since 1882, specifically excluded from United States citizenship. They were Dr. T. V. Soong, the handsome brother of Madame Chiang Kai-shek and head of the Central Bank of China, and Mrs. Soong, a spectacular beauty with exquisitely delicate features.

Mrs. Harrison, seldom at a loss for words, at once began speaking of a favorite author, Lin Yutang, a Chinese writer of American best sellers. Dr. Soong listened politely, with no noticeable enthusiasm, then remarked that Pearl Buck had written some excellent books about the Chinese. There was an awkward pause fortunately interrupted by the arrival of Henry Morgenthau, Jr., the Secretary of the Treasury, whose long thin nose, the subject of many cartoons, provided immediate identification. With him was his wife, a small woman with a worried countenance and a friendly smile.

While the guests valiantly tried to make conversation as they waited for Mrs. Roosevelt, a carelessly dressed man with an untied shoelace walked into the room and introduced himself as Eric Biddle. Remarking that it would never do to be in the White House with an untied shoe, he proceeded to tie his. This prompted Mrs. Morgenthau to confess she had gone walking that morning and had forgotten to change her shoes. We were all gazing at her feet when Mrs. Roosevelt strode in full of apology for her tardiness. She had a kiss for Mrs. Morgenthau, an old friend; a warm greeting for Mrs. Soong, whom she obviously knew from other social occasions, and friendly salutations for the rest of us.

Mrs. Roosevelt singled out Mrs. Morgenthau and Mrs. Soong for further special attention by presenting each of them with a small silver donkey figure (Mrs. Harrison received no donkey, presumably because Mrs. Roosevelt assumed she was a Republican, like her husband). While the two ladies were pinning the donkeys to their dresses, our hostess told us about the enterprising Mexican who owned the donkey that had modeled for the pin. The Mexican advertised the beast as a famous personality—the only donkey model in the world—and charged admission to an exhibition of him.

After we were ushered into a spacious dining room on the ground floor and had taken our places at the table, I rode the back of the donkey story to get into the subject of alien registration. I told of the alien, illegally in the country, who had recently written the Immigration Service an unsigned letter declaring that the only friend he had in this country was his horse; he was the only one who never asked him what country he came from or whether he was an American citizen. Mrs. Roosevelt began describing some of the mail she was receiving from worried aliens, letters as varied and poignant as those that came to our office. In one letter a woman expressed the fear that some of the information she would be asked to reveal in the registration might get back to her husband; he did not know that as a young woman she had served a prison sentence for stealing. The woman had tried to tell him about it before they married but he refused to listen to her then, insisting that "the past was past." Now that they had been married for a long time and her husband was not as much in love with her, she was afraid he might have different thoughts about the past.

Mrs. Roosevelt was also concerned with a letter from a highly respected member of a community who was afraid he would lose his standing when it was learned he was an alien. He had been voting for years under the impression he was a citizen, but had recently discovered he had not fulfilled all the formal requirements of the naturalization law and was subject to the registration law.

Harrison foresaw no difficulties for either of the letter writers. They could avoid the possibility of embarrassment by simply registering in any city where the registration clerks were not likely to know them; nothing in the law required aliens to register in the communities where they lived.

That was all very well for informed aliens, Mrs. Roosevelt commented, but she was concerned about the aliens not familiar with the law, of whom there must be thousands. She reminded Harrison that many had never learned English; they lived among their compatriots and knew only enough of the language to earn their livelihood. Harrison tried to assure her that his office was trying to reach as many of them as possible through the foreign-language press and radio.

As the discussion continued, it became apparent that Mrs.

Roosevelt's main objection to the registration was that it clearly discriminated against one segment of the population. Expressing a similar view, Harrison approvingly cited Mayor La Guardia's stand that all Americans, citizens and aliens alike, should be registered and fingerprinted. Our hostess was uncertain about the advisability of universal registration since it smacked of regimentation; she favored fingerprinting as an infallible method of identification, but conceded there might be some justification for some of the fears expressed by its opponents.

Mrs. Roosevelt must have sensed that a prolonged discussion about aliens might lead into embarrassing territory for she cut it short by turning to Soong, who sat next to her good ear, and engaged him in a private conversation. Without her leadership, the conversation sagged; the rest of us seemed to have little or nothing to say to one another. When, to our relief, she reentered the general conversation, she told of an amusing experience she had during a recent radio broadcast with Archibald MacLeish. While she was listening to MacLeish discourse on the place of the arts in the world today, the producer of the program, feeling that she was doing too much listening and not enough talking, thrust a note under her nose. The first line read: "Be a——"and was followed by the drawing of a lion flexing its muscles; the second line, "don't be a——" depicted a mouse.

Only once were there any conversational fireworks. Mrs. Roosevelt started them by asking Morgenthau, for everyone to hear, whether it was true that we were about to lend the Spanish Franco government the sum of one hundred thousand dollars. "Darling," he corrected her patiently, "they never ask for that little. They probably want one hundred million dollars." Everyone laughed, Mrs. Roosevelt as heartily as the rest. Morgenthau said he was unable to account for the rumor about the loan; that very morning he had asked Jesse Jones (the administrator of the Federal Loan Agency) about it and he too was in the dark. Whereupon Mrs. Roosevelt revealed she had "asked Franklin about it" and he had told her that he wished he knew "what it was all about."

At that point Eric Biddle, who had recently been abroad as the executive director of an American committee concerned with the care of European children, set fire to the discussion by insisting it would be politically wise to help Spain get on its feet, arguing that with millions of Spaniards left destitute by the recent Civil War, we could lend them money with no fear that it would be used for military expenditures. Franco's request for a loan, he believed, offered the United States an important opportunity for winning Spain's friendship, expressing a point of view not unlike that of the British government which had recently favored American aid to Spain on the grounds that it might help keep Spain neutral, uninvolved with the Rome-Berlin axis.

No one at the table shared Biddle's opinion. Mrs. Roosevelt emphatically opposed any loan to Spain, fearing that the money would not be used to alleviate poverty but would be used by Franco and his cohorts for Fascist purposes of their own. Even more vehemently, Morgenthau proclaimed that Spain would never get a loan from the United States, "except over my dead body." Biddle promptly retorted that while he was not wishing Morgenthau any bad luck, he sincerely hoped that Spain would be granted the loan. Replying to Mrs. Roosevelt's objection, he saw no reason why the American government could not stipulate exactly how the money was to be spent.

Nodding toward Soong, Morgenthau declared it was a good idea to give aid "to our friends in China and in South America (a loan of fifty million dollars to Argentina had been announced by him only three days before), but certainly not to Spain." Whether Morgenthau was being naive or paying lip service to Mrs. Roosevelt's feelings on the subject I could not be sure, but it seemed curious that a man of his vast experience in international finance would not realize that a loan made to a South American country, particularly to Argentina which was friendly toward the Franco government, could easily be siphoned off to Spain. Biddle may have had the same thought or known more about the rumored loan than he cared to reveal, for I detected a sardonic gleam in his eyes as he listened to Morgenthau's pronouncement.°

Toward the end of the dinner, while we were eating ice cream and cake, Mrs. Roosevelt, anxious perhaps to leave no doubt in the minds of the Soongs as to how she stood on the question of race relations, suddenly began describing "an embarrassing few moments" she had experienced in Texas earlier in the week while meeting with an assemblage of high school students. A Latin-American youngster who told her he came from a country where there was a great intermingling of white and Negro blood wanted to know how she could reconcile the traditional Southern attitude toward the racial question with the nation's professed democratic principles.

Mrs. Roosevelt confessed to us that the question put her "on the spot," explaining that although she had expressed her opinion on the subject on a number of private occasions, she had never done so in public. While debating with herself whether to be evasive or speak her mind, she decided that as she had "always tried to be honest" she owed the boy an honest reply. Agreeing with him that some Americans were denied certain opportunities because of their race or religion, she said she found the situation a disturbing one because she did not believe that a democracy which did not serve all of its people could long survive. Much to her surprise, she told us, the students gave her a big hand.

The sincerity with which Mrs. Roosevelt described the epi-

° That same afternoon, while glancing through the Sunday *New York Times*, I spotted a dispatch from Madrid which no one had mentioned at dinner. "As a gesture of goodwill the United States has authorized the sailing of a merchant ship to bring 10,000 tons of wheat to Spain. The wheat is the gift of the American Red Cross." The news story went on to say that "The gift has been matched by the British, who granted navicert for 150,000 tons of corn, *which Spain is obtaining from Argentina on credit.*" (My italics.)

sode made me squelch the temptation to comment that a number of the Texas students may have been applauding her courage for making the statement rather than endorsing its content. Harrison asked if the statement had created any "backfiring" in the press. "Not yet," she replied, then dryly noted that "sometimes newspapers don't print ideas they don't like."

On that note we left the table and went up to the second-floor living room where coffee was served. General conversation was no longer possible. A short time later, I was relieved when Mrs. Morgenthau signaled the end of the party by kissing Mrs. Roosevelt good-bye.

Two months later when his work as director of Alien Registration was completed, Harrison returned to his law practice in Philadelphia but remained with the Department of Justice as a dollar-a-year assistant to the Attorney General. At the same time Gilfond became chief of the department's public-relations unit and asked me to join his staff as a writer specializing in informational material dealing with the foreign born, aliens and citizens alike.

By that time we had access to some of the major statistical results of the registration. There were some four and three quarter million aliens in the nation, more than a million more than had been estimated. There was alarm expressed in some quarters that the number should be that large, but Harrison was quick to point out that the number represented the smallest percentage of aliens the country had ever had, and the Attorney General and his staff repeatedly expressed the government's faith in the loyalty of its noncitizen population. Yet in many sections of the country the antialien sentiment remained strong, and despite appeals to the "American sense of fairness," employers were overreacting to the potential danger of a fifth column and firing employees who were not citizens.

The reelection of Roosevelt in November 1940 for an unprecedented third term by a smaller vote than he had received in previous presidential elections did not alleviate the uneasiness that pervaded the country. Nor did the growing influence of the isolationist movement led by Charles Lindbergh and other prominent members of the America First Committee. Nor did the continued barrage of bad news from the European war fronts. The White House added to the uneasiness by using its clout to affect the passage of the Lend-Lease Act of 1941, which permitted the President to sell or lease war supplies to nations whose defense was considered vital to our own.

Meanwhile, the Department of Justice went on behaving as if our entry into the war was imminent. The Federal Bureau of Investigation intensified its effort, begun in 1939, to compile a list of persons born in Axis countries who might represent a threat to the national security once we were at war. Special attention was paid to the membership of the German-American Bund which, under the leadership of Fritz Kuhn, was openly championing the aims of Adolf Hitler.

At the same time the Immigration and Naturalization Service ° was preparing detailed plans for establishing internment camps that would imprison the aliens of enemy countries who were considered potentially dangerous, even though no funds had as yet been officially allocated for such a purpose. In the Attorney General's office, unbeknown to the general public, procedures were being established for arresting aliens and setting up civilian boards to give them hearings. The same office went so far as to prepare, for the President's signature, a series of proclamations directed against nationals of enemy countries which would be issued simultaneously with our declarations of war on those countries.

The department's immediate concern, as reflected in the speeches which my associates and I wrote for its top-ranking officials, was to assure the public once again that the government considered the vast majority of the foreign-born population to be loyal and law-abiding, regardless of where they were

° The Immigration and Naturalization Service became part of the Department of Justice on June 14, 1940, shortly after the passage of the Alien Registration Act. It had previously been in the Department of Labor.

born, and to convince the foreign-born that, notwithstanding the recent fingerprinting of aliens, the government had the highest regard for their Americanism. These two themes were repeatedly expressed with all the sincerity and documentation at our command. Everyone, from the Attorney General down the line, realized that unless there was continued amity between the foreign-born and the rest of the population, Fascist propagandists could make serious inroads into our national security. We also wanted to avert a repetition of the violent anti-German prejudice that became rampant throughout the nation during World War I.

I found that I enjoyed ghostwriting speeches, projecting myself into the character of the man delivering the speech as well as into the psychology of the audience for which it was intended. I began to regard each speech assignment as an opportunity to influence both the official for whom it was written as well as his audience. With the exception of Earl Harrison, who was more conscientious than most of his colleagues, the officials usually had few or no suggestions to make as to what I was to write for them. When I asked an assistant Attorney General if there were any particular points his speech should include, he looked baffled for a moment, then jauntily replied: "Oh, make it like the Gettysburg Address—but a little longer."

Sometimes a speech would be so compatible with the speaker's personality that he would eventually come to believe he had written it himself. One official suggested that the speech I write for him follow the lines of one he himself had "composed" a few months before. With that he reached into a desk drawer and handed me what turned out to be, verbatim, the manuscript of a speech I had prepared for him. Like a good ghostwriter I did not disabuse him of the illusion that he was its author but simply agreed that it would indeed make an excellent model.

The attack on Pearl Harbor put an end to my speechwriting for a while. The immediate task for me and the rest of Gilfond's staff was to let the aliens of enemy nationality know what was required of them. As soon as Congress had declared war on the Axis powers, the President signed the proclamations that designated more than one million persons as "enemy aliens," and the Attorney General issued regulations that put restraints on their possessions and travel.° Within hours after the Pearl Harbor bombing, the FBI arrested some one thousand aliens regarded as "potentially dangerous" and interned them until their cases could be examined by Alien Enemy Hearing boards, each made up of three civilians, which would recommend to the Attorney General whether the aliens be released, paroled, or interned.

Civil liberties took a back seat in those days; in the name of national defense expediency became the order of the day. The department's authority to "apprehend, detain or intern" any alien of enemy nationality for any reason whatsoever was based on an antiquated wartime law, the Alien Enemy Act of 1789, which still had the sanction of the courts. Patently unfair, the law included in its category of "alien enemies" the thousands of men and women who had been victimized by the Nazi and Fascist regimes and had come to the United States for refuge. Another inequity, authorized by the same act, was the department's disregard of due process of law in the procedures set up for the Alien Enemy Hearing boards. No alien appearing before the board could be represented by his attorney. The boards were not bound by any courtroom rules for establishing evidence; nor were they expected to submit a stenographic record of the testimony, which meant, in effect, that hearsay information carried far more weight than it should have.

All of this disturbed me. My only comfort was that the new Attorney General was Francis Biddle, who as Solicitor General had lived up to his reputation as an intelligent humanitarian. Shortly after his promotion to the cabinet post, Biddle decried

° Aliens of enemy nationality were prohibited to possess such articles as short-wave radios, cameras, firearms, and explosives. They could not travel without applying for permission; in no case could they travel by air. The regulations also stipulated that they could not change their place of residence or employment without notifying the authorities.

the "glaring imperfections" of the 1789 Alien Enemy Act and pleaded that a greater effort be made to "separate the sheep from the goats." As an example of the indiscriminate thinking prevalent among Americans, he noted that "to too many Americans our German neighbor is still German, but only German. We have not yet learned to think of him as an anti-Nazi German, though he may have fully as much reason to be as anti-Nazi as we have."

He had the same concern about the Japanese and Italians. After the Pearl Harbor attack, Biddle, speaking in good faith, assured the shaken Japanese-American population that "at no time ... will the government engage in wholesale condemnation of any alien group." He did not know then, of course, that in a few months Roosevelt, submitting to the pressures of the military, would agree to the wholesale evacuation of Japanese Americans, citizens as well as noncitizens, from the West Coast. When Biddle first learned of the plan, he fought it tooth and nail, insisting the evacuation was unnecessary, and urging a continuation of the Department of Justice's established policy of interning only those aliens of Japanese birth who by their activities, affiliations, or relationships in Japan might be considered potentially dangerous. To the everlasting shame of all Americans, Biddle was overruled. In February 1942, the President ordered the wholesale internment of some 110,000 men, women, and children in War Relocation centers in the interior for the duration of the war. Two thirds of them were American citizens by birth.°

In the same month, in a further attempt to separate sheep from goats, the Department of Justice conducted an "identification program" for all German, Italian, and Japanese nationals.

° The ignominy of this sad chapter in American history was compounded the following year by the United States Supreme Court which upheld the right of the military to treat American citizens of Japanese ancestry as though they were enemy aliens guilty of misconduct, despite the fact that not a single act of sabotage could be attributed to them, nor to the Japanese-born men and women interned with them.

Once again they were required to report to post offices, this time with photographs of themselves. In exchange for information about their employment record, organizational connections, and addresses of close relatives serving in the armed forces, each alien received an identification card with his photograph and thumbprint, which he was required to carry with him at all times. The purpose of the program was, of course, to exert tighter control over the alien enemy population, but every effort was made to convince the alien that the identification card was for his own protection as well.

The job of publicizing the identification program fell on my shoulders. I did it as efficiently as I knew how, but it went against my grain; and it must have lowered the morale of the million or so aliens subjected to it for, despite official assurances to the contrary, the program implied a deep distrust of them. The nervousness and indignation it engendered was reflected in some of the messages I received from my Rochester relatives. My uncle Stefano wanted to know if being an "alien enemy" would mean deportation to Italy. They could not understand why the American government would consider them dangerous since by now they had been here so long they could not imagine having any other homeland. One angry relative wrote: "Don't those imbeciles in Washington understand that to have American-born children is to become an American for the rest of your life?" The term "alien enemy" was merely technical, I replied halfheartedly; they had nothing to worry about.

Actually the Italians represented less of a worry to the government than the Germans and the Japanese, despite the fact that they composed the largest of the "alien enemy" groups, some six hundred thousand of them. By February 1942, only two months after Pearl Harbor, 10 percent of them had husbands or sons in the American armed forces, and the number was steadily increasing. Their failure to become citizens could be ascribed to their difficulty with the English language and to the traditional prejudice of Americans toward immigrants from Southern and Eastern European nations, which for many years precluded large-scale Americanization programs. The fact that they had not become naturalized did not prevent them from feeling that the United States was their country. My uncle Stefano put it neatly in a letter to me: "We Italians have become Americans, in spite of the Americans. It should not be held against us that we speak this country's language badly or not at all. The most important language of all is the language of the heart."

As it turned out, the Italians were not stigmatized as "alien enemies" for long. In a surprise move, on Columbus Day of that year, Attorney General Biddle, acting with the consent of the White House, released the 600,000 Italian nationals from virtually all the restrictions imposed on alien enemies. This momentous action, based partly on the statistic that of the 10,000 aliens interned by the Department of Justice less than 250 of them were Italians, had wide repercussions. It accelerated the efforts of Italians to become naturalized Americans, and it flung open the doors of factories which until then had been refusing to hire persons of Italian ancestry, citizens and noncitizens alike. In Italy the effect of Biddle's declaration was to bolster the forces of the Italian underground by an estimated 200,000 volunteers, a development that was to help save the lives of many Americans attached to the Eighth Army there.

My relatives in Rochester jubilantly celebrated the action with a party at which they assured one another that I must have surely helped bring it about. They would not believe me when I tried to explain that I had nothing to do with it. The credit for the idea belonged to Edward Ennis, an Irish-American member of Biddle's staff, who was widely esteemed for his sound judgment. Biddle immediately seized on the suggestion and passed it on to the President, who told him he wished he had thought of it himself.

Even before I knew him personally, Biddle's anomalous personality was a puzzlement to me. How was it possible for the member of an old-line elite American family to talk with genuine compassion about the dilemma of Italian, German, and Japanese immigrants far removed from his social experience? In my effort to answer that question, I made his acquaintance and we became quite friendly, but he did not cease to mystify me. Although he was reputed to be one of the nation's most brilliant trial lawyers, he seemed incapable of conversing alone with strangers without sounding shy and awkward. As I discovered at his home one evening, he was at his best when playing host to a roomful of men, such as politicians and journalists, who could talk shop with him.° And I observed him at his worst during a dinner party when, unable to summon any small talk for the beautiful woman seated next to him, he launched on a lengthy monologue about the Biddle family tree.

My best conversations with him were on the subject of literature, which, he revealed, had been his first passion. Besides writing a novel about a family not unlike the Biddles, *The Llanfear Pattern*, he had married the poet Katherine Chapin. His immersion into the law profession, which began with a stint as secretary for Justice Oliver Wendell Holmes, an American he revered above most, sidetracked him from his interest in writing. He envied me for being able to work on a book even while holding down a job, and longed for the day when he could start devoting full time to his own writing. °°

Like that of Franklin D. Roosevelt, his bearing was more aristocratic than democratic, but whereas Roosevelt had the talent to communicate successfully with persons below his own social level, Biddle did not. While he was undoubtedly sincere when he said in a public address that "one of the essences of democracy is that men of different views and different races and different colors can live together in a union," his temperament suggested that of a snob. His actions did not. It was Biddle who, as chairman of the National Labor Relations Board, aggressively championed the constitutional prerogative of col-

° Drew Pearson and Senator J. William Fulbright were part of the gathering I attended at the Biddle home. The group spent most of the evening deploring the Soviet Union's inept sense of public relations, which they attributed to the Soviet's sense of inferiority in its diplomatic relationships with other nations.

°° In his retirement Francis Biddle published two volumes, both autobiographical: *A Casual Past* (1961) and *In Brief Authority* (1962).

lective bargaining right up to the Supreme Court where, in a surprise decision, his position was upheld. Although this milestone development drastically improved the situation of the American working class, it is doubtful that many workers were ever aware of him as their champion. To what extent Biddle was actually aware of workers as something more than abstract figures in a legal brief was a moot question.

An anecdote reported to me by Gilfond suggested that Biddle may well have been asking the same question of himself. On a train bound for New York Gilfond, to his astonishment, discovered that the Attorney General was riding, not in first class as was usually his custom, but in a coach car. Unable to contain his surprise, Gilfond blurted out: "Why, General, what are you doing in coach?" Biddle, reacting with the embarrassment of a minister caught in a brothel, offered some vague explanation. To Gilfond it was evident that the Attorney General was simply economizing. My own interpretation of the episode was quite different: I assumed that Biddle had chosen to ride coach in the hope of trying to rub elbows with the hoi polloi and possibly establish rapport with at least one or two of them, as his friend Eleanor Roosevelt was wont to do.

One of Biddle's most impressive traits was his disregard of protocol when fighting for any cause he considered just. He once threatened to indict the British Ambassador if any British deserter was shanghaied on American soil. When a Navy medal of valor was being denied to an American sailor simply because he was black, Biddle raised hell at a cabinet meeting until the Navy's decision was reversed. And in one of his most publicized actions, he ordered the chief of Montgomery Ward, Sewell Avery, bodily lifted out of his Chicago office when Avery defied a Department of Justice directive affecting his firm.

To add emphasis to the action, Biddle went to Chicago with his aide Edward Ennis and installed himself in a hotel until the deed was done. Ennis afterward told me of a small incident at the hotel which was as reflective of Biddle's occasional naiveté as it was of Ennis's invariable canniness. Before retiring for the night, Biddle invited Ennis to his room for a nightcap. In the course of their chat the name of J. Edgar Hoover came up. "Tell me, Ed," asked Biddle, "do you think it's true that Hoover is a homosexual?" Ennis countered the question with one of his own: "Tell me, General, who made the arrangements for this hotel room?" Biddle looked puzzled, then replied, "The FBI." Ennis put down his drink and stepped toward the door. "Good night, General. Sleep well," he sang out in a loud enough voice to be easily recorded and made a quick exit.

His innocence about possible machinations of the FBI did not, however, preclude his shrewdness in making staff appointments in the Department of Justice. Gilfond, consistently pragmatic and cool-headed under fire, was the ideal public-relations director for those hectic times. To head the Alien Enemy Control Unit he appointed Edward Ennis, a sagacious young liberal who had already acquired considerable experience handling cases of aliens subject to deportation.* As soon as he became Attorney General, Biddle asked Earl Harrison, who had covered himself with glory by his skillful handling of the alien registration program, to step up to the position of United States Commissioner of Immigration and Naturalization Service, a development that was to affect my future significantly.

In accepting the appointment Harrison, who wanted to be near his family, stipulated that the national headquarters of the INS be transferred to Philadelphia for the duration of the war. He also proposed I join his staff as Special Assistant to the Commissioner in charge of the agency's public-relations program. I readily accepted the offer not only because it represented a substantial promotion but also because of my intense dislike of Washington. On the other hand, moving to Philadelphia meant coming to grips with the question of what I intended to do about my relationship with Margaret, which had continued for almost five years without a break.

* Edward J. Ennis, a longtime champion of civil liberties, eventually became president of the American Civil Liberties Union, later chairman of its board of directors.

Two months earlier Margaret's husband had finally consented to a divorce and allowing her custody of their daughter, and she was naturally assuming we would marry as soon as she was free. Except for separate addresses, we were already living as man and wife, and the relationship appeared to have all the desirable elements of a good marriage. The trouble was that almost as soon as I learned that we could formalize our union I began to have serious doubts as to whether I wanted to spend the rest of my life with her. As my departure to Philadelphia approached the need to let her know my feelings racked me with so much guilt and conflict that I began to doubt my ability to remain sane. In my torment, I sought a one-hour session with a New York psychiatrist, but he was of little help beyond assuring me that as long as I could function in an office eight hours a day, as I was doing, I was mentally better off than most people and in no imminent danger of a breakdown.

Margaret soon became aware of my condition and the reason for it, but she made no issue of it. She continued to be as devoted and affectionate as ever. As usual, she made sure I got enough food and sleep, and when I showed signs of abandoning my manuscript, she insisted I return to the rigid daily writing schedule I had adopted for completing it. Gradually, with her help, I began to recover my mental equilibrium and banish the demons torturing me for my indecision. Yet the conflict remained unresolved. Part of me dictated marrying her; another part of me would not hear of it.

Even after I moved to Philadelphia the problem remained unresolved, but the fear of losing control of my mind was gone, and the manuscript had been completed and accepted by the first publisher who read it. For a while Margaret traveled to Philadelphia on weekends to stay with me, but the visits became less and less frequent and finally stopped altogether. I could never explain my failure to marry her since I myself did not know for certain. My first rationalization was that I craved to have a bachelor life before settling down to marriage. Yet I knew myself to be essentially monogamous, uneasy with casual sex relationships. Gradually it occurred to me that a good deal of my reluctance to marry Margaret may have derived from the antediluvian concept ingrained in me in my Sicilian childhood which held that a young man should marry a virgin, that in no case should he wed one who has had a child by another man. My intellect branded the concept as nonsense, but my emotions took it seriously enough to make me feel that since marriage was a serious step I would want to enter it with a clean slate, with a woman who though not necessarily a virgin was not already a mother. My confusion was compounded by the attitude of my parents who, though now aware of Margaret's failed marriage and daughter, expressed genuine distress at the news of our parting. Were they afraid I might never be able to find a wife as suitable for me as Margaret? And did they think I should marry her because she had saved my life? I would never know.

Throughout the trauma of our separation Margaret, unfailingly sensible, made no effort to extract explanations from me. But once she realized I could not marry her she stopped dealing with me as a lover, despite my pleas, and treated me as a platonic friend. Six months after my departure from Washington I received an engraved card announcing her marriage to a captain in the Army.

TWELVE

The Philadelphia Front

"McCarthyism" became a new word in the American language during the early fifties, but long before then its nefarious techniques were used by the Dies Committee for Un-American Activities and to a more limited degree by the FBI and the Civil Service Commission in their investigation of government employees. These two agencies, operating on the premise that all government employees who were anti-Fascists before the war were either subversive or potentially (what latitude that adverb gave them!) so, provided a field day for ex-Communists turned informers as well as for personal enemies of the employees under investigation. I became one of their targets and had it not been for my superiors at the Department of Justice, who gave me the chance to defend myself, I would have wound up as one of their victims.

I first learned of it from one of the Attorney General's executive aides who formally notified me that "certain allegations" had been made by "certain persons" concerning my past activities. He would not identify my accusers, but he gave me a list of their allegations and told me that the Solicitor General would be heading a departmental committee to appraise my written responses to the charges. The most serious of them was that in November 1936 I was supposed to have attended "a top fraction meeting of the Communist Party" in San Francisco as a representative of the Federal Writers' Project. This allegation was easy to ridicule since I had yet to set eyes on San Francisco and since I was not employed by the Federal Writers' Project until the spring of 1937. The implications of the other allegations were also false, and I had no trouble disposing of them. Parenthetically, I added that I had never been a member of the Communist party under my own nor any other name.°

On my own, I sent a copy of my defense to Earl Harrison who promptly replied that my statements were "categorical and specific and they seem to me to knock all the props from under the so-called charges." There ensued a brutal period of waiting for the Solicitor General's committee to meet and render its decision. No important writing assignments were given to me during that time, and I felt like a pariah about to be cast out of his community. When the clearance finally came, my colleagues seemed unduly relieved and congratulated me with an enthusiasm that might have led a stranger to believe that I had won the Irish Sweepstakes.

Although I was grateful to the department for giving me the opportunity to reply to the allegations—not all government employees were that fortunate—it angered me that I could not come face to face with my unknown accusers. And it disturbed me that these enemies, in their effort to get me fired, were able

° Many of the same allegations were repeated when I was summoned to Washington in 1952 by the House Un-American Activities Committee and its Senate counterpart headed by Senator McCarthy. That the Attorney General's office, a decade earlier, had cleared me of the charges made no difference to the committees. At the House committee's executive session I experienced some of its worst skullduggery, being confronted by a false witness I had never seen before who claimed I had attended a Communist party meeting with him. When my attorney, taken by surprise, failed to challenge the witness, I insisted on interrogating him and was able to indicate the falseness of his testimony. After the hearing my lawyer marveled at my action and said: "You should have been a lawyer." To this I could not help replying, "No, *you* should have been the lawyer."

to use the offices of the FBI to cast a sinister light on my past with their distortions and outright lies. Three of them I was eventually able to identify: a former editor on the New York City Writers' Project who had become a paid informer of the FBI, my ex-mistress from Arkansas and the New Deal high official who succeeded me as her chief lover.

Meanwhile, Earl Harrison was beset with difficulties of his own. Senator Guffey of Pennsylvania was singlehandedly blocking Senate confirmation of his appointment as Commissioner of Immigration and Naturalization, partly because he bore an old grudge against Biddle for recommending presidential appointments that had not met with his approval, and partly because he was under the mistaken impression that Harrison was a member of a wealthy family that represented powerful industrial interests with whom he had clashed. All attempts to convince Guffey that Harrison came from a poor family that ran a small grocery in a working-class neighborhood of Philadelphia came to nothing. President Roosevelt had not been enthusiastic about the appointment since Harrison was a Republican with no political clout, but after Guffey had succeeded in preventing confirmation for six months he yielded to Biddle's request for intervention, and wrote the Senator a personal note that persuaded him to change his mind. The note read: "Dear Joe: As one old friend to another I want to ask you to forego your fight on the Harrison appointment. I know how deeply you feel about it, but I do not believe it is a matter of sufficient importance to make an issue out of it and that is bound to embarrass a lot of your and my good friends. Will you do this for me. F.D.R."

By the time Harrison's appointment was finally confirmed the national headquarters of the service had been in Philadelphia for five months. The acting commissioner, for whom I worked until Harrison came into office, was Major Lemuel Bradford Schofield, a bulldog of a man with a thick, square body who was Philadelphia's former Commissioner of Public Safety. His exposé of local police corruption as much as his spectacular

raids during the Prohibition era, which were part of his crusade
to make Philadelphia the driest city in the East, had won him a
highly publicized reputation for toughness. Biddle, who had
chosen him to fill in for Harrison, once described him as "a
sadistic cross-examiner when the temptation afforded," and
recalled Schofield's propensity for stepping on the toes of
prominent Philadelphians, a trait he demonstrated during Prohibition by raiding bars in the city's most exclusive private
clubs, including one to which he himself belonged.

To my surprise, Schofield and I got along splendidly. He
liked the material I ghostwrote for him and I liked his
forthright style of doing business, even though at times it made
me feel I was under military rule. The title "Major" he had
acquired honorably during World War I. The only reason he
was not in the new war was because of a bad leg, the result of
an automobile accident. To ease the stress on the leg he carried
a cane, but the man's vitality was so glaring that it seemed
more like a weapon than a means of support.

No man is all tough and Schofield, I was to soon learn, was
no exception. A middle-aged woman with the title of "Princess" saw through the hard exterior and sensed that he could be
hers for the taking. She was the Austro-Hungarian daughter of a
Jewish toymaker who had acquired her title through a shotgun
marriage to the scion of a family second only to the Hapsburgs.
Her name was Princess Stephanie Hohenlohe-Waldenburg
Schillingsfurst and, at the time of her meeting with Major
Schofield, had recently been adjudged an undesirable alien and
placed in the custody of the Immigration Service until arrangements could be made for her deportation. So far the State
Department had not been able to find a country that would
admit her. There had been forty-two refusals.

The princess seemed destined to languish in the custody of
the Immigration Service's detention quarters at Gloucester,
New Jersey, when the acting commissioner, responding to her
wiles, succeeded in having her released by assuring the State
and Justice departments that she would provide our government with information about the Nazi spy system operating

here and in England—information she had gleaned from her wide acquaintance with top-ranking Nazis. Her release triggered a storm of angry editorials. *Life* identified her as an active Hitler agent who, in exchange for services she rendered in the dissolution of Czechoslovakia, had been rewarded by the Führer with the castle of Leopolzkron located on a magnificent estate near Salzburg.

The *Philadelphia Inquirer* called her "one of Hitler's slickest agents since the Fuehrer started operating in Europe" and credited her with paving the way for the concessions at Munich. Its editorial recalled that the princess had arrived in the States in December 1939 with 106 pieces of baggage, posing as a German refugee. "Since her arrival she has been one of the aides of the noted Nazi fifth columnist Fritz Weideman, who works the West Coast for Hitler. Last December, after enormous public protest, the Government arrested Hohenlohe, moved to deport her. . . . And now it is announced she has been set free, to come and go as she wishes. Reason: Officials say she gave the Government 'information.' Information bosh! . . . The notion that Hohenlohe would sell out Hitler—after her record and his—is stupid, fantastic, and typical of the wishful thinking which has double-crossed the democracies so frequently in the past."

Following the release of the princess, her relationship with the major bloomed to such a degree that it came to the attention of President Roosevelt. Convinced, like most of the press, that the princess was no simple "refugee" but an unscrupulous adventuress, the President asked the FBI to ascertain the extent of her relationship with the major. The report he received prompted him to summon Biddle to the White House at once. With a broad grin he handed the Attorney General a series of photographs showing Schofield furtively entering and leaving a house near Washington where the major had installed her. "Well, Francis," drawled the President, "it would appear that your acting Commissioner of Immigration is pretty busy these days fucking Princess Hohenlohe."

The princess was placed under close surveillance and, as soon as war was declared on Germany, arrested as an alien enemy and held in custody. The major managed to have her placed in the service's nearby detention station in Gloucester, New Jersey, but except for making frequent trips to Gloucester to console and comfort her, he could do no more. On the day that Harrison replaced him as commissioner, the princess was transferred to an alien enemy internment camp near Dallas, Texas, where she remained until the end of the war.

It was there, while touring the detention centers maintained by the Immigration Service, that I encountered the princess for the first and last time. The stories I had heard about her prowess as an international siren were far more spellbinding than the woman herself. The traits which the major and her other paramours found irresistible were not apparent to me; she impressed me as a rather pathetic and drab entrepreneur. °
Having heard I was a writer, she tried to persuade me to use my "influence" to get to a publisher the autobiographical manuscript she had been writing. She was confident it would become a best seller and "make both of us rich." Curious though I was to read it, I explained I was without influence; that, in any case, it was against regulations for internees to be publishing books while in custody.†

My own autobiographical manuscript, *Mount Allegro*, was finally published in January 1943, six months before the allied invasion of Sicily. It was hardly the most auspicious time for a book that spoke favorably of Sicilian Americans but, to my surprise, it was loudly and unanimously lauded in the American press and for a few weeks landed on the best-seller lists. The outpouring of reviews and fan mail was heady stuff.

° Major Schofield's fascination with the princess remained constant. On her release from internment after the war, the major, acting as her attorney, legalized her status as a resident alien, and abandoning his family, began living with her on a farm near Phoenixville, Pennsylvania. Although she was said to have had other lovers at the time, their liaison continued for almost a decade until Schofield's death in 1955.

† The manuscript was never published.

The mail came from hundreds of readers of diverse nationality backgrounds who were able to identify with my Sicilian protagonists. Perhaps the most gratifying letter came from one of my favorite anti-Fascist heroes, the historian Gaetano Salvemini, a former member of the Italian parliament who was now teaching at Harvard. He wrote that reading *Mount Allegro* was "a reliving of my childhood in Apulia 60 years ago. I could see in each of your characters some person who is still alive in my memory. Your feelings are a strong mixture of fun, respect and tenderness which recall Dickens at his best."

Was the book fiction or nonfiction? No one (not even myself finally) was quite certain. On the eve of its publication, the publishers, over my protests, had acted on the advice of its sales department and decided to publish it as fiction, even though it had been contracted for as a nonfictional memoir. The only changes I made in the text were to fictionize the names of my relatives and add a tongue-in-cheek author's note to the effect that since the characters were being presented as fictitious, "anyone who thinks he recognizes himself in it is kindly asked to bear that in mind." To add to the confusion, the book was reviewed by experienced critics both as a novel and as a work of nonfiction. The *New York Times* listed it in its fiction bestseller lists; the *New York Herald-Tribune* in its nonfiction lists. The confusion continued in the bookstores and libraries.

None of the Italian-American readers who wrote me had any doubt that it was intended as nonfiction. My uncle Stefano, who was able to decipher occasional sentences in the text, took great pride in letting people know that he was the "Uncle Nino" in the story. And his wife was grievously hurt that I, one of her favorite nephews, had deliberately given her the name of Giovanna, which I learned (too late, alas) was also the name of a notorious Sicilian queen who enjoyed having sexual intercourse with stallions.

My aunt was not the only one who felt slandered by the book. A group of Rochester Sicilians unable to read English were persuaded by an unscrupulous lawyer that I had vilified their hometown of Carapippi and everyone who came from it.

Their sense of outrage brought them together at a mass meeting where they discussed a two-part plan for discrediting *Mount Allegro* and me: bringing a libel suit against me and my publishers, and getting together a "Spite Book," in which each of them would be afforded the opportunity of expressing his opinion of me. The hate anthology was to be sent to the Department of Justice with the request that I be fired from my job.

Their fury stemmed from a brief account in *Mount Allegro* of the bad blood that existed between the people of Girgenti, where most of my relatives came from, and those of Carapippi. A former high school classmate, the son of a Carapippano, informed me of the situation; he said his people were "fighting mad" and advised me to write a conciliatory article that would "cool their anger." Instead of an article, I wrote him a letter expressing some of my own Sicilian anger for having been grossly misinterpreted, pointing out that anyone who could read English would realize that my text actually satirized the people of Girgenti for having entertained outrageous notions about the people of Carapippi. As for being sued, I indicated that the publishers would welcome the juicy publicity ensuing from such an action, but that it would defeat one of my reasons for writing *Mount Allegro*, which was to show that, contrary to the popular canard, Sicilians are usually not a revengeful people.

My letter had the desired effect. When my friend translated it at the next meeting of the Carapippani, it put an end to the matter. Or so I thought. A few weeks later another ex-high school classmate, now also a lawyer, informed me that "hundreds of Carapippani in Brooklyn" were "angry as hell" about my treatment of their hometown. "I have taken the liberty of defending you," he wrote from Brooklyn, "taking the position that you are too intelligent a man to hold generalized prejudices against the people of a whole town. Will you therefore confirm my position by writing me a few lines which I can read to them at their next meeting?" I sent my defender a carbon copy of the letter I had written for the Rochester group and, once again, it succeeded in cooling the hotheads who were out to scalp me.

Except for this episode, *Mount Allegro* became a steady source of gratification. Both Italian and non-Italian readers responded to it with a warmth that made for scores of agreeable acquaintances and a number of enduring friendships. For the first time I began encountering prominent Italian-American members of the establishment, the artist Luigi Lucioni, the tenor Giovanni Martinelli, the soprano Vivien Della Chiesa, the former Commissioner of Immigration Edward Corsi, the Sicilian-born judge of the New York State Supreme Court Ferdinand Pecora, and various other judges in the New York and Philadelphia areas.

As a token of his affection for *Mount Allegro*, Lucioni presented me with a portrait he drew of me, Martinelli admired the rhythm of my prose, and Edward Corsi took me to dinner at El Morocco in gratitude for publicly taking to task Gian Carlo Menotti, the composer, after he had made a denigrating comment about southern Italians (of which Corsi was one) during an "Evening of Italian Culture" which Menotti and I addressed. Judge Pecora sounded favorably disposed toward *Mount Allegro* when we were panelists on a radio network show called "Author Meets the Critics," but we soon clashed on the validity of the melting pot concept. Like most members of the establishment then, the judge was confident that immigrants could become rapidly Americanized once they put their minds to it and moved into English-speaking neighborhoods, as his own parents had done. I maintained that it was unrealistic, as well as undesirable, to expect immigrants from an ancient civilization to lay aside readily their own culture for that of their adopted country. Neither of us succeeded in convincing the other.

Except for the men and women in the arts, I found I had little in common with most of the successful Italian-Americans I encountered. It seemed to me that in their climb to success they had lost or repudiated the most civilized traits of their immigrant forebears. I much preferred the company of Italian-born Italians, whether they were poor immigrants, like my relatives, or aristocrats like Corrado di Niscemi, a transplanted prince of the Sicilian nobility who, married to a Philadelphian, divided his time between their Philadelphia apartment and his family palazzo in Palermo.°

Our meeting came about accidentally. While dining in a small Italian restaurant, I kept overhearing from a nearby table the unmistakable sounds of a Sicilian dialect intermingling with two other dialects I could identify as Tuscan and Roman. Since my back was turned to the table, I could not see who the conversationalists were, but when I distinctly heard the Sicilian voice say, "When I was in Mount Allegro . . ." I impulsively turned around and asked: "Were you really in Mount Allegro?"

In heavily accented English, the Sicilian demanded: "Why do you ask? Of course, I was in Mount Allegro. I have been there many times. Why does it interest you?" With some embarrassment, I explained that I had just published a book with the title of *Mount Allegro*. "Ah," he shouted, his face lighting up, *"tu sei Gerlando!"* (You are Gerlando). Leaping to his feet he came to our table and bending his six-foot frame so that he could kiss me on both cheeks, he proclaimed in a loud voice for all the diners to hear, "What *Uncle Tom's Cabin* did for ze South your book veel do for Sicily."

Niscemi then insisted that my companion and I join the group at his table. There we were plied with drinks the rest of the night while he and his comrades, a Florentine artist by the name of Carlo Bocciarelli, who was to become an intimate friend, and a Roman baron named Nick Saitto, exchanged pleasantries and insults in a lusty style reminiscent of the sessions in Rochester between my father and my uncles.

Niscemi was the first educated Sicilian I came to know well,

° Prince Niscemi was the first cousin of Prince Giuseppe di Lampedusa, author of the highly acclaimed novel, *The Leopard* (1960).

and I was entranced by his vast fund of Sicilian lore as much as by the complexity of his thinking which alternated between cynicism, idealism, and outright futility. He was not always easy to understand for his attachment to the Sicilian dialect was evident no matter which language he was using. Because of his sense of humor I felt free to suggest that he spoke seven different languages—all in Sicilian. He had advanced degrees in literature, philosophy, and chemistry but was content to spend most of his days in rumination. At one time, he told me, he had undertaken a vast project, a history of the world no less, but had felt impelled to give it up when he got to 1914, "because the world began to go to hell and then I completely lost my perspective."

Like other Sicilian noblemen of the forties, Niscemi was a passionate advocate of Sicilian separatism. He dubbed himself a "Sicilian Sinn Feiner," explaining that he felt a close kinship with another island people, the Irish, since they, like the Sicilians, suffered from the same indignity: "living under the rule of a people far inferior to themselves." But, unlike most other members of the Sicilian nobility, Niscemi was a staunch anti-Fascist. ° He and his wife had concealed many an anti-Fascist fugitive from the Fascist police under the beds in their palazzo. And as soon as the United States was at war with the Mussolini regime, he made frequent trips to Washington to provide the Army's intelligence service with detailed information about Sicily that would facilitate the American invasion of the island.

Publicly, Niscemi could not afford to be too vocal about his anti-Fascist views for fear that the Fascist regime might take reprisals against his mother in Palermo, the Duchess of Arenella, from whom he had been separated by the war. So it was with some surprise that I encountered him in a Phila-

---

° Niscemi became the inspiration for the leading character in my novel *The Ship and the Flame* (1948). He died of an undetected internal injury in 1965 after falling out of his bed at the Villa Niscemi.

delphia radio broadcasting studio where a Voice of America representative had assembled Niscemi, an Italian countess living in Philadelphia, and myself to tape record messages to the people of Italy soliciting their support in overthrowing the Fascist regime. After we had been photographed by the local press, we delivered our messages. Niscemi's was easily the most passionate of the three. Not until we were alone at lunch was I able to express my concern that the broadcast might get his mother into trouble with the Fascist authorities. "Don't worry about it," he said in Sicilian. "We did what we were asked to do and tonight there will be a story in the newspapers proving it, but there won't be any broadcast." To my astonishment, he informed me that the cord connecting the microphone with the electrical outlet in the studio had remained disconnected during all three messages. On pressing him for a further explanation, he would only admit that the whole affair had been a charade prearranged with an understanding Voice of America representative. "As a fellow Sicilian who has read Pirandello, you certainly should be able to figure out at least a half dozen reasons for the charade." With an enigmatic smile he changed the subject by recommending the squid on the menu.

That same fall, almost a year after the Italian-Americans had been exempted from alien enemy regulations, I became party to another kind of charade, this one arranged by Alan Cranston, who would one day become a United States senator from California. We had become good friends while I was on the Attorney General's staff and he was the Washington press representative for the Common Council for American Unity, an organization involved with the welfare of immigrants. Now Cranston was chief of the foreign-language press division in the Office of War Information, anxious to project the image of an immigrant population unified in its support of the American war effort. One of his concerns was that in Philadelphia, where Italian-American organizations were seldom unified on any issue, plans were being made, as usual, for at least three separate Columbus Day parades. As he explained in his phone call to me, it was important that this year there be not three parades but one huge parade that would incorporate all elements of the Italian-American community. Cranston had arranged a meeting in Philadelphia with the Italian-American community leaders to solicit their cooperation. Would I be willing to attend the meeting as a representative of the Department of Justice? All I had to do, he said, was nod my head vigorously whenever he made the statement that the Department of Justice was in full accord with what he was proposing.

Since the cause was a good one, I readily consented to being Cranston's stooge and became a witness to a spontaneous drama as farcical as anything Moliére might have written on the theme of men who, while trying to impress authorities with their intense patriotism for the United States and their willingness to undergo any personal sacrifice, were actually demonstrating their determination not to make any concession that might suggest the slightest loss of position or prestige.

The actors—that is what they became—consisted of a prominent judge and some lawyers who were officials in the Sons of Italy fraternal lodge as well as officers of unions that were predominantly Italian-American. They all listened attentively to Alan Cranston and his deputy Lee Falk (creator of the comic strip "The Phantom"), and outdid one another in agreeing that the Italian-Americans must present a united front in this year's local Columbus Day celebration. But when it came to determining how the three parades would be combined and who would lead the consolidated parade they behaved like small children fighting over the possession of a toy, though with far less innocence. The judge, a father figure in the Italian-American community, outdoing the others in histrionic gestures, actually ripped open his shirt and beat his hirsute breast with clenched fists as he declared his undying love for the United States and democracy. Despite the antagonism among them, no one dared remind the judge that only a few years before he had accepted a Fascist decoration from Mussolini in person.

The speeches on patriotism continued to singe the at-

mosphere while befogging the issue at hand until Cranston
suggested that since they could not agree which of them was to
lead the parade it might be well to revert to the words of the
Bible and choose a child to lead them. As for the order in
which the various groups would march, he proposed that this
be decided by drawing lots. They promptly hailed Cranston for
his Solomon-like sagacity, then began wrangling among themselves as to whose child would head the parade. They were still
wrangling when we left.

In that same year Cranston and his staff were also involved in
investigating the assassination of Carlo Tresca, a tragedy which
I was invariably to associate with the publication of *Mount
Allegro*. Tresca had promised to attend a cocktail party given
for me on the day of the book's publication, but he never made
it. On the morning of the party when I dashed to a newsstand
to read what the critics had to say about my book, I was
confronted by the front-page headlines of his murder. On the
previous evening, while he waited with a friend for the traffic
light to change at Fifteenth Street and Fifth Avenue, a man
stepped up behind Tresca and fired four shots from an auto-
matic pistol, one of which struck Tresca in the head, another in
the back. The killer escaped in a dark sedan. Tresca died on the
pavement almost before the car had disappeared from sight.

The assassin was never found nor was the motive ever
ascertained, though it was generally assumed to be a political
assassination. Both the Fascists and the Communists, his friends
agreed, had ample reason for wanting to dispose of him. Tresca
had been on Il Duce's official blacklist since 1931, the year when
Tresca began his vigorous campaign against Fascist activity in
Manhattan. Moreover, Tresca, in his newspaper *Il Martello*, had
frequently attacked Generoso Pope, the powerful publisher of
New York's daily *Il Progresso*, which had been consistently pro-
Mussolini until the day the United States declared war against
Italy.

Following the declaration, Pope desperately sought to win
recognition as an opponent of Mussolini and his regime. But

with every attempt he made to identify himself with anti-Fascist groups, he invariably found himself blocked by Tresca, who let it be known that the ex-henchman of Mussolini would never be admitted into any anti-Fascist organization as long as he, Tresca, was alive. An Italian-American War Bond dinner in September 1941 was attended by Tresca only after he had been assured that Pope would not be present. But Pope did appear, accompanied by a well-known gangster. Tresca left as soon as he saw them entering the room, saying to the men at his table: "This is too much. Not only a Fascist but also his gangster. This is no place for me."

The next day Tresca received phone calls from two city officials asking him to keep quiet about the incident. Tresca agreed to do so but, feeling endangered, he notified the Federal Bureau of Investigation of the situation.

Tresca's common-law widow, Margaret De Silver, and some of their Trotskyite friends were convinced that Tresca's assassin was in the pay of the Stalinist Communists. They argued that Tresca had fought hard to keep Communists, as well as Fascists, out of the Mazzini Society, the leading organization of Italian anti-Fascists in this country, and that for eight years before his death he had been "an implacable enemy of the Stalinists," who frequently reminded his readers in *Il Martello* that Stalin's GPU agents had assassinated Leon Trotsky and a number of other anti-Stalinists.

As fond as I was of Margaret De Silver, I could not agree with her and her friends, and suspected that their opinon was unduly influenced by parochially political considerations. The report prepared by Alan Cranston and his associates in the Office of War Information persuaded me that the Fascists had far more to gain by Tresca's death than the Communists. One significant section of the carefully documented report identified Tresca as the organizer of the Italian-American Victory Council, in which both Communists and ex-Fascists were anxious to participate. It revealed that although Tresca had little use for Communists, he was not opposed to their participation in the council because he felt that all anti-Fascists should unite until fascism was defeated.

At first the authorities were remarkably active tracking down clues and interrogating suspects. One of the suspects was a gangster with a criminal record, Carmine Galante, who was seen entering the killer's getaway sedan an hour and a half before Tresca was gunned down, the same sedan that had tried to run down Tresca while he was crossing a street two days before the murder. But this lead came to nothing and in a few months the investigation slowed down to a standstill, although many persons with an intimate knowledge of Tresca's political activities had never been questioned. All this gave rise to the suspicion that Generoso Pope's political clout, which extended all the way to the White House where he was considered an invaluable vote-getting power for the Democratic party, was asserting itself with every influential politician who could stop the investigation.

One of the investigation's most questionable aspects was that for almost two years the Italian end of it had been assigned to Louis A. Pagnucco, who had close ties with Pope and had long been associated with Fascist supporters. A group of prominent liberals, which included Morris Ernst, Roger N. Baldwin, John Dewey, Norman Thomas, and Edmund Wilson, called Pagnucco's background to the attention of Manhattan's district attorney Frank Hogan and demanded he be removed from the case. After several months of foot-dragging, Hogan replaced Pugnacco with another assistant district attorney but insisted on retaining Pugnacco as a consultant in the investigation.

The new inquiry was as ineffectual as the first. At a memorial meeting in New York on the second anniversary of Tresca's death, twelve hundred men and women, at the very hour and minute when he was assassinated, rose silently to assert their support for a resolution that demanded the authorities intensify their investigation. After that the meeting voted to offer a five-thousand-dollar reward for any information that might shed light on the identity of the assassin and the motive behind the killing.

The Tresca Memorial Committee also issued a pamphlet, "Who killed Carlo Tresca," with an impassioned introduction by Tresca's labor leader–poet friend Arturo Giovannitti, who wrote: "I am going to add my shout to the tumultuous uproar that demands justice and will not be denied, even if some sacred icons must be toppled from their pedestals and a few pillars of our so-called civilization must lie shattered in the dust of their ignominy." In a second preface to the pamphlet, John Dos Passos emphasized that "it was surely as a fighter for American freedom that he [Tresca] was shot down," and denounced those public officials who allowed pressures, however powerful, to interfere with their duty of finding Tresca's murderers.

All these efforts proved futile. Evidently, the power of those who found it expedient to leave the mystery unsolved far exceeded the passions of those who held that justice should not be denied.

In the summer after the assassination Margaret De Silver wrote me to say that *Mount Allegro* had provided her "with a delightful and substantial bridge to the memory of Carlo," adding that "although he was Abruzzese and therefore, I assume, almost a foreigner to your Sicilian family—blue eyes, fair skin, and all that, nevertheless it is amazing to me how much they have in common." The letter expressed particular interest in a chapter of the book titled "God and the Sicilians," recalling that "Carlo was very violent on the subject of the Church, like all ex-Catholics, but nevertheless would give lovely descriptions of the festas. To be sure, I gathered that the flesh-and-blood women in their country costumes were more fascinating to him than the saints and Madonnas of the procession. Carlo had a wonderful vulgar gesture when he met with a nun, with which I imagine you are familiar. Nevertheless, he maintained that his first sweetheart was a nun and having Jesus for a rival was very exciting."

The social world of Philadelphia, to which *Mount Allegro* as much as my status as an eligible bachelor gave me open sesame, seemed totally foreign to the world of Carlo Tresca. Yet one evening at a Main-Line dinner party I found myself seated next to a socialite dowager of a wealthy manufacturing family who turned out to be Margaret De Silver's sister and an enthusiastic admirer of Carlo Tresca. The contradictions of American capitalism (and radicalism) were never more graphically apparent to me as when she described her final memory of Tresca: In her chauffered limousine she, her sister, and Tresca were passing through a small industrial town in Eastern Pennsylvania when Tresca, who had just enjoyed a luxurious repast, yawningly recalled that some years ago on that very street a mob of citizens had run him out of town on a rail for having tried to organize some factory workers into a union. "I must return here some day and find out what's happening to the workers," she heard Tresca murmur.

The Philadelphia social set, though generally stodgy, was not without its surprises. The only old-line Philadelphia family with whom I seemed to have much in common were the Lewises, John Frederick Lewis, Jr., a middle-aged millionaire, and his wife, Ada. Unlike most of the social registrites I met, the Lewises were liberals active in anti-Fascist and civil-liberties organizations. A Socialist in his Harvard youth and now a staunch New Dealer, John Lewis seemed to regard his wealth as a source of embarrassment and guilt. He was quick to inform me that he had done nothing to earn the family fortune; he had inherited it. Gesturing sardonically toward a group of family portraits, he added: "They did it all." The first of his American ancestors, I learned, was a Hessian soldier who had come to fight against the American revolutionists "but had the good sense to desert."

Lewis's ironical view of life was reflected in part by his compulsion to acquaint friends with a list of all the things he had never done in his life, such as not driving a car, not taking a woman to a hotel for an assignation, not ever engaging in tennis, baseball, football, swimming, skating, or motorcycling. Reading was a passion with him, and his ambition had been to be a college professor, but he had gone to law school instead at the insistence of a tyrannical father. As soon as his father died, he gave up the law, determined that henceforth he would do only what pleased him; but his father's strong influence persisted and he found himself serving on all of the various boards (as many as twenty-six at one point) of the cultural institutions his father had supported.

Although Lewis was the first to admit he was tone deaf, he was president of the Philadelphia Academy of Music for many years, and though he readily confessed to his ignorance of modern art, he was also a longtime president of the Pennsylvania Academy of the Fine Arts. His favorite pursuits were unrelated to those of his father's: collecting Chinese art objects, anonymously supporting a bookstore that sold Socialist literature, and one (the Centaur) that specialized in fine and rare editions of modern literature. I first met Lewis on the final day of the Centaur Bookstore. Having tired of losing money on it, Lewis and its manager, Harold T. Mason, were marking its demise with a cocktail party at which guests were invited to take home whatever books left on the shelves appealed to them. The wake—that was its mood—took place in a room above the store which had long been a favorite meeting place for various Philadelphia authors, among them Christopher Morley, Struthers Burt, Joseph Hergesheimer, Roy Helton, John T. McIntyre, Edward Shenton, McCready Houston. ° Although the leftover books were appealing enough, I took particular pains to avoid one woman with a somewhat dyspeptic countenance, only to discover from a photograph in next morning's *Philadelphia Record* that she was Dorothy Parker, one of my favorite humorists whom I had always longed to meet.

My odd credentials—author, full-blooded Sicilian (the first he had ever known), and free-wheeling bachelor—titillated Lewis

---

° I became friends with Burt, Hergesheimer, and Helton at the Franklin Inn, a Philadelphia luncheon club of authors, academics, journalists, and art patrons founded originally as a literary club in 1902. The publication of *Mount Allegro* produced an invitation to join it, and I remained a member for thirty years, the only Italian American in its history so far.

from the first, and I was a frequent guest at his house. I, in turn, enjoyed his iconoclastic views and delighted in his eccentric behavior, which sometimes included falling asleep at his own dinner parties when the guests around him proved to be boring. After we had become friends, Lewis confided that as much as he loved his wife, he wanted to enjoy the favors of a mistress. "You must have a lot of women in that address book of yours by now," he said. "Why don't you fix me up with one of them?" I replied I would do nothing of the kind; I liked and respected his wife too much to do any pimping for him. He took my refusal with good grace, and I heard nothing more on the subject until some months later when he told me about an affair he had just ended with a pretty clerk he had picked up at Woolworth's.

The affair lasted for about three months, until Lewis tired of her "bird-brain chatter." When he met with her for the last time, Lewis asked her to suggest some gift he could buy her as a farewell token. He was quite certain she would ask for an expensive fur coat or a car. But it developed she wanted nothing for herself but for her brother who had recently completed his first book of poems. Would Lewis pay the printing bill for its publication? Lewis was so charmed by the nature of her request that "it damn near made me want to take her back, bird brain and all."

The Jewish family I came to know best in those early Philadelphia years were the David Sterns, publishers of the *Philadelphia Record*, one of the nation's few pro–New Deal dailies. Their Rittenhouse Square apartment was as intellectual a salon as any I encountered in the city, though Stern himself seldom evinced any interest in anything but business, politics, and chess. The invitations came from his wife and daughter, both named Jill, who seemed to find the company of authors a necessary condiment in their lives. At their home I met Pietro di Donato, whose first novel, *Christ in Concrete*, published four years before, had made him the best-known Italian-American novelist in the country.

Di Donato was a handsome man of Napoleonic stature with primitive emotions and sophisticated literary aspirations who, until the publication of his best-selling novel, had worked as a bricklayer to support his seven orphaned siblings. Largely autobiographical, *Christ in Concrete*, which I had reviewed for *The New Republic*, on its publication in 1939, dramatized the excruciating death of his father who as a construction worker was buried under a stream of mortar in a collapsing building, as well as the trials and tribulations of the eldest son who, at the age of thirteen, became the sole breadwinner of the family.

Di Donato's personality was not unlike that of his literary style, which was striking for its volcanic evocation of scene and character. Intensely emotional, he was still immersed in the patriarchal role he had assumed while still a boy, even to the extent of expecting his siblings to require his permission before marrying. When he spoke of his relationship to members of his family and to the non-Italian widow he was considering marrying (he was furious that she had been married before), he sounded more like an Abruzzese peasant just landed at Ellis Island than the American-born son of immigrant parents. Except for the similarity of our ethnic origins and for our Italian-American books, we had little in common. We managed to strike up a friendship of sorts, but I found him too humorless for my taste and he undoubtedly found fault with me. On a train trip to New York, we had so little to say to each other that both of us slept soundly most of the way.

At the time of our meeting Di Donato was living in Philadelphia as a conscientious objector assigned to the job of male nurse in a Philadelphia sanitarium. It was filthy and agonizing work which he could barely tolerate but having chosen it over service in the Army, he grimly accepted his fate until the Sterns, whose patriotic fervor sometimes approached hysteria (when a girl of German ancestry who had accompanied me to their apartment made a disparaging remark about the way the Allies were conducting the war, they promptly reported her to the Federal Bureau of Investigation), began a

spirited campaign to persuade Di Donato to change his status
from that of a conscientious objector to that of a soldier. Unless
the Allies won the war, they repeatedly pointed out, the Nazis
would rule the world. "Is that what you want?" they would ask
him in a tone of voice suggesting that the outcome of the war
depended on him. Their zeal, together with Di Donato's
increasing disgust with his male nurse chores, finally paid off.
One evening to their delight he announced that he had decided
to join the Army. But the Sterns' sense of triumph lasted only a
few days for when Di Donato presented himself for induction,
he was rejected for some minor physical disability.

My experience at Army induction headquarters had its own
surprising denouement. Reporting early one morning, without
breakfast (as instructed), I felt absurdly like a sacrificial lamb
presenting itself for slaughter, incapable of letting anyone share
my secret that as a combat soldier I would not be able to kill
another human being, even in self-defense. In my wallet was a
statement from my orthopedic specialist, in whom I no longer
had any faith, which described an old back injury that, after ten
years, still necessitated my wearing a corset, a formidable
object with metal ribs that made it resemble a medieval
torturing device. I arrived wearing the corset, hoping against
hope that somehow it might result in my being drafted for a
noncombat assignment.

A young sergeant directed me to remove everything I wore,
including the corset, but on taking a look at my thirty-four-
year-old nude body underweight by some twenty pounds, he
must have decided the Army would be better off without me;
he urged me to carry the corset with me throughout the
examination, in the hope, I suspect, that it would clinch my
rejection. But none of the doctors found anything physically
wrong with me. The report from the orthopedic specialist was
disdainfully brushed aside; the corset was treated as an invisible
object. My skinny body, the appalling state of my teeth, my
incredibly flat feet—all won their complete endorsement. By the
time I reached the last doctor on the examining line, an

unmistakably WASP psychiatrist, I was trying to figure out how to wear my corset under the uniform of a combat soldier.

The psychiatrist began by asking me to follow the motions of a pencil which he moved jerkily within inches of my eyes. He finally stopped and grunted: "Pretty nervous fellow, aren't you?" I retorted that being poked and prodded for several hours on an empty stomach was not exactly conducive to a calm state of mind. "Ordinarily I'm not nervous," I said. He asked me to recall some episode in my past that had especially ruffled my calm. For a few seconds my mind was a blank, but then my memory came up with a scene of entrapment and hysteria, almost forgotten, in which I was the sole protagonist. The setting was the small vestibule of a Bank Street house in Manhattan where I was to dine with some new friends.

I entered the street door of the house, expecting that in the vestibule I would find a doorbell or knocker with which to announce my presence. Not finding either, I tried to open the door I had just shut behind me but it would not open. Beginning to feel trapped, I pounded on the door leading directly into the house, hoping my hosts would hear me. When no one came, I panicked and in my desperate need to escape the suffocation of the vestibule performed a gymnastic feat that ordinarily would have been beyond my powers. Somehow, I managed to scale the full height of the tall door long enough to beat my knuckles against the glass transom above it. I was on the floor panting for breath when my hosts opened the door.

Trying to suggest what had happened, I pointed to the front door and gasped that it would not open. My host went to the door and opened it without the slightest difficulty. Apparently, I must have turned the doorknob in the wrong direction. In my distraught condition, I had regressed to my childhood when I, a born lefthander, was being trained by parents and teachers to be righthanded. "In a time of crisis I had reverted to my original instinct as a lefthander," I told the psychiatrist.

The psychiatrist regarded me with wary blue eyes. "You certainly described that experience very graphically," he said,

and I thought I detected a note of suspicion in his voice.
Although it had never occurred to me to let the Army doctors
know of my susceptibility to claustrophobia, I immediately
began feeling guilty. Stammering, I ventured the explanation
that if my description of the experience struck him as
"graphic" it might be because I was a writer.

He seemed unimpressed. "What kind of a writer?"

When I informed him I had just published my first book and
mentioned the title, his whole demeanor was transformed. His
eyes brightened, his face glowed, and he exclaimed that his
wife was reading it and "loving it." She would be thrilled to
learn he had met its author, he said, and congratulated me on
the enthusiastic reception the book had enjoyed in the press.
Then, resuming his professional stance, he asked if I could
recall other experiences similar to the one I had described. I
cited various instances when, out of fear of suffocation, I had
felt impelled to leave elevators and subways before reaching
my destination, but added that although I had suffered from
claustrophobia as long as I could remember, it seemed to have
abated in recent years.

In his final question he asked how I earned my livelihood,
and after I had told him, he passed sentence. "There's nothing
seriously wrong with you," he began. "If you were in the Army
assigned to an airbase, you wouldn't be a problem to anyone.
But suppose you got assigned to the tank corps and in the
middle of some maneuver you suddenly felt you were suffoca-
ting and needed out, you would be endangering your life and
the life of every man in that tank. I'm rejecting you."

I was too stunned to say anything. My immediate reaction
was one of deep depression. It must have been noticeable. "Not
everybody has to be a soldier," he said. "It seems to me that
you're helping the war effort with the job you have." With
that, he shook my hand, promised to read *Mount Allegro* as
soon as his wife relinquished it, and turned to the next man in
line.

The depression continued as I found myself reflecting that

while most of my male friends were in uniform risking their lives and making personal sacrifices of all kinds, I would be living the comfortable life of a well-paid civilian. Earl Harrison saw no reason for brooding over my 4-F status. "Frankly," he said, "I think you'd make a miserable soldier. You're better off— and so is the country—doing exactly what you're doing."

A few weeks later, perhaps as a way of making me feel closer to the war effort, Harrison sent me on an inspection tour of the Immigration Service's major internment camps in the western and southwestern areas of the country. By that time the entire civilian internment program, which consisted of sixteen camps housing some ten thousand individually arrested German, Italian, and Japanese nationals, had been transferred from the custody of the Army to that of the Immigration Service.

The program, which was to become the service's chief wartime activity, involved the agency in a number of unfamiliar and complex problems, not the least of which was coping with the American public's attitude toward interned aliens which grew increasingly antagonistic as the list of American casualties lengthened. Already there had been several instances of violence threatening the lives of internees as well as the government's commitment to the Geneva convention, the international pact governing the treatment of imprisoned alien enemies.

The main objective of my tour, Harrison told me, was to absorb enough firsthand information about the internment program to cope with the onerous public-relations problems which the program was presenting almost daily.

THIRTEEN

Concentration Camps—American Style

The mass internment of 110,000 West Coast Japanese in February 1942 gave no comfort to the thousands of anti-Nazi refugees in the country who found themselves categorized by the United States government, their supposed protector, as "alien enemies." Although the Department of Justice had announced that it would intern only those aliens of enemy nationality whom it had reason to believe might be disposed to endanger the national security, the refugees were afraid that what had happened to the Japanese would happen to them.

As the Attorney General discovered on the first day we were at war with Germany and Italy, their fear was not groundless. Biddle tells about it in his memoir, *In Brief Authority*. Arriving at the White House with some proclamations that required the President's signature, the Attorney General found Roosevelt with his physician, Admiral Ross T. McIntyre, who was busy swabbing out the Chief Executive's sinus-infected nose. While the President was signing the proclamations, he asked Biddle how many German nationals there were in the country.

"Oh, about six hundred thousand," replied Biddle. (Actually there were half that number; Biddle had apparently confused their number with that of the Italians.)

319

"And you're going to intern all of them," said the President in a tone that suggested he approved of the idea.

"Well, not quite," replied Biddle.

"I don't care so much about the Italians," continued Roosevelt. "They are a lot of opera singers, but the Germans are different; they may be dangerous. . . ."

Biddle, who was determined that German and Austrian nationals be spared the fate of the West Coast Japanese, became apprehensive as to what the President would say next. Inadvertently, Dr. McIntyre, who was having difficulty working on the Chief Executive's nose, came to his rescue. "Please, Mr. President," he pleaded, and Biddle promptly used that as an excuse to withdraw, unwilling to hear the President make any further statements about wholesale internment.

I never learned what made the President go along with Biddle's policy of selective internment, but he was undoubtedly influenced in part by the mail the White House was receiving from scores of anti-Nazi refugees, among them Thomas Mann, Albert Einstein, and Bruno Frank, who emphasized the ironical fact that many of those categorized by the American government as "alien enemies" were among the first and the most farsighted adversaries of the governments against which the United States was presently at war.° In any case, there was no mass internment of them.

As a result of the Department of Justice's selective internment policy, less than 1 percent of the more than one million aliens of enemy nationality in the country were interned during

° The Attorney General's selective internment policy was derived from the experience of the British government with its own aliens of enemy nationality. In the panic that seized the British when the Low Countries and France collapsed, the government mass-interned almost eighty-five-thousand German and Austrian refugees, many of them avowed enemies of Hitler who had fled to England for safety. After a few months the public came to its senses and began condemning the government's wholesale internment policy. In turn, the government admitted it had victimized "some of the bitterest and most active enemies of the Nazi regime," and returned to its initial policy of selective internment.

the course of the war—some 10,000 altogether. Of that number approximately 5,000 were German, 5,000 Japanese, and 250 Italian. In addition to those aliens who had been individually arrested as "potentially dangerous," there were interned several hundred German and Italian seamen who had been seized, along with their ships, as soon as we went to war with the Axis countries.

Actually, the Department of Justice's selective internment policy was not nearly as selective as it might have been. As I discovered in my two-month tour of the alien enemy camps, many of their occupants represented no threat to the national security; had they been accorded due process of law, they would probably never have been interned.° Some had been arrested because of their close ties with their native countries, some because they were members of pro-Axis organizations, such as the German-American Bund, which they had joined for purely social reasons, some because they had not understood the alien enemy regulations and had in their possession radios or weapons forbidden to them. Others were interned because they were known to have opposed American intervention in the war. I encountered one Italian who had been arrested on the day we went to war with Italy because he had written the White House a few months before Pearl Harbor, begging the President not to go to war with Italy "since Italy is my mother and the United States my father and I don't want to see my parents fighting."

For me, one of the most curious aspects of the internment program was the presence in the camps of several thousand men and women (with their children) from Latin-American countries who, at the request of our State Department, had been seized by their own governments as potentially dangerous alien enemies and handed over to American authorities. Compounding the bizarreness of the program was the Machiavellian

° The Department of Justice's policy of reexamining regularly the cases of interned aliens led to the parole or outright release of many aliens before the war was over.

device that was contrived to legalize their detention by the Immigration Service. This consisted of escorting the Latin-Americans over our borders, then charging them with "illegal entry" into the country. As an Immigration Service camp commander told me, "Only in wartime could we get away with such fancy skullduggery."

The rationale for this international form of kidnapping was that by immobilizing influential German and Japanese nationals who might aid and abet the Axis war effort in the Latin-American countries where they lived, the United States was preventing the spread of Nazism throughout the hemisphere and thereby strengthening its own security. However, the project turned out to be something of a farce for as the internment camp commanders became better acquainted with their Latin-American charges, they learned that a number of them were not the "potentially dangerous" Germans and Japanese originally arrested but impoverished peasants who had been paid to act as substitutes for them.*

The media knew nothing of the Latin-American phase of the internment program, but even if they had known it is unlikely they would have revealed it. At the outset of the war, in the interests of national security, the media had cheerfully acceded to the Department of Justice's request that as little as possible be said about the arrest and detention of alien enemies since any publicity given to the subject might seriously interfere with the government's observance of the Geneva Convention of 1929. Based on the concept of reciprocity, the pact provided the government with its only means of assuring the safety and humane treatment of Americans who became prisoners in enemy countries. It protected all interned men and women from acts of violence as well as from insults and public

---

* Although there is ample documentation regarding the internment of men and women from Latin-American countries in the official records of the Immigration Service, I could find no recorded information about the presence of proxies in the internment camps. Presumably, the subject was too embarrassing to receive official recognition.

curiosity, and unlike previous agreements of its kind made it possible for its signatories to determine whether or not the enemy nations were abiding by its provisions.°

To drive home the significance of the Geneva Convention in our operation of the internment camps, I sometimes shared with members of the press an off-the-record report of an explosive situation that developed in Santa Fe in the spring of 1942 after a local newspaper had published an account of the disastrous defeat the Americans suffered in the Philippines, which reported that among those killed were several members of the New Mexico National Guard. In a spirit of vengeance, a mob of angry New Mexicans armed with a variety of weapons ranging from hatchets to shotguns marched on the Santa Fe internment camp with the intent of murdering all of its two thousand Japanese occupants.

The mob would have had its way had it not been for the camp's quick-witted camp commander, Ivan Williams, who, realizing that his small contingent of guards was no match for it, confronted the men alone and talked to them about the consequences of killing or injuring any of the Japanese. Williams emphasized the reciprocal features of the Geneva Convention, pointing out that any action they took against his charges might result in the death of their sons, brothers, and friends who were prisoners of the Japanese. After he had spoken for about an hour, the ringleaders were persuaded he was right and ordered their followers to disperse.

Unfortunately, not all newspapers in the country were aware that the Department of Justice was anxious to avoid having its internment program publicized. From time to time a newspaper published near one of the internment camps would print

° This was accomplished by delegating neutral powers to inspect the camps regularly in behalf of the warring nations they represented. In the United States, representatives of the Spanish government acted in behalf of the Japanese, the Swiss government represented the interests of the Germans, and the Swedish government looked after the interests of Italy and the rest of the nations at war with us.

an angry editorial to the effect that the aliens in the camp were eating better than most Americans. Usually, the writer of the editorial received a visit from one of the camp officials who would explain that the Geneva Convention stipulated that as part of the "humane treatment" guaranteed to interned aliens, the food they were served had to be "equal in quantity and quality" to that of the United States troops at base camps. The official would also point out that food costs for internees averaged less than fifty cents per person per day and that much of the food consumed they raised themselves at a cost to the government of only ten cents an hour for their labor.

This would often end the matter, but the readers of the angry editorial were not likely to forget it. When casualties of American soldiers were headlined, their antagonism toward the interned aliens was liable to ignite to a perilous degree. In Bismarck, North Dakota, where the service operated a large internment camp for Germans and Japanese, the hostility of neighboring Americans became so intense that when one of the German aliens escaped from the camp, they formed a posse and went hunting for the escaped German, eager to kill him. Fortunately, the service's border patrolmen were able to get to him first and return him to the camp unharmed.

I began my tour of the major camps by interviewing Willard F. Kelly, a colleague in the Philadelphia office who was directly in charge of the internment program. At the outbreak of the war Kelly had headed the service's border patrol whose primary function was to prevent the smuggling of aliens and goods into the country by patrolling more than eight thousand miles of American land and coastal boundaries. Then one day Major Schofield told him that he wanted the border patrol to establish and operate an internment camp in Texas for a group of German seamen who had been apprehended by the service at the outset of the war. Kelly argued strongly and, he thought, convincingly that the border patrol should stick to its primary function, but the major was not convinced. "Get going," he told him. And Kelly, the most diligent of men, got going with such speed and efficiency that from then on he bore the burden of the service's internment program.

The success of the border patrol in doing their new assignment well was largely due to the deep respect that Kelly engendered among the patrolmen. A decent man who was long on wisdom and short on formal education, he was an instinctive leader of men and a good judge of them. Although he had not gone beyond high school, he expressed himself with a clarity and succinctness that persons with far more education might well envy. I could not be in his presence without thinking of the strong men with few words that became my Hollywood heroes in the Saturday afternoons of my youth.

Except in the movies, I had not expected to encounter the likes of Kelly but at the very first camp I visited, in Kenedy, Texas, I found his soul brother in the camp commander, Ivan Williams, the same Williams who had stopped a mob from massacring two thousand Japanese in his charge at the Santa Fe camp he then headed. Nothing about his outward appearance suggested the man's talent for asserting authority in thorny situations. No movie director would have cast him to play the lead in a movie dealing with Williams's exploits. Except for his Texas Stetson and the varied hues of his neckties, he lacked color. Yet behind the mundane facade was a steady strength that no one could mistake. He applied his strength so judiciously that his reputation for fairness spread even among aliens who had never set eyes on him.

The year before, while Williams was still in charge of the Santa Fe camp, Kelly, cooperating with the Army, had sent him to Tule Lake, a huge War Relocation Center housing 16,500 West Coast Japanese, to investigate the actions of a group of troublemakers who were disrupting the life of the community. Williams found that some 100 American-born Japanese, who had received their early education in Japan and had recently taken steps to renounce their American citizenship, were the core of the problem. After jailing them, Williams made arrangements for their transfer to his Santa Fe camp. One of the men refused to budge. He sat on the floor of the jail naked, preparing to commit hari-kari with a butcher knife someone had slipped him.

"You're a coward," Williams told him. "But if you're going to kill yourself, go right ahead. I'll watch you, so that no one gets blamed for your death."

"I am not a coward," the man protested.

"In my book you are," said Williams. "Because, unlike your friends, you're taking the easiest way out. But go ahead and get it over with."

"You are a strange man, Mr. Williams," the man said, obviously puzzled. "I have heard people talk of you. They say you are a strict man."

"Yes, I'm plenty strict but I run a decent camp."

The man was silent for a while, then he rose from the floor and handed Williams the knife. "I am not a coward," he said.

"I guess you aren't," Williams conceded. "Now get your clothes on and let's get going."

My favorite story about Williams dealt with a different kind of confrontation, this one with an Army bigwheel, Lieutenant General John L. DeWitt, military commander of the western defense area, the same general who had championed the mass internment of West Coast Japanese. In August 1942, shortly after Williams had assumed charge of the Santa Fe camp, he was informed that the general was arriving at the railroad station with more than one thousand Japanese aliens who, having been judged "too dangerous" to be interned in the War Relocation centers, were to be transferred to his custody. So obsessed was the general with the dangerous character of the aliens that he had ordered an armed escort of one thousand soldiers with fixed bayonets, almost one guard for every prisoner.

When Williams arrived at the Santa Fe railroad station with his contingent of sixteen border patrol guards, who were to escort the one thousand aliens to the camp, DeWitt began to admonish him for not providing a larger guard, shouting that with so few patrolmen the Japanese could easily break away. "What kind of a fool are you?" he stormed.

Without raising his voice, Williams stood up to the general. "Suppose the Japanese do try to run, what would you and your thousand guards do about it?" he asked. "Fire at them and endanger the lives of innocent bystanders? With all that shooting somebody would be bound to get hurt and it might not be the Japanese. No, General, I'm not a fool. You are the fool," and with that Williams ordered his sixteen patrolmen to march the Japanese to the camp.

He was the first camp commander to tell me that the Japanese presented fewer problems than any of the other interned aliens. The most difficult were the Germans, particularly the pro-Nazis who had been members of the German-American Bund. The convinced Bundist, he said, liked to dream up "complaints" to present to the camp authorities, mainly to enhance his prestige with fellow Bundists. The more fanatical of them kept insisting they had the right to observe all German political holidays, such as Hitler's birthday, with mass meetings, demonstrations, and displays of Nazi emblems. Williams, as well as the other camp commanders, forebade such activities, much to the relief of the other internees. "For many of the interned Germans it is the first time they have had any direct experience with hard-core Nazis and they find they have little in common with them," Williams observed.

Although the Germans and Japanese constituted most of the Kenedy camp's population, there were seventeen different nationalities represented among the 2,700 men in the camp. Most of the diversity occurred among the prisoners who had been brought to the camp from Latin-American countries, Williams pointed out. "It seems to me that those heads of governments in Latin America arrested anybody not born in their country and sent them to us as alien enemies. A lot of them don't know what they're doing here. I can't say I do either, but we try to keep their minds off their troubles."

At Kenedy, as well as in the rest of the camps I got to, the most insidious evil of internment was boredom—"the barbed-wire sickness," it was called. The camp commanders did everything possible to keep their charges fully occupied. In addition to the chores they performed to maintain the camp, such as operating the mess halls, carpenter and plumbing shops, the laundries and vegetable gardens, the prisoners were also encouraged to engage in farming, forestry, and road-building projects outside the camp for which they were paid prevailing wages, most of which were withheld from them until their release from the camp. There were also sports facilities, flower garden projects (at which the Japanese excelled), a library, and weekly movies. Occasionally prisoners with musical skills provided concerts, and the artists among them gave group exhibitions.

The most gifted of the amateur artists at Kenedy was a German Catholic priest from Central America who was putting the finishing touches on a mural that covered an entire wall of the camp's improvised wooden chapel. In the manner of Italian medieval painters the mural vividly depicted scenes from the life of Christ, including his crucifixion. Above them was a radiantly triumphant portrayal of the resurrected Christ in the kingdom of heaven. It was the only visual symbol of hope I was to encounter in any of the camps. When I asked Williams why the priest had been interned, he replied that according to his dossier "he is supposed to be a Nazi." But Williams did not believe that. "He's no more of a Nazi than I am." No one else in the camp had been of greater help to him and to the prisoners, Williams added. "He does a lot for their morale—and for mine."

There was nothing in the physical appearance of the compound to inspire optimism. The tall barbed-wire chain fence and guard towers surrounding it dominated the desolate landscape like a harbinger of doom. For some of the prisoners the fence became an intolerable symbol of frustration. In the gnawing anxiety of not knowing how long they would be imprisoned and what was happening to their wives and children, they succumbed to barbed-wire sickness. One prisoner was caught trying to dig a tunnel from his barrack to the fence, several hundred feet away. He readily admitted the futility of the project, but explained that for months he had not had any word from his wife and child and felt he had to take some action that would prevent him from becoming insane.

Another prisoner, in a letter to his wife, begged her to release their pet canary from its cage. (All outgoing and incoming letters were closely scrutinized by camp officials.) "No living thing should be caged up," he wrote. "When I am free, I want to live in a house without locks, even without doors. It will be a house made up of windows, and the view must not be obstructed by anything, not even mountains."

Attempts to escape were surprisingly few—a dozen in the entire history of the service's internment program. Three had occurred at Kenedy while Williams was in charge. Like all other attempts, they were unsuccessful. Except for a prisoner from Nicaragua who eluded twenty-five FBI agents and Williams's border patrol guards for three days, the escaped men were usually caught within a few hours. The hunt for the Nicaraguan precipitated a sharp disagreement between the FBI agents and Williams who, knowing the prisoner to be a highly resourceful individual, was quite certain he was hiding in the vicinity of the camp, waiting for his chance to head south for the Mexican border. Unwilling to accept his advice, the FBI agents took off in various directions. Theirs was a wasted effort; the border patrolmen found the Nicaraguan only three miles away from the camp. Williams modestly attributed the capture to "good luck" but could not resist suggesting that border patrolmen were apt to be smarter than FBI agents. "The FBI guys never got near him," he said with uncharacteristic smugness.

From Kenedy I traveled to Crystal City, a sun-baked town in southern Texas that called itself "The Spinach Center of the World" and emphasized the boast with a larger-than-life statue of Popeye in the town square. In contrast to Kenedy, the

Crystal City camp had a lively, almost cheerful atmosphere. Except for the barbed-wire fence around it and the absence of passenger vehicles, it resembled a thriving southwestern town, complete with a school, hospital, a bustling community center, a bakery, and various other stores. What distinguished this camp from all the others operated by the service was that its population of three thousand consisted of families, nearly all of them with children.

The family camp was established out of humanitarian considerations early in the internment program when it became evident that confining husbands and wives in separate camps, especially when there were children involved, created unnecessary hardships. The idea grew out of the fact that the aliens being imported from Latin-America often included families with children. Later, the service took the idea one step further by permitting wives who had not been arrested to live with their interned husbands, along with any children they might have.

To oversee the complex social-service problems of the family camp, Harris acquired the services of Evelyn Hersey, a leading social worker and a warmhearted New Englander. In addition to mobilizing the assistance of social-service agencies, she supervised the formidable task of fusing into a community a polyglot population of all ages and condition, ranging from recently born infants to old people verging on senility. Medical care, schooling, recreation, and work projects had to be established. There was also the problem of feeding a community from many different countries with diverse dietary habits. This was finally resolved by providing each family a weekly allowance of camp money with which it could buy (and cook) whatever kind of food it preferred. The camp administrators also established a clothing store where families could find a wide selection of materials for making clothes to suit their own individual style. All in all, everything possible was done to make the prisoners feel they were not in a prison.

With the guidance and encouragement of the camp officials, the community had achieved self-government with democratic procedures, including elections, followed at every level of its operations. Each language group in the camp elected its own council; in turn, each council elected a spokesman who acted as an intermediary between the prisoners and the administration. His main job was to listen to the grievances of the aliens in his group and pass them on to the camp officials and, if they seemed to infringe on their rights under the Geneva Convention, to present them to the Swiss, Spanish, or Swedish emissaries who visited the camps regularly for the express purpose of hearing such complaints.

As I learned from a German council spokesman, the job of handling complaints was not an easy one. He described to me what had happened that morning: "Mr. X came to see me and said he wanted to register a complaint. It seems that his wife had told him he ought to make a complaint because yesterday their next-door neighbor made one. His complaint was that the prisoners were not given pajamas. I said to him, 'Now look, Mr. X, if I pass on your complaint that you are not receiving pajamas, the Swiss government will have to tell the German government and maybe the German government won't know what "pajamas" means. And if they went to all the trouble of looking it up in the dictionary right in the middle of a big war and finally found out what "pajamas" means, I think the German government might just say, 'Oh to hell with the whole business.' "

That the camp ran as smoothly as it did, despite the presence of a fanatical pro-Nazi group that tried to stir up trouble whenever possible, was largely due to the unique talents of its camp commander, a former border patrolman named Joseph O'Rourke who, with no college education or special training, combined the skills of a seasoned diplomat with the expertise of a first-class social worker and psychologist.° He also exuded more charisma than any government employee I had ever met.

° The disruptive activities of the fanatical pro-Nazis in the camp were often curbed by other pro-Nazi prisoners who did not go along with their tactics. When any of them became too obstreperous, the camp officials transferred them to some other camp.

The prisoners considered him the most popular man in the camp, and their children responded to him as though he were the Pied Piper reincarnated.

Whenever I walked with O'Rourke around the camp, gangs of tots would follow closely behind, vying with one another to have a word with him or shake his hand. He returned their love in full measure. The children were his primary concern; he was determined to imbue them with the sense of freedom being denied to their parents. Looking ahead to the time when the camp would be shut down, he wanted the children to have happy memories of the place so that "they can grow up to be good American citizens." It was a matter of pride with him that many of the children seemed unaware that they were imprisoned; they were under the impression that the fence around them was intended for the people on the other side of it. "Of course, sooner or later they'll find out the truth but meanwhile it's something that doesn't have to prey on their minds."

Out of their love for O'Rourke the young children were the staunchest pro-American group in the camp. Earl Harrison, who visited the camp earlier, had told me how, during a tour of the compound, he and O'Rourke had encountered a group of excited children who informed them that they were about to "play war." "Okay," said O'Rourke, "but I hope nobody gets killed." On their way back they passed the same spot again and noticed that the children were sitting around looking dejected. "What happened to the war?" asked O'Rourke. "Anybody get killed?" The children glumly explained the war had never begun because nobody would agree to be the enemy; everybody wanted to be on the American side.

It was a different story with the older children who were all too aware of the implications of the fence and, in most instances, were in the camp only because their parents had the legal right to insist they live with them. I met with a group of them. "We're supposed to be Americans," their spokesman told me. "We were born here. So why should we have to live in a prison camp like we were criminals? We haven't done anything to be punished for." One of the teen-agers added, "And neither have our parents."

O'Rourke worried that their bitterness would have a permanent effect on them and also that the resentment they expressed might infect the younger children. "It's a tough problem trying to explain to the older children, as well as some of the adults who claim they've done nothing to deserve internment, that they are simply victims of a lousy war and the only thing to do is to make the best of the situation." He and his staff, he said, were doing everything possible to make things easier for them. "This camp has something to keep everybody busy—lectures, courses, sports, gardening, all kinds of hobbies. We've got people making tables, beds, mattresses—or learning how to. There are thirty teen-age girls getting nurse's aid training in the camp hospital; after the war, they'll be able to get jobs in any hospital. If I could persuade everybody to keep busy, they'd be a hell of a lot more relaxed . . ."

By this time we had become good enough friends so I could ask O'Rourke, who was separated from his wife, what he did for relaxation. "As far as I can tell," I said, "you're working from dawn to dark every day of the week." He replied that he couldn't help it, but that about once a month he went on a Saturday-night drinking binge in some town where no one recognized him and tried to forget about the camp. "My family are the people in this camp, but, hell, you've got to get away from the place once in a while and let go. The only way I can keep my head straight is to do a little drinking now and then and try to find some loving woman." He told me about a woman he had picked up at a bar on his last binge. "She was in her forties, about my age, and so damn grateful."

On the last night of my visit, O'Rourke and I had a couple of beers in Crystal City. As we were driving back to the camp in the dark, the flood-lighted compound came into view, almost a mile away. From that distance in the black of the night it looked, not like a prison camp, but like a magical city

immersed in a glorious celebration. As we approached the
camp, O'Rourke sang the first line of a currently popular song,
"When the lights go on all over the world," and followed it
with a second line of his own, "The Crystal City camp will be
dark again." ° He added, "And a damn good thing that will be
for everybody concerned."

My last stop in Texas was a former federal minimum-security
reformatory known as Seagoville, on the outskirts of Dallas. The
new and attractive $1,800,000 facility, which occupied only a
small segment of its 830-acre tract, resembled a prosperous
college campus. At the outbreak of the war, after it had been a
reformatory for barely a year, the facility was transferred to the
Immigration Service, staff and all, for the internment of aliens
who would be repatriated at the close of the war. The first
group of prisoners arriving there were families from Latin-
American countries. After their transfer to Crystal City, Seagoville was used mostly for female aliens, but within a couple
of days after my arrival the service's new policy of permitting
husbands and wives to be interned together went into effect,
and the population of the facility almost doubled. The single
women remained in the comfortable dormitories of the facility,
the couples were ensconced in some sixty prefabricated one-
room, eighteen-foot-square living quarters sold by the manufacturer as "Victory Huts."

I was lucky enough to be present on the morning when the
spouses were first reunited. It began with the arrival of several
busloads of German aliens from other internment camps. Their
wives waited for them, lined up about fifty yards away from the
buses. As soon as the buses were unloaded, the couples rushed
toward one another, hugging and kissing, crying with the joy of
being together again. Then, still holding on to each other
tightly, they proceeded to the mess hall to lunch together.

When the Japanese husbands arrived a little later, I wit-

° O'Rourke's prediction was not accurate. Crystal City was the last of the
Immigration Service camps to be shut down. It was in operation until
November 1, 1947, two years after the end of the war.

nessed a totally different scene. There was no show of emotion; the encounter was sedate, ritualistic. On leaving the buses, the men lined up opposite the line formed by their wives and the two groups solemnly bowed to one another. Then the men turned their backs on the women and marched toward the Japanese mess hall, while their wives, still maintaining a respectful distance, followed. Unlike the Germans, they did not dine together. The men sat at the tables waiting to be served; the wives crowded into the open kitchen at one end of the mess hall, preparing the meal and giggling like children as they identified their husbands for one another. Only after their men had been served and left the mess hall did the women sit down to their own lunch. And only in the privacy of their own quarters did the spouses finally come together.

None of this surprised Dr. Amy N. Stannard, the officer in charge of Seagoville, who had been observing the differences between Occidentals and Orientals for more than a year. The arrival of the German and Japanese husbands would accentuate the differences and complicate the station's administrative problems, she thought, but it would do a great deal for the morale of the women. A psychiatrist by training, she believed that internment was a greater ordeal for women than it was for men, but she admired the women for their strong community spirit, particularly for their concern in trying to help those who found internment especially hard to take. Seagoville was equipped with various facilities to ease the strain of confinement—an auditorium with a stage where the women performed ballet and theatricals, an extensive library with books in Spanish, English, Japanese, and German, a weaving room where prisoners could learn to make drapes and rugs, and a completely equipped garment factory where they could learn, teach, or engage in dressmaking. Most of the women made the best of their internment but for some, as Dr. Stannard observed, the trauma of having been plucked from their families and imprisoned in a distant place had inflicted a wound that would not heal.

As the former warden of Seagoville when it was a women's reformatory, Dr. Stannard was a more experienced administrator than the other camp commanders I was to encounter. Working closely with her assistants, she was able to keep a close check on what was happening in the camp day to day. Part of her information came from the staff censors who read all letters written or received by the prisoners. The more revealing of the letters were by the prisoners who had been uprooted from their native habitat in Latin America and brought here for internment. Many of them had been living in poverty under primitive conditions, and expressed enthusiasm for the good food and housing they now received, which was far superior to what they had known before internment. Some of the letters expressed considerable fondness for their American keepers, whom they described as "considerate" and "gentle." Occasionally there were amusing misinterpretations. Writing to a Peruvian relative in Spanish, one woman said: "The ladies are so kind they even put out food at night for the *cucurachas*" (cockroaches), apparently unaware that the "food" was poison. Yet for all the comforts available to them at Seagoville, most of the letters dealt with the anguish of being parted from loved ones.

Among the letters Dr. Stannard received was one from a recently paroled German woman who had spent a year at Seagoville and was now living in San Diego. The letter thanked her for "all your kind words and deeds, for the smile you had for each of us," and described being interviewed by her San Diego parole officer. "The man must have expected me to resent the past year because he seemed so very much relieved to get my report on Seagoville," she wrote. "I told him I never had it so good in all my life—no work unless we wanted to, no worry about food—it's good and served regularly three times a day."

Unlike all the other internment camps I visited, the Seagoville staff included a trained dietitian, a beautiful blonde named Marian Brooks, who made certain that the food served to the approximately seven hundred German and Japanese internees (in separate mess halls with separate menus) conformed to their ethnic tastes and contained enough vitamins to maintain their health. "Miss Brooks is one of the main reasons why no one ever thinks of escaping from this place," one of her colleagues told me.

Because of Miss Brooks, with whom I went dancing at a Dallas nightclub, I too had no desire to leave Seagoville, but one morning there was a telephone call from the camp commander at Santa Fe, my next stop, urging me to get there as soon as possible, explaining that through the grapevine the Japanese aliens there had learned of my forthcoming visit and were anxious to talk with me about urgent problems. I left Seagoville the next day.

After I had been in the Santa Fe compound for less than an hour, Seagoville, by comparison, seemed like a relaxed and convivial country club. I had barely arrived when a three-member committee representing the two thousand Japanese in the all-male camp presented Lloyd H. Jensen, the camp commander, with a petition asking that the barbed-wire fence surrounding the compound be made at least a foot taller. The petition was motivated by the fear that the residents in the surrounding area might become incited by recent reports of heavy American casualties in the Pacific and try again to storm the camp, as they had the year before.

The internee committee spokesman then turned to me and, explaining that there were a number of Japanese in the camp with pressing problems that only I could handle, asked that I meet with each of them. I pointed out that they were crediting me with powers that even the head of the Immigration Service did not have, and Jensen vouched for the fact that I had no judicial authority whatsoever. But the spokesman and his associates kept addressing me as "Honorable Commissioner" and politely but unrelentingly kept requesting that I listen to the petition of their "clients." We finally reached an understanding: if they would explain to their "clients" that I lacked the authority to solve their problems, I would agree to listen to them and pass on their petitions to the proper authorities.

While two of the committee members went about the camp rounding up the men who wanted a hearing, the spokesman produced an empty crate and a chair which were to serve as courtroom props and now began addressing me as "Honorable Judge." Planting the two props in the middle of a street, he flicked away some imaginary dust from the chair with a grandiose gesture of his handkerchief and invited me to be seated. "The court is in session," he shouted and clapped his hands like a character in an Alice-in-Wonderland scene.

In a matter of minutes some twenty-five Japanese, young and old, were lined up in front of me. With my self-appointed tipstaff sometimes acting as interpreter, I listened to each of their stories. Nearly all of them evolved around the tribulations of families who had been cruelly separated by the petitioners' internment. Their wives and children were suffering. When could they be reunited? It had been many months since they had applied for admission to the family camp at Crystal City, and still no word from Washington. Meanwhile, they were alarmed to hear that the family camp was rapidly filling up and would soon reach capacity. One man was too filled with emotion to talk. He wept as he showed me the copy of a letter his wife had written the Attorney General: "My husband is still detained. I am not in good health and have two children, 8 and 10 to look after. My sisters are in different camps and my brother is in the American Army. I do not know why my husband is detained there, but could you please tell me if it is possible for him to be with us?"

Many of the men were fishermen who had been arrested at the outset of the war because they fished off the California coast in radio-equipped boats. A paranoiac United States Attorney in California was able to convince the Attorney General's office that the fisherman could conceivably communicate with and assist any Japanese submarines which might be operating in those waters. On the basis of such flimsy conjecture, 545 Japanese fishermen were ordered interned as "poten-tially dangerous to the national security." °

There was anguish and anxiety in nearly every man. By the time I had listened to all of them, I felt depleted by their despair, but I had to inform Earl Harrison about some of the cases that required immediate attention. I spent all evening working on a report in my hotel room at La Fonda and got it posted shortly after midnight. The next morning every bone in my body hurt and I was hot with fever. The hotel physician diagnosed the ailment as a severe case of the flu and ordered me to stay in bed for at least ten days. No better the next day, I morosely tried to resign myself to the dreary prospect of being confined in a hotel bed until I recovered, but that afternoon two Good Samaritans, total strangers to me, unexpectedly came to my rescue.

They were the writer Dorothy Thomas and her mother who, learning of my illness through the hotel doctor, recognized my name as one mentioned to them by a mutual friend, another writer named James Still whom I had known at Yaddo. The two women insisted that in my condition a hotel was no place for me and over my halfhearted protestations took me to their ranch house on the outskirts of the city. For the next two weeks, until I was completely recovered, they treated me with all the care and tenderness of devoted old friends.

My erstwhile tipstaff was among the first to greet me when I returned to the camp. Purporting to speak for all of the two thousand internees, he informed me that my recovery would be celebrated that evening with a theatrical presentation at which I was to be the guest of honor. The camp's acting company, I learned from Jensen, was the most popular of the camp's cultural activities; not even the movies were as well attended. Many of the actors were professionals; several had been in

° Eventually, after the fear of Japanese submarines on the Pacific coast had subsided, most of the arrested fishermen were permitted to join their families at the Crystal City camp or in War Relocation centers.

Hollywood movies. The theater group was held in such high esteem by all the prisoners that by common consent the actors who played female roles were exempted from all menial camp chores that might roughen their hands.

The performance I witnessed took place outdoors on a stage constructed by the internees themselves. Before the curtain went up, the Japanese sitting next to me, a bearded ex-college professor, explained that rather than risk boring me the players had decided not to perform one of their customary six-hour dramas but to limit themselves to two brief sketches.

The first and the shortest of the plays had but one actor in it: a uniformed Japanese infantryman equipped with a large pack over his shoulders and a stage rifle by his side. When the curtain rose, he was at the far end of the stage, flat on his stomach, sniffing the air for danger. On a backdrop was painted an ominously dark forest suggestive of invisible enemies. As the soldier began to inch his way across the stage, his whole being alert to every sight, sound, and smell, his fears became the audience's fears and the tension mounted. By the time he had reached the center of the stage, the suspense was almost unendurable. At that point came the most stunning surprise I have ever seen in the theater: the soldier abruptly stopped crawling, faced the audience, and *grinned*—the exultant grin of someone who has succeeded in fooling everyone. He was still grinning as the curtain came down to the frenzied accompaniment of cheers, exclamations, and applause.

The second presentation was pure farce, a spoof that demonstrated the prisoners' ability to laugh at themselves. The war has ended and as the curtain rises we see two Japanese returning from an internment camp, lugging heavy valises. Their wives receive them with shouts of joy that become even more jubilant when they are told that the valises are filled with presents for them. On opening them, the wives find they contain nothing but rocks that the husbands had collected during internment. The curtain falls as the disgusted women begin pelting the men with the rocks.

There was also wild applause for this sketch. As the ex-professor pointed out, the audience could easily identify with its theme since rock collecting was the favorite camp hobby.

"The best internment camp I have seen anywhere in the world" was the way a foreign representative of the International YMCA characterized the Sante Fe camp under Jensen's command.° Jensen attributed the camp's smooth operation to the prisoners themselves. "They would make any camp commander look good," he said. "They do all the work that has to be done—maintenance, gardening, cooking—and they're very good at it. Of course, sometimes it takes a bit of psychology to figure out how to deal with them . . ."

To illustrate, Jensen told me of a group of prisoners, expert gardeners, who had volunteered to landscape the area around the camp's hospital. They were doing a fine job but were handicapped by the absence of nearby water outlets, which necessitated lugging bucket after bucket of water from a considerable distance. Finally tiring of this, the men asked Jensen if he would supply them with enough pipe to convey the water to the hospital site. Jensen told them he could not justify the expense of the extra piping. The men left disappointed, but a little later Jensen's assistants began reporting that small sections of pipe around the camp, intended for other purposes, were mysteriously disappearing. Jensen knew at once who the culprits were but on thinking the matter over decided not to interfere. A few weeks later the leaders of the project came to his office and smilingly reported that a completely laid pipe line now connected the hospital grounds with the water supply.

Jensen did his best to express astonishment. "How in the

° In the last year of the war, after Jensen had been promoted to an administrative INS post in New York City and Ivan Williams had resumed command of the Santa Fe camp, there was a pitched battle between 16 border patrol guards and some 350 rock-throwing Japanese militants who had insisted on conducting military drills and Japanese flag and bugle ceremonies within the compound. The guards put the rioters on the run, locked up their ringleaders, and quietly disposed of all Japanese flags and bugles on the premises. It was the only instance of collective violence in any of the INS camps.

world did you do it?" he exclaimed. The men went on smiling until their spokesman tapped a forefinger significantly against his brain, and then everyone roared with laughter.

The vagaries of Japanese humor were a constant source of amusement to Jensen. After I had seen and admired the paintings produced by one of the prisoners, Jensen showed me the admission form the artist had filled out on his arrival at the camp. Under the heading marked "Assets," he wrote in bold letters: "One billion dollars in unsold paintings." Under the heading "Cash on Hand," he wrote "Thirty cents."

On the eve of my departure from Santa Fe, Jensen, aware of my interest in art, proposed a trip to the home of Frieda Lawrence in Taos where I could see some of D. H. Lawrence's paintings. Jensen had become acquainted with Frieda Lawrence, he explained, in the course of handling her application for United States citizenship. I readily agreed to the expedition but on our way to Taos had second thoughts about it when Jensen informed me that Frieda Lawrence's citizenship application had been denied on grounds of "moral turpitude" for having lived with Lawrence without benefit of clergy. After expressing disgust that our government should presume to judge an applicant's application for citizenship on such absurd grounds, I pointed out that Lawrence was dead. Jensen's rejoinder was that she was still guilty of "moral turpitude" in the eyes of the INS since she was now living with another man to whom she was not married.°

In Taos we went directly to the Lawrence home, and Jensen knocked several times on the front door. Finally a hoarse voice bade us enter. My fears about the reception we would be

° He was Angelo Ravagli, a wily Neapolitan whom I met in Taos the next day. He was said to have seduced Frieda Lawrence in 1925 while she and Lawrence were in Italy, a circumstance which may have well inspired Lawrence to write *Lady Chatterley's Lover* (1928). Ravagli began living with Frieda shortly after Lawrence's death, and eventually married her. After her death, he became the heir to the Lawrence estate which, ironically, included royalties from the continuing sales of *Lady Chatterley's Lover*. He died in Italy, a wealthy man, in 1976 at the age of eighty-four.

accorded were realized at the instant that Frieda Lawrence recognized Jensen. Without a word of greeting, she backed into a wall, holding a rumpled bathrobe close to her portly torso, and glared at us through a frame of gray and unkempt hair limply scattered around her face. She looked like a witch out of *Macbeth*.

Quite obviously, we had intruded on her while she was in the throes of a bad hangover. When Jensen introduced me as a writer, she simply grunted and went on staring. I felt very sorry for her and could hardly wait to leave. Out of deference for Jensen, who seemed indifferent to her hostility, I took a cursory look at the paintings that crowded the walls, all by Lawrence. They struck me as coarse and inept, obviously intended to shock, more expressive of Lawrence's shrill contempt for bourgeois sexual mores than of his sensibility as an artist. Begging Frieda Lawrence's pardon for our intrusion and getting no reply, I hastily made my exit with Jensen behind me.

From Santa Fe I traveled north to the INS internment camp at Missoula, Montana, which quartered an equal number of Italians, Germans, and Japanese. Most of the Italians were seamen who had been captured in American ports on the first day of the war; only some 250 were civilian aliens, residents of the United States who had been arrested because they had been pro-Fascist journalists, active members of pro-Fascist organizations in the United States, or simply because there was some reason to suspect that their loyalty to Fascist Italy might be stronger than their loyalty to the American government. Among the latter were fathers of sons fighting in the American armed forces.

The Italian civilians I spoke with were invariably bitter about their internment. "Six hundred thousand Italian aliens in this country get the Attorney General's blessings for being good Americans—and they had to pick on me," one of them lamented. "So what if I did write in a newspaper that I thought Mussolini was doing a good job? Does that make me a Fascist? I was finished with that son of a bitch as soon as he teamed up with that other son of a bitch in Germany, but I can't get that through the skulls of those people in the Attorney General's office."

I had come upon him while he was painting a landscape at an improvised outdoor easel. The prickly quality of his remarks was at odds with the soft blend of colors on his canvas. "I see you're an artist as well as a journalist," I said.

He laughed but there was no mirth in his laughter. "I never painted a goddamn thing in my life until I got to this place. It was the fucking FBI that made an artist out of me."

I was attracted to one of the prisoners because he looked so much like my father. I thought he must be a Sicilian, but his birthplace turned out to be Venice. When I asked him in Italian what he was doing in an internment camp, he shook his head dolefully. "I'm here because I'm unlucky. I've always been unlucky. I'm even unlucky about my children." He showed me a letter he had recently received from a daughter in Detroit named Gladys. "Dear Dad," it read, "I was sorry to hear of your detention. I wouldn't worry about it though. You being an Italian and unnaturalized has put you in an enemy classification. But there is no need to worry as long as you have done nothing. There is great satisfaction in knowing that Uncle Sam is on the job, isn't there? I'm just tickled pink they aren't letting anything slip past them. I do hope you will soon be out though."

"She takes after her mother," he grumbled. "A woman with the brain of a *cretina*. What can you do to get me out of here?"

I told him I had no authority and no influence with the Attorney General's office.

"That figures," he replied. "If you had, you wouldn't bother talking with me."

Later, when I examined his file I learned he had so antagonized the Civilian Hearing Board which handled his case that the board characterized him "as dangerous an alien enemy as could be found in the United States." Yet the most serious charge they could point to was that government agents had found two contraband articles in his possession, a radio equipped with a shortwave band, and a Graflex camera. The only other charge against him was that, according to "a confidential source," he had been heard to make some anti-American remarks, one to the effect that Hitler would one day conquer the United States.

An assistant U. S. attorney disagreed with the Civilian Hearing Board; he did not consider their charges substantial enough for interning the man, especially as he had never belonged to a pro-Fascist organization. Swayed by the Civilian Hearing Board's strong indictment of the Italian, the Attorney General's office overruled him, and ordered the man interned until a careful investigation could be made of the case. As a result of the investigation, he was released from the camp shortly after my encounter with him.°

The most cheerful of the Italian internees were the seamen. Not that they liked being confined (some of them complained that being deprived of women was a definite breach of the Geneva Convention which protected war prisoners from "cruel and inhuman treatment"). Nor were they happy with the camp's heavy reliance on canned foods, which they regarded as potentially poisonous and for a time refused to eat them. Yet none questioned the American government's right to intern them for the duration of the war—an attitude which enabled them to accept their detention with far more grace than the civilian Italians. Some were openly pro-American. One seaman told me he was grateful to the American government for interning him for otherwise he would be risking his life in the war for a philosophy of government he despised. He and several others wanted to know what steps they could take to

° By 1944 about half of the interned Italian civilians were either paroled or released unconditionally. (One man was released a few hours after it was learned that his American soldier son had been killed in action during the invasion of Sicily.) The rest of the civilians, about one hundred hard-core admirers of the Fascist regime, remained in internment until the end of the war. Nearly all of them, willingly or not, were then deported to Italy.

become permanent American residents after the war.

The camp's favorite Italian was a gentle elderly ship captain, the official spokesman of the seamen, who served as their father away from home. From his numerous trips to the States in the course of a long career, he had acquired a fluent command of English and a host of American friends who, on learning of his internment, kept bombarding him with gifts of clothes and cash. The clothes he passed on to the seamen who could fit into them. The money embarrassed him; he would try to return it but more often than not it came back. When that happened, he would accept it as a gift for his dog who, as he wrote his friends, was addicted to desserts. This was no mere whim on his part. Every day he and his dog, inseparable companions, would visit the camp PX where the captain would order a single-scoop ice-cream cone for himself and a double-scoop one for the dog, while explaining to the clerk that it was the dog who was treating.

The captain's engaging personality undoubtedly influenced the camp commander's opinion that of the three nationality groups in the camp, he preferred the Italians, despite their occasional indulgence in temperament, because he considered them "the most human." Yet, like all the other camp commanders, he found the Japanese the easiest to deal with; no other prisoners were as willingly cooperative and as democratic. He noted that while some of the Italians and Germans considered it demeaning to their social rank to do such menial chores as washing dishes or scrubbing floors and toilets and would pay compatriots of inferior social rank to do the work for them, the Japanese took no notice of social rank. The millionaire business-men and the poorest fisherman uncomplainingly worked side by side at whatever menial work was assigned to them.

The camp commander marveled at the efficiency of the Japanese in organizing themselves as a community. "The Ger-mans have the reputation for being good organizers, but they can't compare with the Japanese." At his suggestion I tried to interview the man whom the Japanese had elected as their mayor but was told by one of his assistants that the mayor was on vacation. "And how is he spending his vacation?" I asked, certain that he must be joking. But the assistant was perfectly serious; the mayor, he explained, was spending most of it on the miniature golf course the Japanese had built in the camp. The assistant was willing to take me to his chief but requested I desist from discussing camp business with him since he had been working hard for many months and deserved a complete rest from his duties. When we reached the golf course the assistant pointed him out to me and offered to introduce us, but the mayor seemed so immersed in the game that I decided not to disturb his concentration and postponed my meeting with him until he had returned from his vacation.

The longer I remained at Missoula the more aware I became of the lack of love between the Japanese, Germans, and Italians. The Japanese, who had their own mess hall, behaved as though the other two groups did not exist. The Germans and Italians, on the other hand, expressed open contempt for the Japanese, whom they regarded as an inferior people, but they also had a low opinion of one another. They were compelled to share the same mess hall, but since they could not agree on a common menu, they maintained separate cuisines, with the Italians turning up their noses at sauerkraut and the Germans disdaining spaghetti. Their general incompatibility sometimes resulted in fisticuffs, at which time their leaders would feel obliged to remind the men that they were allies, not enemies. All in all, the relationship between the three groups hardly augured well for the solidarity of the Axis alliance. "If, God forbid, the Axis powers should win the war," an Italian seaman told me, "there would soon be another war between the winners."

After leaving Missoula, I made a quick trip into Idaho to inspect an all-Japanese camp of internees near Kooskia, a tiny village in a canyon, where the internees were building a road through a wilderness so thick that no fence was required to contain them. Here, in the midst of primeval forest and swift streams, the Japanese had little fear of hostile Americans, only of hostile bears and snakes. Although they grumbled about the low wages they received for their strenuous labor, the men were doing an excellent job building the road and maintaining a tidy camp, with only a small contingent of border patrolmen supervising them.

The last internment camp on my itinerary was Fort Lincoln at Bismarck, North Dakota. After the vivacious atmosphere of Missoula, the camp seemed dreary and listless. The general gloom was accentuated by the flatness of the surrounding landscape and, to some degree, by the tight-lipped personality of the camp commander who appeared to derive little satisfaction from his job. Yet for all of his grimness, his staff members described him as a fair-minded commander with a compassionate heart. I was told that shortly before my arrival his attention was drawn to a German prisoner who was walking up and down the length of the barbed-wire fence like a caged tiger. When he asked the German what was wrong, the prisoner showed him a letter he had received that day which indicated that his grandmother was ill and without help. Since she spoke no English and lived alone, he worried that no one was likely to come to her assistance. Promising to do what he could, the commander made a long-distance call to a social-service agency in the town where the grandmother lived. Within a few hours the old woman was getting the help she needed, and a report about her condition was on its way to the camp.

After I had been there for a few days and met the camp commander's family, I realized how much his personal problems may have contributed to his sense of gloom. After being a widower for several years he had recently acquired a second wife who could be a substitute mother for his two young sons. She was a handsome woman in her late thirties with dark flashing eyes and a voluptuous figure. St. Louis had been her home from the time she was born and now, as she told me, she felt as if she were in Siberian exile, cut off from all her friends and from all the cultural diversions she enjoyed in the city. Her stepchildren had not warmed up to her and it was apparent to me, as it must have been to her husband, that unless he were soon transferred to a post in a more urban area, their relationship would be in serious trouble.

Adding to the camp commander's difficulties was the ornery behavior of some of his German charges who systematically created as many problems as possible for their American keepers. Internees who became troublemakers in the other camps often wound up at the Fort Lincoln camp. One of them, who had arrived in the States in 1935 as a propagandist for the German Travel Bureau, had been in three other internment camps before being transferred to Fort Lincoln. His record indicated he had been "a source of trouble" ever since his arrival there, spreading false rumors among the internees and "instigating unreasonable demands on the camp administration." While in the hospital malingering, "he complained unduly about hospital food and opened windows to discomfort other patients." On one occasion he painted an obscene picture on a wall, then refused to remove it. The writer of his report described his attitude as "arrogant and overbearing." Yet the report was careful to point out that he was probably not a Nazi, that his unfavorable record was a result of his personality, not of his political beliefs. He was judged to be a "product of Imperial Germany," which he had served as a navy captain in World War I. There was little about his camp behavior that escaped the attention of the guards. "At Christmas time," one sentence of the report read, "he burned candles on Christmas trees, though he knew full well that it was against fire regulations."

A constant complainer in the camp was a former chemist who had committed the terms of the Geneva Convention to memory, so that he could make certain the Americans were living up to their obligations. Attorney General Biddle, who had met him while visiting the camp the year before, described him as "a herr professor type." Biddle reported that the chemist had only one complaint but one which he pressed obstinately: they did not get enough butter. Biddle asked him how much they got, then told him that it was substantially more than he received under rationing. The chemist's rejoinder was "wonderfully Teutonic." "But that's not the point, Mr. Attorney General. Under the Geneva Convention we are entitled to as much butter as the American troops—and we are not getting it!"

Among the most disgruntled prisoners in the camp was a group of Germans who had been seized a few days after the United States declared war on Nazi Germany and hustled off to Fort Lincoln without a hearing. Twenty-five of them addressed a strongly worded petition to the President and the Attorney General demanding their immediate and unconditional release "unless warrants charging specific law violations can be sworn to against any or all of us." Although the writer of the letter did not know or pretended ignorance of the Alien Enemy Act of 1789 which empowered the President to arrest and confine aliens of enemy nationality without regard to the Bill of Rights, it was an admirably articulate statement of the questions and objections which must have occurred to the hundreds of aliens who were confined without proper explanation within a few days after Pearl Harbor.

One of its most forceful paragraphs read:

From a letter written by the Hon. J. Edgar Hoover we are led to assume that we will "be accorded every opportunity" to establish our "loyalty to the United States." Who accuses us of disloyalty? What is the evidence of disloyal acts on our part? We insist upon the elementary right to be confronted with our accusers, to examine the evidence against us, and thereafter prepare our defense and refutations accordingly. We believe that our imprisonment, the seizure of our papers and effects, the freezing of such funds as are necessary to the maintenance of our families, the refusal to grant us the elementary right of legal counsel, the imposition of strict censorship upon letters addressed to us, the failure to inform us of specific charges against us, all to be wholly without the sanction of any law applicable to us as permanent residents of this country and an abrogation of the fundamental guarantees of our Constitution and the lawful acts promulgated thereunder.

All of the signers shortly thereafter received hearings before Civilian Hearing boards but for those who were not ordered released the hearings only served to illustrate the government's abrogation of constitutional guarantees since the aliens were not permitted legal counsel nor the opportunity to face their accusers. In the interests of national security, we had suspended these and other rights which, presumably, we had gone to war to preserve. No one at Fort Lincoln, or at any of the other camps, with whom I could discuss this crude irony, could tell me to what extent it may have influenced the pro-Nazi attitudes of the internees, but no one could dispute the bitterness it must have engendered.

The signers of the petition, along with the German seamen who had been confined since 1939, constituted the most militantly pro-Nazi group in the camp. They were eager for Germany to win the war and enthusiastically looked forward to their repatriation. Meanwhile, their chief project was to make the lot of the camp administrators as difficult as possible. The camp commander told me that every time the news of a German victory was reported on radio, the group would invariably present his staff with a fresh set of demands which exceeded the bounds of the Geneva Convention.

"It's their way of fighting the Americans," the camp commander explained. "We don't mind because we know we are living up to the provisions of the Convention. We also know from experience that when the Swedish representative hears what their demands are on his next trip here, he'll tell them they're unreasonable and that will put an end to it—that is, for a while." He kicked away a stone in his path. "I guess that if I were in an American internment camp over in Germany I'd be raising the same kind of hell."

I was glad to leave Fort Lincoln. Of all the camps I visited and would be visiting in the months to come, it was the grimmest reminder that we were engaged in a war of hopelessly conflicting wills. It was also one more reminder that the war had thrust us into the shameful position of locking up people for their beliefs.

FOURTEEN

White House Weekend

In April 1944, just a year before Franklin D. Roosevelt died, I spent a three-day weekend at the White House as the guest of Eleanor Roosevelt. The invitation had been issued without forethought at a dinner party in her honor given by John Frederick Lewis, Jr., and his wife, Ada, one of Philadelphia's few wealthy families that favored the Roosevelt administration.

It was a large dinner party with some twenty guests in attendance, a surprising number of them Republicans who kept asking one another why they had been invited. My own explanation, which I kept to myself, was that it probably appealed to John Lewis's maverick sense of humor to see how many fat-cat Republicans he could lure to a dinner that honored the wife of a President they heartily loathed. Whatever the reason for their presence, their uneasiness was all too evident at the dinner table where, too often, the company became submerged in a well of silence broken only by the shrill inflections of Mrs. Roosevelt chatting about retarded children with the guest next to her good ear, Dr. Edward Strecker, an eminent psychiatrist of the Republican faith. All through the interminable dinner I could observe John Lewis at the head of the table quietly fidgeting under the watchful gaze of his wife, not daring, for a change, to be himself lest he offend his guest of honor.

Except for having greeted Mrs. Roosevelt briefly on her arrival at the Lewis home, no communication with her was possible until after dinner—that is, not until the men and women, in accordance with Philadelphia social ritual, had separated for a while, the women to fix their faces, the men to smoke cigars and talk of matters presumably unfit for mixed company. Moments after the two groups rejoined in the living room, I found my opportunity to approach her. Four years had passed since I was her Sunday-dinner guest at the White House and, except for a few perfunctory greetings through the mail, we had not communicated since.

I began the conversation by inquiring about our mutual friend Mrs. Margaret Fayerweather, who continued to be the main link in our relationship, precipitating a nice example of Mrs. Roosevelt's spontaneous nature, for in the middle of informing me that our mutual friend was about to begin her annual two-week sojourn at the White House, she interrupted herself to propose that I join them there the coming weekend. Thrown off guard by her naturalness, I became a victim of my own, replying that, unfortunately, I had already made another engagement. There was nothing in Mrs. Roosevelt's facial expression or comment to indicate that I had blundered; she simply said she was sorry I was not free and turned to another guest waiting to talk with her.

Some five minutes later, while chatting with friends in another part of the room, I was suddenly overwhelmed by the realization that my refusal was a gross expression of stupidity. Hastily excusing myself, I rushed back to Mrs. Roosevelt and blurted out that I had been completely mistaken: my weekend was absolutely free and I would be delighted to accept her invitation. The blue eyes twinkled, and she asked if I could manage to get to the White House on Friday afternoon when Mrs. Fayerweather would be arriving. I assured her I could and I would.

The original weekend plan that occasioned the blunder was my annual April visit to my parents in Rochester, which coincided with their wedding anniversary and my father's birthday. I dispatched a special delivery letter to them explaining why I was obliged to postpone my trip, expecting them to be pleased by the White House invitation. But my news had the opposite effect. In a deeply worried voice my mother telephoned to express her fear that Mrs. Roosevelt had asked me to the White House for the purpose of enlisting me in some dangerous war assignment overseas. She was convinced that either the President or his wife would ask me to become a secret agent in Sicily. Nothing I said to her would shake her belief that this was the real motive for the White House invitation, and she begged me to feign illness and break the engagement. In vain I tried to convince her that the invitation was inspired by purely social motives; she kept repeating her worry that as a secret agent I would surely be caught and shot.

My father sounded less nervous when it was his turn on the telephone. He asked me to send him some memento from the White House, some tangible proof I had been there which he could show our relatives. He recalled the skepticism that my first visit to the White House had aroused. "Why," asked my uncle Peppino at the time, "would the head of the world's richest nation want to sit down with a young man who earns less than I do as a bricklayer?" Surprised, my father's feeble rejoinder to that was "Have you ever known your nephew to lie?" He anticipated that a White House stay as long as a weekend would stir up even more skepticism. I promised him documentary proof this time, a note on White House stationery which he could show the disbelievers, and, if possible, a packet or two of White House matches.

Although he sounded more resigned to the prospect, my father also believed that the purpose of the weekend invitation was to brief me for some secret Sicilian mission I would be asked to undertake. "Your mother is right. You are much too naive to be a secret agent. You always believe what people tell you. Do me and your mother a big favor and try to avoid the assignment."

Anxiety was a common trait of all my relatives, myself included, and the war worried them as nothing else in the United States ever had. Even the years of the Depression, when many of them lost their homes to the banks, were not as fraught with anxiety. It worried them that their adopted country, the birthplace of their children, was at war with their native land, dropping American bombs on their own kin. They worried that their sons might be drafted, killed, wounded, or taken prisoners, all of which was happening with increasing frequency. They were not the only ones in the nation who had such worries, of course, but their capacity to emotionalize their anxieties seemed to surpass that of any other people I knew, and I could not help wondering if this was a peculiarly Mediterranean legacy of theirs, an instinctive anticipation of tragedy germinated through the centuries by frequent traumas and tears. In any case, their worries loomed distinctively large and black compared to ·the general mood of the nation which was bizarrely optimistic.

The extent of the optimism worried the Administration. Shortly before my White House weekend, the *New York Times* had staged a forum entitled "We Still Have a War to Win" in which an undersecretary of state and an army general warned Americans against "a smugly optimistic assumption of assured victory." The undersecretary complained there was too much talk of postwar planning, not enough awareness that the nation was still in grave danger. I doubted that the forum would affect many consciences. By now the war had become a routine aspect of the American way of life, an established element of the booming economy. The newspaper headlines about battles lost, the casualty lists which now numbered 190,000 Americans, and the occasional glimpses of wounded or departing soldiers were not enough to instill in the American psyche the terror of being engaged in history's bloodiest war.

My recent exposure to the alien enemy internment camps had sharpened my awareness of the nation's general state of complacency. Yet I perceived that if the national mood was at odds with the devastation abroad, it was not because of the average American's lack of heart but because of the mind's habitual inability to project itself into horrors that go beyond the realm of personal experience. Except for the families of dead, wounded, or missing sons, brothers, and husbands, there was an absence of pain; there was also the casual assumption that the responsibility for continuing the war to its successful conclusion could safely be left to the father figure in the White House.

The cheerfulness persisted inside the White House. It seemed singularly free of the war tensions which had already begun to kill Franklin D. Roosevelt who, I was told, was in Warm Springs, Georgia, for a brief rest. The only obvious indication that there was a war in progress was the presence of armed guards patrolling the sidewalk in front of the White House. Once I got past the front gate, where two of the guards cursorily examined my luggage, the Presidential mansion appeared to be as peaceful as it had been when I first went there in 1939. Even the spectacle of the armed guards quickly lost its ominous implication, for moments after I had been ushered to a third-floor bedroom and was starting to unpack, I heard, diagonally across the wide hall, one of FDR's grandchildren receiving a sound scolding for having paraded with the guards on the sidewalk. "If you do that again, I'll spank you," a woman's voice threatened. "If you spank me," the boy retorted, "I'll kick you . . ."

The heated exchange, which ended in a stalemate, was the only bellicose note of the weekend. Considering the relaxed atmosphere that prevailed, I could quite understand why the little boy had difficulty regarding the White House guards as anything more than life-size toys. Despite FDR's absence, the Roosevelt family exuberance was amply represented, especially by Franklin D. Roosevelt, Jr., on leave from the Navy. Another Roosevelt present for the weekend was his sister, Anna, who had just arrived with her young children and her second husband, Major John Boettiger, a Seattle newspaper publisher with conservative leanings. On Saturday there was a surprise guest, the writer Martha Gellhorn, a long-time friend of Eleanor Roosevelt's, who, in the turbulence of breaking off her marriage to Ernest Hemingway, had telegraphed that morning to ask if she could come to the White House for "a weekend of rest." Mrs. Roosevelt, while still giggling at the notion that anyone could consider the White House suitable for resting, showed me the telegram, then telephoned her friend to urge her to get there in time for lunch.

Throughout my sojourn I had the dreamlike impression of observing some surrealistic operetta that required no story line and no arias. There were rapid and constant changes of scenery: a large drawing room where extrapotent cocktails were served, rooms of assorted sizes to accommodate the varying number of guests served at mealtime, a basement room where we watched movies, a second-floor reception hall where a throng of young college graduates, members of a government internship program, were fed coffee and cakes, and a reception hall on the ground floor where Mrs. Roosevelt poured tea for scores of guests until she was reminded of an urgent radio broadcast engagement and was replaced by Mrs. Fayerweather. Little of the scenery stuck to my memory, but I recall vividly one rather nondescript dining room because it was there that Mrs. Roosevelt and I found ourselves breakfasting alone on Sunday morning.

The cast of characters changed almost as rapidly as the scenery. At the Saturday-afternoon tea party I met Josephus Daniels, the distinguished editor and statesman from North Carolina who had served as Woodrow Wilson's Secretary of Navy in both of his administrations. Daniels, then eighty-one, told me he had finished writing the first of a two-volume work about the Wilson era and thought he had time enough to write one more book.° I also spoke with two close friends of the

---

° In 1947, a year before he died, Josephus Daniels published *Shirt Sleeve Diplomat,* an autobiographical work which dealt with his long tenure (1933–41) as ambassador to Mexico.

Roosevelts, Mr. and Mrs. Davison, who discussed with me their criticism of the American military command for starving the French people with a blockade. Mrs. Davison argued that a well-fed people were far more likely to be friendly to the Allies than a people demoralized by hunger. The President, it developed, had listened sympathetically to the Davison viewpoint but felt it was up to General Eisenhower and his generals to plan their strategy as they saw fit. Mr. Davison hoped to discuss the subject with Eisenhower but did not feel optimistic about the outcome.

On Sunday there were more new faces, among them Judge Samuel Rosenman, a member of FDR's famous "Brain Trust" of the early New Deal years, who came as a dinner guest with his wife, and Mrs. John Curtin, wife of the recently arrived Australian Prime Minister, who had been deposited at the White House by her husband while he went on to more official functions. Mrs. Curtin was a short, melancholy woman whose napkin I kept retrieving from the floor all during dinner (much to Mrs. Roosevelt's amusement) and who, at every opportunity, would go off by herself to play nostalgic Australian tunes on one of the White House pianos.

Throughout the weekend Mrs. Roosevelt, as befitted her role of leading lady, kept lending an air of suspense to the whole operetta. At the least expected times she would rush out of the White House to participate in some conference or radio broadcast. If the tempo of the production seemed unduly frenetic at times, no one could question the expertness with which it was produced. Guests were fed at the proper times, groups of them arrived and departed when they were supposed to, and everyone, with the exception of Major Boettiger whose views were often sharply at odds with those of the other guests, appeared to be having an enjoyable time. FDR, Jr., bantered wittily with Martha Gellhorn, who was both sexy and sharp. Judge Rosenman regaled the company with puns; *On Whom the Belles Told* was his suggested title for a book of memoirs by Errol Flynn, whose headlined difficulties with tattling ex-

360 AN ETHNIC AT LARGE

mistresses were currently titillating the nation. Even Mrs. Fayerweather, who was not given to much levity, entered the spirit of the occasion with a joke or two, and several times I distinctly heard the First Lady laughing like a teen-ager.

The potent whiskey sours Major Boettiger prepared for the company just before the Saturday dinner may have accounted for the singularly spirited conversation around the table. Out-talking and outcharming everyone else, FDR, Jr., held the center of attention during most of the meal. Not all of his stories were for amusement. One of them described the problem of trying to find accommodations in Miami for himself and his family. It was a strong indictment of the Navy for its failure to act in a responsible manner. The situation so upset him that he had spoken to "the old man" about it, and when that produced no result, he staged a press conference to air his complaints and those of other Navy men with housing problems. The next day the Navy commander of the Miami area, Admiral Monroe, sent for him and tried to assure him that "definite steps" were being taken to provide more housing; a project with a capacity of two hundred living units was being rushed through. Roosevelt, unimpressed, pointedly asked the admiral how many Navy families in Miami were in need of housing. The reply was twelve hundred.

His candor obviously annoyed Major Boettiger, who told his brother-in-law that if anyone else in the Navy had dared call a press conference without first obtaining the permission of his superiors, he would have been court-martialed. Resenting the implications of the remark, young Roosevelt replied that if he ever gave the Navy justifiable grounds for a court-martial, he would demand one.

The subject of Roosevelt energy came up during a conversation I had with Mrs. Fayerweather about the Roosevelt family. She agreed with me that the President and his wife must be the most energetic couple ever to occupy the White House. In Mrs. Fayerweather's estimation, their sons were even more energetic—"energetic to a degree beyond the patience and capacity of most mortals, especially if they happen to be married to them. Each one is a human dynamo who sets a pace that most people cannot keep up with. It explains why there is such a high divorce rate among them."

When I remarked how much FDR, Jr., reminded me of his father, Mrs. Fayerweather said that it was John, the youngest son, who was most like the President. It seemed a pity to her that John had gone into business instead of politics and had broken with family tradition by becoming a Republican. "John has his father's intelligence and magnetism; he would have gone far as a politician."

For me, I told my friend, the President's most impressive quality was his consistently optimistic attitude, which seemed to transcend the professional optimism of politicians. Mrs. Fayerweather, who had known FDR all of her life, attributed the genuineness of his optimism to his deeply religious nature. Religion, she added, was far more important to him than it was to Eleanor Roosevelt; although Mrs. Roosevelt was religious, her husband relied on faith in God to a far greater extent than she did.

Toward the close of our conversation, I observed that it must have taken all of his energies and optimism to have headed the nation three times during some of its most trying history, and marveled that he might seek a fourth term, as the newspapers were reporting. Mrs. Fayerweather was certain he would run again. "He's bound to; he can't help himself because he knows enough about the presidency to realize that a new man, no matter how brilliant and dedicated he might be, could not possibly be as effective as himself while the war is still on. And the voters know the same thing."

The subject of the fourth term came up again the following morning while Mrs. Roosevelt and I, without waiting for other guests, breakfasted on eggs, toast, and café au lait (the beverage I most associate with my Sicilian childhood) and shared the same copy of the Sunday *New York Times*. The editorial page of the newspaper included a column by Arthur Krock headlined: "IF NOT ROOSEVELT, WHO?" I read aloud the paragraph that struck me as the core of the piece:

"The fundamental problem of the Democrats is whether the President can or will accept a fourth-term nomination, this time by a real draft in contrast to the sham draft of 1940. Nature and his physician may furnish a negative answer to that question, for his health has been giving concern and the burdens of the next four years will tax a man in the first flush of his maturity."

In her comment, Mrs. Roosevelt disregarded the point about the President's poor health (I gathered from Mrs. Fayerweather that it was the reason his physician had ordered his current vacation in Georgia) and confined herself to the question of whether or not he would run for another term. She began by informing me he had not yet made up his mind; he was having great difficulty reaching a decision. He had tried to consult with her on the question, but she had declined to advise him on the grounds that it was a decision which only he could make. Usually, she added with a smile, she had no hesitation letting him know exactly what she thought. She paused a moment, as though her remark had triggered off a memory, then told me an anecdote about herself and the President which struck me as a classic commentary on that phase of the human comedy known as marriage.

Mrs. Roosevelt was about to retire late one evening when she was joined by the President, who wanted her opinion on a matter of foreign policy seriously affecting British-American relations. He listened carefully to what she had to say on the subject, then proceeded to disagree sharply with nearly all of her arguments. Mrs. Roosevelt tenaciously stuck to her opinion. No less tenaciously, the President attacked her viewpoint until the late hours of the night. When they finally parted, they were still completely at odds with each other. The next day the British ambassador and his wife came to the White House for tea. While pouring, Mrs. Roosevelt became aware that the President, conversing nearby with the ambassador, was discussing the same subject they had argued about so heatedly during the night. She suddenly realized that the President was stating as his own opinion her side of the question with the very same language she had used. "I was so astonished," Mrs. Roosevelt said, "that I almost dropped the teapot."

My delight with her story encouraged my hostess to tell me another, no less revealing of her relationship with the President. This time the setting was their Hyde Park home. They had gone there on a Sunday for a week of rest but no sooner had they arrived and had their midday meal than the President revealed that he had promised some leaders of the Oxford Movement, who were staging a rally on a nearby site across the Hudson, that he would put in a brief appearance that afternoon and address a few words to their conclave. The President took it for granted that his wife would accompany him but, as Mrs. Roosevelt put it, she had "wickedly decided" not to have any part of it, especially as she was not committed by any promise to attend the rally. She told him she preferred to stay home and catch up on some of her correspondence.

Miffed by her refusal, the President drove away in a grumpy state of mind. His mood was even worse when he returned some two hours later; in Mrs. Roosevelt's words, "he was fit to be tied." For a while he was too angry to talk but gradually as his sense of humor became restored, he was able to describe what had happened. Everything had gone well until he was ready to leave, but at that point his car refused to start. After he had unsuccessfully worked the starter dozens of times, one of the rally leaders stepped forward and offered the assistance of his group. Thinking there was a mechanic in the group, FDR said he would be grateful for any help. But a mechanic was not what the leader had in mind. At his signal, the men and women around the car fell on their knees and in unison began to pray aloud for divine intervention. When the prayer was over, the leader asked the President to try the starter again. This time, to FDR's amazement and disgust, the engine started up immediately.

The real reason why the engine had finally responded occurred to him while driving back to Hyde Park: his repeated

efforts to start it had flooded the carburetor with gasoline; the
engine simply needed a few moments of inaction—the moments
taken up by the group prayer—to allow the excess fuel to
evaporate. He told his wife that apart from feeling like a fool
over the "miracle" the group thought it had performed, he was
deeply annoyed that it would presume to use the power of
prayer for as mundane a purpose as starting an engine. Then,
with the Alice-in-Wonderland brand of logic often characteris-
tic of husband-and-wife relationships, the President concluded
his report of the experience by declaring that if she had done as
he had suggested in the first place and attended the rally with
him, nothing of the kind would have happened.

Just before some of the other guests joined us at the breakfast
table, Mrs. Roosevelt spoke of another aspect of his personality,
which explained, at least in part, why his reputation was often
impugned by some of the same men who had been his staunchest champions. She was referring to his habit of listening so
closely and sympathetically that people were often misled into
thinking he was in full accord with what they were telling him.
Time and time again, according to Mrs. Roosevelt, persons who
had private interviews with him for the purpose of selling him
on some idea would emerge from his office with the distinct
impression that they had won his support when, in point of
fact, the President had made no commitment whatsoever. In a
number of instances, Mrs. Roosevelt said, she had tried to curb
their elation by warning them that unless FDR had specifically
said yes to their proposal, it would be a mistake to count on his
consent, but her warning had seldom been taken seriously. She
believed that the failure to appreciate this side of the President
had led to "a great deal of unfortunate bitterness and recrimination," even among those who thought they understood
him well.

Mrs. Roosevelt's revelations about her husband made me
reflect that no biography of a famous man could ever be
complete without the kind of intimate information that only a
wife of long standing can provide. With her ability to perceive

him objectively, Mrs. Roosevelt might have been her husband's ideal Boswell. The dictates of her conscience, I realized, precluded that possibility. As much as she respected truth, she was a loyal wife incapable of revealing anything about her husband that might detract from his public image as a heroic figure. She was, after all, a creature of convention.

I was reluctant to part with her the next day. She had an instinctive wisdom about human nature and a zest for life that warmed my heart. In her presence, I liked being an American, and I did not feel like an outsider. Her basic values, I was convinced, were not unlike those of my parents. My mother had had little education and spoke little English; yet I was certain that were they to meet they would recognize each other as sisters.

I never saw her again after that late Monday afternoon when I returned to Philadelphia. My final memory of her was that of the gracious hostess urging me to stay another day or two. ("John Hersey will be here tomorrow. You would enjoy knowing him.") I was tempted, but my worry that Harrison might become annoyed by my further absence from the office, as well as the old adage about fish and guests smelling after three days, persuaded me to take my leave.

As soon as I arrived in Philadelphia I telephoned my parents to assure them that no one had asked me to go to Sicily or anywhere else as an agent, secret or otherwise, and that I would be coming to Rochester the following weekend to give them a full report of my White House sojourn.

FIFTEEN

A Not-So-Final Note

My thirty-fifth birthday came about a month before Franklin D. Roosevelt suddenly died of a cerebral hemorrhage, and six months before World War II ended with Hiroshima. It marked the end of my apprenticeship as an American.

By then I was well into the process of discovering who I was and what I was up against. I had learned how to protect myself from the bruising paradoxes of everyday American life, and how to cope with the ever-recurring sensation of being a foreigner in my own native land. That I had managed to hold my own in the American mainstream struck me as something of a miracle but one which I could in part attribute to a growing awareness of my own worth as well as to a propensity for the comic. Humor was essential for it enabled me to put distance between my psyche and the various assaults made upon it.

Time has pulverized the memory of nearly all the assaults, but one of them, though inflicted indirectly, made an indelible impression on my ethnic soul. I learned of it on the same day I returned from my White House weekend. As I was lugging my valise up the stairway to my apartment, the middle-aged ex-Follies showgirl who lived below me greeted me with the

words "They're investigating you." She paused melodramatic-
ally (she had studied acting at one time) while my mind leaped
to Kafka's "Joseph K." in *The Trial*, then added: "Two government agents. While you were away. Asking me all kinds of
questions."

I had been investigated by government agents before (all
federal employees were routinely subjected to investigations by
the FBI or the Civil Service Commission), but never before had
anyone they questioned been as eager to talk about it. Morbidly
curious, I urged her to tell me all. She said that the questions
dealt mostly with my personal life and that she had answered
all but one of them with a "no" or "don't know." Did I have a
steady girlfriend or a number of girls? Did I go to bed with any
of them? Had she ever seen any radical literature in my
apartment? Had she ever heard any left-wing songs coming
from it? Had she ever noted any foreign mail addressed to me?

After a few more such questions they asked her the only one
for which she had an affirmative answer: Had she ever seen any
"foreign-looking persons" coming to visit me? She had indeed.
The agents, with eagerly poised pencils, then asked, "Do you
know who they were?" She nodded and replied: "They were his
mother and father."

Through the filter of my neighbor's Irish wit the episode had
already lost some of its sting, but enough of it remained to
remind me once again that in my own country I was an
outsider, a quasi-American with foreign-born parents. While no
employer, to my knowledge, had ever discriminated against me
because of my Italian ancestry, I could not say the same of my
brother, whose application for a job with a major Rochester
factory was torn up in his presence as soon as the personnel
clerk noted his Italian name, nor of a cousin who had been
offered a teaching job with the stipulation that she change her
name to an Anglo-Saxon one, nor of many other relatives with
similar experiences.

Their anger became mine but since I knew something of the
history of immigrants in this country I saw no cause for

bitterness. With the exception of the earliest American settlers, who received a friendly enough welcome from the Indians, every arriving immigrant group was pelted with the insults and assaults of the immigrants who had come before them. The Irish suffered badly in the hands of the Yankee settlers; the Germans were denigrated and attacked by the Yankees and the Irish; then all three of these groups vented their bigotry and hatred on the immigrants from southern and eastern Europe who were arriving in droves at the turn of the century and who, even before they experienced the hatred, sought refuge in crowded ghettos where they could be among their own, away from the strangeness of those who did not speak their language.

They did not all survive. A good many died before their time. Among the Italians, more than one million men and women returned to their native land after a brief sojourn. Those who chose to stay, or had no other choice, planted roots in their adopted land by having children, even while enduring the most excruciating hardships. The pain of uprooting themselves and trying to survive in an alien land where they were not made to feel welcome eventually stopped hurting. But in their children there emerged an unexpected kind of pain—the pain of confused identity. Unlike their immigrant parents, who always knew who they were, their children could not be sure—not as long as they remained locked into the ghetto psychology of the immigrant mind. For all their wisdom, none of the Italian immigrant parents I knew grasped the dilemma of their children, who from early childhood were pulled in one direction by their parents' insistence on Old World traditions and in the opposite direction by what their teachers told them in the classroom. In this inadvertent tug of war, the parents often prevailed and the children were left with confused impressions of identity that were never resolved.

I resolved mine by becoming an ethnic at large, with one foot in my Sicilian heritage, the other in the American mainstream. By this cultural gymnastic stance I could derive strength from my past and a feeling of hope for my present.

Rarely did I encounter in the American world the sageness and love of life I found among my Sicilian relatives; but theirs was an old and static world which lacked the spirit of enterprise and faith in the future that firmly attached me to that admixture of compatriots known as Americans.

The future seemed to have temporarily come to a dead stop when Franklin D. Roosevelt died. For twelve years, through the scourge of the Great Depression and the flames of World War II, he had functioned as a valiant and reliable father figure for millions of his constituents. For most immigrants, no other American President was as deserving of their affection and kinship. And the President knew it. Always the astute politician, he must have had them in mind when, addressing a convocation of the Daughters of the American Revolution in the thirties, he opened with the words "Fellow immigrants."

The news of his sudden death reached me while I was attending a concert by the Philadelphia Orchestra at the Academy of Music. In the midst of a symphony the conductor Eugene Ormandy interrupted himself to read the momentous announcement just handed to him. My companion that evening was a piquant, blue-eyed brunette from Virginia, a direct descendant of one of the nation's founding fathers. Earlier in our relationship, she had revealed I was the first Italian she had ever dated. Our tears intermingled as the orchestra commemorated the audience's grief with a rendition of Beethoven's *Eroica.*

Index

371